UPROAR

UPROAR

JACK MACLEOD

The Porcupine's Quill

Library and Archives Canada Cataloguing in Publication

MacLeod, Jack, 1932 –
    Uproar / by Jack MacLeod.

ISBN 978-0-88984-306-6

    I. Title.

PS8575.L463U67 2008   C813'.54   C2008-904641-2

1 2 3 4 · 11 10 09 08

Published by the Porcupine's Quill, P O Box 160, Erin, ON N0B 1T0.
http://www.sentex.net/~pql

Readied for the Press by Doris Cowan.

Represented in Canada by the Literary Press Group.
Trade orders are available from University of Toronto Press.

We acknowledge the support of the Ontario Arts Council and the Canada Council for the Arts for our publishing program. The financial support of the Government of Canada through the Book Publishing Industry Development Program is also gratefully acknowledged. Thanks, also, to the Government of Ontario through the Ontario Media Development Corporation's OMDC Book Fund.

ONTARIO ARTS COUNCIL
CONSEIL DES ARTS DE L'ONTARIO

Canada Council   Conseil des Arts
for the Arts   du Canada

For Cynthia

With hugs all around for
Heather, Adrienne and Andrew,
Genni and Jeffrey,
and all the good people at Dooley's

And to the memory of Jack McClelland

'There is nothing stable in the
world; uproar's our only music.'
Keats, *Letters*

Calamity, when it hits, is usually a surprise. The troubles you half expect, and most worry about, are seldom the troubles that do appear; it's the unanticipated ones that sneak up on you quietly and grab you by the throat. When they whack you, they shatter all your preconceptions, leaving you shocked by their simplicity and by that sting of the bizarre which makes them so harsh and bewildering.

For many years Professor J. T. McLaughlin believed he had everything. Not fame or wealth, but everything he'd ever wanted. He had a loving wife and three wonderful children, solid friends beyond his wife who was his best friend, health, a pleasant and comfortable house, as well as a secure tenured position at Chiliast University, Toronto. What more could he want? He assumed he could relax and just get on with living happily ever after.

And then, suddenly and without warning, Trish left him.

McLaughlin was dumbfounded. He felt as though he'd worked for years to strengthen his foundation and refinish his floors, and plop – his roof fell in. That he had a stable and happy marriage was to him a given, a certainty. Is there anything so upsetting as a smashed assumption? Everyone has some worries, sure, but what can drive a man crazy is not so much what happens, because stuff always happens, but rather what *doesn't* happen when it has never crossed your mind that it might not, like walking into a familiar open elevator door, and there's no elevator there, just void.

Where he thought there was order and certainty, abruptly there was pain and fear. He found the needle on his compass spinning, his bearings lost, and nothing seemed to make any sense. Trish had been gone several months now, and he was still bewildered. He thought of all this as he drove to the university that morning, remembering the old adage: If you want to make God laugh, tell him your plans. Lately it seemed that God was chortling a lot, and that J. T. could do nothing right.

It was a hot and humid morning in early August and he was late for an appointment with Tony Mazzioni, the departmental Chair. Mazzioni's door was closed, and the secretary, who pointedly informed him that the door had been open until ten minutes ago, said the Chair was 'not to be disturbed'.

Back in his own office, J. T. awaited the Chair's summons. From his briefcase he took review copies of two new works on economic theory, and a bottle of vodka. The books he dropped into the chaos on his desk; the bottle, he placed with care on a bookshelf behind Schumpeter's massive *The Business Cycle*; yesterday's empty he put into the briefcase. Scotch was his usual tipple after five p.m., but during the day he touched up with frequent references to Schumpeter. Vodka, he reasoned, was odourless and undetectable, although he failed to notice that his clothes and even his skin gave off the unmistakable whiff of stale whisky from the night before. His six-foot frame was slightly bent not only with a bookish slouch, but with the round-shouldered stoop of emotional depression.

A year ago, Trish had suddenly got her own afternoon TV talk show and plunged into show biz. Then, eight months later, she left him. Nothing seemed right with his world. Visibly he had aged. He had lost some weight over the summer because he paid scant attention to meals. His face, sometimes termed 'pleasant' or 'interesting' but not handsome, presented a high forehead, brown curly hair worn rather shaggy, a stubborn chin recently clean shaven in an attempt to look younger (the previous beard had been turning grey), and slightly bloodshot blue eyes peering myopically over pouches turning purple from booze. His nose was becoming, if not red, veined and distressingly too pink.

McLaughlin had always been a cheerful sort, laughing and grinning rather too much than too little, but in recent months he had approached most of what life offered with indignant disapproval, his expression often one of unsmiling befuddlement.

Much of his difficulty, he now believed, was that he was too credulous. Possessed of a tolerably high IQ and a well-stocked academic mind, he had assumed that the rational was the real and the real the rational. Like many intellectuals he was more of a theorist than a practical man, and a bit feckless. Believing that life made sense left him vulnerable to the casual madness and duplicity of panhandlers, door-to-door salesmen, politicians and even some of his colleagues.

Making up his mind and getting on with it presented frequent difficulty, for as a classical liberal he could always see the other guy's point of view, the other side of any argument, often leaving him in disgruntled ambivalence. He found unfairness as surprising as it was distressing. When feeding his three cats he would scrupulously give each the same measured amount, exactly the same share of gravy. When reading a student's exam he tended to agonize a long time, debating with himself the case for an A – against a B+, then reading the entire paper a second time ... before putting it aside to reconsider tomorrow.

His office reflected his mentality, looking like the aftermath of a typhoon in a stationery store. Piles of papers and clippings littered the place, stacks of books perched precariously on the edge of the desk and the window ledge, threatening a biblio-avalanche if nudged. Pictures of Trish and the kids had pride of place in silver frames by the telephone, and a photograph of Sidney Bechet in Paris sat on top of an overflowing filing cabinet beside a cartoon image from *Punch* of Bertrand Russell.

In an attempt to establish some order in his life he made daily lists of things to be attended to. Today's list, which he pulled from an inside pocket of his rumpled jacket, read:

> Apologize to editor of *Econ. Journal* for late
> submission of book review
> Meet B.J. Gandy for lunch
> Pick up dry cleaning
> Prepare revised book list for Eco. 213

After considering the items disconsolately, he took a pencil and added:

> Work out in gym
> Give up drinking
> Kill self

The phone rang. Frank, his cheery broker, wanted to know whether he'd decided to sell those two hundred shares in an asbestos mine. 'No', said J.T., 'I calculate it's a hold.'

'It's down 29 per cent in a rising market since we talked last.'

'But the fundamentals are still there. The supply is static, and I'm sure the demand is rising.'

'Well, the company has big unsold reserves, and asbestos just isn't favoured by the market. Oil, yes, gold, maybe, but not this stuff.'

'Frank, I've looked at the numbers and done the analysis. The smart boys will see the light. Hold.'

'J.T., your trouble is, you neglect obvious trends and want to believe that the market is, ah, rational. It ain't.'

'So you're telling me to give up on the numbers? To give up on *thinking*, for gawdsake?'

'Maybe you think too much.'

'Huh. "Over-ratiocinate", that's what my father-in-law used to say to me. Said that my financial and investment model was Cartesian: *Cogito, ergo zero sum*. Well, could be I'm stuck with it, Frank. But it'll work out. It's a hold.'

'They're your numbers. I'd sell.' He hung up.

McLaughlin stared out of the window for a while. With a sigh, and rubbing his eyes, he pulled from a drawer the Xerox of a long, long letter he'd written to Trish days ago, mustering all the arguments against divorce, reciting his views yet again, demonstrating in the most reasonable terms how and why they'd be better off together, worse off apart. It read more like a balance sheet of social accounting than a plea from the heart, but he didn't know that; to him it seemed a nine-page expression of the most compelling analysis and logic. He was folding the pages neatly back into the drawer when the Chair (once the Chair Man, now the Chair Person) appeared at his door.

'Ah, McLaughlin, it appears we missed each other at ten o'clock.'

'Sorry about that. I was delayed by, er, a bit of car trouble.'

'A frozen battery in summer, was it? Or a flat tire?'

'No, actually, I'd misplaced my keys. Took a while to find my spare set, and I was, you know.... So what did you want to talk about?'

'A committee. The principal of Burke College retires after this year, and the administration thinks it a good idea to start the process of finding his replacement early, as soon as term opens next month. I've nominated you as departmental representative on the search committee. You'll give it your best attention, I trust.'

'Oh, well, the thing is, I'm already on a whole gaggle of committees that take up a lot of time. I'm on the library committee and the parking committee and on, er, some other ones. And faculty advisor to the college yearbook. And I'm still on the advisory committee for investments of the pension fund. They needed an economist, you know, what with those dim philosophers and anthropologists always spouting off.'

'Maybe that's why the pension fund is in such bad shape,' the Chair replied ambiguously. 'But none of those duties take up much time, I'm sure. So, I'm counting on you for this search. You are, after all, with Cuttshaw, the only economist cross-appointed from the University department to Burke College, and Cutty is already overburdened this year. So,' he added as he walked to the door and McLaughlin sputtered ineffectually, 'keep me informed, won't you?'

Right, thought McLaughlin, *I won't.*

- 2 -

Anxiety is a condition now endemic in our crass, hot-wired commercial society. Pressures on the job, longer hours required in the workplace, a frantic pace and constant fear of 'downsizing' gnawed at the mental health and confidence of all who thrashed around to keep their salaries and make the monthly payments on their mortgages and credit cards.

Prof. J. T. McLaughlin had never expected to be subject to such fears.

He'd always made a decent salary and managed on it fairly well. He never doubted that the world was his oyster. But now he was experiencing attacks of panic. He knew it was irrational, but he didn't know how to deal with irrationality. Clearly alcohol was no answer, but what was the question? Trish had seldom complained about him, never denounced him, but still she'd gone. The most frustrating thing was that he didn't know how to fight for his family, because he didn't know what the problem was or what to fight against. How do you battle fog, a cloud of unknowing?

On that unforgettable morning months ago when Trish had announced that she was leaving the hearth and home, he hadn't known how to react. So he didn't; he simply went to his office as usual. His nerves were jangled, his hands unsteady as he drove home from the campus at six p.m. that day, saying to himself, *Please, God, let her little red sports car be in the driveway.* But it wasn't.

He'd stumbled into the empty house and looked around disconsolately. No one there. He stowed his briefcase in the hall and went up to the master bedroom to see whether her clothes were gone. Her dresser was bare. One side of her closet was vacant, the other side still full. What could that mean? Maybe she was only partly gone, only half moved out? Temporarily? Coming back? He sat down on the edge of the bed and stared at the wall. The blank wall conveyed no message of encouragement.

Soon he went downstairs to the kitchen and looked in the fridge.

No meal or sandwich had been left for him, no note on the fridge door with a phone number or forwarding address. Nothing. Do people just vanish? he asked himself. Yes, I guess they do.

He went to the bar and took down a bottle of Plymouth gin and a bottle of vermouth. Went back to the fridge and filled the ice bucket. Reached into the cupboard and by habit took out two martini glasses. Looked at them for a long time, then slowly put one glass back. Then he sat down on the floor and laughed at his own folly, laughed and laughed – until the tears came.

He'd always thought of himself as level and quite sensible, possessed of stamina. But after only a few days of worry, sleeplessness, inability to eat and an excess of alcohol, his stomach went into spasm. Intestinal convulsions made his insomnia worse.

He developed intense apprehensions, particularly the feeling that people were looking at him strangely. Whispering about him? Avoiding him? It's a short step from anxiety to paranoia.

It was hard to keep up appearances. He tried to affect an outward cheeriness, but the undertow of his emotions kept dragging him down. Simple tasks often seemed too much trouble. Put them off till tomorrow, till the weekend. And so he couldn't be bothered to take in his dry-cleaning or to change his sheets, with results that soon became olfactorily disturbing, although even that didn't rouse him from his gloom.

Even a trip to the grocery store became a daunting chore. Whenever he thought he could take enough Pepto-Bismol and Rolaids to allow eating without eruptive consequences, he still could not bring himself to shop for only one. His fear was that the cashier would identify him as a hopeless social reject, and he dreaded admitting the truth: that he had become a lonely, single man. With grim resolve he would buy two steaks, two packages of macaroni and cheese, two frozen dinners, and if any acquaintance or neighbour glanced at his shopping cart and its superfluous dualities, he would smile as convincingly as he could, as if to say: see, I'm happily married, part of a couple, just a regular family guy. But this cheery front was of interest to absolutely no one, and never fooled his rebellious bowel, which would often seize up and threaten painful rebuttal before he got his groceries home.

One evening when he returned from just such an excursion to the

Summerhill Market (where one young widow and one knowing blonde divorcee had attempted to chat him up, although he was too uptight to notice), he stepped inside and caught a whiff of Trish's perfume. *She has been in the house, again.* In the fridge she'd left him a chicken pot pie and a bowl of fatigued salad, plus a note on the kitchen counter. 'Dear J.T., I have taken those 14 shirts from the bedroom floor for the laundry and left you some gubbins in the fridge. It doesn't look as though you're eating sensibly at all. Why not phone me? You could take me out for dinner Saturday, oh no, sorry, *Sunday* night, OK? Love, Trish.'

He sat down to reread the note, searching for signs and signals. What lovely handwriting, he thought. How nice of her to leave a meal for me. Saturday night was probably bridge with the girls. Or not. His gut gave him another jagged twinge. But she wanted to see him, wanted to have dinner, together.

As he sipped a scotch and looked at the note and pondered, his mood flipped from euphoric to wretched, from optimism to dread. He decided not to eat the chicken pot pie, not to eat at all. *Something is sure to change,* he thought; *it's bound to, got to. This can't be happening to me. Can it?*

* * *

Three nights later J.T. sat staring at the TV. He'd sunk two large martinis while waiting for a package of unspeakable frozen dinner to heat in the oven. Dinner was the hardest time of the day; eating alone seemed to him a defeat. After the first glutinous half of whatever it was, minced raccoon tails and rice or something, he gave up, munched part of a stale chocolate bar, and by seven-thirty wandered back to the TV carrying a glass of Talisker's dark smoky single malt. From a mindless sitcom he flipped to the Weather Channel; at least that was about something real. There was a freak early snowstorm in Alaska, heavy rain on the prairies from Kansas to Alberta, an earthquake in Chile. Maybe, if Nostradamus and Edgar Cayce were right and California plunged into the sea, he and Cuttshaw, another economist in the department, and his pal, could buy some ocean frontage in Oklahoma. They could become beachcombers. Cutty would like that.

Presently he found himself standing in the basement. He had gone down to find something – but what? Sat down on a suitcase and tried to remember. Was he experiencing what the geriatric set called 'a senior moment'? Surely not, he was only fifty-one. Ah, a screwdriver. To fix something, yes. But what? A loose chair leg, maybe, or a door handle. Gotta keep the old house in good nick. Might have to sell it. The thought depressed him further – though his mood had been grim enough before.

He sat down again on the bottom stair and considered: where does memory go when it wanders? To the attic, back to childhood, to Tibet? Perhaps it just went out to the garage to rest there in the dark like the car until someone came along with a key to turn on the ignition again and get it moving. It might be a good idea to go out and wash the car if he could find the chamois. Or some piece of cloth. Where did Trish keep the cloths? He had no idea. More and more he felt like an old T-shirt that had been torn and discarded. The bog of despond is easy to slip into, easy to wallow in, hard to climb out of.

Twenty-four years they'd been married. Since he was twenty-seven. Half his life almost. Did that mean nothing? Probably.

He had never expected life to be a bowl of cherries, but that didn't mean he accepted the bad with serenity. On the contrary, he confronted both the big disasters and the daily niggling little vicissitudes of life with equal dismay. He could see little sense or redemption in a universe that accepted as 'normal' the perverse stupidities of clear-cutting, vegetarians, Bible-thumpers, Disney, basketball, tofu, prostates, global warming, TV advertising, Andrew Lloyd Webber, arms sales to poor countries, telephone solicitors, recording instructions for VCRs, Republicans, the CIA, and divorce lawyers. Reality, not the mysterious, is the true Unexplained.

In search of reassurance he shambled up the stairs to the second floor and went into the bedrooms of his three children. Sitting on each of their beds in turn he looked at the various posters, shelves of books and stacks of CDs that displayed their individualities. These warm and secure rooms, where they had studied and slept and dreamed for years, gradually worked their magic, comforting him and bringing a deep sense of satisfaction and calm. The father of such wonderful kids could not be a total failure. No matter what happened to the family the children would have a shimmering future and his pride in them was a constant that would last forever.

Later McLaughlin was in the kitchen when he heard the front

door open. Frowning, he went to look and there stood Trish.

'It's just me. I thought I'd drop in and see how you're doing. Have to look for a few things in my closet, too.'

'Jeez. Why didn't you phone, or come by in the afternoon when I'm not here? I thought we're supposed to be separated, and you walk in casually like it's the laundromat.'

She only laughed and shrugged off her coat. Patricia was a tall, slender, bosomy woman with a carefully contrived tousle of blond hair, her face cosmetically lifted and tucked to make her look younger than her fifty years. Her bright eyes were green, her red dress ill-advisedly a little too tight, too short, her jewellery a little too heavy, heels just a little too high.

'Buy me a drink, sailor?' She laughed again.

'I guess so, if you want.' He mixed her a martini and poured himself one too.

'I thought I told you to get that pile of junk out of the back driveway. It looks terrible.'

'That's not junk, Trish, that's a '29 Ford Model A Roadster, a classic car. Be worth a mint some day.'

'Some day. It doesn't even run.'

'It will. I'll get it going. That's my hobby.'

'My hubby with the hobby,' she sighed. 'Your whole flipping *life* is a hobby. I don't know why you don't give up on this teaching nonsense and use your precious economic degrees to make some real money, maybe in something like investment banking or currency trading. I'd buy you some red braces. I had a fellow on the show last week, a broker, with an Hermès tie and the *cutest* red braces.'

'I guess I'm not the type. Anyway, you're not running my life any more. You're filing for divorce, remember?'

'Oh, that. Don't take it all so *seriously*, J.T. Of course we're separated, and of course there's the three-year waiting period before the, ah, arrangement, but we're still friends, aren't we? After Molly, you've always been my best friend. Don't be so *moody*.'

'I'll soon be your divorced best friend, and of course I take that seriously. It's a very heavy step, Trish.'

'It's not. People get divorced every day. It's nothing *personal*. I just started that action to give you your *freedom*. Aren't you enjoying your freedom? Aren't you dating lots of women? Isn't it fun?'

'No, and no. If I'd wanted "freedom" I'd have let you know and moved to Tahiti. But what you call freedom, I call hollow misery. Can't you just imagine me in a singles bar? Krist. We're both too old for this crap. You don't see men my age in singles hangouts.'

'But you do, even older guys. Lots of lively ones, maybe who look after themselves better than you, but upbeat, having a good time.'

'Forlorn old losers, you mean. It all strikes me as sad and forced and vulgar.'

'Oh, you do go on. It's a lot of laughs.'

'Shit, I could have more laughs at a Presbyterian funeral. Anyway, I hear you're having a thing with that TV sports producer.'

'Pish tush. We're just friends. Business associates. You shouldn't believe everything you hear. And people tell me you've been dating. Tell me about it. I'd *love* to hear.'

'Not really. The thing is, Cutty steered me into a couple of places that seemed to be singles bars. One girl, young enough to be my daughter, came on to me a bit, but it turned out she couldn't carry a conversation other than on Britney Spears' wardrobe or Harry Potter films.'

'That might at least put you in touch with the younger generation. We should both pop off in exciting new directions. Our kids are all grown up and away in university, after all. Let's *live* a little. What's to lose? If you tried at all, you could get *lots* of dates. You could be out every night roaring around and having a helluva time.'

'Hell. That's about right. Hell.'

'There you are again, being staid and poopy. Why don't you put a zippy ad in the Personals? Nice, well-fixed professor, newly liberated…'

'Sure. Swell. I can see it now: "Older despondent male, chain smoker, usually half-cut, not too smelly, soon to be bankrupt, into fantasizing and frozen dinners, seeks rich myopic soul mate who owns a distillery"….'

'What's with "soon to be bankrupt"?'

'Well, divorce means that you get half of everything and I'll get skint; that's how it works.'

'Is that what you're worried about? Have I asked you for anything? You really don't understand me at all. I wouldn't *dream* of taking any *money*. I haven't even asked you to sell the house, and I wouldn't – unless, you know, later I became unemployed or something. But I make as much as you do, and soon I'll probably make more. It's just *fabulous.*'

'Get real, Trish. Of course you'll take money. Lawyers are expensive and make demands. They'll want steak, plus two ears and a tail. I've been trying to tell you for months that women of, um, a certain age don't have long-term prospects in front of a TV camera, no matter how good their plastic surgeons.'

'Huh! Look at Barbara Walters. She's doing fine.'

'Right, LOOK at Barbara Walters. She's been snipped and sliced so much that she can barely move her mouth. And you don't even have a pension.'

'*Pension?* How boring. I can't begin to look *that* far ahead.'

'You should. Once we're over fifty there are certain realities. Look, together we earn enough, but half of enough is never adequate.'

'That's what it's all about to you, isn't it? Money, your silly economics again, and *lecturing* me about money.'

'It's bloody *not* what it's all about. What I'm saying is that you're being as realistic as a fruit fly, and it scares me. What it's about is I don't *want* a divorce, not that I seem to get a vote in this thrash. I don't *want* to lose the house, the family, our extended family at the cottage. I don't *want* the kids to come back from university at Christmas, or later on with grandchildren, and have to go to two different places, probably two cold condos, neither really a home.'

'What in the world is wrong with condos? I *love* my condo.'

'Real homey, is it? Has a nice garden?'

'At least it has a pool, a heated indoor pool, which you could never afford.' She beamed a triumphant smile. 'But, do let's stop talking about all this. Believe me, I have no wish to ruin your precious finances, and we're just going round and round in *circles.* Gosh, I've left, for now, but it's no big deal. Maybe not forever, who knows? Call it a sabbatical.'

'What are you saying? You're coming back? Are you?'

'Oh, I don't know. I told Molly maybe I'd be here at Christmas when the kids are home, for a sort of holiday, you know?'

'Jesus, Trish, I . . . I . . .'

'Wait, now. Wait. All I said was that I *might* be coming back. We might think about it again when the waiting period for the divorce is up, say in a couple of years.'

'A couple of YEARS! Dammit, you can't say that to a dog, a couple of years. You can't say that to a cat. You can't say that to a fucking GERANIUM.'

'OK, OK, forget it then. Hey, have you had any dinner yet?'

'Some.'

'Can't a girl get another drink around here? Mix me another martini, will you ... you always made a killer martini. Then, tell you what, I'll take you out for dinner. We can be on a date.'

'A date? You're kidding.'

'No, you and me. We'll go out. I'll be your date, it'll be kicky. We should maybe think about going out on dates together.'

'Plural? Dates. I can't believe this. We've been married for twenty-four years, we're still legally married, we have three kids, and you want us to bloody well DATE? By God's grubby galoshes, I believe you've gone mad. Maybe we're both flaming mad.'

But he mixed more martinis, then sat looking at her with round staring eyes. She chattered away cheerfully and asked him to suggest some questions for a guest she was having on her show the next day.

The evening careened further downhill from there. They drove to Pappas Grill on the Danforth to eat souvlaki, but he couldn't pay attention to the food. Try as he might he couldn't begin to comprehend what was going on. Try as he might, he couldn't make any sense of it. He felt as shattered as a dropped light bulb.

Trish continued to burble away about the joys of being on TV as though she had not a care in the world, as though the situation was 'normal' and his emotional distress non-existent. It was always her carefree high spirits, her childlike enthusiasm and laughter that got to him, disarmed him. Confusion and amazement blunted the edge of his hurt and impatience; hope snuffed the flame of his simmering anger. It was hard to stay angry in the face of such blithe insouciance.

She gave him a perfunctory kiss on the cheek when she said good night, with the casual suggestion that they go out together again soon.

That night his chaotic emotions and groping mind permitted him very little sleep. The scotch bottle provided no relief. He knew that the evanescent evening had written him a cheque that would bounce in the lonely morning.

- 3 -

'I have a collect call from Mr Francis Z. Springer in Prince Albert, Saskatchewan. Will you accept the charges?'

The telephone roused J. T. from a drowsy evening stupor induced by a bad day at the office and, although it was only nine p.m., half a bottle of single malt scotch. He blinked uncertainly at the receiver in his hand.

'Zinger,' he muttered. 'Holy leaping Jesus.'

'Will you accept the charges?'

'Yes. Well, no.' He sighed. 'Whatthehell. I suppose so, yes.'

'Go ahead, please.'

'Hello. J. T.? Are you awake?'

'Of course. Somewhat. Hey, you stubble-jumping old bastard, Z. How the hell are you? Haven't heard from you in years.'

'Yeah. Been a while, I guess.'

'Why are you calling collect? Broke again, eh?'

'No, no, nothing like that. Truth is, I'm rolling in it. That's why I called. Things are on the upswing. I'm still at the office, but the new owners don't allow calls outside the province from the news desk. Terrible way to run a newspaper. Fact is, I'm clearing out of here. Coming down to Toronto.'

'What?' McLaughlin almost choked on his scotch. 'You're what? You haven't been out of Saskatchewan in decades. But right now might not be the best time. I mean, I've got some troubles here. Everything has gone bugfuck. My life isn't just perfect at the moment and I don't know how much time I could spare with you. So maybe not just now, eh?'

'Well, I'm locked in and can't change my dates. Pulling up stakes. I'll be there in a few weeks. I guess I'm running out of windmills to tilt at here, and I've signed up for a new caper down your way. Got a fixed contract. I'm going to be a Canadian Journalism Fellow at your Chiliast University ... sort of like a Nieman Fellowship at Harvard, you know, a sabbatical year for, ahem, "distinguished" journalists to read or write or study whatever they choose. I'm looking forward to it, I admit. Might be a hoot.'

'Wait. This is amazing. I *know* the Canadian journalism thing. My college, Burke College, runs it. You've applied for a fellowship?'

'Won it. No sweat. There are six of us from across the country. The managing editor here put in the forms for me last spring, I guess in a frantic attempt to get rid of me.'

'I'll be damned and detonated. But this is bloody marvellous, Zinger. Saying "I just won a fellowship" is like saying "I just bedded Cindy Crawford."'

'Better. It lasts longer, and less risk of prosecution.'

'Great stuff! This is swell! I couldn't be more surprised. But I thought you had to be younger than forty to win one of those?'

'Might have lied a bit about my age. Shit, what's a decade or so between friends when you're lined up at the academic trough?'

J.T grinned and sat up straight. Fully awake now, if rather muzzed by alcohol, but beginning at last to take it all seriously, he shook his head and belched and added a couple of inches of Glenfiddich to his tumbler.

'You don't sound just right, J.T. A bit slow and thick. Into the sauce, are you?'

'No, no, I'm fine. Z., it will be tremendous to have you here. Great. What are you going to do with the year?'

'Oh, I'm not sure yet. Thought I might do a sociological study on Depression among Feminists Over Thirty-five in Urban Singles Bars, sort of a social uplift thing, or I might toss off a little paper on Hegel's Theory of Phenomenology as Applied to TV Sitcoms. Then again, I've been trying to reread some McLuhan, so I might take a course in media and communications. Or I might use the time to, I dunno, write another novel.'

'Hold it. Stop right there. "Another" novel?'

'Yeh. I've got one coming out in the spring, from a big perspicacious Toronto publishing house, which is another reason I decided I'd uproot and come down there. They'll want me for some publicity shit, probably put the old Springer kisser up on billboards or some such. Don't you love it? I are a author. They seem to think I'm the next Jim Harrison ... well, maybe the next Sweet Songstress of Saskatchewan, or the next dark and stormy Bulwer-Lytton at least. As long as their cheques don't bounce, I could care less.'

'Incredible. You never cease to astound me, Z. What's the title? What's it about?'

'Tell you all about it when I get there. We'll sit up late for a few nights over a bottle of the old infuriator and catch up, eh? There is one little thing, though, one tiny way you might help me out, ol' buddy, just to smooth my petal-strewn path to the buttertub of academe.'

'As soon as you call me "ol' buddy" after all these years of never a postcard, my nostrils begin to twitch at the scent of prairie rodent. What's the catch?'

'No catch, J. T. Nothing like that. All systems are go and glowing. It's just that I could use a trifling bit of bridge financing. Only for a few weeks, of course. Now, wait, stop with the laughing. The thing is, I have to get down there, and clearing off some of my, ah, existing obligations here at home has left me with a temporary shortfall. The lovely Fellowship lolly is certain and secure, absolutely guaranteed and up front. You could check it out at your end. But first I have to make the trip and show up before I get the goodies. So I was hoping you'd lend me just a few travel dollars. You fat cat economists always have lots on hand, eh? Just a bit of financial facilitating, you might say. You'll get it back the day after I arrive, a promise. You know *me*, buddy; my word is my bond, on my honour as a journalist.'

'Good to hear that journalists still have honour, tho' you'd never notice that in the media most days. And I *do* know you, as a rogue and a con artist with the biggest unpaid bar tab in the West.'

'Harsh, J. T., very harsh. I always make it a rule to pay my debts.'

'Sure, with money borrowed from other pigeons. How much is this going to cost?'

'Only a few coins. A mere bagatelle. Couple of thou should do it.'

'A *couple* of thou? Don't shit me, Mr Rockefeller. An airline ticket costs only a few hundred, tops.'

'Yeh, but see, I'm driving down. Need my wheels. Should be a nice jaunt. Remember the red '55 Thunderbird, Rosinante, that I won in a poker game back in '78? Still runs like a deer, and I've had her all reworked and polished and ready to roll. The perfect touring car for my eastern exodus. Be a shame if some mingy professor with bags of bucks to spare should spoil it all now. I'll even lend you the car some weekend. It's a ladykiller.'

'Look, you old fraud, I might see my way to letting you have, say, one thou, I suppose. Short term. A signed I O U. With the firm understanding that I get it back in September when term starts.'

'Stingy, J.T., very stingy. Must be your Scottish blood. Call it fifteen hundred for auld lang syne and we've got a deal.'

'A deal? You've got your hand out like a Bangkok beggar and you want more and you call it a *deal*? A thou. Max. And only because it'll be good to see you.'

'You're a mean and disappointing tightwad, McLaughlin. You've hurt me. Beggar, is it? You've wounded my pride. Just another small slice from your privileged academic pot roast and I'll forget what you said.'

'A thou. Period. And if you forget to pay it back smartly the next slice I take will be from your spavined nether regions. The fact is, I'm in some real trouble here myself. I'm down and dragging these days, if you want the truth. Very down. My whole life is on hold, and barely holding.'

'You sound low, in fact. Not much snap. I used to think of you as fat and sassy, and now you sound slow, as though you were talking from the bottom of a rain barrel, or maybe the bottom of a bottle. Not quite right. You haven't been burned in the penny stock market again, have you, or caught in a compromising position with one of those delectable coeds?'

'Worse than that. Shit. My wife, well, the thing is, Trish up and left me a while back, after she got her own show on TV. I haven't gotten used to it yet. And yeh, I guess you could say I've been leaning on the booze a bit. More than I should. But I don't rightly know what to do. Or what else to do.'

'Flaming hell. Sonofabitch. I'm truly sorry to hear that. I used to think you had one of the last happy marriages left in North America. Whaddya know, dead wrong again, eh? Never a merry thing, divorce. Always a big pain all around, in my experience. Grinds you down, and not just financially. If I ever talk about getting married again, hit me with a shovel, will you? Compared to divorce it would be easier and cheaper to find a sexy girl you don't much like and just give her a house.'

'I hear you talking, Z.'

'Well, as Plato said, the best laid wives of mice and professors gang aft a-gley. How are the kids, how are they taking it? It's always toughest on them. Fucks with their heads.'

'The kids are fine. A little confused and concerned, but they're OK. They stayed at home with me.'

'Good, good. So why did Trish walk? After all these years. Must be a serious reason. Fill me in.'

'Um, no, not now. This phone call is on my dime, remember? And it's already cost me your bloody thou. Anyway, it's a long story. The damnable thing is that I don't *know* why she left. She wouldn't say why. Just some vague stuff about "wanting a change". I'm some perplexed and shook up, I gotta tell you. When you get here we'll sit up a few nights and melt some ice cubes.'

'Right. Hang in there, daddy. Ol' Francis Z. knows all, and has been around *that* track more than most. You'll be OK. I'll just clear things up here and see you in a couple of weeks. Did I hear you say you were sending me fifteen?'

'No. Goddammit, no. My own finances are no hell, and they tell me divorce is never cheap. Just get your ass down here and bring a chequebook. Jeez, in an antique car yet. Sometimes I think you're more outta your gourd than, um, I've been lately. But it's a longish drive, take you most of a week. Just climb in your ancient vehicle and head 'er east. Hey, remember what we used to say, Z.? Remember when I had that '29 Chevy when we were undergrads, and you had that impossible '30 Nash with three fenders? We'd say ... my gawd it's a time ago ... we'd say: keep the rubber side down and keep 'er between the ditches. Remember all that?'

'I do. Yeh. I'll try. But if you break into a chorus of "Those Were the Days" I may barf. Don't forget to express me a money order here at the paper. And thanks. Gotta gallop. Be seeing you.'

For the next two hours McLaughlin stared into the cold empty fireplace and let his mind wander and finished the other half of the Glenfiddich bottle before falling asleep in his easy chair, again.

- 4 -

On a Saturday morning it did not take McLaughlin long to do his weekly grocery shopping. Just a few bags. Into the back of his car he dumped potato chips, Shreddies, milk, cat food, a round of Polish sausage, pickles, macaroni and cheese, aspirin, some frozen dinners, two steaks, and a carton of praline ice cream. Also some dish soap and Javex just in case he might get around to cleaning his kitchen. But he didn't much want to go home to tackle that, or anything else serious. With nothing but time to kill, he drove north on Yonge, idling along until he found himself almost to Richmond Hill. Too early for lunch, and he wasn't hungry anyway. On impulse he swung into a new car dealership. Looking at cars sometimes cheered him up.

The first car he saw was red, of course, as dream cars ought to be. A lipstick red convertible with a white top and white leather. It seemed to be made of one part gleaming paint, one part steel, and two parts rocket shaped testosterone. What struck him most was that ineffable new car smell, that perfume of leather and stunning newness, that subtle but compelling scent that tickled the senses with the promise of open roads and vast skies and a limitless expectation of untamed, blameless days in an unscathed future.

The salesman who approached him was all exuberance and gleaming teeth displayed in an excessive commercial smile. He wore a cheap brown suit, screaming pink tie, a mauve shirt and large glass cuff links.

'If it's zip you want, real fun, then this is your baby. Nifty, eh? Twin carbs and 427 cubic inches, enough to blow away anything else on the road. Great beast of a motor. D'you like to take it for a spin?'

'Well, maybe. How much is it?'

'Hey, I can let you have it for less than the recommended sticker price. I'm sure we can work out a deal. Easy terms. After we work out any trade-in, options, you know. Won't be a problem at all.'

'But what sort of base price are we talking about?'

'It's all negotiable, not to worry. My name's Roberto, by the way.

Call me Bob. What's yours?'

'McLaughlin.'

'No, your real name, your first name.'

'McLaughlin.'

'I mean, just so we can talk, you know, what does your family call you?'

'My kids call me Dad, or Sir.'

'Uh huh. And what does your wife call you?'

'Stupid Prick, mostly.'

'Funny, hey, that's funny. Well, anyway, let me tell you more about the vehicle.'

Bob rambled on about the CD sound system, the upholstery, the side-impact safety features, the four-wheel anti-lock brakes.

'I guess I'm less interested in that stuff than I am in the style, the design, the presentation. And performance and speed, of course.'

'Of course. The speed will blow you away, blow anything away. This baby can really roll. Zero to a hundred in nanoseconds. And I gotta tell you, it's a real babe magnet. Er, did you say you have kids? You married or single?'

'I don't know. Um, I'm not sure.'

'You're a great kidder. See, when I said babe magnet, I meant ...'

'What about a test drive. Can I take it for a spin?'

'Are you sure this is a good time for you?'

'How do you mean? I'm here, aren't I?'

'The thing is, well, I hope you don't mind my asking, er, are you sober?'

'Sober? Of course I'm sober. It's still morning for gawdsake.'

'I was just wondering. People do get hangovers, eh? There is, though, and no offence, just a slight whiff of scotch that made me wonder whether, you know, this might not be an ideal time for you to take off in this car. The company's insurance might not cover if ...'

'Dammit. I've never been so insulted in my life. You can take your babe magnet and do you know what you can do with it?'

'Wait, hang on. I was only trying to be safe, protect you, and ...'

But McLaughlin had already walked away in an indignant huff, a mode of transport much favoured by men with a certain kind of problem. The experience had not cheered him up at all. He thought, maybe I should stick to the '29 Model A.

Zinger was in Prince Albert, at his office desk, sorting and discarding old files, offensive threatening letters from readers, and unpaid bills. His round file was overflowing. A brisk young summer intern and gofer named Jimmy approached him with a sheaf of papers.

'Mr Dowie says you're to attend to this. We need a lot of filler for tomorrow's women's section, sorry, lifestyle section, and the usual "Miz Morals" copy hasn't come through. Can you do a quick take on it?'

'Me? No way. In another two hours or less I'm collecting my pay and I'm gone, outta here for a year. Don't bother me.'

'Dowie says, no copy, no cheque. Says, quote, he's always goofing off but I'm going to squeeze a few more drops out of him before bidding him a fond good riddance, unquote.'

'Shit. He said that, did he? It's only three-twenty and I'm not due to ascend bodily into heaven till five. I'll show the bastard. Are those the questions from the mail?'

'Yeah, this lot. Plus e-mails, which I just sent. If there aren't enough real letters, Dowie says just make up some questions on your own. You've done *that* before, God knows. Keep them short. Dowie says when you handle this stuff your answers are too long anyway.'

'My boy, when will you learn that wisdom doesn't come in sound bites? Now buzz off and let the resident genius do his thing. Let's see, here.'

* * *

Dear Ms Morals,

I am a man greatly interested in athletics and fitness. My aerobics instructor gave me an old copy of *Weekly World News* which reports on a man who can turn his head a full 360 degrees. Is this a good exercise? How could I learn to do this?

Jock

Ms Martha Morals replies:

Yoga. This interesting technique can be learned through the excellent self-help booklets available from the Prince Albert College of Yoga, Chiropractic and Upholstery. Send $20 to the College care of Dean Francis Z. Springer, P.O. Box 627, Prince Albert, Sask.

But no, unless you intend to take it up seriously as full time employment, as with a circus, Ms. Morals cannot recommend this practice wholeheartedly. If your neck turns 360 degrees you risk damaging certain nerves and veins, cutting off the supply of blood and oxygen to the brain, and thus rendering yourself unemployable as anything but a TV announcer or newspaper editor.

There is also the considerable hazard of confusion: you may lose track of whether you are coming or going and end up bumping into yourself or pouring drinks down the back of your collar on social occasions.

* * *

Dear Ms Morals,

Our class is doing a project on ecology and the environment, which I care about very much. But in recent years even some socialist politicians have criticized such wonderful organizations as Greenpeace, which causes me confusion. Could you please recommend some reliable sources of information on global warming?

Joey

Ms. Martha Morals replies:

In general, most newspapers don't take pollution very seriously because most pollution is caused by our biggest advertisers.

What we laughingly call 'nature' is all very well, but at the northern lake where Ms Morals usually vacations, the environment has been turned into a noisy hell of power boats, motorcycles, power mowers and weed cutters, not to mention incessant loud thumping boom boxes. If a cottager wants to avoid noise, fumes, and oily water, she must flee from 'nature' and return to the tranquillity of the city. This reinforces my basic view that we are all doomed. Sometimes I think we should abolish the environment because it takes up too much space and is too hard to keep clean.

Zinger looked up at the clock.

'Hey, Jimmy, does this copy have to go to the editorial desk, or can I bang it right in?'

'We're running late for the Saturday edition, so dump it right into the system.'

'Real good, then, James. No problem.'

'Are you writing real answers this time? Or are you playing at it?'

'Well, well, are you telling me to take all this bullroar seriously?'

'This is a newspaper, after all.'

'Ah, the idealism of youth. That this *should* be a newspaper is precisely my point. But do you really think it is? A proper newspaper, my young friend, should be about facts and truth and investigative reporting and shit disturbing. Journalism should glow with craftsmanship and analysis and alert social conscience. It should not be filler for ads and shallow ideology and smelly little orthodoxies.'

'I agree. That's why I want to be a journalist. But are you really helping the cause by being funny?'

'I only satirize what I care about, Jimmy. The root of humour, as Mark Twain said, is anger and sadness. So the proper journalist should keep his tongue in his cheek and cock snooks at those who debase real newspapering. Filling the pages with horoscopes and celebrity cleavages, lifestyle fluff and this advice to the lovelorn crap is only cheap infotainment, not to be taken seriously. So I don't.'

'But do you take *anything* seriously, Zinger? Your copy is always nonstop jokey.'

Zinger regarded the lad with a sharp gaze. 'How old are you, Jimmy?'

'I'm nineteen, why?'

'Nineteen. Well, well. By the time you're my age you'll see that there are only two possible responses to life and to journalism. Listen, you can view life as a tragedy or you can see it basically as comedy. Those are the choices. I believe the tragic view is too easy, and not much fun. Tears clog the mind; laughter eases the soul.'

'OK, but recognizing tragedy doesn't mean you have to be solemn and dreary. Can't you just be serious?'

'Almost never advisable. So-called "reality" may be too distressing to be taken seriously. Humour may be your best defence.'

'I can't see that you need much defence, eh? You're leaving for the big city to have a whole year off. You've got all the luck. I envy you.'

'Envy? Dear God. Jimmy, Jimmy. Let me tell you, you see before you a man with, um, a few problems.'

'You? Problems?'

'Me. Let me level with you. I'm a lapsed idealist, a failed romantic. I'm a man facing a third divorce. My children are barely speaking to me and I'm dragging an alimony payment or two and some unpaid bills and bar tabs, hoping to leave town one jump ahead of the bailiff. That the sort of thing you envy?'

'Well no, gee, I didn't realize ...'

'And you don't want to know.'

'Sure, I do, but ...'

'What have you been studying at university, Jim?'

'Uh, some history and some poli sci, but mostly English lit.'

'Lit. I see. And does the name John Newlove mean anything to you?'

'Some kind of a writer, isn't he?'

'Right. A poet, and one of the best. A Saskatchewan boy, like you and me, only better. He wrote a poem once, in a book called *The Night the Dog Smiled*, with a title of "Concerning Stars, Flowers, Love, Etc." A favourite of mine. You put me in mind of it. You might like it. I'll copy it out for you and leave it on your desk, later. Now, piss off, lad, and let me finish my labours before the time is up.'

'Sure. Anything you say. And good luck to you, eh?'

'Thanks. Damn. Where was I?'

* * *

Dear Ms. Morals,

When my older sister Louise came to visit, she brought her new baby boy. One morning I woke to find the baby crying and Louise gone. That was almost five weeks ago. What should I do?

Concerned in Meadow Lake

Ms. Martha Morals replies:

Possibly by now you'll have fed the baby and maybe changed its diaper. Cleanliness is next to godliness, although both tend to be a damn nuisance.

Ms Martha would suggest that there is often a lively market for babies, so you might be able to sell it on eBay. However, you might make more if you sold tickets and held a raffle.

When Jimmy came back to the office the next day, this is what he found on his desk in Zinger's scrawled handwriting:

Make it easier, they say, make it easier. Tell
me something I already know, about stars or flowers or,
or happiness. I am happy sometimes, though
not right now, specially. Things are not going
too good right now. But you should try
to cheer people up, they say. There is
a good side to life, though
not right now, specially. Though the stars
continue to shine in some places and the flowers
continue to bloom in some places
and people do not starve in some places
and people are not killed in some places
and there are no wars in some places
and there are no slaves in some places
and in some places people love each other,
they say. Though I don't know where. They say,
I don't *want* to be sad. Help me not to know.

John Newlove

- 6 -

McLaughlin's oldest daughter Jocelyn, a senior at Queen's University, was due home for the weekend to attend a friend's party. J. T. was eager to see her. He'd made sure he had extra food in the house, particularly fresh vegetables, and even made an attempt to clean up the kitchen, shifting some dirty dishes into the sink, and to put some order to the books and newspapers strewn around the living room. He'd asked the cleaning woman to come that day, but she said she couldn't come till the following morning.

Although it was a warm, brilliant early autumn evening, he decided to make a fire in the fireplace. That would be welcoming to Joss. There is an agreeable ritual, almost a sacrament, about laying a fire, lighting and enjoying it, something comforting and reassuring, securing the bond between man and place, denizen and his den.

He smiled to himself as he lit a match and ignited a cheery blaze and thought, 'Be it ever so humble, there's no ache like home.'

Music, that would help. His daughter always said he had no music from after World War II, and it was true he was a traditionalist and a square about most things in life. Were there any discs here less than two decades old? Probably not. He laughed at himself. He loaded the player with a few things by the Clash, Van Morrison, the Stones, and an old Beatles anthology, then settled into his leather chair with a tall glass of scotch and water, just a light one. Joss had said she might arrive late in the evening. He picked up his current favourite novel, *The Road Home* by Jim Harrison, and began to read it for the second time. At page ninety-nine he found Harrison, who was no stranger to alcohol, writing: 'It was as if the dreams needed to be sedated in this atmosphere of turbulent darkness.... At such times we drink so as not to go mad, but then we have only found another sort of madness.' Too right, J. T. thought, good on you. But soon the book slipped from his hand as he fell asleep. When he roused himself to go upstairs to bed he noted that his daughter's jacket had been dropped on a chair and her presence was in the house.

In the morning, J.T. was sitting at the kitchen table in his pyjamas drinking coffee and nibbling toast when he heard her coming down the stairs and rose to greet her with a kiss and a hug.

'Hey, ol' Joss, what time did you get in?'

'It was after eleven-thirty, Dad. You were snoozing in your chair and I didn't want to wake you.'

'Yeh, thanks. When I went up to bed, I checked that you were safely tucked in, of course. I sure am glad to see you. You look great.'

She poured herself coffee and said, 'You, on the other hand, don't look so great. You're too thin, I think, and a bit, um, haggard. Are you all right?'

'I guess I didn't sleep very well, but I'm fine.' He didn't want to tell her he had anxiety attacks and nightmares.

'Are you and Mom getting along any better?'

'Maybe, some. We had dinner together recently.'

'Do you think she's all right? I mean, she's been acting a bit strange recently. Last week, for example, she sent me a box of clothes, things she'd worn once or twice on TV. We're the same size, you remember.'

'Right. So what's strange about that?'

'Well, they were sort of glamorous-older-woman stuff, you know, stuff that doesn't suit me, things you might wear to a big fancy party but nothing I could wear on campus. Some of them were quite bare, showed a lot of flesh, and when I asked her about that later on the phone she just laughed and said "If you've got it, flaunt it." Not exactly a very motherly thing to say to a twenty-one-year-old college girl, would you say?'

'Perhaps not, but she's just doing her show-biz thing, I'd say. It may not last.'

'I sort of hope it doesn't. I liked it better when she was a real mom and not coming on like something from Rodeo Drive. Toronto is scarcely Hollywood, TV show or not. She's getting carried away by it all, over the top. I guess it all worries me a bit.'

'God knows it worries me, too, Joss.'

'So what are you going to do about it?'

'Do? I guess I don't really know what to do. Whatthehell am I supposed to do?'

'Not just sit here at home and fall asleep in your chair and do *nothing*, for pete's sake.'

'Well, I can tell you that months ago, just after she left, I went to see a shrink, who's a friend, someone your mother had consulted years ago, before we were married, so he had a good handle on – what we're dealing with here. And all he recommended, after long talks, was "guard the hearth". That's about all he had to say, repeatedly, "guard the hearth".'

'Not a wonderful plan for action, I'd say. And I don't suppose he had any wise words for you about, you know, drinking?'

'He did, yeh. Said it wouldn't help anything, was counter-productive. Urged me to cut back.'

'Good. And you should. It's no accident that Rob and Davey and I all found summer jobs out of town this year. I mean, being at home has not been all fun for us lately. And we look to you for, I don't know, something, some action.'

'Uh huh. Action. Like what?'

'How do I know? But, Dad, you've been left, dropped. You're being pushed around, and you've got to shove back, hard.'

'Easy to say, Joss. I've tried everything I can think of, really. I've tried to reason with your mother. I've talked about how a life on camera is not the sort of thing a fifty-year-old woman can count on for long-term career or secure income, and that the Peter Pan crap may be OK for a while, but Peter Pan didn't have to pay rent.'

'So how does she respond to that? What does she say?'

'That's just it. She doesn't say *anything*. She just shrugs and blows me off. No reaction, except maybe a yawn and cheerful indifference. I might as well be talking to the refrigerator.'

'I know what you mean. She won't talk about it seriously with me either or tell me anything. But what about you? You're getting worn down and depressed. You mustn't blame yourself, Dad. I don't believe you've done anything wrong to Mom, and she's never said you have.'

'I should hope bloody not.'

'I have a friend at school who's a grad student in psychology and she says that a number one cause of stress is being blamed for, or blaming yourself for, things you didn't do or can't control. And rejection. Both of which apply to you. Is that a fair analysis?'

'Yes, that makes some sense. I'll admit to being a bit depressed.

But who's to say what's "normal"?'

'Not much to me seems normal around here. It struck me when I walked in last night, the house is empty. I mean, I'm used to coming home to mom and you and my brothers, five people, but now there's only you. Just one. I realized how lonely you must be.'

'True. But I'm OK now, Joss. Really. And it's not all about me. Look, marriage is not just about two people, a man and a woman. After years together, plus children, a marriage becomes a family, a unit. It becomes organic, a living, growing organism like a tree, with new branches and deeper roots, with the whole greater than the sum of the parts. But if you chop off half the trunk, the tree will die. Love? Sure. But it's also about responsibility and mutual support and, well, survival.'

'Aw, Dad, what I'd say is … oops, ohmygawd, look at the time! I have an appointment. I'm supposed to be downtown to get my hair done in, like, ten minutes. Quick, call me a cab.'

'No, take it easy. I'll drive you down.'

'What? Not in those ratty old pyjamas you won't.'

'Sure, I'll just put a trench coat on over top, no problem. Come on. No one will notice or care. I've got my extra set of car keys right here. Let's go.'

'I dunno, Dad. What about house keys?'

'Hey, I'll be gone for only a few minutes, and I've got to leave the door open for the cleaning woman. Hop it, kiddo.'

He delivered Joss to Yorkville Avenue and was back within twenty-five minutes. But he found the front door locked. Clutching his coat around him, he hurried to the back door. It was locked too. He pounded on the back door. No answer. Returned to the front and pushed on the doorbell. No answer.

Mrs Koulosac had arrived ten minutes earlier. A rather shapeless and lumpy grey-haired woman, a recent immigrant still rather timid about this strange new society, she looked warily up and down the street to be certain she had not been followed by purse snatchers, rapists or serial killers before she entered, locked all the doors, changed into work clothes and turned on the old noisy vacuum cleaner.

Having failed to make her hear him, McLaughlin cast about for some way to get in. Maybe his sliding bedroom door to the upstairs sundeck was unlocked, if he could climb to it. A long extension ladder in the garage was half buried behind boxes and car parts, but here was a shorter stepladder that might do. He carried it to outside the sunroom and set it up in a flower bed by the window, then shucked off his trench coat and began to clamber upwards. The ladder was unsteady. It had rained during the night making the earth soft, and the front legs of the metal ladder began to sink into the ground. 'Shit!' he bellowed, clutching at the eavestrough and losing his footing as the ladder fell away. He clung by his fingers to the sharp edged trough and his legs thrashed about in the air for a foothold. Then the elastic on his old pyjamas gave up and the bottoms fell away. He tried to haul himself up, but couldn't, and just hung on.

At this moment, prompted by a moving shadow at the window, Mrs Koulosac looked up from her work, blinked, couldn't believe her eyes, gaped at the dangling spectacle of the bottom half of a naked man, emitted several small yelps of fear and dismay, and ran for the telephone to dial 911.

McLaughlin had to admit defeat and dropped nine feet to the ground, striking his knee on the edge of the ladder when he landed, opening a gash on his leg which bled profusely. Sitting prettily among the petunias he cursed a blue streak, reached for his pyjama bottoms and used them to staunch the blood. Minutes later he was still sitting there, swearing loudly and wondering what the hell to do next when two cops appeared with drawn guns.

'Boy, am I glad to see you guys,' J. T. shouted. 'The feeling is not mutual,' said one of the cops, thinking this must be a madman or an addict very high on drugs. The other cop handed J. T. the trenchcoat, insisted that he put it on, now, and demanded to see ID, which in his trouserless state McLaughlin could not produce.

'But I live here,' he protested, 'this is my house.'

'Sure it is, pal,' said the first cop. 'Shall I cuff him, Harold?'

'Might as well, Ray,' said the second cop, 'until this whole scene makes some sense.'

'But officer, the woman inside can identify me as the owner and bring out my wallet with ID. She's my cleaning lady, just ask her.'

The first cop went around to the front door and rang the bell repeatedly before Mrs Koulosac finally opened it. She unleashed a long loud volley of indignation in a guttural central European language, but the only words Harold and Ray could make out in

English were emphatic enough: 'I quit. I QUIT!' She plunked a hat on her head and stalked off down the street, refusing to look back.

Things began to calm down and get somewhat sorted out when an elderly neighbour lady, Mrs Wilson, ambled across her lawn to the squad car and identified the man in the trenchcoat as Professor McLaughlin. 'Yes, he lives right here.' One of the cops accompanied J. T. into the house while ID was found and presented. Meanwhile the other cop explained to the neighbour as much as he understood about the incident from the 911 call and what McLaughlin had said about the ladder on the ground. 'I'm not entirely surprised,' Mrs Wilson sniffed. She looked around to see if anyone but the cop could see her, then put her hand to her mouth and made a tipping motion. Then she giggled and said, 'His wife left him, you know. It's just what this neighbourhood needs, officer, an inebriated flasher who's an acrobat. May I offer you some tea?'

J. T. and his pal Cutty Cuttshaw were driving home together from the university. 'Your old friend Zinger?' said Cutty. 'Really? For the whole academic year?'

'Yeh, that's what he said,' J. T. muttered.

'That's good. He might cheer you up, maybe a lot.'

'I doubt it. He couldn't be coming at a worse time.'

'But he's very upbeat. You've always told me what an amusing rogue he is.'

'Yes, but he's always causing trouble. The sort of free spirit we sometimes envy, or imagine we wish we could be. But he's a loose cannon. He can be a real pain in the ass.'

'Your oldest friend, and you can say that?' George (nobody called him George) Cuttshaw had steel-grey hair and the fresh open face of a cherub, which contrasted nicely with his bulky shoulders, thick waist and even larger chest. He looked at J. T. quizzically.

'Cutty, I really don't want him here now, not while I'm so preoccupied. Oh, he's basically a good guy, sure enough, and I've known him since high school, since the time I was in grade nine and he was in grade ten, and yes, you bet, all through university in Saskatoon, we were close. We had great times together, we were on the debating team, both wrote for the campus newspaper, read a lot of the same books, hell, chased the same girls. But when I went off to England to try for the Ph.D. and he decided to stay in Saskatchewan and move to Prince Albert as a newspaperman, we both changed, I guess, and grew apart. Well, we corresponded for a while, sometimes quite regularly – but then even that stopped. We lost touch. And now he's suddenly showing up. Never left the province, never visited me in the east, and when I visited my parents back home and dropped in to see him in Prince Albert, he seemed a little, um, distant, impersonal. He was cheerful enough, but something just didn't feel quite right, not the same. This is a man who hasn't left Saskatchewan, ever.'

'Really?'

'Really.'

'Nothing ever stays the same. You know that.'

'You think? Or maybe nothing ever changes. He was always utterly unreliable. He's been divorced at least twice, you know, and from really good women. Bad track record, I'd say. On the phone the other night he just wanted to borrow money for the trip down here. I dunno, the idea of seeing him just makes me uneasy, maybe even sad.'

Cutty considered that for a few silent moments, keeping his eyes on the road.

'Well, nostalgia and disappointment aside, friends is friends. But even if you can't go back to what you were in bloody high school, the bond is still there, somewhere. Could be he needs the same emotional support we all do. Does it occur to you that maybe he's not entirely the happy camper he pretends to be?'

'Well, on the phone the other night he sure seemed relentlessly cheerful.'

'I dunno, J. T. Sometimes I think you don't realize that *everybody* is having a hard time. Not just you, everybody. We all get hassled and tired and desperate, it's just a matter of how well we conceal it and roll with it. Give him a break. Give yourself a break. Nobody has an easy time of it. It's a struggle.'

'Shit, Cutty, and "say not the struggle naught availeth", and other uplifting bromides, eh? Give it a rest.'

'I'm entirely serious. And about the male bonding thing, too. I've thought about it a lot recently. I think it's bred into us from the pre-historic hunt and from wars, battles where males needed to collaborate with each other in a fight, guard the other guy's back for him, pick him up if he falls. So the bonding thing is rooted in a tough code of loyalty that helps men survive. Come on, isn't that the sort obligation you feel to Zinger?'

'Could be. Some, I guess. But it can be a bloody nuisance.'

'Sure, but necessary. Bonding means you can't refuse a buddy.' Cutty paused. 'Look at it this way. Between grade nine and marriage, how many girlfriends did you have? Thirty?'

'I guess twenty or more; why?'

'But only one Zinger. Just one more important male friend. I rest my case. Friends can provoke the hell out of you, but if we don't guard each other the wolves will get us.'

41

'You may be right.' J. T. lapsed into a resigned silence. After a few moments' thought he continued, 'And I suppose this male-bonding thing that you brought up has to do with all the things you can't talk to women about much, like sports, cars, drinking in bars with buddies, sexual experiences in the past ...'

'Or in the future?'

'And can only talk about with men. I always found it hard to talk to Trish about, um, you know, fears. Male egos are so fragile. We're afraid of rejection, eh? It's hard to admit to a woman, particularly your wife, that you're afraid you might not be good enough.'

'Yup, you've got it. Rejection is a basic fear, maybe the biggest. Where the world expects, and women expect, men to be bold and strong, full of macho confidence and bravado, a guy can only talk about the real black dog doubts and fears with another man. Women would judge us, think we were being weak. But a man would understand. Hell, we all have fears, we'd be stupid if we didn't; fear that you won't get the job, can't do the job, can't succeed the way we hope, can't get it up, can't say all the right things and meet the emotional demands of the female, can't handle the debts, hell, can't be heroes. At bottom, is there anything more frail than the average male's self-esteem? Fear is a terrible thing if you have to face it alone. So, male bonding. You might call it a kind of reciprocal support, maybe a kind of love.'

Surprised by his friend's direct openness, J. T. considered for a moment, staring at his shoes and then at his buddy, thinking that this was an unlikely exchange and a helluva ride home, before he said, 'Even love dies, Cutty.'

'Does it? Does it really? I don't think so. Not if you are glad it happened. It just becomes changed, that's all. You may leave it, but it never leaves you. Regret may replace hope, but memory won't let go.'

'You think so? Maybe that's it. Maybe that's why we dream about the past. Aw, Cutty. Ol' Cutty. You're a good guy, you know? You're all right.'

- 8 -

On Friday morning, in a hallway of Chiliast U., Cutty came face to face with Z. Even though they hadn't met in many years, they exchanged greetings cordially, then stood back and regarded each other with curiosity.

To Cutty's eye, Zinger, though older, looked just the same. A lean and spare six feet two, loose-limbed but erect as a lamppost. His face was now craggy and rough textured as a ruined barn, but it was still long and narrow, with a sharp pointed nose above rather thin lips, snapping grey eyes, and thick black hair combed straight back in a Brylcreem pompadour. His smile was bright, but rather a sardonic grin. He wore a light summer suit of bright blue, a dark blue shirt with a white tie, and white shoes: the full Winnipeg.

Cutty led the new arrival into his office to sit down.

'Good trip?'

'Fine, thanks.'

'Glad you made it. Term begins Monday. I think J. T. was getting worried about you.'

'So where the hell is J. T.? I left a message on his voice mail saying I'd show up by Friday. What sort of shape is he in, anyway?'

'Hard to say. Even when he's here he's often not all here. Distracted, sort of blunked. And drinking like a refugee from the Sahara. How much has he told you about his, um, recent circumstances?'

'Well, he told me that his wife walked, and he doesn't seem to have accepted that at all. On the phone, I could tell he was into the sauce. That's a steady thing, is it?'

'Yeh, fairly constant. Sort of sad. He doesn't much appear "drunk", at least not at the office, but he hasn't been exactly sober for more than a year, since Trish left. Not blasted, exactly, more like well-marinated. I'm pretty sure he keeps a bottle in his office or his briefcase.'

'How the hell can he teach if he's lit?'

'I'm not sure how much longer he can get away with it. He's

relatively level and OK till five o'clock or so, maybe till four; just keeps topped up till evening when he opens the sluice gates. Around here and in class he speaks very deliberately, EE-NUN-ciates very carefully, and I guess he gets away with it tolerably well in lectures, but his colleagues know he's half in the bag and not all with it. Much tut-tutting, of course. He may have to take a leave of absence if he doesn't straighten 'round. Doesn't look well, sort of bleary and bluish. Hasn't written a thing in more than a year. Damned shame, really. If he's not careful he's going to have a great future behind him.'

'Been to a doctor for help, I suppose?'

'Yeh, oh yeh, but he doesn't listen or take advice. I think the only hope is to resolve his problem, his divorce, one goddam way or the other. But he's not facing up to reality. He insists that he still loves Trish, although sometimes I wonder if he isn't just stubborn and a loyalist, and can't understand it when others aren't. And the poor bastard is delusional. You'd swear he was the only guy in North America who ever had to face divorce. To say he's a terrible bore about it is a vast understatement, like saying the Grand Canyon is a ripple in the landscape. Last month I went over one night to take him out to dinner and a Blue Jays game, and he loves baseball, right? But he didn't want to go, wouldn't go. Shit, he just wanted to sit there and stay home and guzzle and talk about his marriage and how it would all work out. Ain't love *grand*? The big-deal intellectual who can't count up to zero. And if you ask me, Trish is playing him like a trout on a line, keeping him on the hook in case her escapades don't work out. But he's going on about guarding the hearth, for the tenth time. And he slam-dunked a whole bottle of scotch while doing it. It's hard, Zinger, very hard. You'll see. Could we change the goddam subject?'

'Sure, yeh. I don't much like what you're telling me, Cutty, but somehow I'm not surprised. The silly prick was always naive and full of emotional over-reactions when I first knew him in high school. A hopeless romantic. Used to fall in love with every female who let him fumble with her buttons. Always moaning about some dizzy broad and leaning on trees and reading poetry. Maybe I can be some help, most prob'ly by fetching him a brisk kick in the ass.'

'He'll be glad to see you, too.... Anyway, when did you get in?'

'Last night, kinda late. Bloody long drive it was. I've been on the road almost two weeks, zigging and zagging across the map of the northern U.S. till I crossed back into Canada at Detroit and got into range of CBC radio, thank God, and got here about midnight. Luckily it was easy to park. There was a free spot with a sign that read "Reserved – Board of Governors", so I pulled in and left a note on the windshield saying "New Member, Bank President".'

Cutty expressed doubt that his Saskatchewan licence plates would lend much credibility to that, but Z. waved his concern away. 'And Gandy – let's go find B.J.' Cutty guided Zinger through the building to the office door of Professor Emeritus Gandy, tapped, and swung it open to reveal a short little fireplug of a man with a finely trimmed white beard, a prominent nose and a ruddy complexion, a very high shiny forehead and white hair down to his collar. His Donegal tweed suit looked as though it had not been pressed in a decade. Although he was at least eighty, his movements were vigorous and his eyes danced behind small glinting spectacles. 'Francis, my dear fellow,' he exclaimed in a gruff voice. Warm handshakes were exchanged and, it being Friday and almost noon, Gandy suggested a quick drink. The three of them agreed to go to the P.O.E.T.S. Corner (Piss On Everything, Tomorrow's Saturday) at Dooley's; probably McLaughlin would show up there. Cutty drove, and before turning south they gave Z. a quick tour of the main buildings with running commentary by the voluble Gandy. The east campus, particularly Burke College and Trinity, he pronounced 'most agreeable'; the west campus he damned as mostly 'Stalinist Gigante', great slabs of concrete vulgarity that were an embarrassment to a civilized community, although recent plantings along St. George Street softened the stunning blows to the senses of the monstrous science buildings. Z. remarked how formidable the main library ('Fort Book') appeared, but Gandy assured him it was a fine institution, particularly the Fisher Rare Book Collection, and that the interior of the main building 'worked' and even had a certain austere charm. No building filled with books can be all bad, he said.

As they drove downtown Zinger declaimed loudly on the horrors of Toronto traffic.

'Holy jangling Jesus, I've never seen anything like it. Apparently you've gotta be stark raving mad to get a driver's licence here. When I came in on the 401 Thruway I was belting along at a fair clip, over the posted speed limit and in the middle lane, and cars passed me on *both* sides, left and right, like I was standing still. This is the only town I've

45

ever seen where you get inside the city limits from the highway and everybody speeds up! They swerve in and out changing lanes without signalling, like rockets on a video game. Krist almighty! Crazed drivers, insane. When I got down to the lakeshore, looking for a motel, I saw cars zooming through red lights. Even taxis. Terrifying. Bloody mayhem and warfare, it is, more dangerous than being a mallard in duck season. Do you have to be demented to drive here, Cutty?'

'It helps. Or aggressive as a kamikaze. It's just the big city. You'll get used to it.'

'Never,' said Z. 'Never.'

At Dooley's, presided over by the legendary owner-philosopher-chef Steve Barootes, they settled themselves at a large round table, 'Reserved', with covers of books by members displayed under the glass table-top. P.O.E.T.S. had been a casual but flourishing lunch group every Friday since 1980, a haven for thirsty journalists, novelists, editors, disillusioned ad men and dyspeptic academics. Once there had been some serious drinkers gathered; now almost as many drank Perrier or diet Coke as draft beer. It was an erratic feast, sometimes as few as three or four showing up, sometimes as many as twenty, people just dropping by when they felt like it, including several scribblers from out of town who knew they'd always find a few congenial souls gathered. J. T. McLaughlin, one of the initiators of the circle who regarded this Friday gathering as a cheerful ritual, always said that if you were invited once you were a member and if you came more than twice you were automatically a Founding Member.

Zinger, of course, knew nobody. He smiled tentatively at nine strangers around the table. Introduced by Gandy, he met two novelists, a photographer, an actress, a distinguished professor of classics, three journalists and a bright and bouncy woman who was an associate professor of fine art. Gandy effused that Mr Springer was his favourite student from years ago in Saskatoon. Cutty suggested that he thought J. T. was his favourite. A good man, B.J. acknowledged, perhaps too often lumbered with the label of 'promising', but he'd begun to despair of McLaughlin unless he snapped out of it and shaped up. Where was he, anyway? Not like him to miss a Friday.

Talk around the table turned to Bob Fulford's latest essay and how Canada would be a diminished place without newspaper columns by Rick Salutin and Joey Slinger. Remarking on Z.'s home base, someone observed that his origins won him points, and that maybe he would join Fotheringham and Pam Wallin as Saskatchewan's best exports since W.O. Mitchell. On one side of the table a dispute arose as to whether John Newlove or Al Purdy had been the finest poet since Louis MacNiece. 'Tie,' cried a voice. Draft Guinness and Smithwick's Ale flowed, while B.J. ordered another Beefeater martini and urged shunning newspapers for a serious rereading of Gibbon. Fisticuffs almost broke out among the journalists as to whether the most beautiful singer was Shania Twain or Diana Krall. When Cutty began a long disquisition on economics, somebody threw at him a celery stick from a Bloody Mary, and B.J. explained why Cutty was wrong and Schumpeter and his disciple J.K. Galbraith should be reckoned the most important economists of recent decades. Cutty said that Galbraith was to economics what Jackie Kennedy was to politics, and much roaring ensued. A lot of braised short ribs of beef were consumed. Someone spilled beer on the actress.

It was a normal lunch.

On the drive back to the campus Zinger said how glad he was to meet such lively people, and wondered aloud how he'd make out this year, surrounded by so many heavy-duty intellectuals. I guess I'm not used to talking to professors, he allowed. Cutty said he'd do just fine, since J.T. often said Z. was to bullshit what Clinton was to interns.

B.J. snorted and cut him off. 'Intellectuals? Har! By God I wish we had even a few more real intellectuals at this university. Another dozen would help, a lot. You mustn't be taken in by professors and Ph.D.s, Francis. Clever chaps, of course, but mostly technicians who know more and more about less and less and don't give a sweet damn for anything beyond their own narrow "professional" fields. Like most universities we've been squeezing out people in philosophy and classics and swelling the faculty ranks in accounting and business studies. But we have English lit scholars who don't read contemporary writers, historians who focus on one decade only in the nineteenth or the twelfth century and wouldn't know Beethoven from bebop. More and more we're emphasizing "professionalism" to the point of tunnel vision. Younger faculty are pressured to stay within their own minuscule "fields" and spend every waking moment accumulating brownie points toward promotion by publishing papers on the left kneecap of the tsetse fly but know little of their own government or history or culture. Oh my. Trained, they are, but not educated, not intellectuals. Technicians. Plumbers.'

'Come on now, B.J., it's not as bad as all that. There are lots of bright people in the universities, certainly in this one,' said Cutty.

'Bright, I grant you. I'm saying, not civilized. I used to tell you lads to hurry and collect your Ph.D.s so that you'd then have time to acquire an education. Nowadays they tend not to do that, but to remain within the narrow ruts of their "specialties".'

'But with the knowledge explosion it takes most of a guy's time to keep up with the flow of information in his chosen "rut".'

'It does, indeed. But did you ever think of simply deciding *not* to keep up? To stop reading the petty dross in most academic journals that is written by specialists only for other specialists? Does it occur to you that you could back up in order to get ahead, and to read and reread the great books and pitch the journals? "Information", you tell me. I say, "Where is the wisdom we have lost in knowledge? Where is the knowledge we have lost in information?"'

'You quoting McLuhan?' Cutty asked.

'T.S. Eliot,' muttered Zinger.

'Har!' laughed B.J. 'Good guess, Cutty, but Francis has it right. There you are. A good generalist who cares is often more of an "intellectual" than rows and rows of specialist chaps. That's why you Journalism Fellows are so refreshing, Francis; that's why you have nothing to fear from the plumbers. Bless me, I can remember when there were giants here, scholars who could bestride many disciplines, like Harold Innis, like McLuhan and Norry Frye and Brough Macpherson and Des Conacher ... I knew them all, Francis. Minds that ranged over the universe. Civilized chaps. Do you recall what Frye said, by the way, at the memorial service for Brough?'

'Can't say that I do,' said Cutty.

'Norry said, "Macpherson and I first came to know each other through a mutual love of Bach. We'd take coffee together after our lectures and talk of music. In those early days we could come together for a meeting of minds rather than as a collision of monuments." Do you like that, Cutty? Oh, I like that exceedingly.'

'There are still some around, though,' Cutty observed, 'intellectuals as you'd say, like Polanyi or Sparshott or David Cook ...'

'Exceptions that underscore the rule,' B.J. insisted. 'Why, in your own department, look at what happened to Sam Hollander. Our most internationally renowned man in economics, probably our only hope for a Nobel Prize in your field … his line is the history of economic thought, Francis … and they squeezed him out. Told him his field would no longer be required in the graduate program, he'd no longer have Ph.D. students, so of course he left and took a major position in Israel, and we lost our best man. The plumbers won again.'

'J.T and I both voted against the majority and for Sam. We objected.'

'But did you organize a protest? Write public letters scorning the technicians? Picket the economics building? Threaten to resign?'

'Well, no, but …'

'I rest my case. Disgraceful business. What sort of a world is it, I ask you, when universities become anti-intellectual? Clever little narrow vulgarians ease their way into power and trample the intellectuals.' He shook his head. 'Now tell me, Francis, what are you going to read while you're here?'

'Well, Professor Gandy, I thought I might do some media courses, Innis, McLuhan, Chomsky, that sort of thing.'

'I've asked you before, please call me B.J. Everyone does. I can certainly tell you a lot about McLuhan. When I was here on a sabbatical, oh, some forty years ago, I sat in on his celebrated Monday evening seminar, and we became friends. Lovely man, Marshall. I knew Innis's work quite well, so there wasn't much trouble following Marshall's line of thought. But now I must be off. You have my numbers, Francis? Splendid. I'll look forward to seeing you next week.'

When they had dropped Gandy off at his apartment on St. George, Z. pressed Cutty for information on where to find some people he'd need, such as the registrar, the bursar and a good bookie.

'Thanks. Good. And while we're at it, tell me something about J.T.'s erstwhile wife.'

'You never met Trish?'

'Only once, when they were first married and he brought her out west to meet his folks. She never came back west with him again, I guess.'

'That's a fact. She complained about that one trip; didn't much like any part of it. J.T. went back and forth to Regina a lot, particularly when his parents were ailing, but she declined.'

'J. T. used to show me snapshots of her and the kids. One of the things that bothers me about this whole situation is the way I've always thought of J. T. as such a happy critter, cheerful, always smiling, God knows an optimist. I think some people regarded him as rather casual, IQ notwithstanding. Certainly not gloomy. I always thought he and Trish were solid. I remember her as good-looking and bright and vivacious.'

'Vivacious isn't the half of it. A dynamo who can turn on the charm. She could charm the stripe off a skunk. Lots of snap and flash, but if you want my opinion she's like a pinball machine that lights up and goes boing-boing but doesn't really get anywhere. Dynamite figure, though. After she became, well, glamorous, she cut a wide swath. Didn't lack for male attention around the TV studios, and that may have made her think she was destined for greater things, the fast lane and showbiz and all that. Maybe she was. Domesticity began to pall, I think. Alice – that's my wife – has friends who work in TV, used to give me reports, not always flattering. Alice says Trish tends to be all sail and no rudder.'

'Alice doesn't like her?'

'Oh, sure, likes her well enough, but they were never close. Trish can be great company, great fun, but maybe a short attention span. Wonderful at cocktail parties.'

'Ah. An SCW without much LHP.'

'Sorry?'

'A Silk Coat Woman without Long Haul Potential.'

'Something like that.'

'You said glamorous, Cutty. I remember her as pretty fetching.'

'Oh, absolutely. A striking woman. But over-done, I'd say, more than enough make-up.'

'My old daddy used to say that if a woman wore make-up too thick, before you married her you should take her out to the lake and drag her behind the boat for a while to see what she looked like when she came out.'

'Your dad may have had a point there.'

'Is J. T. feeling – betrayed?'

'There's a lot of anger in him, Alice agrees, but he doesn't want to admit it or let it out. Still holding it in and waiting for a reconciliation that isn't, I'd say, at all likely. Still in denial, is my opinion.'

'Bloody stupid place to be in, denial. So I guess he's still trying to make nice.'

'Well, you know how he is. Sort of guy who says "thank you" to an automatic vending machine. I've said to him, the good news is you're a nice guy; the bad news is you're too nice a guy. Told him two years ago that he should have thrown her out and changed the locks. Might have got her attention.'

'Ah. So that's how it is. I wondered. 'Nuther mule kicking in his stall. Damn.'

'Mules. She doesn't get serious, but she sure does seem to get around. Alice says, Trish seems to be happy if you give her a stool in a singles bar, in front of a mirror.'

'I get the picture.' Zinger considered this a few moments in silence. 'I suppose no outsider can ever see behind the curtain of a marriage, but you have to wonder what any couple does about the basics, Marx and Freud, money and sex. What do you think, Cutty?'

'Damned if I know what to think. On your two topics, though, I'd say money isn't a problem. They're both spenders, not savers, but there's more than enough to go around.'

'And the other thing? Sex? Maybe he's slipping her the limp white asparagus when what she wants is the bright, stiff one-eyed carrot.'

'Who knows? I sometimes think she's become a bit unhinged. Alice says she may have married too young and is making up for lost time. But my impression of him, for what it's worth, is that he's physically OK and apparently much more than willing, but she often said, "No thanks; I already gave at the office".'

'Bloody hell,' said Z., laughing. 'Bloody hell.'

9

That evening, after the two had finally connected by phone, Zinger pulled into J.T.'s driveway, and J.T. emerged from the house to welcome him. They greeted each other warmly, with much back-slapping and whoops of prairie glee. Z. resisted being hugged, but happily took part in the obligatory ritual of comparing cars. J.T. admired the recent paint job and re-chroming of Z.'s 1955 Type 40A T-Bird and murmured, 'Sweet wheels, sweet.'

Zinger returned the compliment with: 'If that Model A Roadster in the back doesn't run, what do you drive regularly, this heap?'

'Yeh, it's a Chev station wagon.'

'I can see that. A pile of shit.'

'It's OK. Gets me there. But you don't have the hard top on your 'Bird, just the rag top. Maybe a bit breezy for travelling, eh?'

'Nah. I left the hardtop shell at home. I always say, anybody who'd go "motoring" in a sedan would go boating in a submarine.'

They went inside. J.T. put some old Jimi Hendrix and Van Morrison CDs into the player, poured two large drinks, and set a bottle of scotch, a bucket of ice and a pitcher of water on a coffee table between them.

Z. looked around at the house, which he found quite spacious. To J.T. it was just the standard midtown Toronto sort of structure; he and Trish had bought it twenty-four years ago when prices were still low. It was just a serviceable dwelling. You entered from the left side on a few cement steps. Living room, kitchen and dining room, sunroom off the dining space. Sliding glass doors to a small deck. Four bedrooms upstairs. In the basement, McLaughlin had built an office-study of modest size, lined with bookshelves. The walls were made of plywood and stained a rather dirty walnut, a red shag rug on the floor. His desk was large but old and scarred, with a cork-panelled wall over it to which he had tacked clippings and cartoons and postcards plus some photographs, mostly of his three children and a blow-up of a snapshot of Trish in a scanty white bikini. Between the study and the laundry room were a shower and a toilet, partitioned off in plywood, unpainted, and both in need of a serious application of Javex.

The living room was broadloomed in a middle-green carpeting, just a little too bright. Couches along the two long walls upholstered in an indifferent beige. At the far end was a large brick fireplace with built-in bookshelves on both sides, a large painting by Teitelbaum of a family group over the mantel, and dark green leather wing-back chairs on either side of the hearth, where the two men now sat. Not an elegant room, not notably tasteful. Functional. Comfortable.

'Tell about your trip. What took you so long?'

'Marvellous trip. I might have taken a small detour here and there, and stopped a while in Chicago. Great town, that. Saw a game at Comiskey Park. You know the art museum there, eh? and the aquarium, and the bar at the Drake? And the lakefront blew me away. Now that's what a city should look like. Can you tell me why Toronto has turned its back on the lake? I got a few glimpses of the water last night driving in, and when I drove around this morning I saw rows and rows of ugly bloody high-rises cutting the people off from the lakeshore. Alarmingly stupid.'

'There'll be things you'll like, too. Give it a chance.'

'Already I think I like the university. They've given me a nice room in the college.'

'But the trip, Z. How'd you like travelling?'

'Ah, the driving.' Z. mulled at this for a moment or two, and then said: 'It was amazing. I never knew roads could be so long. Once I got the hang of it and got into a rhythm, it was lovely, with perfect weather and wind in the face and the road stretching out like a river and the scenery flashing by and Satchmo or Mozart on the tape machine or laughing at the loonies on U.S. talk radio and stopping anytime, anyplace, to nose around, and country breakfasts at truck stops and the only problem in the whole world being to choose a motel near a good roadhouse and grinning at how fat the moon was over the trees and getting up with the birds and rolling on again without a deadline or a care in the universe and a cooler of beer in the back and the 300 cubes of my thwacking great motor just thrumming along like the pulse of God and just, you know, going, and being gone and being high on it. It was, I tell you, it was glorious. It was just aces.'

J. T. smiled, and refilled their glasses.

For the next two hours they talked in a catching up way about old friends and old places and old times, each circling a bit warily around the other in search of new paths into old shared experience and former intimacy. J. T. fetched more ice and another bottle.

Zinger reverted to the subject of his cross-country drive. 'Wouldn't have missed it for the world, not for all the crampy airplanes at Kennedy airport, wherever that is. We should take a driving trip together one of these days, since we're both bachelors.'

'Hey, I'm not a bachelor. It's only a pause, an interval. Trish is already talking about coming back.'

'Funny, I don't see her around at the moment. You told me she walked, months ago, and now you say she's coming back?'

'Well, um, maybe in a year or so.'

'A year? Uh huh. As Richard M. Nixon said, there's one born every minute.'

'Barnum, he said that.'

'You got something right, at least.'

'Sure. Don't be cynical, Z. She means well, really. She's just *gotta* come back. She's my best friend, she always tells me that. Just this week we had a serious talk, and you want to know what she said? She ...'

'No.'

'Whaddya mean, no?'

'I mean, no, I don't want to hear it.'

'Of course you do. Look, even on the day she first left, moved out, Trish sat on those stairs, those stairs over there, and she cried, and she said: "I'm not sure why I'm doing this, and I'm uneasy and I'm scared, but I must."'

'That inspires great confidence, eh? Such clarity of good sense and purpose. Jeez. I'll admit I can see how that sort of talk would leave you a bit buffaloed.'

'Sometimes I think she's confused. It's got me flummoxed, true enough.'

'Anyway,' Zinger said, reaching for the ice bucket. 'You said on the phone that you wanted to hear about my novel.'

'Did I? Novel. Right. Of course I do. What's it about?'

'The usual stuff – God, Life, Love and Destiny. And tenure.'

'Wait. Whatthehell do you know about tenure?'

'A fair bit. Years ago you wrote to me, a lot, complaining about it, or about not having it.'

'Huh. That's years ago. I don't much see the point to that. What's the title?'

'Oh, I was thinking about calling it *War and Peace*, but I settled on *J. T. and Me*. Written as an exchange of letters, epistolary.'

'You can't be serious. I don't believe it. Are you going to sit there and tell me that, from the days we used to correspond, you'd actually take letters, my letters, and screw me around by putting them into a book?'

'Fiction. No harm in it. A lot of facts changed and some names changed to protect the guilty. Prob'ly won't sell much anyway. Over the past winter I played around with the notion of doing a novel – write about what you know and all that – based on letters, partly on some I found in an old box, partly from memory, with a lot of artful distortion and hyperbole, and quite a bit of plain lying thrown in. Fiction is mainly lying, they tell me. I might have some slight talent for prevarication and buggering about with the truth.'

'Too right, you do. If bullshit could fly you'd be a 747. But you're having me on, aren't you? For a minute there you had me going, about letters I mean, but you're just funnin' the ol' perfessor, aren't you? Ho ho. Have another drink. I should have known better.'

'Whatever you say, buddy. I hope you're still ho-ho-ing when the publication date comes around. If you are, you can break a bottle of champagne over my head to celebrate my fifteen minutes of fame. It may be good for laughs.'

'It's good to see you, Z., great to have you here, laughs or not.'

'And did they tell you that our old high school is gone? Yup, they tore down the whole damn building a few years ago.'

'No. Old Central Collegiate. That's a shame.'

'It is, in very sooth. Now there's a real Canadian thing, come to think of it. Why did they call it "Central"? How bland can you get? Shoulda called it Louis Riel High, or Sir John A. Macdonald High, or W. O. Mitchell Collegiate ... no, I guess it was built too early for W. O. But they coulda changed it ... something with some character, personal, real. But no, hadda be "Central". Shit. And when I drove into Toronto last night and saw that great Jeezly tower downtown, I thought, why is it called the CN? Why not the Marshall McLuhan

Tower? He's famous for communications throughout the world, for kristsake, and they call it the CN. Sometimes I despair of this country. It seems to doubt and dislike itself and its greats. "Central". "CN". Gimme a break.'

'You've got a point. But what's say we do the old school yell. Remember those leggy cheerleaders? Wow. I always had the hots for that boobiferous one named Nancy. Come on.'

They got up and linked arms over each other's shoulders and went into the chant:

> Che hee! Che haw! Che haw haw haw!
> Rip 'em, smear 'em, eat 'em raw.
> We've got the zip, the pep, the thirst
> To light the flame, put Central first.
> C–E–N–T–R–A–L, CENTRAL.

'Again,' Zinger shouted. 'Again!'

And they bellowed and capered and lurched across the room, knocking over only one lamp and a small table, enjoying themselves hugely. When they fell back into their chairs, Z. realized he was out of puff, maybe more than a little tight.

'You feeling at all swacked, J.T.? Soon we should call it a night. Will you empty these bloody ashtrays, at least? Well, yeh, maybe just one more. Have you got an honest bottle of rye whisky out in the kitchen? Can't say I like this scotch as well as rye.'

'Sorry, I'll go find some. But no, I'm not tight. Never seem to be able to get really tight these days. I just hold it at a steady level, you know, keep the gauge at "normal".'

'Doesn't seem entirely normal to me, and you've thrown back more than I have.'

'Used to it, I guess. The thing is, I can't seem to sleep, or stay asleep when I fall in. I keep waking up with, well, the panics and the dreads. Then I pace the floor and pour in some more hooch until I get back to sleep.'

'I don't much like the sound of that. Couldn't you read, or maybe write?'

'Yeh, I do, I write a lot. Look, here's a letter I wrote to Trish the other night.'

'I meant serious writing.'

'This is serious. I want you to read it, tell me what you think.'

'I don't want to read it, J. T. This is private. I don't want to know.'

'It's OK, we've never kept secrets from each other. And see, it's only a few pages.'

'A few? Eight, I make it, no, nine.'

'I haven't finished it yet. Maybe could use some editing.'

'Whatthehell you writing, here? Seems like an endless *Apologia Pro Vita Sua* to me. Jeez. I'll take it into the john with me, read some of it there. I gotta take a Mulroney.'

'A what?'

'A crap, a dump, a Mulroney.'

Z. sighed and ambled off to the can. When he returned he grabbed his glass and began to shout.

'You're out of your tiny mind, McLaughlin! Clearly you've gone bugfuck! You shouldn't let me or anyone else, never mind Trish, read this cow-flop. Bloody awful! You're just so relentlessly *reasonable*, or so you seem to think, falling all over yourself trying to *explain* to her. This isn't a love letter at all, you're fucking philosophizing at her. Spare me such idiocy. I may not know much, but I know marriage isn't about reasoning. You can fight her or you can fuck her or declare love for her or bang her upside the head, but you can't *reason* with her. No sense to that. Women are people too, you know, and there's no reasoning with people when they've got their emotions up.'

'Aw, you don't understand. Trish goes off on tangents, but she's bright. A barrel of laughs, too; headstrong, and a free spirit, you might say.'

'I might, eh? J. T., please, I ask you, extract your learned head from between your buttocks and tell me, what part of "no" don't you understand? She's gone. Departed. Split. Out.'

'Wait till you meet her again. You'll love her. Never a dull moment, great fun.'

'Fun? In a pig's pattoot. You don't sound to me as though you're having much fun. From what you've told me, and Cutty told me, she sounds kinda sad, actually. Thrashing around and always taking off and not knowing how to land. But she's got you down and dirty and chained to the trough, for sure. No, it's sad.'

'How can you say that? She's having a wonderful time.'

'I wonder. Sad, I'd say, because like most people she's so self-centred that she doesn't even know she's hurting other people. This crappy world and maybe your over-indulgence of her have conned Trish into the view that she can have continuous pleasure even if it means giving up happiness. It's the "consumer mentality", the Disney mentality, in which you're persuaded that you can have everything, instant jollies, but that turns out to be only diversion, sensation without real satisfaction. And you, you poor sap, either you don't see it, or you've bought into it, and you're trying to deal with it rationally when the world is never rational, and you're so goddamn busy trying to protect her that you've forgotten to keep your dukes up and protect yourself. You're a mug, J. T., a self-deluding chump. It's a cinch you can't fight reality with a bottle or a theory; you need a sword. You've got to cut her off. Shit. Here endeth the lesson. And I do believe I'll have another shot of that rye.'

'Huh? Oh, sorry, Z., I didn't notice your glass. Help yourself.'

'I always do. I always make it a rule to help myself. You should too, that's what I'm saying. Did you hear what you just said, again? "Sorry." Fuck that. Women. Disney. Fuck the lot of them, and shape up and grow up. I know, let's sing.'

'Sing?'

'Yeh, anything to cheer up this wake.'

And Zinger led them into a rousing rendition of an old favourite song from their undergrad days:

> School days, school days, dear Progressive school days,
> No readin', no writin', no 'rithmetic,
> Never a sign of a hickory stick;
> Mornings we'd play and loaf and chat,
> Afternoons, tours of this and that,
> Or tests to find out what you're gifted at.
> They never found nothin' for me.

J. T. eventually mustered up a grin and joined in.

> ... dear Progressive school days;
> Map reading, rhythmics and untidy art,
> Taught to the tune of a Guidance chart.

> I was a boy with a low IQ,
> You were a bit subnormal too;
> Though none of us worked we all got through,
> Though how is a mystery to me.

'We never did find out who wrote that, did we?' asked Z., rather pleased with himself. 'But now I think I'll just crawl over to this couch here and grab a little shut-eye.' He kicked off his shoes, flopped out, and was soon snoring. J. T. poured himself another inch and began to doze off in his chair. A calico cat jumped onto his lap, and he stroked it. It was, he thought to himself, quite a nice reunion.

10

Next Tuesday morning Zinger sat in McLaughlin's office trying to choke down a cup of bitter institutional coffee.

'Krist, this tastes like the sort of thing they use to remove tattoos. Anyhow, there I was in the main library looking up stuff, and I found one of those silly economic journals you write for. And the subjects, and the titles, good God! Whatever happened to real topics in the real world, like power, or poverty? "Studies in the Minutiae of Marginal Mini-phenomena in Minor Aspects of Micro-economic Theory".'

'You rehearsed that,' said J. T., permitting himself a small smile.

'Some, maybe, but it's all such shitteroo, and the monetary stuff is worse.'

'You're not all wrong. Which reminds me, there's that thousand bucks you said you'd pay me back on arrival.'

'Oh, that. I'll have to open a bank account today …'

They were interrupted by a brisk knock and a pretty and perky face poked around the door.

'Hi,' said J. T. 'Come in.'

'Excuse me, I didn't realize you had someone with you. Shall I pop in another time?'

'No, no, perfectly all right. What can I do for you, Jessica?'

'I wanted to mention that you missed yesterday's meeting of the search committee. We barely had a quorum. The Dean is on sabbatical and the Vice-Provost seems to be away on sick leave. Since you were the next most senior person left we elected you committee chair.'

'You didn't. Damn. I didn't even want to be *on* that group of numb … I mean, numerous luminaries lumbered with the search.'

Z. eyed this newcomer with some interest. She was tall, well-rounded but trim, with dark curly hair pulled back over small alabaster ears and small, discreet gold earrings, and she wore a dark blue suit and a skirt whose moderate length did not entirely conceal shapely legs. Her complexion was pale and perfect; her eyes were large and luminous, arrestingly dark blue, almost purple. Z. rose rapidly from his chair and thrust out a hand.

'Hi. I'm Springer, an old friend of McLaughlin's. Here on a Journalism Fellowship.'

'Pleased to meet you. Any friend of J.T. is all right with me. I'm Jessica Pemberton. My friends call me "Pepper". Cutty mentioned that McLaughlin was expecting a friend from back home. Welcome.'

'Thanks.'

'Sorry,' said J.T. 'I was so nonplussed with Jessica's news that I didn't intro...'

'It's OK. I was just passing by. But make a note of the next meeting. It's already set for eight a.m. Monday.'

'So early? Sure, I'll try.'

After the door closed, Z. shook his head.

'Who the hell was *that*?'

'Her? Oh she's a colleague from down the hall. Associate prof. of history.'

'Go on....'

'Ph.D. Princeton, I think. Writes about the eighteenth century. Also does some Canadian history. Gandy says she's one of the best in the department. And plays the cello, I'm told.'

'Looks real good to me. Very classy. No rings. She married?'

'Was. Divorced a while ago. Two kids, I think. A rather nice colleague.'

'I didn't think that professors came in shapes like that these days. Thought they were all scruffy like you and Gandy. She's elegant. "Pepper". Well, well.'

'Now, about that money.'

'I think she likes you, J.T.'

'We're friendly.'

'I think she really likes you. Such a pretty little number, and brains into the bargain. Do you think maybe she has the hots for you?'

'For me? Don't be loony. Why do you say that?'

'The eyes, man, read the eyes. Real high-beams. Hell, the straight goods walks right in on you and you're too dumb to see it. Why aren't you dating her?'

'For Kristsake, Z., I'm not dating anybody. I'm a married man.'

'Not much evidence of a wife at your house the other night.'

'Well, no, not at the moment. But there will be.'

'Don't bet the farm on it. You should be dating.'

'At my age? Dating? I'd feel ridiculous.'

'Not so ridiculous as sitting around at home with your thumb up your ass.' Just then, Z. had another thought, and decided to play it. 'Besides, it might make Trish jealous, make her worry.'

'Really? I hadn't thought of that. You think so? Nah, that'd just be playing a game.'

'Sure, life's a game and you gotta be a player. Spectators are mugs, and as a cheerleader you wouldn't cut it.'

'She does have a great smile, I'll give you that. But you really think it would make Trish sit up and take notice?'

'Absolutely. Sure thing. Trust me on this; I didn't write the Advice to the Lovelorn column in my paper because I'm stupid, you know. I'm a bloody expert.'

'Well. If you say so, Z. I'll have to think about it.'

- 11 -

Later that day Zinger dropped by B.J. Gandy's office. B.J.'s large oak desk was clear, as neat as a paperknife; a trim stack of correspondence sat on one corner, a copy of W. Jackson Bate's *Samuel Johnson* on the other. Bookshelves lined the walls, the volumes all arranged in reassuring order, and on the hardwood floor was a worn but good Turkish rug. Two photographs were set to one side of the desktop in silver frames, the larger being of Gandy's late wife, the smaller of T.C. Douglas, Tommy, Saskatchewan's late Premier and the father of Medicare. A large window afforded a pleasant view of the college quadrangle. B.J. rose from a battered and cracked leather swivel chair to greet his visitor.

'Ah, Francis. It's most agreeable to see you. Come in, come in. Pull up that old wing chair, there's a good fellow. I trust you've had time to settle in a bit, unpack and all that. Have you enjoyed your new surroundings so far?'

'Thank you, yes, B.J. I'm quite comfortable and beginning to find my way around.'

'Excellent. Well done. It takes a while, of course. And I hope you and McLaughlin have found time to get reacquainted and swap lies, eh? Always a treat to see old friends from Saskatoon, I've no doubt. How do you find him, his mood?'

'A bit depressed, I'd say. Not in great shape. What's your reading on him?'

B.J. paused to consider. 'On hold, I'd suggest, not entirely himself. I keep thinking of a line by your namesake, Francis Bacon, a line I had to dig up and reflect upon. It goes: "He that is used to go forward and findeth a stop, falleth out of his own favour, and is not the thing he was." Apposite, don't you think?'

'Absolutely. I agree. But maybe I can shape him up some.'

'I do hope so. And what brings you along to my musty digs on such a fine sunny day?'

'Well, I dropped in to a couple of classes yesterday, to get the prospectus and reading list on one or two that seemed promising, and size up the instructor, get the feel of things. Just to sit-in and audit courses on various subjects that sounded worthwhile. But I was surprised how few classes there seemed to be available on McLuhan, communications, media, that sort of thing. Any suggestions?'

'But of course. Yes, yes. There are several classes available at the graduate level in the McLuhan Institute, although I'm not well-informed about them. Undoubtedly worthwhile. The best man I know here, in the field, is Robert Logan, charming fellow, author of a fine book called *The Sixth Language*. He was a friend and disciple of McLuhan and pushed on with many of Marshall's ideas, but his appointment was initially in the Department of Physics. I'm not sure where or what he teaches this year, although I can find out for you. And there's a chap in Pol. Sci., what's his name? who offers a course on Media and Politics; listed in the calendar, don't you know.'

'I think that's one I sat in on yesterday. Seems interesting enough. Big tubby man, maybe fifty, with a small ginger beard?'

'That's the fellow.'

'He wants us to start by reading McLuhan's *Gutenberg Galaxy*.'

'No no, that wouldn't do at all, I think, not for starters. First you should read chapter 2 in Logan's book, on Innis and McLuhan, then brush up on your Harold Innis, and start with Marshall's celebrated interview in *Playboy*, 1969. It's reprinted in a book titled *The Essential McLuhan*, and most helpful.'

'Wait, B.J., I'll jot some notes. But why Innis? I thought he was the historian who wrote ponderous tomes on Canadian economic development – on cod and furs and timber and all that natural resources or "staples trades" stuff – that bored me to tears when I was an undergrad. With respect, where's the relevance?'

'A very great scholar, was Harold Innis. A genius, I think. You see, he showed us how to study the staples trades, you're right, but not the materials of the trades. Rather, the patterns, the implications for political economy, the *effects* of the trading arrangements. Later, when Harold turned his attention to communications, he used the same analytic approach, so that with "information" regarded as the staple, he again studied the *effects*, not the content, of methods of communication.

'Innis's young colleague Tom Easterbrook, McLuhan's closest

friend from undergraduate days in Manitoba, introduced Marshall to Innis and the Innisian view that the staple is the key, the pattern and method of communication is the key, or the medium of communication – carving on stone, writing on clay tablets or papyrus, writing on parchment, then printing – is the key. The method of transmitting information is the key. Each medium will shape the content and the impact differently. McLuhan, being one of the nimblest minds this country ever produced, quickly picked up the Innisian approach, and from "the technology is the key", formulated the catchier "the medium is the message". So what Marshall picked up from Innis, the crucial importance of studying the *effects* of the means of communication, not the content communicated, was the fundamental insight, don't you see, and McLuhan was off and running, never looked back. And he acknowledges, in *The Gutenberg Galaxy*, that his own work was an elaborate set of footnotes to Innis.'

'Hold it, B.J., wait. I'm still scribbling here. From "the staple is the message" to rephrasing it as "the medium is the message". Hmm. Damned clever leap, that. So if I'm following you right, the medium, the technology with particular effects to focus on, can be writing on parchment, or printing, or radio or TV? What matters is *how* it is communicated, not *what* is communicated, have I got it?'

'Precisely, dear boy. That's it, that's the Innisian springboard from which Marshall bounced so high. *Quod erat demonstrandum*, Q.E.D. Simple, of course, once you see it. For centuries scholars studied content, which is important and fair enough, but the big breakthrough was to abstract from the content to perceive the various impacts and effects of each medium, a whole new field of inquiry. Don't you love it, Francis? Oh, I like that immoderately. With intellectual puzzles, often the simplest solution is the best.'

Gandy chortled and hugged himself.

'You know, B.J., I've tried off and on to read McLuhan for years and never been sure I had the hang of it. This helps. But I guess you weren't entirely serious about reading him in *Playboy* – were you?'

'Oh, totally serious. McLuhan is very hard to read at first, for the uninitiated. You see, he decided that print was obsolete. Print, being linear, mechanical, logical, rational, had been displaced by electronic communication, particularly TV, which he saw as non-linear, impressionistic, full of images and fleeting movement mainly conveying emotion, but not rational continuity or analysis. So to interpret the effects of TV, Marsh wrote and talked in quicksilver impressions, probes, one-liners, images.'

'Which made him hard to follow. I often thought he wrote like a pinwheel, zapping off in all directions like fireworks, leaving me dazzled but without – what you said – continuity. I guess he usually made me feel slow, stupid.'

'Exactly, that's it. Like the students of formal, classical painting in the nineteenth century suddenly confronted by impressionism. That's why the *Playboy* interview was so important and helpful.'

'I'm not sure that I....'

'Again, it's simple when you see the clues. That magazine, scarcely an intellectual journal, had made so much money in the skin trade that it could hire the best journalists and pay top dollar to any celebrity who'd submit to a feature interview. They brandished their cheque-book at McLuhan when he'd become famous, and he said no. But they persisted, and finally he succumbed to the cash and the appeal of a major pop platform. A crack interviewer came up to Toronto and followed Marsh around with a tape recorder for several days, while McLuhan fired off comments and aphorisms – the famous ones: that print was obsolete, that TV was non-linear – and probes and oblique jokes as he loved to do. The journalist took a transcript back to his editor in Chicago, and they agreed that all they had was fun and – you'll pardon me, Francis – zingers and verbal pirouettes. Makes no sense at all, the editor protested, and sent the journalist back to try again. Same result. More largely unconnected and incomprehensible snap and flash, verbal pyrotechnics, but little that was usable. In desperation, the journalist, a very bright and persistent fellow, reread all of McLuhan, took careful notes, and then cut and spliced the previous tapes and patiently shuffled his clips and quotes until he could render McLuhan's talk into logical, linear form: a, b, c; 1, 2, 3. The editor was delighted, but Marshall was furious. That's not me, he steamed; that's not at all the way I talk, or write. Still, some of his friends persuaded him that the printed "interview", a contrived artifice and a phonus balonus, was the most clear and accessible presentation of McLuhanism yet available, and a great boon to students.'

'Huh. Seems pretty strange and devious to me. Concocted.'

'Certainly. Yet isn't that what scholars call "the historical record"? An artful contrivance?' Gandy chortled again, delighted with Zinger's moralistic doubts and reservations. 'Enormous fun, all this,' B.J. insisted. 'Adds spice and the personal touch to what we laughingly call "truth". So that's where I insist you begin. History made informal and personal, Francis. After all, if you're not interested in people, then books are little use.'

Z. shook his head, but agreed he'd start where Gandy pointed him. Soon he departed, but as he walked out into the quadrangle he was muttering to himself, 'Holy dissembling shit, have I come back to university after all these years to read lies in bloody *Playboy*?' Then he laughed. 'Good old Gandy. Wisdom is where you find it. And in the damnedest places.'

12

Cutty and J. T. left an evening meeting of the Faculty Association and shot a few frames of billiards at the club before starting the drive home. On the way, Cutty suggested they stop at the bar of the Windsor Arms for a nightcap, knowing that was something J. T. was always up for.

'This used to be one of my favourite cocktail lounges,' said Cutty. 'Still looks good. Close enough to Bloor Street and the university to attract the right sort of people, and pricey enough to be elegant.'

'If you say so,' J. T. said, 'but all those women on the bar stools, do you think they're upscale hookers?'

'No way. The management wouldn't allow that. They're mostly just single women I guess, unattached, some nice-looking ones, maybe models or actresses, wouldn't you say?'

'I'd say I think you've steered me in to a singles bar, Cutty. It's really not my sort of thing. You know that.'

'Aw, just trying to expand your horizons a little. Come on, come on, trust me on this. Bring your drink and let's lean on the bar and make a little conversation.'

'Conversation, oh sure. Like "Do you come here often?" "What's your sign?" "Are you a terrorist in drag?" Is that how you're supposed to do it?'

'Just chat. Be relaxed and be yourself and chat up one or two of these beguiling ladies.'

Soon Cutty was ordering more drinks and having an animated conversation with a tiny, attractive blonde about the relative merits of Plymouth vs. Tanqueray gin and how Hemingway always ordered his martinis 'not too dry.' When he discovered she worked in a brokerage firm Cuttshaw was immediately carried away by a discussion of the stock market and its imponderable dips and swings. J. T. meanwhile shifted from foot to foot and tried to smile hopefully at them both until Cutty introduced them, saying that McLaughlin was a well-known economist and market forecaster. The blonde, however, contrived to focus on Cutty, nodding and laughing just a little too loudly at everything he said. Amazing, thought J. T., how easy it all is when fundamentally the guy didn't give a damn.

Presently a twenty-something brunette, wearing glasses and displaying an arresting cleavage, appeared at McLaughlin's side and jolted his elbow.

'Sorry,' he said and stepped back.

'No,' she said, 'I was trying to get your attention. I'm Joyce, hi. I overheard your friend say you were an economist. Is that right? I think I've seen you around the university.'

'Could be,' said J. T. smiling at his own dazzling repartee.

'And your name is McLaughlin? You must be the one who wrote that, um, unusual book on Harold Innis?'

'Guilty,' replied J. T.

'I had to read it in my undergrad program at the University of Alberta. I found it quite, um, interesting, you know? Now I'm here at Chiliast, just started this fall to work on an M.A. in economics. I guess we have a lot in common, being in the same department and all.'

'Oh, doubtless, yes.'

They talked for a while and she managed to keep the conversation moving, if slowly, without finding anything else much in common apart from his evident interest in her scooped neckline and her inquiries about other members of the economics faculty.

'Do you know whether Professor Rogers is gay?'

'I don't know, might be. Why do you ask?'

'Well, I know he's fortyish and a bachelor, so I kind of assumed…. See, I'd never take a class with a gay instructor, because they don't, um, appreciate women and I don't do so well.'

'Uh huh?'

'So can you tell me whether any other of the professors, like, fool around?'

'Fool around? I don't suppose. How would I know? Why?'

'Just asking. But I guess you do, right?'

'Not really.'

'I mean, here you are in a singles bar at ten-thirty and all, so it seems to me a fair question.'

'Hey, I didn't know this was a singles place, I just walked in with my buddy for a jar. Does that make me the Kinsey Report or something?'

'What's the Kinsey Report?'

'Never mind. Before your time.'

'Now don't get upset,' she murmured, leaning forward over his arm dramatically, 'it's simply me being inquisitive, that's all, and getting to know my way around a new place, new people. I was thinking I could use some help with my international trade course, maybe some guidance on my research paper on the E.U., so if you were willing, I thought we might be able to work a little something out, a little friendly accommodation, you know, to our mutual advantage.'

He stared at her blankly.

'I mean, you're not half bad-looking for an older guy, and we might enjoy each other's company, and …

'No, I'm sorry, Joyce, but no. It's out of the question. Besides you must understand that a fellow could lose his job, with or without tenure, if he got caught even laying a glove on a student.'

'Surely that only matters with undergrads, not graduate students?'

'Any student, any level. Dear God. And the other thing is, I'm married.'

'Oh. Since when did that matter to a guy? Not to most guys it doesn't.'

'Well. You may be right. Anyway, if you'll excuse me I've got to go to the men's.'

'Sure. But think about it, OK?'

He moved away and started towards the facilities. As he passed by where Cutty was sitting, deeply engrossed in the little blonde, J.T. whispered, 'Come on, I've got to get out of here.'

Cutty looked startled and asked, 'Why the rush?' He objected that he wanted to finish his drink and his conversation.

J.T. rolled his eyes and marched briskly to the john. When he emerged he avoided Joyce and took a seat at the very back of the room where it was dark and he could fret in silence. A waiter asked if he wanted anything. He ordered a scotch, a double, neat. He was not having a merry and joyous time. Instead J.T. felt about as lively as roadkill on the 404 and hoped that Cutty would hurry it up so they could go home.

His dreary thoughts were interrupted by the arrival at his table of a tall slender woman in a tight black jumpsuit, white makeup, and shiny black hairstyle in a rather severe pageboy. Would she be thirtyish? forty? Hard to tell in this light. Certainly a wide confident smile, though, very self-possessed.

'I hope you don't mind if I sit with you for few moments. I'm Katarina. I'm trying to avoid that man at the bar who thinks he's God's gift to women. Jeez. Is he wrong.'

'May I offer you a drink?'

'Sure, thanks. And would you shift around a bit so you're blocking his view, and maybe try to look a bit interested, as though we're old friends? That's better. Thanks. This place is usually very casual, but it's turned into a zoo tonight and I seem to have been stood up. But my friend may show after a while. She's always late.'

'Sorry to hear it, although I should say that my buddy and I intend to leave quite soon.'

'Just give me few minutes. You may be rescuing a damsel in distress.' She laughed.

'That's me. I'm Sir Galahad,' he said with a shake of his head.

'Take it easy. You're doing just fine, professor.'

'How'd you know I was a professor? Is it that obvious?'

'No, no, you look like a regular guy. Actually it was the fat turkey at the bar who said that. Pointed you out as a neighbour of his. Says your name is McLaughlin and that you live a block and a half up the street from him.'

'Can't say as I recognize him.'

'He seems to think he knows you. Says you're well-known in the neighbourhood as a flasher who gets visits from the police. Can that be true?'

'WHAT? He said that? That's preposterous! I can explain why he'd ... I can explain how he might have got that ... but damn, it would take too long, and you'd never believe it anyway. I really must drink up and be going. It's been nice meeting you miss, ... Katarina.'

'Wait, hang on just a second. Our fat friend also said your wife is Trish McLaughlin the TV star.'

'I wouldn't say "star" but she's on TV, yes, a daytime show.'

'Right. I've seen her, had her face on a billboard outside a TV studio near where I live. Quite the looker. Rather a dish if you like the mature woman. That's really interesting.'

'If you say so. It's just a job, I guess. Now I really must ...'

'Could I interest you in some supper? A snack? It's early yet, only about eleven. What do you say? I am sort of peckish.'

'Very kind of you to suggest, maybe another time, but I really must call it a night.' He drained his drink and started to get up.

She put a restraining hand on his arm, gazed at him searchingly, laughed again and said, 'Just half a minute. What I thought I'd ask you, since we're just talking bar talk or whatever, might be a fun idea.'

'I'm not sure that I …'

'Listen, why don't we, why don't you arrange something with your wife. You know? Like a little get-together. A rendezvous.'

'I don't get it. Why would …'

'You're not all that quick, are you? A meeting. A threesome.'

J. T.'s jaw dropped. He opened and closed his mouth like a goldfish but no words came out. Abruptly he got up and left the table, shuffled down to Cuttshaw and said he was outta here. Now.

In the car on the way home Cutty pressed him on why he was in such a flaming rush, so J. T. filled him in, babbling about both Joyce and Katarina in disbelief and a great flop sweat. But Cutty only laughed. He laughed so hard he had to pull over and stop the car. He clapped J. T. on the back and said, 'I told you you were irresistible. Well, I'll be damned. Wait till I tell all that to Alice.'

'And wait till I tell Trish. She'll never believe it.'

Cutty thought, don't be too sure. She might. But he said nothing.

13

The meeting of the search committee was at eight a.m. in a small college seminar room. McLaughlin, unaccustomed to such a startling early hour and fortified only by vodka-laced orange juice and a stale doughnut, rubbed his eyes and looked around the table apprehensively. Among those present were Pepper Pemberton, looking bright-eyed and bushy-tailed in a smart green pantsuit; Sam Osbourne from English, tall and lanky and tweedy with a perpetual grin; Myrt Gold from Classics, a square-shaped sensible woman in sensible shoes and a thick tartan skirt covered in cat hair; Norbert Norton from Psychology, an owlish little man in a shaggy, stained Shetland sweater and oval wire-rimmed glasses behind which he seemed to blink, or wink, almost constantly.

Not a prepossessing lot of decision-makers, thought McLaughlin, and walked over to introduce himself to the two student members of the committee. The short brown man in neat shirt and tie and plaid jacket was Winston Kennedy Ramsammy, a contained and confident-looking undergraduate in history with alert black eyes, vice-president of the student council. The other student, a large woman in a T-shirt, slacks and Greb Gorilla boots, at least five foot eleven and probably packing two hundred and thirty pounds, as ill-favoured as a Russian street-sweeper, glowing with good health and malice, was Theodora 'Teddy' Kravnik. She was registered as a 'Women's Studies' major in an M.A. program.

'J.T.,' Pepper urged in a stage whisper, 'we'd best get on with it. It's already eight-ten. As chairperson ... '

'Oh, right. Thank you. Yes, I'll call the meeting to order. How do you want to begin?'

'As secretary of the committee,' said Teddy in a gruff voice, 'I'll read the minutes of the last meeting.'

'Oh, I think we could accept the minutes "as read", Ms Kravnik,' said J.T. 'I gather you were all present last week, and Professor Pemberton has informed me of what went on. I doubt we need to stand on formality and rules at this early stage of our discussions. Our time might be better devoted to, um ...'

'Highly irregular, Mr Chair,' snapped Kravnik. 'I must insist that the rules ...'

'Oh, very well,' sighed McLaughlin. 'Proceed.'

So Kravnik solemnly read her minutes, with what J. T. thought was excessive emphasis on his having been made Chair 'pro tem'. Clearly Kravnik was going to insist on throwing her not inconsiderable weight around.

'We're conducting this search, and that ad in the papers has apparently brought in some applications for the position of principal. Is that right, Pepper?'

She nodded, but before she could utter a comment or even a sound, Kravnik cut in again.

'I have all the files on the applications, and Xerox copies of the list of names are right here. Shall I read out the names?'

'No,' said J. T. 'That won't be necessary, Ms Kravnik. Just pass around the list. We're all capable of reading, I think, even at eight a.m. Let's see, here. Hm. Pottelby, Blobkin, Bouchard, Shack, Bromhead, Scheiskopf, Bloufart, Dorkins ... Dear God. Well, at least we won't need to waste time on this cavalcade.'

'Waste time?' sputtered Kravnik. 'Surely you're not serious! These're all valid applicants who've expressed interest and submitted their names in good faith for our consideration so that ...'

'Does any one of them deserve lengthy consideration, do you think, Ms Kravnik? Seems to me a list of incompetents and psychological basketcases that need not detain us. After all, would we really want to choose anyone who actually put forward his own name?'

'His or HER name,' snapped Kravnik.

'And no fewer than three on the list, do you notice, from one department, Women's Studies,' Sam Osbourne observed.

'Some members of the committee,' Kravnik retorted, 'may have encouraged certain people to put forward their names.'

'Oh, did you?' asked Pepper. 'How helpful.'

'What possible reason can there be *not* to give these names, all of these names, a fair review?' Kravnik persisted. 'To use the word "incompetents" might, I remind you, be libellous.'

'Happily our deliberations are entirely confidential and private,' suggested Osbourne, 'so libel cannot be an issue, although we must of course keep our language, er, moderate. But I do agree with the Chair that the list is not impressive.'

'Impressive,' snorted J. T. 'A bunch of ..., never mind.'

'Star Chamber!' Kravnik growled. 'Secrecy! Our proceedings must be entirely above board and publicly transparent. We should be, above all, we must be, democratic.'

'Were you elected to be a member of this search committee, Ms Kravnik?' asked Myrt Gold. 'No? Then none of us was. We're all appointed. I don't believe democracy is an issue here. We're concerned with excellence, quality, that cannot be measured by ballots in a popularity contest. Democracy indeed,' she sniffed.

The Chair gave Myrt a grateful smile, but Kravnik declined to be diverted.

'Possibly the Chair would specify why he finds these candidates "unimpressive".'

'Why, Ms Kravnik? Why? I could, yes. Pottelby and Blobkin are both aged sixty or more, just looking for a plum before retirement. Bloufart, Dorkins, and Bromhead are nice enough people, but none of them, I think you'll find, has any administrative experience whatever. Shack has all the personality of a hubcap; scarcely a leader. Bouchard teaches courses under the rubric of, what is it? "Studies in Sexual Diversity".'

'What in the world is that?' Norbert Norton inquired. 'Never heard of it.'

'Damned if I know either,' said McLaughlin. 'Probably a way to avoid learning any philosophy, history or serious literature. I expect it's a study of the Kama Sutra, doubtless taught on swings and mats in the gym.'

'Really, Professor McLaughlin. Really,' said Myrt, but permitted herself a small smile.

'The other three, I believe,' J. T. continued, 'are names dredged, ahem, derived from the faculty of Women's Studies but, I hasten to add, quite worthy colleagues – except they scarcely have a single scholarly publication among them.'

'Outrageous! Defamation! They have all published in important feminist magazines. I will not sit here and listen to my teachers abused like this!'

'Would you prefer to stand, Ms Kravnik?' Pepper purred gently. 'I'm sure the committee would be interested to hear how your views differ from the Chair's and, may I say, mine. My experience on other searches had been that people who actually seek the job and nominate themselves are seldom the best available.'

'I demand,' said Kravnik, struggling to control herself, 'that we review all these files and interview all these candidates.'

'It would take far too long,' said the Chair. 'There's not enough time. We must really get on, I think, with looking around for the best person, and fully expecting that members of college will think about the appointment, the sort of person needed, and submit nominations, serious nominations, probably supported by several signatures.'

'Hopelessly elitist,' Kravnik sputtered.

'Of course,' said McLaughlin. 'It's an important position and we'll doubtless want to fill it with some recognized figure of proven ability. If that's "elitist", that's just fine with me.'

'Hear, hear,' Sam Osbourne put in.

'Objection! I protest,' erupted Kravnik. 'This whole thing begins to seem like an exercise in sexist and elitist and reactionary anti-democracy.'

'Would you say a cabal?' suggested Winston.

'What's a cabal?' Kravnik demanded. 'If it means ruthless exclusion of good people and probably railroading through some pre-selected WASP suit, then I'd guess it's a cabal, damn right, like you say.'

'It might be desirable,' said Sam Osbourne, 'to review our terms of reference and what we're supposed to be searching for. Maybe get us back on the rails.'

'The terms of reference,' Pepper Pemberton said, 'were sent to us all from the office of the Vice-Provost. As secretary of the committee, Ms Kravnik may have brought a copy along.'

'Didn't bother,' muttered Kravnik. 'Incomprehensible bumpf.'

'Then Mr Chairman, may I remind the group,' Pepper continued, 'that we are asked to find a person recognized as a scholar, with a track record of published work, and with demonstrated ability as an administrator. He or she should have a pleasing personality in order to get along with, and lead, both students and faculty, a commitment to the educational role of the college, and the ability to, shall we say, win the confidence of alumni and granting agencies in the role of fundraiser.'

'To schmooze, you mean,' snapped Kravnik. 'To kiss behinds. To have nothing to do with the masses.'

'Fundraising,' said Myrt Gold, 'in these lean times of government cutbacks, is a not inconsiderable function. Need we be reminded that the college's new art gallery was totally funded by the alumni, or that the restorations of the exterior stonework...'

'Frills,' Kravnik grumped. 'Cosmetic bourgeois frills.'

'I like the art gallery,' said Winston.

'Me, too,' Pepper agreed. 'Apart from programs and training, we need some ornaments to civilization, don't you think?'

'Training?' said Kravnik gruffly. 'Training B.A.s to be cheerfully submissive and unemployed, or to be civilized while driving taxis.'

'Come on,' insisted the Chairman, in a voice slightly louder than he'd intended. 'We're not here to debate economic problems or to swap opinions on political ideology. We're here to find a person, I hope the right person.'

'Quite right, quite right,' Norbert Norton nodded. 'So may I suggest, Mr Chairman, that since it's almost nine o'clock, and perhaps others have nine o'clock classes to get to as I do, that we break off for now, to meet again at the same time next week. I think we should all think hard, and that each of us should be ready with one name to put forward seven days from now.'

All agreed with that, their faces registering various degrees of dismay, none more than McLaughlin's. Dear God, he thought, can nothing around here be quick and simple and straightforward? This damn business could go on for weeks. Months? I could use a drink. But then, as they were trooping out, he suggested to Pepper that they have coffee together, which seemed a much better idea.

14

J. T. was sitting at the bar on the roof lounge of the Park Plaza Hotel. He was to meet Zinger there at seven before they'd go out to dinner. McLaughlin had arrived fifteen minutes early and ordered a double scotch on the rocks, Bell's, and downed it smartly, without thinking, then stared at the empty glass as though not comprehending where it had gone. He gestured at the man behind the bar, who stepped over and blinked at the empty, then said:

'Same again, sir?'

'Yeah.'

'Some water on the side?'

'Hm, no, thanks.'

He twirled the second glass idly before knocking back half of it, wiped his lips and promised himself to slow the pace. But since a quarter to seven at the bar, he'd had at least two doubles. It was seven-thirty-five. Possibly it was three. Who's counting, when you're having fun? But he wasn't. Where the hell was Zinger?

'Bartender!'

'Sir.'

'I'll do the same again.'

'Sir.'

'I see you mix a serious martini. Did I ever tell you about the first martini I ever had at this bar? Krist, that was an evening. 1959, I think it was. I was here with another grad student, we were both just off the train, you know, new in town, and my new friend, "Martini" Macomber was his handle, from California, U C L A, and he was very fussy about his drinks. Ordered a martini, Beefeater, very dry, straight up, no garnish. But when our drinks arrived, his had an olive in it. He sent it back.'

'I'm sure he did, sir. Now if you'll excuse me?'

Shit. Not very friendly, this barman. That bastard who was waving his glass could have waited. Probably a goddamn lush, making demands on the barman like that. Thank God I'm not a drunk.

Certainly not. I merely like the taste of a good scotch, he told himself. Why, I could quit any time, no problem. Just stop, cold. The thing is, I like the hit, the rush. Warms the soul, reinforces the body, calms the mind. If I went home, there'd be nobody there. No bloody reason to go home to an empty house. No one to talk with. No fire in the fireplace. Memory and melancholy took him by the throat.

'Would you like something else?' The barman's question really meant, would he like to settle his bill and depart.

'Oh, sure. Hit me again. Same.'

What's a waiting man to do? Might as well occupy the time with a jar. Bloody Zinger never punctual. When the bartender put the glass down on a new cocktail napkin, J. T. said:

'So my friend Macomber got his second martini, but when it came it had a small twist of lemon in it. I said, No garnish. Pure. Sorry, sir, force of habit. Macomber grabbed him by the lapels and shouted, Look, Sparky, if I want a lemonade, I'll ask for it! Not a bad line, eh? Great guy, Macomber.'

The bartender managed a wan smile.

'Will that be all, sir?'

'All? No, that won't be all. I'm thinking about it. Do you have any peanuts? Pretzels?'

A tiny dish of nuts, slightly soggy, was rather grudgingly provided. When the bartender had his back turned, McLaughlin leaned down and dumped them on the floor. Just to show who's boss around here, he smirked to himself. *I'm* in charge here, he thought with his best Alexander Haig imitation. The customer is always right, and other patent lies of commerce. 'I am the master of my fate/I am the captain of my soul,' and other naïve untruths of the poets. Master, hell, I don't even get a vote in this fracas; Trish acts unilaterally. I guess I'm just the cabin boy on the leaky ship of matrimony. 'God's in Her heaven, all's hell with the world.' Ho.

'Did you say something, sir?'

'No. Didn't, no.'

Where the hell was Zinger? What to do? Damn, after eight-twenty now. Probably chasing some mini-skirt around the college. Should he wait any longer? Not a promising option, but what was? Maybe some friend, or former student, or some solo good-looking woman would wander into the bar, keep the party going. Or should he

- 15 -

It was about twelve-thirty the following Thursday that J.T. and Zinger decided to walk over to the Faculty Club for lunch. The Club is a squat but pleasant building on the west side of the campus, consisting of two handsomely panelled lounges with Group of Seven paintings gracing the walls, several plain and badly furnished meeting rooms, often in use as chess or card rooms, a large main dining room decorated in lamentable light blue with white trim, and a downstairs pub with a fireplace where they settled in. They ordered club sandwiches and got comfortable in a corner with a couple of pints.

'Now, this pub is a nice place, a snug,' said Zinger. 'You mean we can actually smoke here?'

'Just in the pub, but yes. It's almost the only place on campus you still can, although I'm told they're trying to ban it next year.'

'Dear God, this university, this city. I can't believe it. Stephen Leacock used to say that to create a university you needed, first, a library; second, a smoking room; and third, maybe some teachers. But this damned institution, like most of the city, seems to think that almost anything goes – drugs, sex, perversion, stock market fraud, violence – anything, except smoking. It's the most grave new sin. Can't understand it. I always thought that a real professor, like Gandy, was incomplete without a pipe in the seminar room, if not a cigar or a cigarette. A pipe is so real, you know, a symbol of thoughtful reality, wisdom. But banished. Dreadful social fascism, it is. I swear, when I'm invited to a serious orgy in this town, there's always a big sign on the door: No Smoking.'

'Have you been invited to many orgies yet?'

'Not too many, no. A fellow can but live in hope.'

'Yeh,' said J.T. 'That's where we all live, I guess.'

'The big city will provide, I believe,' Zinger muttered. 'Not much so far, but I'm enjoying it.'

'Good. I'm glad, Z.'

'So how are you, J.T.? How're you doing?'

'Oh, not so bad, I guess. Just fair-to-middling. Trish phoned again last night to ask how things are. Had I arranged to have the furnace cleaned and the hedge trimmed? I guess I'd forgotten. But she invited me to a party.'

'A party? She invited you to a party? Jeez, J. T., this is not what I call being separated. I'll bet she got stood up and just wanted a man to go with. Any man. You're being used, ol' buddy. Dangled and diddled.'

'You think so? Could be. Anyway, I didn't go.'

'I'd bloody well hope not. Don't be a fucking patsy, J. T.'

'I hear you talking. But Trish is not like that, you know? She's OK. I think she misses me.'

'Misses, schmisses. If she really missed you she'd be home. And she ain't. Screw the party scene. That's ridiculous. But look, I didn't ask how your marriage was, which I take it is a misery. I asked how *you* are.'

'Oh, I'm OK. A bit flat, I guess. This waiting and waiting is getting me down. It's very wearing.'

'But you're coping better?'

'Not enough to brag about, no. I'll tell you, I up got this morning, a bit tired and underslept, groggy I suppose ...'

'Grog fog. I know. Been there. Hung over.'

'Well, not exactly. I find if you keep the old bod topped up just enough, you don't get hangovers. Just the regular float, the standard fog, like you said. I dunno, Z., it's like trying to make coffee and you can't find the filter. It's like putting your underwear on backwards and there's something vital you can't find and you know something's wrong but you're damned if you can figure out what's missing. Always something missing.'

'Uh huh. That's not good.'

'It isn't, no.'

'You'll get over it,' said Zinger, lifting his glass of Smithwick's. 'But you've gotta stop acting like Laocoon when really you're just another Joe Average divorce statistic. Divorce just isn't that big a deal. It just takes time.'

'Time, you say. And where the hell were you the other night when you were supposed to meet me on the Plaza roof and go for dinner? I waited for you to show, maybe two hours.'

'That night? Sorry, I was detained by a disputation with a young professor of media studies about the role of journalism in the Global

Village. Sorry to have missed you, but I can never pass up an argument. What did you do to beguile the time?'

'Went home. Microwaved some frozen muck. Took apart the carburetor from the Model A so I could clean it. I think I've lost one part. Trish keeps telling me to drag it off to the junk yard.'

'Trish tells, Trish wants ... Are you ever going to tell her to belt up and piss off and stop interfering? It's none of her goddamn business if you want to restore the roadster or build a rocket ship or chase women. Reminds me, how're you getting on with the grand pursuit of the delectable Pepper?'

'You'd be surprised, Z. I've already taken her on a first date.'

'You have? Great stuff. How was it? How far did you get?'

'Whaddya mean, get?'

'I mean did you get her into the sack? No, scrub that question. Clearly she's not that type. A real lady, that one. Not on a first date. But she's all there, all female.'

'It's a bit difficult,' J. T. cut in, 'to think about bed at nine a.m. in the cafeteria after a meeting.'

'Nine a.m.? Cafeteria? You call that a first date? Holy cavorting Krist, McLaughlin, you're hopeless. Here's a woman who probably deserves lotus blossoms and hummingbird tongues and you whisk her off, with bold and imaginative scheming, to the college cafeteria? Jesus wept. Why I've had coffee with her twice myself.'

'True? You have? Twice?'

'Sure. Once in college with Cutty, once when I bumped into her on Bloor Street in a bookstore.'

'So what did you talk about? Did you talk about me?'

'You? Not at all. We tried to talk about cheerful things, not about dopey downers.'

'Oh.' J. T. looked downcast.

'I entertained her with the surpassing Zinger wit and charm. She's a lovely wench. Charming. Bright and buxom, very self-possessed.'

'Women professors aren't "wenches", Zinger.'

'Course they are. My old daddy used to tell me, treat a wench like a lady and a lady like a wench. They eat it up.'

'So how would you treat Trish, oh all-wise Romeo?'

'Trish? We're not talking about Trish, for godsake! Screw that noise. She's, she's, irrelevant, don't you get it? Past. Gone. Of no consequence.'

'Wait. Don't badmouth Trish. She's still my wife.'

'Legally, yeh, but not in reality. And don't you put down my ol' daddy, either. He was a veritable fountain of good advice. I remember when I went off to university he told me to keep my mind and my bowels open. He told me always to read biographies and poetry more than textbooks, and never draw to an inside straight.'

'I wonder why I bothered getting a Ph.D. when all I needed was to listen to you and follow your stupendous advice. God, but I wish I knew everything, like you, and never stumbled over doubts. But I don't know whatthehell to do.'

'Ah shit, J.T., no one knows what to do. Not me, either, of course. All I know is it's a tough go, but if you can't be happy, be cheerful. When you go around moping, wearing a grim look on your face as though you're about to pass a kidney stone, the world will heap more crap on you, partly because you look and act like a crap receptacle, as though you're asking for it. And I do know that slouching around is a serious waste of time. Precious time. Or were you planning to live forever? That's not the deal. What we've got is now, and now is all we've got.'

'Sure, and just now I feel like a reject. But I'll be better. I'll be fine when Trish comes home. Absolutely.'

'J.T.?'

'What?'

'Do me a favour. For auld lang syne and all the years we've known each other, do me a favour, OK?'

'Anything, pal. Name it.'

'Just shut up,' Zinger said with a broad grin. 'Just SHUT THE FUCK UP. You're setting off my maudlin alarm, you're triggering my bullshit detector, and that's a serious sin. Oh, I know, you think I'm a great one to talk about sin, and you have a point, yes, past any question as the world rates these things. But I staunchly believe that there's only one primary sin, one, and that's cruelty. And I say, Trish's being cruel. To you. Maybe to herself, but to you. And I care about you, ol' buddy, and I think you're more sinned against than sinning, and I want you to see that, admit that, and shut the fuck up and get over it. I'm telling you that when the world kicks shit in your face, you gotta get up and kick back, and rationally or irrationally, the only possible response is to be happy. Not carefree, no. With regrets for a certainty. But happy.'

'I see what you're saying,' J.T. nodded, and blinked. 'You make some sense.'

'Of course I do.'

'You sometimes do.'

'Always. Except about my own life, of course, which keeps reeling about. I've no perspective on that. But other people's lives, your life? Easy. I always make perfect sense. Now before you get up off your arse and go over to the bar and order another couple of pints, let me ask you a couple of questions. Did you and Trish quarrel about money over the years?'

'No, almost never. There was always enough to go around, and I often did some freelance work for extra bucks.'

'And were there problems in the bedroom? I mean we're no longer boys, after age fifty and all. Any trouble in the old erectile department?'

'Not at all. I could always rise to the occasion, and often wished there were more occasions. Now, well, I've still got lots of lead in my pencil, but I've got nobody to write to.'

'Yeh. Maybe I can help you find a pen pal. It's just that I'm trying to understand what the problem is.'

'Ask me about TV.'

'How do you mean? Squabbling over control of the remote? But you have two sets, don't you?'

'Sure, but the on-camera thing seems to be beguiling to her, irresistible, a real hit like being on speed, shooting up.'

'Holy shit, I never thought about that. So she takes it all seriously and gets off on it?'

'Too right, she does. It's the celebrity thing.'

'Bloody hell. Some pair, you two, one hooked on booze and the other hooked on the boob tube. Terrible damn thing, addiction. Hard to kick. I'll have to think about this. Now, about that beer?'

- 16 -

As he plodded down the hall toward his office, McLaughlin passed the open door of a classroom and heard the unmistakable drone of young Jane Aptworth, a fresh-caught assistant professor of Literature from Harvard whose serene self-confidence was exceeded only by her vapidity. 'And so we must posit, following Barthes, a homological relation between sentence and discourse insofar as it is likely that a similar formal organization orders all semiotic systems, whatever their substances and dimensions.' McLaughlin stopped and listened. 'We must of course be cognizant that the theory of levels – as set forth by Beneviste – gives two types of relations: distributional and integrational. But distributional relations alone are not sufficient to account for meaning. In order to conduct a structural analysis, it is thus first of all necessary to distinguish several levels or instances of description, and to place these instances within a hierarchical or integrationary perspective.'

McLaughlin poked his head into the lecture room and, with thumbs in his ears and waggling fingers, shouted: 'BOOGA! BOOGA!'

He wandered off down the hall and muttered to himself, 'Another blow struck for intellectual freedom.'

- 17 -

Since he'd left his newspaper job at the Northern Light and moved to Toronto Zinger had not received much e-mail so he did not check it often, but there, on his return from lunch, was a signal that he had messages. Most were just spam of course and one awkward communication from his accountant about some bloody tax problem or other, something about expense claims being rejected by Revenue Canada and a demand for some fifteen hundred dollars. Did he have receipts for those expenses? Maybe, maybe not, but certainly not with him in Toronto. He'd think about that if and when he got around to it. The tax man would have to wait in line behind his other creditors. A man's reach should exceed his grasp or what are credit cards for?

What startled him though was an e-mail from his son John the Bear, the only child of his first marriage, whom he had not heard from for months. It was more than somewhat abrupt and it made him blink.

Dad,

you're fired. you're not my dad any more. I reject you as firmly as you seem to have rejected me. mom divorced you and now I divorce you. you're a poor excuse for a father. there you are in the east being a student, for God's sake, and getting paid for it – there's a laugh – while I am being a real and serious student in saskatoon and not getting paid a dime, certainly getting no help from you. Mom gives me free room and board so I can continue my studies and maybe finish my B.Comm. do you even care that I'm within a year of graduation? summer work at the brewery earned me enough to pay the tuition although I have a sizeable student loan, but last week I was embarrassed not to have enough money in my pocket to buy coffee in the cafeteria for my girlfriend. it's one thing not to send maintenance cheques to mom but don't you realize that she gives me those dollars for my education costs? i'm flat broke. you seem to think you're a smartass. i think you're a dumbass. what the hell are you afraid of – growing up? so i don't want to have anything to do with you any more. You're not a disappointment, you're a total fuck up. it's not that I feel neglected, it's that I feel abandoned.

good bye,
John

Francis Z. Springer was rocked, devastated. He'd really intended to talk to the lad before coming east, had driven by John's mother's apartment before turning his car south for the long trip, but his son wasn't home. Zinger avoided 'phoning because he really didn't want to talk to his ex who always answered the ring, but how many months was it since he'd talked with John? Jeez. That long? Maybe five or six months was his guess. And he was totally sorry about that. Events had conspired against him before he had left Saskatchewan. Where does the time go when you are emphatically not having fun?

And the money. He hadn't realized how far behind he'd become on support cheques. Very far.

What to do? Bloody hell, what to do? It was improbable that his publisher who, come to think of it, he hadn't even met yet, would stand him another advance and he'd long since spent the first one. But he'd have to raise some cash for John, and fast. He had nothing he could sell quickly and God knows, he already had debts here in Toronto, not least the thou he owed to J. T., and his credit cards were maxed out at staggering rates of interest.

In something of a daze he filled a paper cup with a jolt of rye and went out into the college quadrangle. He sat on a bench with his head in his hands. It seemed obvious that he couldn't phone John or even bring himself to e-mail him until he could raise a significant chunk of money.

It occurred to him to sell his car, the T-bird, but that would be like selling his receding youth and his freedom, a dreadful prospect that made him shudder. Besides, he thought, back-pedalling and rationalizing at a brisk clip, you could never get top dollar for a classic convertible except in spring, not now, with winter coming on, and by spring he'd have lots of money anyway. Money squeezed out of his university stipend. Money from his book, most probably. No doubt about it. Spring was a long way off, though, and now was now. Crunch time.

The last resort of the desperate poor is often the pawn shop. That was it. That had to be it.

An hour later he was in McTamney's Jewelers and Pawnbrokers on Church Street. 'Up to one year term', their window sign said. His intention was to hock his laptop and his best camera, although they were both (well, technically) the property of his newspaper. The pawnshop said the laptop was by no means up to date and offered only a laughable price on it, so he kept it and threw in instead the wristwatch his father had given him which fetched a surprising amount. He took a six-months ticket and left the shop with a fistful of cash, several hundred, enough to wire to John. With the great relief of having that done, Zinger sat down at his computer to write a message to his son. He said that some money was arriving. He said he was sorry it was so little and so late but that there would be more coming along.

What to say next?

OK, so I'm fired as a father. I guess I deserved that. It really got to me. I'll make it up to you, I promise. You've heard that before, I know, but I will. There are job offers here that show how my talents are valued in the bigger market. Everything will work out. I'll attend your graduation in the spring and be very proud of you and buy you a grad present that you'll like and take you on a fishing trip. Just the two of us. It'll be like old times.

Should he leave it at that? Was there anything more to say? Everything to say? He gritted his teeth and cracked his knuckles before facing the computer screen again.

You took some heavy shots at me in your e-mail. I guess I deserved them and more because it's true I haven't been a good father. It's true I didn't get a chance to speak with you before I left because I was too busy trying to clean up my own affairs. It's true that I don't much like to think about money because my debt level is so gloomy. I'll change. I'll do better. That's all spilt milk.

Sorry that you see me as 'dumbass' afraid of 'growing up'. I'm not. As I've tried to tell you before it gives me the chills to think of you in commerce when you could be studying something more satisfying like history or literature or philosophy. If you are so 'grown up' do you really want to be a businessman or a banker or a bloody accountant? That's no life. Bankers aren't too frisky.

89

I guess I don't have to worry about you falling into many of the seven deadly sins. Clearly you're not the type. But I do worry about you getting trapped into what GBS – that's Shaw to you, old son – calls the seven deadly virtues: duty, obedience, chastity, thrift, abstinence, probity, caution ... I can't remember them all, somewhere in *Man and Superman*, and worth a look. Don't always try to play it safe. That way lie tears and torpor. Life must be lived as an experiment, not a formula. Don't be afraid to bash about and take risks and damn the torpedoes, otherwise you'll end up with a cellar full of regret, old before your time. And keep in mind the reliable motto: RIBTR, remorse is better than regret.

For myself I'll tell you what does scare me most. I'm afraid of being bored. I'm afraid of falling into the conventional lockstep, marching meekly to the beat of everybody else's tedious commercial drum. I'm terrified of subsiding into a middle-class torpor and mindless acceptance of the world's stupendous madness.

'Acceptance'. Now there's a word. Almost everybody I know seems to suffer from the numbing disease of wanting to be accepted, narrowing and debasing their lives by grovelling for acceptance. As a case in point I offer you my friend McLaughlin. He scuffled for years just to obtain 'tenure' or academic acceptance and is now using it as a shield and an excuse for not writing. As a reward for his compliant dullness his wife has smacked him around and ignored him and kicked him in the balls. I find that sad and comical.

Zinger poured out more screens of rant and advice and tenuous self-justification before he hit the send button. A few hours later he received this reply.

Dear almost dad,

ok, ok, I almost forgive you. I hear you, o socrates, but even with the money you wired, the bottom line is I'm still broke as of next Thursday. should I 'accept' that?

John

With nothing much else to pawn, Zinger decided he didn't know the city well enough to drive a taxi at night and after a few days hadn't had any replies to his applications for jobs on Toronto newspapers. An appeal to B.J. for advice led to mutual embarrassment, the offer of a small loan which he couldn't accept, and a bright suggestion that he offer himself as a tutor in English and essay writing to foreign students in the college. Fifty dollars an hour might be earned that way and it was worth a try.

Within a few days his notice on the bulletin board (of another college – with no name, only a phone number) brought in nine clients with requests for help, mostly from Asian students. He found it easy and quick to improve essays with crisp writing, but soon began to receive offers of more serious money to actually write the essays and even one M.A. thesis from scratch. Ghost writing for gelt was utterly immoral, of course, but soon he yielded to the financial temptations. He tried to justify this academic deception to himself thinking that if he didn't take the jobs, somebody else would. When he collected his fees, always in cash, he felt more than somewhat besmirched, but mused that the three things that have utterly no conscience are a stiff prick, a conservative politician and an overdraft at the bank.

- 18 -

Trish got the news from the building superintendent that her lease would not be renewed because the owners of the condo were returning from Europe and wanted to move back in by January first. They really wanted to be home for Christmas and accordingly offered to skip the rent for the last month if Trish could be out by the December fifteenth so that they could resettle for the holidays and put up a Christmas tree.

This presented Trish with an unexpected dilemma. She didn't want to move. She hadn't anticipated being pushed into moving, certainly not during December. The superintendent and the rental agency both told her that no there weren't any other vacancies available in the building now or in the foreseeable future.

The future was something she didn't want to think about. It was true that the novelty of living in a condo was beginning to wear off. It was true that in the neighbourhood singles bar she liked best, the Sassafras on Cumberland, she was beginning to be regarded as a regular, if not a fixture, rather than an interesting fresh face. Not many of the men there or many of the women, for that matter, seemed to be her own age. The women were mostly under thirty-five, elaborately dressed, coiffed, and on the make. The men tended to be, well, brash and under forty or over fifty, but wearing alligator shoes and bad ties, or no ties but heavy gold chains that clanked disagreeably. Whenever she allowed herself to be picked up in the bar, which wasn't all that often, she usually ended the evening bored or disappointed. There were men who were more interesting at the TV station where she worked, apart from the sleek but blank announcers, but they all seemed to be married or gay. The gays were friendly and certainly nice but Trish shuddered when she thought that most of her social life might turn out to be as a fag hag. She had to admit that, apart from her best friend Molly and some friends who were widows or rather desperate divorcees, she was often lonely.

Should she be concerned about money? Well, no, that wasn't an issue. Clearly, finding an apartment as nice as this one would not be cheap, unless she was willing to move away from Yorkville, which she was not. Why should she? Her salary was large, even generous, and if she was careful not to run her Visa debt up any higher for clothes from Holt Renfrew – after all, she must appear fashionable on camera – and if she got a raise next year, there'd be no problem. Unsettling though, when she'd asked her producer last week about how much of a raise she could expect for next season, he seemed a bit evasive.

Not to worry. She'd think about it tomorrow. Maybe she'd run it by Molly, just for perspective. But what could Molly tell her? Trish really didn't want advice. She just needed to decide what *she* wanted. J. T. wanted her back, naturally. Her children, obviously, wanted their parents back together. Her G.P. and her accountant urged her to go home. And her divorce lawyer warned her not to do anything rash. They just didn't understand. Whatever. She poured herself a glass of port and decided to turn in early. There were quite a lot of reasons in favour of going back to her husband, but it still seemed just too simple, some sort of admission of, well, defeat.

To hell with it. She'd have time to think about it tomorrow while she was getting her hair done before the show.

The next evening, while she was dressing to go to a party with her gay friend Marc, Trish was till fussing at her problem like a tongue probing a sore tooth. Her feelings remained ambivalent, too confused to put her into a party mood. As she looked grimly into the mirror, checking her makeup and looking for insidious wrinkles, she admitted to herself that maybe it would be best to pack it in and go back to J. T. The thought was scarcely exciting but it was reassuring that she had the option. If it didn't work out she could always turn around and leave again. No big deal. Nothing is irreversible.

Yes, she thought, might as well go back. And yet, to be on the safe side, she'd keep the decision to herself for a few days, not even tell the children. No need to rush. Let it be a surprise.

- 19 -

Monday mornings were a problem for J. T. The eight o'clock meetings of the search committee were just too damned early for a man who never got enough sleep and they threatened to go on for weeks. The committee could not agree on anything or anybody, yet they all assumed that they had to choose a perfect specimen, if not a Messiah. McLaughlin found this search for perfection exceedingly tiresome, believing as he did that anyone who wanted to be an administrator was *ipso facto* flawed anyway.

McLaughlin's tendency to say what he thought in blunt or dismissive terms did not make the interminable search process any smoother or win him any prizes for diplomacy. His eyes often drooping with fatigue, his cerebral cortex usually still inflamed by the weekend's alcohol, his need for some morning stimulant not assuaged by the institutional coffee that tasted like boiled rat-tails, he was often choleric and prickly. At one point Kravnik was heard to whisper to Ramsammy that McLaughlin was 'a negative smartass'.

Still, it had to be admitted that the early list of candidates, self-nominated or put forward by departments wanting some advantage for themselves or simply to be rid of academic dead wood, appeared more a list of encumbrances than of talented assets. Not many people of real ability were eager to accept administrative office in a time of declining budgets; financial stringency would make new initiatives or innovations difficult if not impossible.

The associate director of the main library, Mary Nickerson, for example, was put forward by the head librarian in a clear attempt to rid himself of a troublesome and incompetent colleague. Even the genial Sam Osbourne of the English Department was moved to say: 'Dreadful woman. No, no, wouldn't do at all.'

Professor Myrt Gold (Classics) asked that the committee consider one Lionel Munge of the Geography Department, a decent sort, but whose name was met with no enthusiasm. 'Bright, don't you think?' asked Myrt. 'No,' said J. T. 'I sat beside him recently at a Faculty

Association meeting and, when I whispered in his ear, I swear I heard an echo. Got a mind like a conch shell.' This did nothing to endear J. T. to Professor Gold.

The meeting considered four other names, two at some length, but none seemed strong enough to be a plausible. McLaughlin grew more and more impatient and irritable, and couldn't help thinking of the old academic principle that the higher the IQs on a committee, the more they will nit-pick and prolong discussions, showing off how bright and committed they are. He began to doodle idly on a notepad.

When he forced his mind back to the business at hand he heard both Norton and Pepper Pemberton saying very positive things about one Tremblay, a pleasant enough member of the Department of Mathematics. Norton observed that mathematicians, dealing with so abstract a field, were seldom practical people likely to be bold leaders. It would be like, Ramsammy put in, expecting an accountant to be charismatic. McLaughlin thought that was one of the most sensible things he'd heard since eight a.m. But then, his mind wandering again, he started to giggle. Myrt Gold looked at him sharply.

'Sorry,' said J. T., 'I was just thinking of an old joke about – oh, never mind.'

'Do share it with us,' said Gold. 'We could do with some levity.'

'I'm not sure that I ... Oh, whatthehell:

A mathematician named Hall
Had a hexahedronical ball,
And the cube of its weight
Times his pecker, plus eight,
Was four-fifths of five-eighths of
Boo all.'

Sam Osbourne grinned, Norton merely blinked, and Myrt Gold almost smiled, but only said 'Really'. Kravnik flushed and snapped her notebook shut, while Pepper put her hand over her mouth and kicked J. T., hard, under the table.

'Maybe,' said McLaughlin, 'we should, ah, given the hour, ask the Chair to adjourn us for this week. Who is in the chair, anyway? Oh. Yes. Me. Right. Let's adjourn.'

The only good thing about the committee's meetings was that, when they were over, J. T. and Pepper went off for coffee together. He always looked forward to that.

Previously over coffee they'd chatted idly about university problems and how to make the search process go faster, but this morning they started discussing the problems of the students and soon found themselves talking about their own kids. Pepper produced photos of her two from her purse and McLaughlin dug into his wallet for snapshots of his three. They laid the pictures out on the table like Tarot cards, exchanged compliments about how good looking they all were, and beamed at each other and nodded and grinned as proud parents will.

McLaughlin also complimented Pepper on the excellent reviews her last book had received and she glowed. She mentioned that she'd read his volume on Innis and admired it – was it three or four years ago? – but wondered why he'd stopped at the economic history material and not gone on to Innis's later work on communications? She'd been poring over that stuff herself, she said, because it helped her to understand McLuhan. Their mutual friend Gandy was giving her pointers on McLuhan and now she was writing about media.

'And what are you writing about these days?' she asked.

'Oh, I guess I'm between books at the moment, in sort of a lull.'

'I see. You've got to keep at it, though.'

'Uh huh. Well, I've started, a couple of times, to write a piece on Schumpeter, but it's not going well; can't seem to make it hang together.'

'It will if you keep trying,' she said, 'it will work out. Things will get better.'

- 20 -

Looking around for a new apartment, just in case, proved very disappointing to Trish. Anything she liked proved more expensive than her present sublet, and nothing at all in her immediate area turned up. She became discouraged, and more resigned to the cheerless prospect of going back to her marriage. That decision still seemed premature to her, damnably practical but not entirely enticing.

So, when she talked to her daughter Jocelyn on their weekly telephone call and Joss pressed her again about her plans for Christmas, Trish finally allowed that yes, OK, she was thinking of moving back, probably by the fifteenth of December.

'Probably?' asked Joss. 'What's that supposed to mean?'

'All right, girl, all right. By the fifteenth.'

'Great. That's a big relief. Awesome. Have you told Dad?'

'Not yet, and don't you say anything to him either. I'll tell him myself. Christmas is still a long way away, there's lots of time and I still have a few, um, personal and business obligations to clear away, numerous details to attend to. But, not to worry, it will all work out.'

Joss was so excited that she barely listened to anything else her mother said. Just wait till she told her brothers, although she'd promised not to say anything yet, or thought she had. Her dad, though, would be delighted. What a huge relief it would be to him. He always said that there was nothing more important than family, and now they'd all be together again after the fall term at school was over, together for Christmas. She could relax. They could all relax.

The only thing that worried her, however, was that her father would be taken too much by surprise. Maybe he wouldn't have the house cleaned up in advance, maybe there'd be empty bottles strewn around or even a girlfriend to shove off at the last minute. Was there a risk? She couldn't let that happen.

So the next time her dad phoned, as he did every Sunday evening, Joss turned the conversation to how much she was looking forward to the holidays and let drop casually, in case he hadn't heard yet, that it was good Mom would be there too.

'Wait? What did you say? Joss, do you know something I don't?'

'I thought probably she'd told you herself by now. Mom told me she's coming home. Isn't that good news?'

'I'll say it's news! Are you sure, Joss? When? I mean, soon, now, tomorrow, when? Did she mention a date?'

'Something about the fifteenth of December.'

'Well, I'll be ... that's still weeks away, but ... hot damn, Joss, this is the best news I've had since I don't-know-when.' J. T. let out a whoop.

'You'd best do some cleaning up, Dad, before then.'

'Cleaning: oh yes, sure, I thought of that, of course.'

'Uh huh.'

After he put the telephone down, J. T. began to thrash about and pace up and down, taking an inventory of what he'd have to do to get things presentable. A list, he'd have to make a list.

He'd phone Alice, Cutty's sensible wife, for suggestions and to get the number of her cleaning lady, and a painter, he'd get painters in to redecorate the living room, and the master bedroom, possibly the main hallway while they were at it. He'd rent one of those machines people use to shampoo rugs and the furniture. Window washers might be a good idea.

Bottles. He found a trash bag and filled it with empties, admitting some surprise when he found he needed a second bag. A case of forty-ounce bottles of Teacher's scotch that he'd had delivered yesterday, he decided to stow away in the furnace room. Out of sight, out of mind. He wouldn't be needing it.

More problematic was to think of what he'd say to Trish when she arrived. He spent a long time, off and on for days and not a few restless nights, making mental notes of greetings and snappy opening lines to use when she walked in the door. None of these seemed entirely right or adequate:

'Hi there. I hope you notice how spotless the house is.'

'Trish, I'm so happy to see you that I'm cold sober, have been for days.'

'I still love you.'

'It's about time.'

'Trish, I forgive you. If I've been wrong, do you forgive me?'

'The children will be very happy to have you home. Do you like the new colour of the living room?'

'Let's fix some martinis and go up to the bedroom.'

'Trish, I have no idea what in the world to say to you ...'

Later, when he had pushed these thoughts from his mind, he was interrupted on a quiet Thursday night while he was working on his Schumpeter article for the *Canadian Journal of Economics*. He was trying hard to concentrate on the Theory of Creative Destruction when the phone rang just after eleven o'clock. Not the long-distance ring, so not a call from one of the kids. Let it ring. Ignore it. His writing was going well for a change and it seemed a shame to stop. But when it rang insistently for the eighth time he grumbled and reached for the phone.

'Hi, it's Trish.'

'Hey, I'm so glad to hear from you. Is everything on schedule? When are you coming back?'

'That's what I want to talk about. Joss said she told you my plans and that I'd be home for Christmas. Is that what she said?'

'That's what she said. Right. By December fifteenth, and she was so happy about it when she told me, just so happy; it did my heart good, let me tell you.'

'Wait now. Joss wasn't supposed to tell you that, not until I'd had a chance to talk to you myself.'

'Aw, she was just bubbling, knowing she'd cheer me up. She absolutely couldn't wait.'

'Well, there's been a glitch. There might be a little delay. Something has come up.'

'How do you mean, delay? I don't get it.'

'Listen, just try to calm down and listen, OK? Joss spoke too soon, and I have to change my plans.'

'No.'

'Yes. It's a bit complicated. The producer of my show is sending me to Vancouver to do some special interviews, a series, that might run nationally and not locally and be great for my career, but they have to be done around mid-December. I am sorry about the timing, I truly am, but this could be a great break.'

'Yeah, a break for you, a bust for me, for us. Damn it all, Trish, I thought you had to vacate your apartment by December? How the hell can you move if you're in Vancouver? That doesn't make sense to me.'

'Well, there's another thing. I can move on December first.'

'Here? Home?'

'No, easier than that. Just down the hall in this building. It will take only minutes. To my friend Marc's apartment.'

'Who the fuck is Marc?'

'Was. A friend and neighbour. Sweet gay man. He was killed. Beheaded. Poor guy.'

'I'm having trouble following this. Am I supposed to believe he was beheaded? Where was he, Iraq?'

'Let me explain. As I was told the story, he was driving up to Wasaga Beach on the 400 in his Jag convertible, top down, following a speeding SUV with a canoe on its roof. The canoe broke loose, straps broke or came off or something, and it flew back and hit him, sliced his head right off.'

'Bloody hell.'

'His apartment is suddenly vacant and available. It's fully furnished and beautifully decorated, the nicest one in the building, I think, so I signed a sub-lease from his estate, from his sister, to take it over the first of December and I hardly have to move at all. It's a darling place and simply too convenient to resist. You can see that, can't you? It worked out marvellously. The lease is only for six months, well, seven, if you count December.'

'I do count December. I count it very heavily. So will the kids. Christmas.'

'Oh now, don't be difficult. It's only a few months. You're enjoying yourself aren't you? Dating? One of my friends says he saw you utterly surrounded by women in the bar at the Windsor Arms recently. Having a lot of fun, I'll bet.'

'Not exactly. Some weird woman came on to me, but only if I'd arrange for a threesome with you. I was stunned.'

'J. T., really. I don't do threesomes.'

'Well, there you've struck a great blow for the sanctity of marriage.'

'Who said anything about marriage? Please don't start in on all that. You can be such a bore sometimes. Marriage is OK, of course, and probably for when we're, you know, older and all that. It's just not where I'm at, not at the moment. I don't need the pressure, for now at least. You understand, dear, don't you?'

'No. I don't, no. What I do understand is that you're not coming home. Not for Christmas. I think that's awful, Trish, awful. You said you were but now you're not. I don't know that I ... I don't think that I can talk about this any further. Enough is too much, I'm going to hang up now. Good night.'

'But, but J. T....'

He put the receiver down.

He sat a few minutes, rigid with disappointment and anger and fear and regret. He felt as though a shock wave had swept through him, numbed him, knocked him over.

He put out the light on his desk and sat in the dark, for how long? Maybe half an hour. Then he went down to the furnace room and retrieved a bottle of scotch. Thought of the old line 'Malt does more than Milton can/to justify God's ways to man.' Who wrote that? Housman? Didn't remember. Tried to laugh. Couldn't.

* * *

The next day at the regular Friday lunch at Dooley's, he took Zinger aside and told him the whole story, recounting the conversation in detail. For once, Zinger listened patiently, letting his friend get it all out.

'That's a pretty raw tale, J. T. Shit. I am sorry, ol' buddy. What do you do now?'

'Nothing much to do is there? I bloody well can't see anything likely.'

'No. I guess not. But you *do* see the humour in it? Aw, come on. Quite funny really. A reconciliation is stopped dead by a flying canoe. Amazing I'd say. Like most reality, that's damn hard to believe or take seriously. Life is so droll, don't you think? It's the fluke vicissitudes of life that'll get you every time. There's no defence. It's beyond anyone's control.'

'Beyond mine, anyway, thanks a whole lot for finding it funny. You're a riot, a great bloody help. I'm grateful.'

'You're welcome. It's another goddam illustration of Springer's law. You know, LRUC, the Law of Random Unexpected Consequences. You expect one thing, plan on it, count on it, and instead you get the unpredictable and the bizarre, the unforeseen kick in the balls. This is the explanation for earthquakes, banana peels, divorce, Enron, arthritis and why the innocent suffer – at least I can't think of any other good reason. Always the freak imponderable, where only death is safe but safe is death.'

J. T. fetched up a wan smile and heaved a sigh. 'Whatever you say, Z.'

'Indisputably. But always remember, it can work in reverse, too. I mean there can be good fortune and startling benefits from LRUC as well. Consider the irritated oyster producing the pearl. Think about, I dunno, showing enough body bags on TV news to stop a war; or successful blind dates, or unexpected wins in the lottery. I think that's why most people abandon religion and don't much believe in anything any more, nothing solid. Maybe all we can believe in is luck. Erratic randomness. Chaos. And I do wish you good luck, old friend. Despair doesn't last long. Anyway, you'll bounce. Believe me, this too shall pass. Things will change. Cheerfulness will break in. Come on, whaddya say, I'll buy you another beer and we'll drink to the lovely unpredictables.'

- 21 -

Zinger greatly enjoyed walking through the streets of Toronto. The sights and sounds and smells of the big city at least partly compensated for the dirt and urban blight. He had a lively appreciation for the pretensions of Bloor Street, the bustle of the Danforth, the hustle and chatter of the mixtures of brown, black, yellow, and pink people in the Kensington Market or on Queen Street West. It was, he thought, a great town to stroll in, not least for the people-watching, notably for the girl-watching, from the graceful saris of the South Asian women to the sleek hat-box-toting brittle matrons of Forest Hill going in and out of Holt Renfrew's.

Now there, he observed, walking just ahead of him on Queen Street, was a striking young woman, a delectable. Long glossy auburn hair down her back, elegant legs, and a dynamite bottom undulating most affectingly under her snug miniskirt. He speeded his pace to come up beside her for a closer look, but was disappointed to discover that she was creased and lined, over forty going on fifty, the face inappropriate to the body. Damn, he thought, how unfortunate, a 'Butterface', everything but her face, proving once more that hindsight is usually better than foresight. This demonstrated to him again the wisdom of the familiar philosophical principle – was it Heidegger or Kierkegaard? didn't matter – that life must be lived forward and understood backwards. Pleased with his firm grasp of essential ontological truth, he winked at the woman anyway, then veered off and headed north toward the campus, whistling a chorus from that old Dixieland classic, 'You Need a Docta, Take the Wrinkles Out Yo' Birthday Suit'.

Zinger's loose-limbed stride carried him briskly north along Avenue Road. 'Absurd name,' he thought to himself, 'utterly without meaning or character. Why not just call it Road Road, or Street Street? No sense of place or of history, these dull Upper Canadians.' He smiled when he got to Queen's Park and approached the statue of Canada's principal founding father, Sir John A. Macdonald. 'There you are, you old rascal,' he mused: 'They should have named this avenue after you.' Z. tipped his hat to the statue. 'You were a much better and brighter chap than the wooden-toothed, wooden-headed George Washington. Great fighter, George, but not very amusing, not very interesting. Had to rely on the brighter boys to write the Constitution for him. Even then those brainy boyos managed to get it wrong, setting up such infernal checks and balances as to make effective government almost impossible, to create such log-jams and legislative gridlock that little can be accomplished.

'But good old John A., on the other hand, drafted his own constitution and nudged and bribed and cajoled the lads into accepting a form of government that actually works. 'A form of government similar in principle to that of the United Kingdom,' he wrote, and with that one ambiguous deft stroke established effective majority rule, responsible parliamentary government, under the jolly fiction of monarchy. A system you could understand and count on to be functional.

'Come to think of it,' Z. reflected, gazing at the bronze image of Macdonald, 'maybe that's the key to the differences between the two countries. The Yanks got it wrong, got the rules wrong, and bash ahead anyway with the confidence of God's chosen dummies, while the Canadians got it right, but after 1900 employed their superior system with all the balls of Swiss watchmakers, performing prodigious feats of timidity and inertia. Or did, at least, till Saskatchewan and Tommy Douglas took big risks on Medicare and shamed them into grudging action.

'I wonder if I've got that all right,' muttered Z. to himself. 'Must ask B. J.'

He walked on toward the campus, humming happily to himself and ogling the passing co-eds.

> In olden days a glimpse of stocking
> Was looked on as something shocking
> Now heaven knows, anything goes.
>
> In present days a flash of pantie
> Is just 'nother ploy to up the ante
> For snogging and blows,
> Anything goes.

'Doesn't quite scan,' he conceded. 'Needs a little work. Seems everything does, these days. Except being – what was he? – a "mature" student, and a Journalism Fellow. This is the life,' he grinned. 'Not too bad at all.'

He was bopping along so cheerfully that he almost didn't notice Professor Jessica 'Pepper' Pemberton sitting on the front steps of the college, wearing a chic tan suede suit, engrossed in conversation with an undergraduate. This worthy, a boy with sleek hair and an expensive leather jacket over a white shirt and rep tie, was loudly pressing an all-too-familiar argument on her.

'But you've gotta admit, Professor Pemberton, that in order to keep up with globalization we've simply got to privatize and deregulate industries, almost all industries, and reduce the tax burden on corporations so that we can compete in world markets.'

Pepper shook her head and replied in a voice too soft for Zinger to hear. Looking over at Z., she smiled and beckoned to him to join her. After some further rant about 'common sense' and the imperatives of globalization, the student noticed the newcomer and, taking the hint, said good day and walked off.

'Mind if I sit with you a bit?'

'Please do. The sun is so warm and pleasant. Much too fine a day to be harangued by students who think that the voice of the market is the voice of Jehovah. You rescued me.'

'I thought students tended to be lefty radicals. That fellow seemed to spout the right-wing dogmas of the standard economics textbooks, market *über alles*.'

'There are still some of the save-the-world lefties around, but the activists these days are mostly post-Reagan, post-Thatcher types who spout the gospel according to Conrad Black or Rupert Murdoch. I think I liked it better when they refused to bow down to Mammon and shouted at me about how one day's U.S. military spending could feed the Third World for a year.'

'I know what you mean, yeh. But you have a nice way with students. I snuck into the back row of one your lectures recently. Enjoyed it. You have a nice touch.'

'Saw you. Yes, I do try, and it's easy because I really like the students, most of them. They're nice people, nice to work with, in spite of the reactionary ideology they spout.'

'J. T. and Cutty keep telling me that they come to university barely able to read or write. That must be a drag.'

'Makes it difficult, sometimes, yes, but on the whole I feel sorry for them.'

'Sorry? I'm not sure that I ...'

'Well, in this huge city, most of them commute to the campus. Suburban commuters. They can't afford downtown rents if they're from out of town, or they're the offspring of immigrants who live far out on the fringes, so they're on buses and the subway for maybe an hour or more each way, to and from. To pay the heavy increases in tuition fees, imposed by red-neck yahoo governments that cut back on education, they tend to have part-time jobs, nights and/or weekends. "Part-time" usually means no benefits and no overtime pay. I talked to a girl the other day who said her "part-time" job, in a doughnut shop at minimum wage, was fifty hours a week. *Fifty.* Imagine how much time she has to read, except on the bus. Time to read, and think, and write essays? Hardly. And no matter how much they work and scuffle, they graduate with crushing burdens of debt that take them years to work off. I can tell you, it's not much fun being a student these days, and terrible pressure. So, yes, I feel sorry for them. They're being sadly short-changed on their education. I think it's scandalous.'

'Hadn't seen it that way, actually. It sure is different from my undergrad days. I thought that in most European countries, university education was free, zero tuition.'

'Of course. In civilized countries, or even countries that regard education as an investment, tuition is free. But not here. Here they get hosed. Rich kids are OK, of course; their parents pay to send them – generally not to Chiliast, not to a big commuter school, but to smaller out-of-town elite colleges, away from the sweaty multitudes.'

'So far I like it here, I must say.'

'I'm glad. It's a good place. Compared to the commercial world downtown it's open and intellectually free, bubbling with ideas and optimism and research. After they graduate and get jobs, a lot of my former students tell me that they feel like galley slaves chained to their oars. Deeply in debt. Unfree.'

'I know what you're saying. Peons for "progress", whatever that is.'

'Sometimes I think that universities today, the better ones at least, are like the cathedrals in medieval times: they give hope and sanctuary, although that's little enough defence against the barbarians at the gates.'

'Aren't they inside the gates? I'm surprised here at Chiliast to walk from the IBM Building to the Nabisco Building and into the dedicated "Coca-Cola Lounge", and then see advertisements for Nescafé and, er, condoms over the urinals in the washrooms. It's getting so a fellow can't even take a leak, if you'll excuse my bluntness, without getting hit in the eye by Madison Avenue.'

'Uh huh. Soon I expect that the carillon in the bell tower will be playing singing commercials instead of *Gaudeamus igitur, juvenes dum sumus.* Oh, sorry, that means ...'

'"Let us rejoice, while we are young." An old German student song. Brahms used the tune in his Academic Festival Overture, right?'

Pepper fixed him with a level gaze. 'You know, Zinger, you're not exactly what I expected. When Cutty told me that you were arriving from Saskatchewan, and J.T. said this would be your first trip east, I guess I thought you, um, might be a little bit – different.'

'You expected maybe some hayseed?' Z. bristled just a little. 'Did you think I'd say things like "by cracky" and "oh dogies" or "fetch me the moonshine, Mabel"? Like Jed Clampett?'

'No, no,' Pepper laughed – and Z. found it a most engaging musical laugh – 'I just thought, or sort of assumed, you might find the big city campus experience quite, um, challenging.'

'Sure. Somewhat. But I can handle big city pretentiousness.'

'*Touché.* But all I meant was ...'

'You meant, "You can take the boy out of Saskatchewan, but you can't ..."'

'No offence, Z., please. None intended. I was only trying to compliment you on the music thing. But, well, you must admit that even your friend McLaughlin can be a bit, er, unpolished? Wears Hush Puppies? Needs a haircut? I suppose I didn't expect many people to know Latin or Brahms.'

'And I don't, much, but I can fake it with the best of them. I went to school, too, you know, and can come in out of the rain without being told by some culture vulture with a Ph.D. And I was a student of B.J.'s for four years.'

'Dear B.J.'

'We have libraries in the west, even back home in Prince Albert.

And we watch the same programs on cable TV, godhelpus, as you watch.'

'So we all live in the same world.'

'And the long winters give us plenty of time to read. Nothing better to curl up with on a cold prairie night than a good librarian.'

'OK, OK, I admit I was wrong. Your point is made, even if you had to trounce the misconceptions of a blinkered easterner to make it. I was raised in a small town myself, although I seldom admit that.'

'You were?'

'Sure. In Muskoka.'

'You seem very private school to me.'

'Oh yes, guilty. But that came later. Modest origins, and all that. Not from what the Old Torontonians call "a good address".'

'Hey, they tell me that to people in London or New York, *Canada* is not a good address.' They both chuckled a bit, and sat for a while sunning themselves in companionable silence. Z. wondered whether he should shove off, but neither of them made a move to leave, and Z. was pleased when Pepper reopened the conversation.

'The boys tell me that you're a writer. I do know that you're a journalist, but you're an author, too, did J. T. say?'

'Yeh, I scribble some. Whether I'm an "author", as you call it, may be decided when my novel is published, in a few months.'

'How exciting for you. What's it about?'

'Oh, that will all come out soon enough. Matter of fact, I've just come back from applying for a job downtown at one of the big newspapers.'

'But the Fellowship thing is supposed to be full-time, isn't it?'

'It is, yes, but my cash flow is temporarily rather trickly. I applied for some minor evening work, and used a – don't let on about this – phony name. My by-line you see, is F. Z. Springer, so I invented a mythical brother, Fred; same initials on my clippings for show-and-tell.'

'Fred? I love it. And did you get the job?'

'No, they said I didn't know enough about accounting and marketing, state-subsidized building construction, tax-deferred incomes, TV contracts, that sort of thing.'

'I didn't know you were a business reporter.'

'I'm not. I applied for a job as a sports writer.'

'The ubiquitous commerce thing again,' she laughed, with that musical trill of hers.

'Absolutely. Who was the classical figure who, everything he touched turned into gold, so he couldn't eat?'

'Midas, I think. Starved to death.'

'Right. Midas. Old Mr Greed.'

They both sighed.

Just then, two leggy young girls, clutching their books, walked by them wearing miniskirts of arresting brevity. Z. did an involuntary double take. Following his eyes, Pepper shook her head.

'I swear, on this campus it's often hard to tell whether the girls are off to a lecture or on their way to the gynecologist.'

Z. guffawed, and looked at her again, more narrowly.

'I really like you, Pepper. You're quite rompy, you know? Wicked.'

'Thank you. I try not to let it show too much, but I guess it sometimes peeks through. I'm forty-two, and we old academic broads often need some relief from the stereotype of the staid bluestocking. So maybe we've each corrected a preconception, don't you think?'

'I do, right enough. Staid, or a broad, or old, you ain't.'

'And a hayseed, you're not. Let's call it a draw.'

'A push, as they say in Vegas. Say, let's go out for dinner sometime. Would next Friday night be all right? Cocktails and supper?'

'Why, Mr Springer, or Francis, or Fred or whoever, are you suggesting a date?'

'I guess I am, yeh,' Zinger grinned.

'Well, well. Bless your heart, I haven't had a "date" in I don't know how long. Except with gay friends, of course. A woman's got to get out and about – I've got two kids, you know, so I'm not exactly a social butterfly.'

'So we'll have dinner?'

'Francis, really, I hope we'll be friends, but I don't date married men.'

'Oh, I'm not married. Least, I don't think I am. My divorce will probably come through from Prince Albert any time now.'

'A divorce? How distressing. You'll get over it. Your first?'

'My third.'

'THIRD! Now here's a guy with a swell track record. My, my. How can you afford all that alimony on a journalist's salary?'

'Can't, really. That's one reason I sometimes get short of cash. I might have missed a few payments along the way. But my divorce lawyer gives me a group rate.'

'You'd need it,' Pepper laughed heartily. 'But don't get me started on that subject. I really should be going. On that subject, I mustn't start.'

'Never a joyous thing, divorce.'

'Don't I know it. Such agony, all 'round. If often makes people despondent, twisted sometimes. My husband was, well, not a nice man, even to his own kids. We were all scared of him. Temper? Like a volcano. I had to boot him out. His parents did help me a bit, and my own parents did too, enough that I could get by, working nights as a librarian and going back to school to finish my Ph.D. But it was all pretty lean and rough, particularly hard on the kids. Divorce is no fun at all.'

'Sounds bad.'

'It was. And now your friend J.T is going through it. How do you think he's making out?'

'Not too well. Bit of a case, J.T., quite depressed. Sometimes I think he's off the rails, but he's a very good guy, in fact. Just not a realist.'

'And he's separated? For a fact?'

'Well and truly separated. Why?'

'Just curious. And depressed, you say? That's my impression too. I've read that depression is often anger that you turn against yourself. Wrong target. Is that why he drinks? Oh, it's noticeable you know. People make cracks. Sort of sad, I think. You've known him a long time?'

'Shit, I mean, dear me, we do go back a fair piece, yes. I was in grade ten and he was in grade nine when we met. He'd skipped a grade, so he was two years younger, but he always hung out with my older gang. He was obviously bright, precocious even, so we let him. We always got along.'

'Would you say he was, well, shy?'

'Maybe some, yeh. Shy, but trying to cover it up with bluster, you know, and fast talk. Glib. I think, looking back now, that the older girls — two years is a real gap to high-schoolers — the older girls treated him as something of a pet, a tame boy to hang out with and take them to proms when their older boyfriends were away at college. So he became,

I guess, a bit diffident with my crowd. Clever enough, but reluctant to lead. Deferential, you might say, and I think it became a habit. A born 2-I-C, second-in-command; always willing to help, lots of ideas, but not the take-charge guy. When I think about it, typically Canadian. But "shy" might not be the right word. I'd say, at bottom, lacking in confidence. Can a guy lack confidence but still have will and determination? I guess so. Doesn't realize how good he is. Though don't tell him I said so. He'd be insulted; deny it.'

'It's not hard to tell you're rather defensive about him. I expect you love him like a brother.'

'Nah! Maybe somewhat. He's an OK guy. Like I say, we go back a lot of years. Sure. And Cutty, too. So why do you ask? About J.T., I mean.'

'Why? Just casual interest. We're on a committee together. I used to regard him, from only a marginal acquaintance, as one of the up-and-coming scholars around here. If he got his nose out of the booze, he might still be, or so B.J. says. I suppose I feel kind of sorry for him. But look, let's leave it at that. I really must be off. Another class to prepare for at four.'

'Of course. Real nice talking with you again, Pepper. And about Friday night, for dinner?'

'Thanks for suggesting it. Nice of you, really. I'll think about it. You took me a little by surprise. But I'll think about it. 'Bye.'

- 23 -

There seemed to be an unusual number of students waiting to see J. T. in his office that morning after his ten o'clock lecture. Some were freshmen (freshpersons?) who wanted directions for readings toward an upcoming mid-term exam. Two were third-year students who wanted to consult with him about outlines for term papers. The real difficulty, as usual, was to get them to shift from the merely descriptive to the analytic, to state an argument or thesis and set about demonstrating, proving it.

Two fourth-year women in full Muslim garb came in together. They'd come in to ask for guidance in applying to graduate school, and J. T. gave them advice, promising to write letters of reference to support their applications. He thought they were smiling when they left, but he couldn't be sure, because except for the eyes their faces were covered.

He thought he'd dealt with the line-up, and was about to reach behind Schumpeter for the vodka bottle when another knock at the door made him pause. He knew that alcohol tended to loosen the tongue, so he took only a small, quick swig before opening the door again.

In came three young men, together, one with a shaved head, one with wispy blond hair, one with dark brown hair curled over his collar. All wore earrings, and two of the three had rings in their pierced eyebrows.

'Come in, fellows. How can I help you? I don't recognize you from my classes, but ... are you all together?' They said, 'Yes, together.' J. T. grinned, and prompted by vodka couldn't resist saying, 'How about a chorus of "Sodality Forever"? Haw. You guys have more rings on than a counter at Tiffany's. What's the occasion?' They were not amused, and looked at each other uncertainly. 'Ha, ha, just joking, guys.'

They introduced themselves as Billy, Tad, and Mark. No, they were not in any of his classes, but they wanted to ask him about something. None seemed to know how to begin. There was a lot of mumbling and throat-clearing as they found chairs.

'We're told,' said Billy, 'that you signed a petition for Gay Rights last year, is that right?'

'I guess I did, yeh.'

'And you have some minority-group students. We just saw two Muslim women leaving your office wearing the full *hijab*.'

'Yeh, wearing curtains, the whole rig. I was tempted to say, "Hallowe'en's not till next week, gals," but of course I didn't. They just wanted reference letters. Happy to do that. They're both very bright.'

'It's your search committee, for the next principal? That's what we'd like to ask about,' said Tad.

'Sure, ask away.'

'We'd like to put forward a name. We belong to the Gay Alliance.'

'I figured that out,' said McLaughlin.

'We want to nominate, but we're not sure how to do it?'

'Just write down your candidate's name, see if you can get his CV, and put a supporting letter – it needn't be long or formal – into my mailbox here in the department.'

After some hemming and hawing, it turned out they wanted to nominate Professor Morley Snelgrove from the Drama Department.

'Well, I see. Good man, Snelgrove. I know him slightly. Lot of publications, I believe. Is he associated with the Gay Alliance?'

'Oh, he came out years ago. Snelgrove is the most prominent academic in our community.'

'And do you think the College is ready for, what shall I say, an alternative lifestyle principal?'

'If not now, when?' asked Mark.

'Fair point,' J. T. nodded.

'Do you have a problem with that?' Billy inquired.

'Me? Not personally, no. But the thing is, the committee might. I mean Morley Snelgrove is a scholar, past any question, with a book on Beckett that was well reviewed, I think ...'

'And another book on Brecht,' put in Tad.

'Oh, right. Good. But the committee may be looking for someone more, ah, orthodox.'

'Why?' asked Billy.

'Well, um, that's what committees tend to, you know, do. Someone mainstream, representative of the entire scholarly community.'

'And a gay man wouldn't be representative?' persisted Billy.

'Look, you fellows doubtless know about discrimination' – all nodded – 'and I'd argue there's less discrimination in the university than in any other social institution, but ...'

'But?'

'Well, in a position of leadership, being the chief, you have to be sure that the followers are willing to be led. There's also the public image thing, and the necessity of the principal to be able to interact, all right, schmooze, with the big-shot potential benefactors and rich corporate donors on a footing of equality, being acceptable.'

'So a gay principal wouldn't be equal or acceptable?' suggested Mark.

'To me, sure, and to most students; probably to a majority of the faculty. But to the financial community? Hey, I'm not so sure, that's all.'

'You're saying, then,' said Billy with a slight sulk, 'that we shouldn't go ahead and nominate.'

'I didn't say that. No. I'm saying that there might be some reluctance in the committee. But go ahead. So long as you know the odds, place your bet. No guarantees to your man, or to anyone else for that matter, but if you want to try it on, do it. Why not?'

J. T. gave them some suggestions about the nominating process, urging them to collect some signatures from prominent faculty or alumni who might offer support. They shook hands all around and McLaughlin walked out into the corridor with them. At one end of the hall he saw Cutty talking to another colleague, and waved. But at the opposite end of the hall, behind him, he did not notice Teddy Kravnik intercepting the threesome, taking out a pen and notebook as she asked them about the interview.

Later that morning, after turning the matter over in his mind, J. T. phoned Sam Osbourne to sound out his opinion.

'Morley Snelgrove wouldn't have occurred to me, Sam, but he's a solid academic citizen, good-to-impressive publishing record, a former Chair of the Drama department. I think he was a vice-president of the Faculty Association at one time. Very personable.'

'Yes, I see what you mean, J. T. I guess Morley is a popular sort of fellow, and experienced. But it's the gay thing, is it?'

'Uh huh. So I wondered what you'd think ...'

'I'm not sure I'm the right person to ask,' Sam said slowly.

'Why not?'

'You see, I've got a daughter who wants to be an actress. Trouble is, my son wants to be the same thing.'

'Oh.'

Because Osbourne wasn't much help, one way or the other, McLaughlin was glad to bump into Norbert Norton at coffee in the afternoon.

'A delegation, you say? Three of the light-in-the-loafers crowd? My, my. How things have changed. I don't know. I don't think it would fly, but put me down as a definite undecided. I'll see you at the next meeting.'

Zinger and Gandy were walking across the campus on their way to lunch. The golden autumn day was warm, the trees beginning to turn into a display of exuberant colours, nature's lustrous salute to waning summer. B.J. waggled his walking stick at a stand of reddening maples, and pronounced them 'most agreeable, most agreeable.'

They were discussing American politics in a desultory fashion as they strode along. Z. asked a number of questions about U.S. foreign policy, particularly in Latin America, and B.J. began to expatiate.

'It's the old and familiar story of power and hegemony, Francis. It's the contradiction between the rhetoric of liberty at home and the practice of despotism abroad. That's how Roman expansionism began; that's how the British Empire was in the nineteenth century. And now it's characteristic of the American empire, has been since 1945. There's very little new under the sun. Dominance.

'Oh, I know, the ordinary American citizen is very decent and trusting; usually convinced, if he thinks about it at all, that the motives of his government are laudable: to spread democracy and the benefits of market capitalism and consumerism. But power is seldom benign, particularly to the powerless. After 1947 the chief vehicle of U.S. dominance was the giant multinational corporation – an institution which, by the way, Adam Smith abjured, Francis, because it was big enough to rig and manipulate free markets – and the spearhead was the CIA. as the force that could create friendly dependent governments abroad, or break unfriendly independent governments. Meanwhile, poor people who want schools and hospitals can easily be dismissed – or "disappeared" by death squads – as dangerous communists. Spreading "democracy"? It is to laugh. Or cry.'

'*Plus ça change*,' said Zinger.

'Innis was always a realist about this,' B.J. continued. 'The great Harold Innis wrote to a U.S. friend as early as, oh, I think it was the late 1940s, about "the crude effrontery of American imperialism". Don't you like that, Francis? Oh, I like that prodigiously. Strange how most people, good people like the Yankees and like the ordinary Brits in the nineteenth century, always tend to assume that they are the "good guys" while their governments are committed abroad to militarism and casual atrocities to protect their investments. But if the commercially owned newspaper and TV conglomerates don't report it, or bury it on back pages, or put a patriotic spin on it for the sake of jingoism and profits, how are the ordinary people to know? They cannot. It was Saul Bellow who said, "We Americans are the best-informed people in the world; consequently we know nothing." Much of what we call "news" is such bullroar, Francis, misleading at best. Take the coverage of that cruel farce, the Gulf War of '91, or the media acting like cheerleaders when George W. invaded Iraq ...'

'Yeh, wonderful instances of "news" and entertainment combined to a more reassuring and visually pleasing version of what we laughingly call "reality"'.

'Indeed. It's becoming harder and harder to recognize where "infotainment" leaves off and propaganda begins. Some scholars, of course – like Chomsky and Parenti and McChesney, have you read them? – insist that "news" and propaganda have become indistinguishable.'

'I've read some Noam Chomsky, yes, and I've often come across the quote from A. Roy Megarry, the former publisher of the Toronto Globe and Mail, something about the function of newspapers not being to bring news to readers but to bring readers to advertisers.'

'Exactly. I often think, Francis, that if God ever decides to give this world an enema, he'll insert the nozzle into Washington, D.C. But we flounder along, trying to see the real world through the veil of electronic reporting. We are gulled. And remember, it was our man McLuhan who said, "Only puny secrets need protection. The big secrets are protected by public incredulity."'

'I didn't know that. Good line. But surely you're not saying that McLuhan was a radical?'

'Dear me, no. Bless your heart, not at all. Surely I've told you why Innis broke with Marshall? I haven't? I will. But here we are at our lunch spot. I like this pub, the Duke of York. They pull a good pint. Let's get seated and I'll relate all that.'

Zinger, dressed in a baggy sweater under a nondescript tan jacket, and Gandy tugging at a bright yellow waistcoat worn with a brown tweed suit that had seen better days, slid into chairs at a small round table. When they were comfortably ensconced over their pints, Gandy's a Bass Ale and Z.'s a Smithwick's, they both ordered steak and kidney pie and told the waitress not to hurry. The younger man lit a cigarette while the old professor fondled an unlighted pipe. The burn holes on his waistcoat testified that it was usually lit. Gently Z. tried to pull Gandy back to the subject of McLuhan.

'I dug out his interview with *Playboy* as you suggested, B.J. Took some notes. Here. He says, "… electric media are unraveling the entire fabric of our society …" At another point I have him saying that TV is "incompatible with the survival of Western man".'

'Good lad. That's it. Although he often made light of it all, and of himself. Do you remember him with Woody Allen, scolding some poor chap for "misunderstanding my entire fallacy"?'

'Sure. I'm making some headway with McLuhan, but it's tricky and the students in class keep coming back to the "Global Village" thing as if that's all the man ever said.'

'Oh my, no, of course not. Much more to it. All he was saying, I'm sure you see, is that instantaneous worldwide communication abolishes time and space, surrounds us all in an instantaneous global network, throws us all into the same information system. It's a catchy phrase, but an unfortunate one.'

'Why unfortunate?'

'Because he himself wasn't sure that "village" was the right term. Misleading. I remember when I was teaching here years ago, and Marshall came to lecture to my class – only because I was recommended by Marshall's oldest friend, Tom Easterbrook from economics – McLuhan said he'd take questions after his talk, and he told me that the first question inevitably would be about the "Global Village" tag. He shook his head and said he wished he'd called it something else: the "Global Suburb". He was no great fan of television, you know, greatly preferred much older forms of communication.'

'Print?'

'Older than that. The oral culture, like classical Athens, which Innis preferred too. Pre-print, do you see: debate, verbal reciprocity and intimacy, the common law, parliament, the family, the early universities; all oral institutions before the world was made linear and mechanical by Gutenberg's printing device. Organic communication.'

'And by "Global Suburb" he meant …?'

'Oh, he meant that TV was mainly homogenizing, commercial, shallow, mediocre, vulgar, like a suburb rather than a real varied and human village. Banal, he kept saying; banal.'

'You surprise me, B.J. A lot of writers characterize McLuhan as the champion and guru of the electronic age, its advocate.'

'Bless your heart, not at all. Not at all. Marshall was really warning us about it. "I'm resolutely opposed," he often said, "to almost all innovation." To him, technology took man further and further away from the real, the organic, the natural. Away from God, I suppose, since he was such a staunch Catholic. In almost every sense, his own beliefs tended to be traditional and, well, reactionary.'

'I remember reading that while he was a graduate student in England he became an intellectual fan of Belloc and Chesterton, and a convert to the Roman Church,' Z. nodded.

'Totally and wholeheartedly. I think it was his need for a solid rock of faith in the spinning chaos of the modern world, a world with which he enjoyed playing satiric intellectual games, but of which he profoundly disapproved. No, he was very much in this world but not of it. He loved to cock snooks at it. The Church gave him his perspective as an outsider and his moral foundation.'

'Hmm,' mused Zinger. 'Odd that he became so close to a humanist non-Christian skeptic like Harold Innis.'

'Close? To Innis? Oh dear me, no. Most people assumed that because they worked on the same subject on the same campus, they were friends, but that's not true. He learned from Harold, but Innis didn't like him. Not at all. And it was the Church that caused the rupture.'

'The Church? How do you mean?'

'It's rather a strange story, but … Should we order dessert? Perhaps some pie?'

'OK. But the break with Innis. You said you'd …'

'Quite so. Remarkable tale, remarkable. I got the story from Marshall's friend Tom Easterbrook – lovely man, Easter – who left a tape describing the incident in the university archives, oral history stuff, although he never did put the story into print. Odd, that. I once asked Tom …'

'But the story?'

'Oh, yes. What happened was, let me see, that after McLuhan published his first book, on advertising, *The Mechanical Bride* in 1951, Tom gave Innis the book. Innis read and admired it, put it on his course reading list. So Tom invited Marshall along to Innis's morning seminar. It turned out that McLuhan understood Innis's apparently impenetrable later work better than Tom did, maybe better than anyone did. So they seemed to get along famously. Innis was pleased, flattered I suppose, and suggested that he'd stand lunch for the three of them.'

B.J. paused to stuff and light his pipe.

'As they strolled down Philosophers' Walk from the old economics building on Bloor Street toward Hart House their conversation turned to the topic of war, the Second World War. All agreed that war is hell. Innis said something about how the Spanish Civil War, 1936–39, was a precursor of the World War and that the West should have learned a lesson from that confrontation. The Western nations had abandoned the elected Spanish republican government to the military insurgents, the fascists. Well, said McLuhan, with the zeal of a convert to Catholicism, Generalissimo Franco and the Church saw the traditional order being threatened and they had to keep the Protestants in line. Innis was thunderstruck. Did McLuhan support Franco, he demanded? Yes, certainly, said Marshall. Innis stopped in his tracks, aghast. He said lunch was off. Tom, he said, never bring this man to see me again.'

Gandy relit his pipe and puffed reflectively.

'From that time on, Innis closed the door on Marshall. Although McLuhan wrote several long letters to Innis, suggesting collaboration on projects, the Archives show few if any replies from Harold. So, friends? Not a bit of it.'

'I'll be damned,' said Zinger. 'Is this known, generally? In print somewhere?'

'It isn't, so far as I know. I think Tom didn't write it down because he didn't want to embarrass his friend, particularly after McLuhan became a celebrity, although he put the story on tape for the archives.'

'But you're saying that McLuhan was a fascist?'

'I did not say that. I would say only that Marshall was such a political naïf, so other-worldly, if reactionary, that he just did not know that he'd given offence. A great many intellectual Catholics were originally pro-Franco, you know, from Evelyn Waugh to the Pope.'

'I'll be damned,' Z. repeated. 'Sweet Christ on a skateboard, that's a helluva story.'

'Yes,' B.J. nodded. 'The truth is often in the anecdotes. I've told my colleague Jessica Pemberton all my McLuhan stories – you've met Pepper, I think? – and she's busy writing about Marshall and Innis. Ah, here's our dessert.'

- 25 -

J. T. shuffled around in his kitchen looking for clean dishes, wondering where he'd put the bratwurst, puzzled as to why the mustard was in the breadbox. He found a can of sauerkraut in a cupboard behind some stale cookies. 'I'm not all that well organized,' he thought to himself. The electric can-opener had conked out, but he managed to puncture the can in three places with his Swiss Army knife and a hammer, then to tear the lid back with pliers. The bratwurst turned up when he knocked a pile of last weekend's newspapers off the counter and discovered the four forlorn sausages in Saran wrap, warm but not green, possibly edible. 'Bratwurst and sauerkraut make a good nosh,' he told himself. But in the end he didn't eat much of it and pushed it away.

Half an hour later he found himself looking out the front window, waiting for Cutty to arrive to help him lift the Model A's radiator out of its moorings. The rad had to be sent off to be re-cored. Restoration is a slow process.

He watched some neighbour children skipping rope in the street, wishing that his own children would come home more often, but content that they seemed to be happy and doing well in their schools. 'Wish *I* were more happy in my school,' he mused. He looked at the empty tumbler in his hand; didn't remember pouring it, didn't remember drinking it. Burped up the taste of old sauerkraut. Decided to pour another couple of fingers of scotch.

'Jeez, your house is a mess,' said Cuttshaw on arrival. 'Look at this kitchen. A public health inspector would condemn it.'

'Yeh, my cleaning lady quit. I offered to give her a raise, but she said "no way" and stomped out. Maybe I'll find another one.'

'You'd sure as hell have to clean up, a lot, before any maid would take you on.'

After about an hour they managed to loosen the lower bolts from the frame of the car, detach the hoses, remove the water pump, and wrestle the radiator out. Cutty allowed as how he was ready to stop for a beer. While J. T. went into the house to fetch a case of a dozen Muskoka Cream Ale, Cutty sat on the front bumper, pulled out a cell phone, and rang Zinger.

'Get your ass over here, Z. You said you would. Don't leave me alone with him, because it's still early and I don't think I can stand another night of listening to him talk about his domestic un-bliss. You agreed we'd take a serious run at him. Yeh, give him both barrels, like you said.'

'How is our boy?'

'Half-drunk. Moody.'

'Uh huh. I'll try to hurry.'

Cutty told J. T. that Zinger might drop by. They sat on the back steps with their ales. Cuttshaw talked about a book he was writing on international trade theory. J. T. listened, nodded, but didn't seem much interested. Their talk was desultory until half an hour later. Z. came down the driveway and joined them on the back steps; poured himself a beer.

'Lovely evening,' he offered, 'warm and balmy. Not a cloud in the sky. Autumn leaves in full glory. Damn but it's good to be alive, eh J. T.? Sometimes I wonder if Heaven could be much better than this — because if it ain't, I'm not going.'

'The chances of your going to Heaven are mighty slim,' said J. T., 'even if you pay off your debts, including what you still owe me.'

'Patience, ol' buddy, patience. I have everything under control, and soon everything, as the bard says, will be vouchsafed unto you. My publisher says he's going to pay me the advance on my eagerly anticipated literary work any day now, and then your brilliant and cherished friend will be rolling in it.'

'When will it come out, Z., your novel?' Cutty asked.

'Looks like spring publication, sometime after February. But the advance will doubtless be vast. Fame and fortune are lurking just around the corner. Say, why have you got your shoe off? Rubbing your foot?'

'Henry Ford here dropped his radiator on it.'

'It just slipped,' said McLaughlin.

'I'm not sure why you want to keep farting about with this dumb machine,' Cutty mumbled.

'Model As are classics, and I'll be the proud owner of a splendid vehicle. One that doesn't much pollute, a simple machine that any damn fool can fix and tune with a wrench and a screwdriver, a bright and cheery car that ticks along on minimal gas and will bring smiles of recognition and glee from everyone who sees it.'

'We could use more glee around here all right,' said Cutty.

'He's right,' nodded Z., 'the oldies are the goodies, before cars got so huge and complicated and run by computer chips that even trained mechanics can't fix them – have to drop in whole new units at no end of bloody cost. That's why I take such good care of my '55 T-Bird. But a Model A, now, with a top speed of, what? fifty miles an hour, is not fast enough for the barren thruways, where no life happens, but quick enough to get you there; slow enough to let you see where you *are*, not just where you're going. A pleasurable car. Unsophisticated. Simple. A car for the man who *cares*. I can relate to that.'

'Right, and Trish will be amazed. She'll be delighted.'

'Fuck a duck,' said Z., 'you're not doing this for Trish, are you? Women don't understand these things. Hell, she'd just laugh at you.'

'No, you're wrong. She'll be surprised, I guess, but tickled as all-get-out.'

'Yeh, and she bloody well got out. Can't we for Kristsake,' Cutty expostulated, 'even talk about cars without you dragging Trish into it?'

'Sorry,' J. T. muttered.

'You know,' said Zinger, 'I think what you need is to sell this house, or rent it, just get *out*, for godsake. Shift your gears. Too many memories. And maybe cut back on the drinking, some. Cutty and I are sipping this excellent Muskoka Cream Ale and you're chugging away at a very dark brown glass of scotch. Maybe a bit too much, eh? You should get out more.'

'Oh, hell, I've had lots of dinner invitations from women in the neighbourhood. In the last two weeks I've had invitations from three nice ladies, two divorcees and a young widow from down the street.'

'And did you go?' the two men asked together.

'No, I just said thank you. Well, I did have coffee on Sunday with the widow, here in the garden. She brought over a blueberry pie.'

'And? And? How was it?' Cutty importuned.

'The pie? Good. Home-made.'

'No, dammit, the young widow.'

'OK, I guess. Nice. Boring.'

'Bloody drizzling shit!' erupted Z. 'How in hell do you expect to get anywhere if you turn down invitations and don't pay attention to a woman who bakes?'

'Attention? Get anywhere? Whadd'ya mean? I don't want to get anywhere. Besides, if I got too friendly with women in the neighbourhood, Trish would quickly hear about it and think I was being, um, disloyal.'

'Disloyal! Will you listen to the man, Cutty? By the hairy balls of Esau, his wife takes a walk and leaves him in the lurch, trades him in for a stool in a singles bar, and he sits here making noises about *loyalty!* Mother of God. Let's go inside, guys, where I can pace up and down and shout more without the neighbour ladies tuning in.'

Z. stomped off into the house, grumbling to himself.

'What's up with him?' asked J. T.

'I think Zinger has worked up a full head of steam,' said Cuttshaw. 'I think he's trying to rescue you.'

'From what?'

'From yourself, I'd say.'

'Oh. I guess I don't get it.'

The two of them followed Z. into the house, bringing the supply of drinks with them. They found Z. in the living room kicking a hassock and rumbling darkly in his throat.

'Scotch, fellows?' J. T. asked. 'Who's ready for a scotch?'

Cutty declined. Z. ignored the question and threw himself onto the couch, then got up again and began to march up and down the length of the room. His grey-black eyes glittered, cold as granite. They were the eyes of a man who seemed to have calculated the worth of everything the world had on offer and found it all wanting. He fixed McLaughlin with an incisive glare.

'Do you remember that sundial on the campus back home in Saskatoon, the one we used to walk by 'most every day?' J. T. nodded. 'So you'll remember the inscription on it, eh?

> I am a shadow,
> So art thou.
> I mark time.
> Doest thou?

125

Good lines. But now you're just wasting time. You're morose. You're sitting here comatose. You're a prize N A F A F.'

'A what?'

'A No Ambition Fuck All Fun. A becalmed jerk. You've gotta get stirred up. You've gotta get outta this house. You've turned it into a shrine to a marriage that's over.'

'Well, a shrink I went to said I should "guard the hearth". That's all I'm doing.'

'A shrink yet. How long ago was that? When did he say that?'

'Well, a year or so ago, maybe sixteen months.'

'So it's long past the time for that. It's too bloody late for that. Avoiding risk, playing it "safe", hell, that's how you fall into obsessions. Safety be damned. And you can't "guard" anything with your brain pickled in alcohol.'

'I guess maybe I drink a little too much. B. J. told me that.'

'A little? Sweet Krist on a pogo stick. A little? You're as potted as a begonia, and every day, near as I can see. Oh, I know, I know, you say you need a few drams because you can't sleep, to deaden the nightmares, but prob'ly the booze is making the nightmares worse.'

'So you're saying I should knock off the scotch? Easy to say. I'm not sure I could.'

'I didn't say that. I'd never trust a man who didn't drink at all, and nobody ever called me a teetotaller. But cut back, that's the thing, cut back a lot. You're awash in it. You drink all day, every day, right? You're saturated, and it's oozing out your pores. Your clothes are sour. There's a smell to you, J. T.'

'Jeez, what a terrible thing to say.'

'To have to say. You'll have to dry out for a few days, and then see if you can go back to being a social drinker. Hey, Cutty, tell him that story about Eddie Condon.'

'Have I told you that before, J. T.? No? Well, Condon and I used to talk a bit when his jazz band played here in town at the old Colonial Tavern, remember that? And Eddie was a very large drinker. Yeh, Eddie said that he once had a four-week gig in Vegas, and a guy used to come in and sit near the bandstand 'most every night, and the two of them used to hoist quite a few between sets. At the end of the four weeks, the guy said, "Eddie, I think you and I should back off a bit from the bottle. Come on with me to my spread in Wisconsin, I've got

126

my own plane here, and we'll relax and taper off some." The guy talked him into it for a week of free R-and-R. Eddie said the guy's spread turned out to be a big dairy farm. It was terrible, Eddie said: "For three days I drank nothing but milk – and now I know what makes children so nasty."'

Z. slapped his thigh and hooted. Although in fact he'd heard the anecdote before, even J. T. had to crack a smile.

'So we don't want you to quit, do we, Cutty, we just want you to get a grip, reassess and ease off the sauce, that's all. We don't want you to let the bottle drag you down. God knows you seem down enough.'

'What I'm hearing is that you guys, my two best friends, think I'm a bore and a lush. Is that it?'

'That's not what I said, is it, Cutty? That's too simple. I want, we want, you to face up to some things and take hold of your life.'

'And do you, Z., think you really understand all this, my situation? Do you really think you understand my marriage? You assume it's finished, but it may not be at all. What if Trish comes home at Christmas?'

'Christmas doesn't count. A few sweet choruses of "Auld Lang Syne" at New Year's doesn't count. What matters is now, and she is being marked absent now, has been for months.'

'You don't understand,' mumbled J. T.

'No, I don't, I admit. Nobody understands anybody else's marriage. Humans are den animals, like bears, and no outsider can know what goes on in the den. We just see the mouth of the cave from outside, and most of it is subterranean inside. True enough. Everybody is a mystery, I suppose. But what I *do* see is results, effects. What Cutty and I see is that you're numb, partly numb with the booze, and you're tearing yourself up and dragging yourself down.'

'Oh, I don't know. I don't think you're right. I didn't know that was what you think of me. After all these years ... so negative ...'

'What I think of you!' Z. exploded. 'I'll bloody well tell you. What I think is that you're a victim, and beginning to enjoy being a victim. Wallowing in self-pity. You don't see that when your bloody canoe is sunk it's time to stop paddling and start swimming.'

'Well, hell, if that's what you think ...'

'Just listen to me! Listen and for God's sake take me seriously. What I *do* think, and I'm damned well going to lay it all out, is that you are a smart, kind, loyal, well-intentioned ASSHOLE. I think you're a mass of twitching contradictions, a cerebral idiot, a repressed romantic, a pseudo-intellectual denier of reality. I think you're trying to be pathetically gallant or gallantly pathetic about "guarding a hearth" where the last embers are cold as a polar bear's ass. I think the unexamined life may not be worth living, but that the over-examined life may lead to paralysis. For the last few months I think you've had the world view of a self-absorbed proctologist, looking up your own asshole, and looking at it through a bottle at that. You're just so goddamn *dismal*, McLaughlin.'

Z. paused for breath, grabbed another beer. J.T. looked at him with wide, sad eyes.

'You seem to believe,' Z. plunged on, 'that you're in some kind of tug-of-war. But Trish has let go of the rope. So you've gotta let go too. And you've gotta let go of your anger.'

'I remember my shrink used to say something about anger.'

'I'll bloody bet he did. You've been left, dumped. It doesn't take some flakey shrink to tell you that you're angry. So let it out. I've thought about this, and I've looked this stuff up in a couple of head-doctor books, and they say that depression is often, usually, the result of anger that's repressed, anger that's directed at the wrong target, directed against self and not at the bad guys. So if you unleash the anger, and direct it properly, you're a long way toward overcoming depression. Do you see that, oh brilliant intellectual? Do you see that?'

J.T. nodded and muttered that it might make some sense.

'Of course it does. So I fucking DARE you to face reality. Your emotional reality. It's the subjective that counts. There is nothing, as the Bard said, nothing either good or bad but emotion makes it so.'

'Thinking. It's 'thinking' makes it so.'

'Wrong. The old Spear-Shaker meant *deciding*, emotionally, with feeling. And all the King's horses'-asses and all the King's shrinks can't decide for you, you gotta do it yourself. A shrink is usually a Wizard of Oz, wrapped in pseudo-wisdom, but it's you that's gotta wise up, and act, and do. You've gotta make it bloody *happen*, J.T., not just sit in this grubby and deteriorating house, immobile, lifeless as a bug caught in amber. For Krist's sake, react. For Krist's sake, get angry! Make noise, throw things, get on with the chase, bellow and fight and make demands! Recognize your anger and bang the hell out of it!'

'Jeez, Zinger, you're ranting at me. You may not be all wrong, but you're over-simplifying. You're not being fair. You make me feel, well, small.'

'So grow. I'm pouring the fertilizer on you so that you'll stop shrinking and grow. It's change or die. Like trees or empires, we expand or we die. Them's the rules, Twinky, and you can't change them.'

J. T. scratched his head and spilled his drink and studied the soggy carpet. A silence fell, heavy as wet boots.

'Maybe,' said Cutty, 'we should drop it for now, call it a night.' J. T. looked grateful.

'N O!' Zinger roared. 'We won't call it a night till I've had my say. When you're dealing with a shit-wagon you gotta dump the whole load.' He thumped a fist on the coffee table. 'There's one other thing I gotta get out. It's selfishness, McLaughlin. You're being bloody selfish.'

'Me? Selfish? Hey, that's absurd. That's insulting. I meet my obligations, I look after my kids. And my students. I try to see the other guy's point of view, even yours, Z., bully that you seem to want to be. I, I ... serve on committees, and give money to Amnesty International. No one can say I'm not a good friend, considerate. Who else lends you money? And I've tried over the years, God knows I've tried, to make my marriage work. Maybe I failed. The harder I tried the worse it got. But selfish? I can't believe you'd call me that.'

'I can and I do. You're not just depressed, and angry, but you're expecting us to buy into your excessive grief. You want your friends to accept it and share it. But there comes a time, by God, when depression is not tenable, not tolerable, certainly not interesting. It becomes an affront to friendship and, well, to life, joy. You think you're unique? The only guy a woman ever left? Screw that. No, after a time, grief becomes a, what? a posture, a demand that your friends grieve too. There is an arrogance to prolonged sorrowing that claims that it's exceptional, unequalled, that it passes the understanding of ordinary mortals like Cutty and me. But really it's just self-flagellation, so don't expect us to admire it. There is, lord love us, no end to the selfishness of men, and you're no bleeding exception. Sure, mope and mourn if you like, but me, I've had it up to here, up the ol' wazzoo.'

Z. stopped pacing the floor and drained his glass. 'Come on, Cutty,' he said, 'we ought'a go.'

'Jeez,' said J.T., 'you sure know how to carve a guy up. You're an arrogant bastard, Z.'

'You're welcome,' said Z. 'Any time. The ol' Zinger Truth Machine is always at your service, and let me assure you, it's infallible. Also free, and worth every penny.'

'Our man makes a lot of sense,' Cutty said. 'Rough and unwelcome, I suppose, but good sense. Think about it, J.T., please. And then we'll come back on the weekend and help you some more with the car, won't we, Z.?'

'Sure,' said Z. He clapped a hand on J.T.'s shoulder, but was met only with a shrug and blank stare.

Cutty began to shuffle to the door. Z. turned and followed him, shouting a cordial 'Good night,' as he followed Cuttshaw outside and down the front steps.

'You gave him some heavy whacks,' said Cutty as they drove away. 'I didn't know you intended to be so rough. Maybe too rough.'

'I didn't know myself. But I got on a roll and I decided to hit him with the whole shot. There's something to be said for shock therapy. I love him like a brother, but sometimes I think he has the common sense of a lima bean. He's got a tough core, somewhere in there, if he can just get a grip. Shit, man, what are we talking about here? A dumb dodo? A destitute cripple? Nah, he's a tenured professor, with three good kids and talent and books and articles in print and a house, and even some health, or else the booze would have done him in long before this. Thousands would kill to have his advantages, so why should we protect him? A swift boot in the ass can be salutary, take it from me, and I've had a few. Dammit, I just don't want him on my conscience, with a tombstone that says: Here lies another decent man, ruined by a woman, ruined by himself.'

'You may be right, if awfully harsh.'

'For damned certain I'm right. I'm always right – except about myself, of course. Never could figure myself out, but others are fairly easy. Anyway, Cutty, say not the struggle availeth more than sweet fuck all, but it's lovely to be above ground and laughing. Come on, I'll drive you up to McSorley's and buy you a nightcap, whadd'ya say? We can talk about how many economists can dance on the head of a pin. I didn't much enjoy that, and I've got a terrible thirst on me.'

- 26 -

Zinger phoned his editor, one C.N. Boychuk, at MacDonald-Fraser Publishing. She was the one who'd sent him notice of the acceptance of his novel months ago. She invited him down to the office the next morning at eleven. Zinger showed up in a brown jacket and bright green tie over a pale blue shirt, hair slicked back with more than a few dabs of Brylcreem.

'Hi,' she said, 'I'm Cathy Boychuk.'

'Francis Z. Springer. Pleased to meet you.'

'Come along to my office, it's just back this way. Coffee?'

'Sure.'

'Do sit down. I know you want to talk about your book. It's wonderful. I *did* enjoy it on first reading, and now I've read it twice. I'm not certain, to be frank, that we'll be able to sell it big time, but it's a swell book, funny, plus energy, and I just love it.'

'I suppose you have to say that to every author you deal with.'

'Yes, I do. But in this case I mean it. It has a nice swing and zip, and I laughed a lot, out loud, when I first got into it. Raunchy. And raunchy is good. It works with the sales staff. I had two of our salesmen read it, and they agreed it was eccentric and comic. Hey, let me get that coffee.'

Cathy swirled out of the room. She wore a short dress of electric blue that matched her big round eyes. Compact, maybe only five foot three, her strawberry blond hair cut close and pert. Flat shoes, no jewellery, no wedding ring. Cathy might be thirty-six or thirty-eight Zinger thought, but she moved like a young colt and her bouncy movements gave a noteworthy jiggle to her prominent breasts. She exuded enthusiasm, a most attractive quality in big-city working women, in people, and rare.

When she burst back into the room carrying two cups and a copy of his manuscript, she said that Mr MacDonald, the owner and publisher, would send an imperial summons to them in five minutes.

'Thanks for the coffee, Ms Boychuk.'

'Call me Cathy. And don't get vexed when you meet MacDonald. He barks and he bites, but the staff mostly ignore him. His father had the brains, but he's retired now, so we all try to remember what the old man would have done, and so we're usually able to overcome the worst of the son's bad judgments. Oh, there's the buzzer. Can you imagine getting commanded by a buzzer? So tacky. Come along and I'll present you to himself.'

Cathy led Zinger down a long corridor to MacDonald's office, performed the introductions, winked at Zinger, and departed.

'So, Mr Singer, you're one of the team now.'

'Springer.'

'Of course. Did Boychuk say you were from somewhere in Alberta?'

'Prince Albert, Saskatchewan.'

'Ah, yes. Whatever. And just in town for a few days, are you? We might have fitted in a round of golf. I'll be off to the course by noon, but our foursome ...'

'I don't golf. And no, I live here. I'm at the university for this year.'

'You're an academic?'

'A journalist.'

'Thank God for that. Can't stand academics. They usually write dreadfully. Can't make any money on them. I take it you have a contract with us?'

'Right.'

'Cathy says I signed it last summer. Good girl, Cathy. Great hooters. Here's the file. Give me a minute to review it. Hm.'

MacDonald, on closer inspection, was a man of only forty-five or so, but looked older because of a gleaming bald head with a fringe of iron-grey hair. He was a six footer with a gruff voice and a fleshy face topped by rimless glasses. He wore a dark grey pinstripe suit and a massive gold ring on his right hand and a diamond pinky ring on his left; gold cufflinks.

No wonder the office was so lacking in character: no framed book covers on the walls or photographs of authors. It was a large corner room with the handsome wood panelling of an old building, windows on two walls, a credenza with a wet bar on another, but only a few books in evidence on small shelves on either side of the door. Tacked to the wall above the credenza was a strip of black felt, three feet long, with a sign under it: 'For books that meet a long felt need.' Another sign in a plastic casing on the big oak desk read: 'I'm too busy to be nice to more than one person per day. This isn't your day. Tomorrow isn't looking good either.' Clearly, Zinger thought to himself, I'm not dealing with Jack McClelland or Maxwell Perkins here.

'Contract seems to be in order. Standard terms. We'll owe you another $1,000 advance against royalties on the pub date. That's publication date. Scheduled for March.'

'I understand. But I wonder whether you could push up the pub date a couple of months, say to January, or just let me have that five grand a little earlier?'

'Can't do it. We're locked in. The product is slotted in to our spring list.'

'The product?'

'Your book.'

'Oh. The thing is, I've had some unexpected expenses here in the east, and I have some alimony payments ...'

'Alimony? Dear God, why do you writers always have alimony payments? Seems to go with the territory for most scribblers. Why do you make your lives so chaotic? Damned foolishness. Inattention. Fecklessness. Remember, as Mrs MacDonald always says, life presents no problems to serious and well-conducted persons. A piece of advice, Mr Singer: if you have a choice between marital discord and a double root canal, take the canals every time.'

'I'll bear that in mind – if I ever get a choice. But on the cash advance thing ...'

'Out of the question. See here, I'm a businessman. My ledgers have got to add up. The book business is in crisis in this country. Twenty percent of our population speak French, another twenty percent are functionally illiterate, and no one under forty reads anything if it's not on a computer screen. It's tough sledding.'

'I'd have thought the book business was always in crisis.'

'Seems that way. My father made a living out of it, although most days I'm damned if I see how. Not enough buyers. Too many lending libraries and second-hand bookstores. But do you know what plagues the industry? Do you know? Authors! Damn them, I detest them all.'

'I'm an author, and if that's the way ...'

'You're not. You're a writer. There's a big difference. Most writers I can get along with –'

'They supply the product.'

'Right. But authors are a pain in the ass. I've made money for a lot of them, but do they ever thank me? Hold testimonial dinners for me? Ever mention me with gratitude in their "Acknowledgements"? Not a bit of it! They want their hands held, they expect to be flattered and pampered and cajoled because they're, God help me, "artists". But all they talk about is sales and money. They whine and complain and flaunt their neuroses and bitch endlessly about their royalty statements. If they wanted to get rich, why didn't they go into dentistry? Let me tell you, it takes a hard-nosed businessman to keep them off the breadlines.'

'I'd argue,' said Zinger, his temperature rising, 'that one Al Purdy or one Philip Larkin or one William McIlvanney is worth rows and rows of dentists.'

'Who are those guys?'

'Poets. They're poets.'

'Dammit, if you've got a toothache, do you drop in to see a poet? I do *not* publish poets. Got quite enough trouble, thanks a lot. You should just stick to being a writer, and let me worry about the authors and the royalties.'

'And if the cash advance averages out to around a dollar ninety-eight per hour of work, what do you recommend?'

'Honest labour, that's what, or join the Chamber of Commerce. None of this twiddling with "art". You have to get out and hustle to sell books, and I'll expect you to flog your own product on a sales tour and tell stories, tell jokes, keep the interviewers happy. Sell yourself. Do you think you can do that?'

'Might could.'

'I bloodywell hope so. Damn, sometimes I wonder why I stay in this business.'

'I was beginning to wonder that myself.'

'It's not the money. God knows there's little enough of that. Dealing with every frigging "author" who thinks he's Hemingway, but Hemingway never had to meet a payroll. I could probably make more money selling used cars. No, the main reason I stay in this business, let me tell you, is simple: literary pussy.'

Zinger burst out laughing, then stopped and stared at MacDonald with what he hoped was a semblance of a straight face.

'You mean, the literary women? In the sense that André Maurois said, that to acquire culture is to prepare one's self for love?'

'Don't try to one-up me with some Frog author. You know damn well what I mean. Great gaggles of simpering young female wannabe writers. And the whole publishing industry is staffed by young lovelies with M.A.s in English lit who can't find jobs anywhere else and think that the book trade is glamorous. Therefore, they accept low pay. Frustrated types, dreaming of "art". I've found that frustrated females are usually good for a bounce, and neurotic ones are the best in bed. They're so grateful.'

'Wasn't it Ben Franklin who said older women were the most grateful?'

'Them, too. But never underestimate a publishing house girl. They're the very best perks in the trade. Perquisites are what makes the world go 'round, I say, and if you'd met Mrs MacDonald, you'd know why.'

'You're a cornucopia of advice, Mr MacDonald. Truly a man after my own heart, a pussy pirate with an eye on the doubloons.'

'Call me Mac. I like you, so now I'll give you some further pointers. Listen up. On your book, I mean. First, we'll change the title. "J. T. and Me" doesn't cut it. Put some more boffing and kinky sex in it and we could call it "Zinger and the Zaftigs", something that's a grabber, you know?'

'I don't think …'

'Sure-fire seller. We'll put a nude shot of J. T. on the cover.'

'J. T.'s a man.'

'A man? Dear God, save us.'

'And he's a professor,' said Zinger, beginning to enjoy himself beyond his expectations.

'Worse and worse, a professor. Can't you think of anything *interesting* to write about? Anyway, we scrap the title. There's a story about the journalist who submitted a story to the *Reader's Digest* titled "I Screwed a Bear". Got rejected. Resubmitted it with the new title, "I Screwed a Bear for the FBI". Rejected again. But he hit paydirt on his third try, "I Screwed a Bear for the FBI and Found God". Good, eh? You see my point?'

135

'Perfectly. Sometimes the old jokes are the best jokes. One becomes fond of them.'

'We see eye to eye, then. Good lad. I knew you had sense. Next, we'll change, what was it, Prince Albert to Boise, Idaho, and Toronto to Boston or Cleveland or someplace interesting so that we might pick up some big-market sales in the U.S.'

'Prince Albert stays.'

'Well, think about it. Talk to Cliff in sales. He says he's read it. I didn't have time, you know, to read it right through, but here's another thing. I noticed that you used a couple of letters, like, mail, near the front. The letters will have to go. Agreed?'

'That won't be easy. The entire novel is epistolary.'

'It's what? Like pissing down a pant leg? What's that supposed to mean, epistolary?'

'It means the novel is written as an exchange of letters.'

MacDonald gasped, clutched his throat, went over to the credenza and poured himself a stiff shot of whisky. Gulping, he stabbed a finger at the panel of his buzzer system. In moments, Cathy appeared.

'Boychuk, what in hell have you got us into? I've got to rush off to my next, er, meeting. Review this man's contract, instantly. If you can't find looph ... ways to alter it, you'll have to deal with this man on your own. He needs help, mental help, anything you can give him to salvage this product. If necessary, commission a group of junior editors to do fast revisions, a rewrite, or else we're going to take a terrible bath on this thing. Get to it. Good day, Mr ...'

'I'd like to shake your hand, Mac. You've given me important new insights to the industry. Be assured, I'll take Cathy's suggestions very seriously.'

MacDonald could still be heard sputtering as Zinger followed Cathy down the hall. They got settled in her office and grinned at each other.

'So how did you get on with Big Mac? Wait, don't tell me. It was gruesome, right? Usually he walks all over authors and his shoe size is about the same as his IQ. He prefers 'How-To' books and cookbooks. He's a hemorrhoid on the ass of publishing. How bad was it?'

'Actually, I liked him. We think alike, Mac and I. We have a lot in common.'

'Really? I'll be damned. Like what?'

'Oh, we're both simple pirates, both interested in making a buck. I found him crude, of course, but for a businessman, refreshingly frank.'

'You amaze me, absolutely. I thought you'd say he was crass and insulting.'

'That too. I've known hockey players with more respect for the printed word, but if a guy is ready to publish my stuff and cut me some cheques, why should I take offence? I've taken worse shit from the publisher of my newspaper for years. No problem.'

'I think you're having me on. I can't remember an author saying anything like that in the last decade. What was he so apoplectic about when I came in, the title?'

'He mentioned that, and we danced a small jig around the meaning of "epistolary".'

'Don't tell me. Please say you're joking. He didn't know it was in letters, right?'

'You'd warned me to ignore him, so it was OK. I'm good at that. As long as you and I agree on some of these things, we'll be all right.'

'Well, I'll be hornswoggled.'

Zinger laughed.

'I haven't heard anyone say that in years either. My ol' daddy used to say that, too. He'd have liked you. No, look, in the newspaper business, I had only two rules of thumb. One, don't piss off the advertisers, since they pay the freight. Two, listen attentively to what the publisher wants and what the editor wants, and then go ahead and write what I want. Always found it a good arrangement.'

Cathy shook her head and grinned some more. It was a most engaging grin. For the next few minutes she grilled Zinger on exactly what Mac had said, and he repeated much of it verbatim, to her considerable amusement, leaving out the perks. They also spent half an hour on some suggestions for revisions that Cathy thought might improve the book, most of which Zinger found helpful and agreed to make.

'You're not going to fight me on changes? They're not compulsory, you know.'

'Nope. That's fine with me. But let's stop with the nudging at "the product" and go and get some lunch, shall we?'

'Mac doesn't give me an expense account to take authors to lunch.'

'Doesn't matter. I'm buying.'

'Really? Well, actually I've brought a sandwich with me, it's in the desk here, and you're welcome to half of it, if you like. Only trouble is, I've got another meeting in, damn, about thirty minutes.'

'Dinner, then. How about tomorrow night?'

'Not tomorrow night, I'm sorry, truly I am, but I'm up to my ears in manuscripts I have to read before Friday, so I'll have to work evenings.'

'I understand. So I guess there's not much hope of my taking you to dinner Friday night or maybe Saturday?'

'Friday night would work, yes.'

'Excellent. Done.'

She gave him her phone number and smiled a broad, not very shy smile that made him think of sunrise over the hills.

'Hey, I'm not used to authors taking me out. It just doesn't happen much to a working girl in this shop.'

'Consider it, please, one of the perks of the trade. I certainly do.'

As the weeks rolled on the search committee struggled to reach a conclusion, but agreement proved difficult. There had been a small flurry of interest in Morley Snelgrove after his nomination by the Gay Alliance, but although his qualifications were solid, support for him was not substantial. Although no one on the committee seemed willing to say so outright, there was an evident reluctance and indecisiveness about recommending a person well known to be gay. Much admiration for the man was expressed but with reservations. Myrt Gold said that, much as she personally liked Morley, and respected him, the fact was that with the general academic community and particularly with the alumni, he just would not do. Several heads nodded, glad they hadn't had to say that themselves. J.T. said some positive things about him, but when it became clear that the only voice raised in firm total endorsement of Snelgrove was in the strident tones of Teddy Kravnik, his candidacy got no further.

And so the solemn deliberations of the committee returned to two names they'd considered earlier: Claudia Moldano and Peter D. Cooke. Moldano (D.Phil. Oxon) was currently the chair of Italian and Renaissance Studies and might be a popular choice among the faculty. A well-known book on Dante gave her some intellectual distinction, her reputation as chair of her department was blameless, her stated age of forty-eight was about right, and not least important was her striking appearance, for she was slender and very tall, stylishly dressed, and her quite notable figure glided along under a well-cut plume of jet black hair. She had, it was evident, brains and beauty and presence. Her husband was a well-known banker, giving her easy entry to the downtown business community.

Myrt Gold was against her. She noted that Claudia Moldano's photograph often appeared in the social columns of the newspapers, particularly the *Sun*, as she appeared with her husband at charity balls. The pictures were often full length, displaying her gowns and sleek figure to excellent advantage. J.T. quietly thought to himself that it might be swell to appoint a principal with such great cleavage. But Myrt insisted that this was a search committee, not a beauty contest. What they wanted was a strong executive officer.

Norbert Norton allowed that Moldano rarely spoke up at meetings; but she was a listener, and seemed to canvass opinions, take advice well. Myrt retorted that a leader must be able to do more than take advice, and that Claudia 'might be too soft, maybe a little too, er, ladylike.'

'So now it's a disadvantage to be ladylike?' Pepper cut in impatiently. 'Really, Myrt. As for her looks, I'd note that many CEOs seem to be big handsome men with deep baritones, and that doesn't seem to be a handicap. So why should a woman lose points for being good-looking and smartly turned out? It could be argued that we could use more style and elegance around here.'

'Hm. Point taken,' said Myrt. She paused; her eyes narrowed. 'Say, Pepper, maybe we should consider you for the job.'

'Nope. Thanks, but I'm not much of a one for administration. I don't really like it.'

Myrt Gold suggested that Pepper might later change her mind if the right executive position came along, since after all Pepper was only, what, forty-two? Meanwhile, Gold urged, they should look again at the file of Peter D. Cooke. Here was a man, she said, not much overburdened with elegance – he was bearded and wore leather jackets – but extremely bright and highly experienced, although he was barely forty.

Reconsideration of the Cooke file brought out many murmurs of approval. A professor of philosophy, a Princeton Ph.D., fiercely bright, he had published three books on off-beat topics: *The Political Thought of C.B. MacPherson*, *Technology and Angst*, and *Globalization: The People vs. McWorld*. He had been an associate dean in the Faculty of Arts and Sciences, and for one year acting dean of Graduate Studies when Dean Riddell had died suddenly. Declining to let his name stand for a deanship in either division, he had stepped out of administration, taken a sabbatical leave, and then returned to teaching full time.

Pepper Pemberton commented that Cooke didn't appear to seek office, but office sought him; definitely a plus, she thought. Sam Osbourne wondered whether his publications weren't a bit scattered or possibly erratic, even too 'pop'. Wasn't he a bit of a contrarian, regarded as a radical? After all, he rode a motorcycle. Kravnik snorted that the leather jackets were a pose, and that he was just another establishment man from Rosedale, probably from a wealthy background. He was born in Trail, B.C., J.T. pointed out; his father was a miner. Teddy studied her fingernails. Myrt asked whether the choice really had to be between a woman who wore Balmain and a man on a Harley-Davidson. Winston Kennedy Ramsammy inquired which of these two the chairman would be prepared to vote for? J.T. replied that he'd be very happy with either candidate, which helped not at all, and Winston suggested that the chair might call a vote, if only a preliminary straw vote, non-binding. J.T. sighed and passed out blank slips of paper for ballots.

The result was not a lot of help either. A tie. Three for Moldano, three for Cooke. From the comments that followed it was pretty clear that Pepper, Osbourne and Kravnik had voted for Moldano, while Norton, Ramsammy and Myrt Gold supported Cooke. What to do now?

'Someone didn't vote,' Pepper said. 'Did the chair cast a ballot?'

J.T. shook his head. No. Osbourne pressed him. Evidently, the chair's vote could be the deciding one as to how they'd proceed. J.T. nodded assent to that, but looked at his watch. It's getting late, he said; let's leave it at that till next week. He asked them all to think carefully and reconsider their choice and they'd vote again, but meanwhile he would set up appointments for the committee to interview both candidates.

'Prudent,' said Osbourne, 'but not much of a decision.'

'Well, maybe the best we can do for now. Meeting adjourned.'

J.T. hoped that Pepper would join him for coffee as usually she did after these meetings. Sorry, she said, she had an appointment with a graduate student at nine-fifteen, and a lecture at eleven. J.T. said, Oh, of course, another time, and then surprised himself with what he blurted out next.

'Uh, what about lunch? We could rehash the search proceedings. Would you be free for lunch?'

'Well, possibly. Not till one or one-fifteen. But yes, lunch might be nice.'

'I could meet you at the Faculty Club. No, wait. How'd it be if I came by your office at one – I can wait if you're not ready – and we could walk up to Bloor Street, maybe to that café in the Colonnade?'

Pepper smiled, warmly if uncertainly.

'Fine,' she said. Well, well, she thought, I wonder whether I've got some perfume in my bag in the office?

J. T. thought, I wonder what the hell I'm doing? Whatever. It's only lunch. But he did look forward to it.

- 28 -

'I dunno, B.J. This media course I'm taking is getting me down more than somewhat.'

'Why is that, Francis?'

'Well, some of the material presented is obvious, some of it seems to be academic nitpicking, but mostly I suppose it's the negative approach. Blame everything on the media. Most of the stuff in the readings and in the lectures seems to be some kind of put-down, always critical.'

'Academic work should always be critical, that is, judge what's good as well as what's bad, not critically to destroy, but to evaluate. Analysis, there's the thing, and then deciding for yourself.'

Zinger shuffled his feet and slouched in a chair in Gandy's office where he had sought out B.J., as often he did, when he wanted to try out some thoughts. As his student, years ago, Zinger had often found Gandy elusive, unwilling to be pinned down to any orthodox opinion, usually happy to juggle at least two contradictory theories in the rarefied academic air without dropping either, but without prodding his questions to a final conclusion. Now, in his own middle years, Zinger still found Gandy refreshingly undogmatic, sometimes an intellectual tease, often provocative, which I guess, Zinger thought, may be the mark of the superior teacher.

'Yes, I see that, but I meant that this communications study is critical in the sense of negative damning almost everything. You know, concentration of ownership is squeezing out alternative views and dissent, globalized media are promoting McWorld through cultural imperialism, that sort of thing. And we're always hearing that the book is obsolete, as McLuhan said, and that electronic media are incompatible with, what did he say? the continuation – survival? – of rational individualist Western man. It's all bloody discouraging at best. I got the sense that the voice of McLuhan is the voice of doom.'

'And what if he's right?'

'Do you think he was right, B.J.?'

143

'No one man is ever entirely right, and Marshall was no stranger to hyperbole. But, right? On balance, I think so, yes.'

'That's it, cheer me up. The end of ... Wow. I was never totally impressed by "rational" Western man, but I would be sorry to think that "individuals" were a dying breed. Interesting people, individuals.'

'To be sure, to be sure,' said Gandy, puffing contentedly on his curved white Meerschaum pipe. 'I believe some will continue to exist and flourish. But probably fewer. Just those of us who are throwbacks and cranks, persisting in the old pre-electronic culture, the print culture.'

'And McLuhan himself was one of those?'

'Yes and no. He and Innis both preferred the older culture, the oral, such as classical Athens, the intimacy and flexibility of dialogue and discourse, before Gutenberg and print made communication mechanical. The *results* of print were – you know the litany of effects – individualism and secularism, centralization, nationalism, bureaucracy. Empirical science and technology. All logical and linear, like type. A mixed bag of blessings, wouldn't you say? McLuhan also preferred the pre-Gutenberg, organic medieval world, which was I think a large part of his conversion to the Holy Roman Church. In the face of mad modernism, he wanted, probably needed, stability, a fixed moral perspective, a rock to stand on for a different view of the flux. I'd argue that it was his deep faith, and his ironic humour, that kept him sane in a world called "meaningless". No, I believe McLuhan regarded the modern world as being quite awful, to be endured only with the aid of faith, an outsider's jaundiced perspective, and humour.'

Gandy paused to repack his pipe. Zinger lit a cigarette.

'But I haven't responded adequately, Francis, to your charge of overly critical, the heavy negative slant of so much media scholarship. No. Let's address that. I think McLuhan might have asked us to consider not merely the paltry and meretricious aspects of television, but what TV does well.'

'And it would be a very short list, wouldn't it? I've been told that "educational television" is an oxymoron.'

'Not necessarily. A little list of what TV does well, in contrast to mindless sitcoms, might be instructive. What would you include?'

'Well, sports and some spectacles I suppose. Nature films and travel films. Documentaries – I've seen some wonderful documentaries on PBS on the history of baseball, and on Lewis and Clark, and the U.S. Civil War. Some non-violent children's programs. And I'd argue that political debates and interviews are often revealing of the personality, the character of politicians, if not their ideas.'

'Surely you'd add TV's on-the-spot coverage of great events like the tearing down of the Berlin Wall or JFK's funeral or rocket space launches.'

'Yes, right, there can be a great sense of immediacy.'

'But you're missing perhaps what television does the very best.'

'I'm not sure …'

'McLuhan pointed out that what TV does best is to present the ad, the advertising, the commercial pitch. Think of it: a memorable image, a story, a message in sixty seconds. Well, now thirty seconds. Or ten. Produced at great expense by hordes of writers, actors, make-up and lighting people, location finders, directors, psychologists, and Lord knows what other high-priced talent. All to create a few seconds' worth of hype and selling. TV ads have impact. Nothing to do with truth or falsity, of course, but damned clever. A staggering waste of brains and resources, shameless, but effective. Some call it an art form, and powerful.'

'Some call it intrusive shit.'

'Quite so. It's the ceaseless propaganda of consumerism and the mega-corporations.'

'I try to filter it out, ignore it.'

'Ah, but the point is you cannot. How many ads do you and I see per day? Three thousand, at least, perhaps five thousand – on TV, in newspapers, magazines, billboards, on storefronts, on radio – it's a relentless flood. Try as you may to ignore it, you cannot. It shapes the society. It's what Marshall called an "environment". Advertising is the "ground", and we are merely the figures in the ground.'

'Uh huh. And you've told me before that the voice of television is not the voice of information but of diversion, whether it's music or news or drama or politics, even religion, it's the remorseless voice of entertainment. We're reduced to the passive role of consumers, just buyers of TV images.'

'Not exactly, Francis. If you'll permit me, the "market" for the TV networks is the advertisers, and the "product" of the vast TV industry – do you see? – is audiences. People in audiences are commodified as "product" and sold to advertisers. It's a lovely system, and with oil and arms and drugs, one of the four largest industries in the world.'

'I used to think that at least the news was straight and real, but now I doubt even that. "Infotainment" do you call it?'

'You're the journalist, dear boy. Probably you know what you're producing.'

'Some days I doubt it.'

'Well, at least you're a print journalist and a word man. But do you know how many words there are in a thirty-minute TV newscast?'

'How many? No. Who's counting?'

'Possibly you should. With eight minutes of time for commercials, the number of words in the remaining twenty-two-minute TV news broadcast is not more than 1,400, or approximately the equivalent of two columns, or less, on one page of the *New York Times* or the *Globe and Mail*.'

Gandy permitted himself a dry chuckle when Zinger blinked at that.

'Damn,' said Zinger. 'Compression. Which is why TV news has so little time for background, perspective, interpretation. Hell, for explanation, or analysis.'

'Precisely. I often think that the familiar journalistic lead of the "Ws" – whowhatwhenwhere – tend to omit the "why", and the top of the story might better read, "On the one hand, and on the other." But that would require thought, too many words, too much time, and certainly be less arresting. Good journalism isn't usually good business. It costs too much, appeals only to a small elite, and is harder to sell to impatient audiences conditioned to snappy sound bites.'

'And so you'd argue that the picture of the world we get on TV news is mostly factoids and images, not reality.'

'Exactly. Facile pictorials. Never mind the material that's edited out, never mind the slanted agenda and biases of the corporate owners which are filtered down to the editors and reporters, never mind the grotesque over-simplification of facts, what we the viewers receive is mainly illusion to render us comatose. In a highly ambiguous world, where there are few if any certainties, we are deprived by TV of ambiguous reality.'

'Illusions,' Zinger muttered, still turning that over in his mind. 'There may be something to this "media studies" lark after all.'

'Oh, to be sure. Much of it is merely fashionable bullroar, of course, but there are things to be learned.'

'I took a run at McLaughlin on the subject of illusion and reality the other night. I might even have done him some good.'

'Cutty told me about your skull session with J.T. I dare to hope you may have had some effect.'

'Maybe. Hope so, tho' I doubt it. I smacked him fairly hard. He's not good at facing reality.'

'Which of us is, Francis? The conundrum of the human condition we've been speaking of may cause us to want illusions, need them, wrap ourselves up in them as a protective cloak. Reality might be so unacceptable that it would kill us.'

'Not me. God knows I have few illusions left. I like to think I'm a realist.'

'Quite likely you are, although our ranks are few, and I needn't caution you again of the dangers of mere cynicism as against sensible realism. But I can't recall, when you were an undergraduate, did I ask you to read Hans Vaihinger, *The Philosophy of As If*? No? Not a very good book, really. It was the title that most attracted me, made me think of how we live. We, most of us, go crashing through life's underbrush as if we knew where we were going, but we do not. We act as if work or our jobs are important in the great scheme of things, as though our religious choices or our sexual selections or our tiresome and simplistic ideological delusions were important, but they are not. We want desperately to believe that our lives are significant, meaningful, despite massive evidence to the contrary. A life lived is soon forgotten, last week's news. How often do you think of your grandfather, eh? Dante wrote, "Who knows most grieves most for wasted time." We live as if we have infinite time, will live forever, squandering our days in trifling pursuits, but no, we will not live forever. No.' B.J. paused and rubbed his temples, gazing out the window. His silence hung heavy, as both men reflected that Gandy's life already spanned eighty years or more.

'You put me in mind,' said Zinger, 'of what Dorothy Parker wanted on her tombstone:

Time doth flit.
Oh, shit.

147

'Fair enough,' said B.J. 'Time is a serious matter, however we express it. We spend most of our brief allotted years blundering about, hurting others, hurting or neglecting those we love, usually oblivious to that hurting, or believing we might make it up to them some day or sweep all our ignorance and folly away by saying "I didn't mean to. I'm sorry." But that doesn't suffice, does it? No. My own life has had its blunders, I do confess. Many. It's so distressingly hard to see through our own willful illusions and patently false "As Ifs" and live, shall I say, sensibly, enjoying the lavish sensual banquet of being alive – without causing needless anguish to others and to ourselves. I think we should try to obey that ancient injunction to the physicians: First, do no harm. No harm.'

Zinger nodded, stopped to consider.

Gandy took off his spectacles, rubbed his eyes (was that a tear?) and slumped in his chair. Zinger let a few moments of silence punctuate the old man's obviously heartfelt sentences. He found it difficult to imagine what harm B.J. could possibly have done. There was an ineffable sadness to Gandy's face. Under the bushy eyebrows the eyes, usually piercing, were moist and glowing as from the depths of caverns. The old man had turned inward, perhaps lost in memories. His voice had become soft and slightly fogged.

'Who said,' Zinger inquired, 'Human kind cannot bear very much reality'? Might have been Disney, or Ted Turner.'

'T.S. Eliot,' said Gandy, 'Quartets. And that's my point exactly. That is why men invent religions. The basis of religion, it's been said, is fear. Not merely fear of death, but fear of meaninglessness, lack of purpose. How can you cope with a universe that lacks purpose? That there is none is hard to accept, and on this eternal subject, God is mute. So we make up purposes. Illness and death strike us down in random and cruel ways, "unfairly" we say, ways we can't accept. And thus we cling to life in terror and choose to believe that it must have meaning, and we dream up meanings we crave, creating religious beliefs I might call fanciful. The process may produce solace, diversion from raw reality. Conflicting beliefs also provide jolly excuses to hate and slaughter each other, which diverts us inordinately. Mix in nationalism, ideology and poisonous xenophobia and you develop a whole menu of reasons to pursue cheerfully the most abominable carnage and bloodshed. Savagery, I say, "justified"

by "As If". No, I prefer the meaningless to manufactured delusion.'
'But you'd admit religions also promote ethics and moral codes?'
'Ethics, undoubtedly. And on this point all the major conflicting religions agree. They diverge and contend on almost everything else, but on ethics they speak with one true, if invariably neglected, voice. The Buddha said it: kindness. Hillel said, treat others as you would yourself be treated; all else is commentary. And five hundred years before that bothersome Nazarean pointed out the Golden Rule, Confucius was asked whether there was any one word that could sum up morality, and he answered, "Is not that word *reciprocity?*" No, the fundamentals of ethics have always been clear and agreed, having little to do with organized religion. It's the ritual and baggage of the orthodox theology that are the peripheral and pernicious claptrap, the social commandments, the licence to kill, the grand illusion.'

Gandy paused and fondled his pipe again.

'Ah, Francis. You mustn't mind me. Old men all pretend to be wise, but of course we're no less deluded than others. It's a self-gratifying pose we affect to persuade ourselves that we have learned something through experience, though I doubt most of us have.'

Zinger remained silent. He looked at Gandy with a quizzical gaze. Is this what you get, all you get, from decades of learning? Shall we dance around the pale fire of philosophy and end up only with a will to disbelieve? Zinger lit another cigarette.

'Um, by the way, is it really OK to smoke in this building, B.J.? It's not permitted in most buildings on campus.'

'No. Certainly it's prohibited here too. But I keep a window open and ignore such impertinent idiocies. What can they do to the likes of me? I'm retired, years ago, so I can hardly be fired or deprived of tenure. It's a wonderful position, in which I derive real satisfaction from being able to say to the authorities, if you'll excuse such immoderate language, "Screw you". Gandy winked and tamped his white pipe. 'I hope you live to grow old, Francis. You'll find it has some few but real compensations.'

The two men smiled at each other. Wisps of smoke rose. Soon the accustomed twinkle returned to B.J.'s eyes.

'Har!' said Gandy, straightening himself up, harrumphing, replacing his spectacles. 'Which brings us, my boy, to escapism, intoxication, and our friend McLaughlin.'

'It does?'

'Certainly. Intoxication as a means to protective illusion. Chemical means to "As If" are things that man has always indulged in as ways of altering or escaping the world's bitter facts. We take solace and refuge not merely in delusion but in chemicals that ease our troubles and render the world more tolerable. Wine, alcohol, coca, tobacco, opium, peyote, cocaine mark all ancient human festivals and are as old as man, more reliable and direct routes to hallucination and religious ecstasy and uplift of the dolorous spirit. A man named Ronald Siegel wrote a useful book called *Intoxication*, arguing that a "fourth drive", after food, thirst, and sex, is the drive to – as they say – "get high". It has persisted through millennia. It's not clear that man can live, or wants to live, without fantasy, without chemicals. Siegel argues, by the way, that trying to abolish drug use is like trying to abolish AIDS by banning sex. It does not work, any more than Prohibition worked. Mankind has always embraced its mind-chemicals.'

'I'm not sure where you're going with this.'

'I'm pointing out that whether we wake up with coffee or cocaine, whether we take work breaks with cigarettes or whisky, whether we relax with martinis or marijuana, whether we go to sleep with drugs bought at the pharmacy or on the street, we are all "users", and want to change the way we feel. It's the chemistry of "As If" the world could be sweeter, and most people most of the time find it irresistible. Except for the puritans and fundamentalists, of course, who are the world's dullest people, usually fanatics. Which brings us back, I say, to our friend McLaughlin.'

'Ah. The booze.'

'Yes. Illusion and booze.'

'But, B.J., I don't think he enjoys it much. I don't think he gets high. Seems to me he uses it as a tranquilizer to stay numb, more like a shield than a stimulant.'

'Agreed. And that's precisely when it has the most debilitating effects. What we do not know, I'd say, is how much of his ingestion is addiction, and how much of it is choice. My surmise is that it's mainly choice. There is as yet little or no evidence that he wants to give it up, or that he's ready to square up to reality without a quart of "As If". You can tell him to stop, of course, but my point is that he won't, until he wants to. Until his reality is more agreeable.'

'You may be right. You're making good sense. So how do we get him to want to?'

'Ah, there's the question. I doubt that we can. The motivation must come from within. Isn't that always the case? Nagging, even shock therapy, may be irrelevant and unwelcome.'

'I see what you mean, B.J. I'll think about it.' Zinger stared at a wall for a few minutes, then pursuing his thought, said, 'Tell me, since we're tossing around questions of illusion and reality, what's your basic opinion on whether we all need some "As If"? Can we get along without it?'

'I don't know, Francis, I don't know. Of all the larger questions of life, this is one of the few about which I've had, over the long term, difficulty in making up my mind. It takes some strength and resolve, to be sure, to live as an intellectual orphan, without some beguiling beliefs and delusions to act as crutches when the sting of reality, unadulterated reality, and calamity makes us limp. We have so little, come to that, to keep us from despair. Are we better with our comforting "As Ifs"? Are we happier in our dream worlds, or should we waken to stabs of pain and remorse? Possibly dreams are all that keep most of us alive. I'm not sure. To be candid, I do not know.'

'I can't remember, B.J., I can't recall you ever saying before, "I do not know." Should we leave it at that, for now, and go and drink a beer?'

'A capital idea, Francis. Capital. And if I ever resolve this dilemma to my own satisfaction, you'll be one of the first to know. Come along, then. Let's be off to the bar. We'll drink – moderately – to ambiguity.'

- 29 -

Almost every week the Chair of the Economics Department asked McLaughlin how the search committee was getting on, and invariably J. T.'s answer was evasive. He could hardly say, 'We're at a deadlock' without prolonging the conversation uncomfortably. And so he'd smile and say something to the effect that everything would work out fine, probably soon. But he himself did not entirely believe it.

On successive weeks the search committee interviewed the two leading candidates, Claudia Moldano and Peter D. Cooke. As expected, both proved articulate and poised, well-informed on university finance and politics. Moldano's striking appearance complemented her low-key but self-possessed, confident manner. Cooke seemed more quick and hard-edged, responding to questions with volleys of facts, figures and incisive comments. Each was an attractive person, bright and pleasant, impressive. Each expressed considered views on how the college's daily life and operations might be improved. Both said they were surprised and flattered to be on a short list for such an important position.

But neither seemed to dislodge the committee members from their previous preferences. When another vote was called at the following meeting the result was another tie. Evidently Pepper Pemberton, Sam Osbourne and Teddy Kravnik were still for Moldano. Norbert Norton, W.K. Ramsammy and Myrt Gold continued to plump for Cooke. Myrt muttered to Norbert something about not being willing to support any candidate favoured by Kravnik, while Kravnik (overhearing the remark) exclaimed that she would always prefer to choose a woman over a man, 'another bloody suit,' as she put it – but that in her opinion both candidates 'reeked' of establishment hyper-respectability. Myrt Gold commented that Cooke had appeared for the interview in a leather jacket, not a suit. An expensive jacket, countered Teddy, and she was willing to bet serious money that a week after taking office Cooke would be tailored in fifteen-hundred-dollar three-piecers. Unlikely, Pepper commented, but was the committee really hung up on what people wore? Were they looking at costumes instead of quality?

'I think,' Ramsammy observed, 'that once again the chair has not voted. If he had, the seven votes could not have produced a tie, now, could they?'

'Your arithmetic is impeccable, Mr Ramsammy,' said Pepper. 'Did you vote, Mr Chairman?'

'Just "Chair",' Teddy grumbled.

J. T. shook his head.

'I hoped,' he said, 'that at least one vote would be shifted after the interviews, and that a clear majority would emerge.'

'Doesn't seem likely,' said Osbourne. 'You'll have to weigh in, McLaughlin, one way or another.'

'We have time this morning,' said J. T., 'for further discussion. Shouldn't we talk about the choices some more? Some seem to think that Ms Moldano is too understated, too soft. But she gives me the impression of being a person of inner resources, strong, what we used to call 'a tough broad'.'

'How delicately you put it,' said Myrt.

'On the other hand,' J. T. continued, 'Cooke has obvious strengths and qualities too. A keen, fast mind, analytic, wouldn't you say? But at least two members of the committee have said, weeks ago, that he may be a bit impatient, even abrasive. Is that fair? Am I putting that fairly?'

'You are,' said Osbourne, 'but we've been all over this. I don't believe further discussion is going to help us or change anyone's mind. What we need, it's clear, is a vote from the chairman. You must break the tie.'

'Is that the sense of the meeting?' J. T. asked rather plaintively. 'I hate to cut off discussion. Any further comments?'

Silence. Stares. Glares.

'Oh. I see.' J. T. shuffled his feet and wished to God he could light a cigarette, riffled his notes and cleared his throat.

'Well. Yes. I take it that, um, it comes down to my vote. Damn it all anyway. So.'

Another silence.

'In my department,' J. T. essayed with further circumlocution, 'we have certain understandings about these procedures. It does sometimes happen that an appointment committee will have trouble deciding between two candidates for jobs who have roughly similar qualifications, both strong, but with little to rate one higher than another. We'd be glad, I think, as in this case, to have either one.'

'But we can have one only,' said Myrt Gold.

'Yes. And I think that in my department, in recent years at least, all things being equal, we've usually decided that, because of the imbalance of numbers between male and female faculty, and because of the clear need for more role models for female students, if no other factor seems decisive, we tend to lean toward hiring the woman.'

'Particularly if she's good looking,' said Myrt. 'And so you "tend to lean" ...'

'Yes. To the woman. My vote goes to Claudia Moldano. It may be a grand thing for the college to have a woman, for the first time, as principal.'

Much chatter followed. Teddy told Ramsammy that the chair might not be such a twit after all. Pepper smiled at J.T. as Sam Osbourne reached over and clapped McLaughlin on the shoulder. Norton said it was a helluva way to make a decision, but that Moldano certainly was well qualified and acceptable, undoubtedly more acceptable than further weeks and weeks of committee meetings at eight a.m. on Mondays.

'I move,' Osbourne said, 'that the chairman be authorized to approach Professor Moldano and offer her the position of principal.'

'Second,' said Pepper.

'Do we have to wait,' J.T. wondered, 'until we inform the president of our choice?'

'Damn the president,' Osbourne replied, 'let's just get on with it and present everyone with a *fait accompli*.'

All heads nodded.

'Whew,' McLaughlin sighed. 'I thank, the college will thank the committee for its time and effort. I'll go to see Claudia as soon as I can. I guess the meeting is adjourned.'

J.T. shook hands with all members of the group as they dispersed. Everyone seemed relieved, most seemed pleased. Even the salty Myrt Gold said to Norbert that Moldano might do well because 'she's pretty bright, for a clotheshorse.'

J.T. walked out with Pepper. They beamed broad smiles at each other.

'You sure kept us in suspense,' Pepper said, 'backing into your decision the way you did. But I'm happy with the choice.'

'Uh huh. I'm glad it's over. We might all get an extra hour's sleep on Monday mornings.'

'That too. I need all the time I can find for my writing, and mornings work best for me. But I really believe Claudia Moldano will impress a lot of people with her smarts.'

'Could we have lunch again, Pepper? Maybe try the Kensington Kitchen?'

'Sure, that would be nice.'

'But wait,' said J. T., 'I think this calls for a small celebration, don't you? I mean, um, like dinner?'

'Good,' she said. 'I'd like that.'

They fixed a date. J. T. suggested they go to Bigliardi's. 'Perfect,' said Pepper, noting to herself that she had been promoted from coffee to lunches to dinner. Well, well. Meanwhile, they wandered off to get coffee, J. T. grinning from ear to ear at all the intrepid decisions he'd made in one morning. For a downhearted man with his head so stuck in the soggy past, he began to get a glimmering that there might be a future after all.

- 30 -

Pepper and J.T. settled into a leather banquette in the restaurant. Bigliardi's is a smart steakhouse on Church Street, old and traditional and handsome. Soft lighting and dark oak panelling. Before the stadium was moved it used to be favoured by the Maple Leaf Gardens crowd, before the hockey game or more likely after. At eight o'clock it was only half full, the noise level down to a low buzz.

'Were you able to talk to Claudia Moldano about the appointment?'

'No, she's away this week, giving a paper at a conference in Milan. I hope to catch her Monday. Let's hope it works out.'

'Milan? Nice work if you can get it. Were her classes cancelled?'

'She had a colleague fill in for her, so the classes went on. I checked her out on that sort of thing before. We know, don't we, all sorts of "star" academics who neglect students, particularly their grad students, and don't even keep their office hours, but Moldano isn't one of those.'

A waiter appeared for drink orders.

'I'll have a Tanqueray martini on the rocks, not too dry, with a twist,' Pepper said.

J.T. wondered whether it would be prudent to order a double, but Pepper noticed his hesitation and got him off the hook by telling the waiter to make hers a double.

'The same,' said J.T. with relief.

Pepper looked smart and comfortable in an emerald green wool sweater dress, V-neck, with black pumps, a gold chain necklace, and discreet gold earrings. Her dark hair was short and sleekly styled. Her deep blue eyes were glowing, her complexion radiant. J.T. had put on a double-breasted dark blue blazer, beige Dacks trousers, his favourite Liberty paisley silk tie, but his loafers could have used some polish. He fiddled nervously with his fork.

'Do you mind if I smoke?'

'Not at all, but only one at a time. You've already got one going in the ashtray.'

'I do?' said J. T. 'So I do. Thanks.'

'Take it easy,' Pepper laughed. Her laugh seemed to him a melodious ripple, a sound clear as wind chimes. He was about to offer a conversational gambit of surpassing brilliance, like 'Have you been here before?' when Pepper looked around the room and sighed.

'I've always liked this place. My dad, the Senator, used to bring me here after hockey games. I never much liked the games, but always looked forward to the steaks.'

'Your father is a senator?'

'Yes, he doesn't know any better. He's a lifelong Liberal, God help him, and after being the mayor in Parry Sound and an M P, they stuck him in the Senate, poor dear. I told him I'd never again vote Liberal, if I live to two hundred, because of what they've done to ruin public broadcasting, the CBC. Anyway, I remember the first time he brought me here – I was probably seventeen, still in boarding school at Havergal – I thought I should be the dutiful daughter and ladylike, so when he ordered the sixteen-ounce sirloin, rare, I ordered a low-cal salad. He stared at me for a full minute, called the waiter back, and bellowed at me, "That's not food! That's what food *eats*." I've been a fan of rare beef ever since.'

'That's a line in a Dan Jenkins book, I'm sure it is. He writes novels about sports, mostly football. Do you read Dan Jenkins?'

'No, but the Senator does, and he quotes favourite lines to me. I'm more of a Thomas Hardy fan myself, and Jane Austen, but he loves the humorous writers. Leacock, of course, and Flann O'Brien.'

'Wow, that's great,' J. T. exclaimed. 'I'm mad for Flann O'Brien. What a coincidence. I got Zinger to read him years ago. And Donald E. Westlake. Does your dad, do you, read Westlake? The Dortmunder series?'

'Absolutely. We're both big fans. How about Evelyn Waugh?'

'Of course. And how about Michael Malone, *Handling Sin*, and what's it, *Foolscap*?'

'Heard the Senator speak of Malone, but I haven't read him.'

'You've a treat in store,' said J. T., waving at the waiter for another round.

'I do hope so,' Pepper smiled. 'But make mine a single, will you, with Perrier on the side?'

* * *

'Cutty tells me that you play the cello.'

'Play at it,' said Pepper. 'I wasn't good enough, not quite, to get to concert level and I didn't fancy being second chair in a second-class orchestra, so I went on to grad school in history. But I still play for relaxation. Right now I'm learning the concerto by Saint-Saëns. My favourite is the Dvorak, finest concerto ever for the cello.'

'Oh, it's my favourite too, absolutely,' J. T. lied, never having heard of it.

'I try to get my kids off rock and pop radio. On commercial radio you never hear the classics, so most young people just don't know.'

'How true,' J. T. agreed warmly.

'I remember when I was little, maybe twelve, the first time I heard Beethoven, and then later, "Ode to Joy". From the Ninth, the choral? Transported me, utterly. And now they use that theme on TV as background music for a milk commercial. Disgraceful.'

'Awful,' J. T. nodded vigorously. 'Vulgar. Wow, the Ninth. It is, as the man said, "miracle enough to stagger sextillions of infidels" – and maybe even a few Chicago economists. Imagine writing that. Jeez, imagine a grumpy old Kraut writing that when he was deaf! Zinger and I used to play, I don't know, a game about the greatest human achievements. We used to correspond about such things, apart from jokes and stuff, about "pinnacles" of man's creation – swapping notes and impressions, dumb exchanges I guess ... playing the game of choosing what was "best".'

'I like games,' said Pepper.

'Me too. So we agreed on the Ninth and the works of Shakespeare, and I voted for the Parthenon, but he'd never seen it, apart from photos, I mean.'

'Too bad. I'd vote for the cathedral at Chartres.'

'Good! And we kicked around Euripides, and Sam Johnson and Boswell's *Life*, great favourites of ours.'

'Sure. I've read Boswell and the other great biography of Dr Sam by W. Jackson Bate.'

'You have? Outside of the department of English, and B.J. of course, I don't know many people who've read Bate.'

'Just us good people,' Pepper beamed. 'We're a secret society. Did you know that in his Dictionary he defines "network" as, how does it go? "Anything reticulated or decussated, at equal distances, with interstices between the intersections." Don't you love it!'

'Wonderful,' said J. T.

'Can I nominate?' She sipped her drink. 'Right, how about Mozart's *Requiem*? And Joe Green?'

'Who?'

'Giuseppe Verdi!'

'Aw, you got me.'

'And Thomas Jefferson. And Louis Armstrong. The envelope, please, and the winners for painting are: Goya, with a grateful nod to Monet's waterlilies.'

'Dickens should get a nomination,' J. T. offered.

'Mark Twain,' Pepper threw in. 'Maybe F. Scott Fitzgerald.'

'*Tender Is the Night*, my favourite.'

'Not *Gatsby*?'

'Too polished. I tend to like the magnificent failures.'

'Should we vote for the computer? Maybe not. I know, Thomas Crapper and the flush toilet!'

'Brilliant. Was his name really Thomas Crapper?'

'Don't ask me.'

'Kraft Dinner.'

'Excellent. And Richard M. Nixon, and George W. Bush. And Post-it Notes. The electric toothbrush.'

'I think you've got the hang of it,' J. T. said.

'And Saran wrap,' Pepper chortled. 'And the anchovy-stuffed olive.'

By this time they were both breaking up with laughter.

* * *

The waiter brought their starters, twelve fresh oysters on the half-shell, one dish to split.

'Yum,' said Pepper, reaching for a lemon. 'Look, don't start that again. My sides are aching, and I might vote for Homer Simpson. I can certainly tell you're not a rich man.'

'That obvious, is it?'

'Of course. When I was newly divorced and dragging, psychologically, my friends used to set me up – they meant well – with rows and rows of eligible men, mostly rich men, brokers and bankers and tycoons of self-proclaimed importance. I'd get all gussied up and put on my late mother's best diamond earrings and trot off to dinner with these guys, largely because it was expected of me, and single women with two kids aren't supposed to turn down dates and fancy French dining rooms, now are they?'

'Bigliardi's isn't very fancy, I suppose.'

'No, wait. The cuisine these men chose was always expensive but usually indifferent; I can cook as well as most of those chefs with my eyes closed and have Béarnaise left over, so I was much less than blown away by it all, and I'm sure it showed. Two or three dates and I'd get dropped, if I didn't drop them first, as I usually did. Then the Senator told me that women in search of a fortune should simply ask these successful men about the subject that fascinated them most: themselves. And their money. Dad is a good guy, very, and he didn't exactly tell me to keep my mouth shut and my legs together, but that was the message I got. So I listened to their life stories, deal by financial deal, or inheritances, mostly. And do you know what? Bo-ring! It was all so – as B.J. would say – tiresome.'

'I wouldn't have minded if my dad had been rich.'

'Might have ruined you. These men, particularly private school men, seem to think that being born rich and handsome – since their rich fathers married beautiful women – gave them special entitlement, a licence to be arrogant and superior and loud as a matter of right, birth-right. Dear God but they tend to be, you know, so predictable.'

'I hadn't thought of it that way.'

'You should.'

'Oh, here's the soup. Did you order soup?'

'Nope.'

'Me, either. But what's say we eat it anyway.'

* * *

'You mentioned Zinger a couple of times. He says you've known each other since high school.'

'True, yeh. Seems a long time ago. I'm fifty-one.'

'I'm forty-two.'

'I know. I looked you up in *Who's Who*.'

'A girl can't hide anything these days. My book on Thomas Jefferson won a prize, so they put me in there.'

'And your book on Sir John A. Macdonald got excellent reviews.'
'Not bad. And so did your book on Innis.'
'Pretty fair. But I couldn't give away the monograph on Karl Polanyi. Cutty and I made a few bucks on our textbook, though.'
'Lately I've been working on a history of TV, and with help from B.J. reading McLuhan. What are you writing now?'
'Now? Oh, not much, not at the moment. I seem to be becalmed. Can't make it go.'
'There must be a reason for that. You shouldn't waste too much time. Time is all we've got.'
'Uh huh. I've been, I guess I've been a bit out of sorts lately.'
'I believe you. Is it anger? Depression is usually just misplaced anger, without the right focus or outlet, don't you think? It squelches enthusiasm, which is too bad. Enthusiasm matters. That's one of your friend Zinger's best qualities, I'd say.'
'Probably. He just doesn't seem to give a damn, or believe in much, yet he hurls himself into everything like a halfback running off-tackle. When I first left Saskatchewan and we used to correspond a lot, his letters were always, what should I say, upbeat, breezy. I used to look forward to them. A certain mutinous derision about the world and journalism and ideas and even himself. For a while we lost touch. And now that he's turned up here, in Toronto, now he seems to be set on giving me a hard time. Raked me over pretty badly again just recently.'
'What does he say?'
'Oh, the usual.'
'Such as?'
'That I should shape up. That I drink too much. Maybe I have been drinking a bit.'
'All your friends know that, J. T.'
'It's that obvious?'
'It's that obvious. But you'll do what you like, until ... well, until you sort it all out. Drinking for a lift can be good, but drinking as a repressant, a hole to hide in ... But it's not my business. Look, here come our steaks. Great.'

* * *

'Do you see a lot of movies?' Pepper asked, spearing a sautéed mushroom.

'Not a lot. Mostly I rent videos. Make my own popcorn at home.'

'You have favourites?'

'Action stuff, mostly. *The Man Who Would Be King*, rented that again last week, and *The Four Feathers*. I've seen *Zulu* seven times.'

'The Senator likes that one, too. I prefer Fellini, and some early things like *Kane* and Eisenstein. Fred Astaire and musicals, too.'

'I'll make a terrible confession,' said J. T. 'I can't stand Ingmar Bergman. Depresses me ineffably.'

'Good, though. Without Bergman, what do you do for cocktail party conversation?'

'I'm not much good at that.'

'Me, either. It doesn't matter. If God wanted us to communicate, he wouldn't have invented the cocktail party.'

'Your steak good?'

'Fabulous. And Bigliardi's does a great pickle.'

'Never underestimate the joy of a garlic pickle. You sure have a good appetite on you, Pepper.'

'I do. When I get turned loose, I eat everything in sight. The Senator says I eat like a sparrow most of the time, and then go nuts like a starved hyena when I'm on a roll.'

'We could come back here again. If you like.'

'Really? That might be nice. The wine is good. I'm enjoying all this.'

'It's a Châteauneuf du Pape.'

'One of my faves.'

'Shall we order dessert?'

'Why not?'

* * *

'There's this other thing I have to confess.'

'Beyond Bergman?' said Pepper, spooning crème brûlée. 'What a night for confessions! Let me guess. You're a vegetarian?'

J. T. shook his head.

'You've got AIDS? That would be just my luck.'

'Nothing like that.'

'You subscribe to the *Reader's Digest*.'

'No, but ...'

'When the bill comes you'll say you've forgotten your wallet.'

'Pepper, really, I've gotta tell you. I'm not divorced yet.'

'And won't be till twelve more months go by. I know that. Dear God, I know that. Does it matter?'

'Well, I thought I should say ...'

'The honourable thing. You're the type, and there aren't many of you left. Look, when I got, so it seems, promoted from coffee after meetings, to lunch – where you never talked about anything much but university matters – to dinner, well, I checked you out with Cutty and Zinger and they both said you're separated and in the tender care of a divorce lawyer. So you're a free man, which is good, because I don't go out with married men, clear? You're a good guy. I like you. That's all. Can we agree that we're both too old to play games? Dating is for teeny-boppers, and older marital losers often embarrassed by it all, usually a bore. You're not a bore. If you want us to go out together again, that'll be good. Can we leave it at that?'

'It's a shame you're not direct, Pepper.'

'Damn right I am. I've been around the track and bumped a few fences. For most women over forty the rat race is over and the rats won. Hell, the last guy I dated for any length of time turned out to be a switch-hitter, played for both teams. I was not flattered. Singles bars? Don't ask me about singles bars, playgrounds for forlorn losers. So I'm glad to be having dinner with you with nothing but steaks and Ingmar Bergman between us.'

'I guess so. Yes. Should we look at the cheese tray?'

'Just coffee, thanks, I'm stuffed.'

* * *

Reluctant to have the evening end, J. T. ordered a liqueur, a Drambuie; Pepper said she'd have an Armagnac. They sat a while in easy silence.

'I've looked at your wife's TV show a couple of times. She's very attractive. Quick-witted.'

'My erstwhile wife.'

'Does Erstwhile give you a hard time?'

'Some. Yes. She means well. But it's a strain, probably on her, too. Never was much interested in the academic game, and the TV thing is beguiling, I think. Probably it's turned her head. Celebrity, even just local celebrity, can twist your attention away to, um, different things. But it may not last.'

'No, it may not last. I realize that. Does she?'

'I'm not sure.'

'Cutty says,' Pepper said, regrouping, 'that you're restoring an old car.'

'Yes! Adelaide. My pet. It's an old Model A, a roadster, 1929. At the moment it's all in pieces, in my garage, but I think I can get it together, make it go.'

'I'll bet you can.'

'I'm sure I can,' J. T. said, with more conviction then he'd felt in recent weeks. 'For damn sure. I'll take you for a ride in it, in the spring.'

'I think I'd like that.'

* * *

When they left the restaurant, Pepper suggested that he leave his car in the parking lot. Wasn't he a little too tiddled to drive? Not at all, he insisted, although he knew he was in no great shape to walk. It was clear she didn't want to drive with him, semi-loaded, not all the way to the West End.

'Tell you what, J. T., just put me into a cab. I'll be fine, but you'll have to decide on your own means of transportation. I hope you won't drive.'

'I'm used to it. Been driving after a drop taken since I was sixteen in Saskatoon. I'm all right, really.'

'Here's a cab. I do thank you for a most enjoyable dinner. It was truly a good evening.'

What do you do, McLaughlin wondered, with a lady professor at eleven-thirty at night on Church Street? He gave the cabbie a twenty. He gave himself a reminder not to slouch and not to protest too much. He gave Pepper a fumbling kiss on the cheek.

'Tell you what,' said Pepper, smiling warmly. 'When we spoke of Sam Johnson earlier, I remembered a quote, from his *Meditations*, I think, that the Senator particularly liked. I'll find it, and see whether you like it. Might be appropriate. Good night, and thanks again. Good night.'

J. T. drove home, slowly and deliberately. When he got to his house he parked, with only one wheel off the driveway and on the lawn. Went back to the garage and patted the Model A. Sat on the back steps for a few minutes. Looked up at the stars, the Big Dipper and Orion. Went into the kitchen and poured a scotch, just a small scotch. In the living room he kicked off his shoes. Put on a CD of Jack Teagarden at the Club Hangover, San Francisco, 1954. Wriggled his toes when Teagarden swung into the 'St. James Infirmary Blues': 'Put a twenty dollar gold piece on my watch-chain, to let the boys know I died standin' pat.' Yeh. Turned off the player. Put out the cats and the lights. Went up to bed, feeling better than he'd felt in some time.

* * *

In the morning, in Pepper's strong and distinctive handwriting, he found in his office mailbox this quote from Dr. Sam:

> My indolence ... has sunk into grosser sluggishness,
> and my dissipation spread into wilder negligence.
> My thoughts have been clouded with sensuality: and,
> except that from the beginning of this year I have, in
> some measure, forborne excess of strong drink, my
> appetites have predominated over my reason. And a
> kind of strange oblivion has over-spread me, so that I
> know not what has become of last year; and perceive
> that incidents and intelligence pass over me without
> leaving any impression. This is not the life to which
> heaven is promised ...

Johnson in 1764, age 55.

Thanks again for dinner.

31

Claudia Moldano pleaded pressure of work, some problems that had arisen while she was away in Milan, and a writing deadline. She could not possibly see McLaughlin till Wednesday morning. What's two more days? thought J. T.; no sweat.

When he arrived at her office at the appointed time, J. T. was beaming with pleasure. The long search was over, and he could make a handsome offer. Moldano would doubtless be delighted. She was looking very chic and European, he thought, in a trim black pantsuit, heels, a thin gold chain at her throat.

He put to her the committee's decision and outlined the conditions, careful to note that financial terms, which he understood to be very favourable, would be worked out between herself and the president. Wasn't it all good news? Good for her and good for the college. He gave her his biggest grin and offered congratulations.

'I'm not sure that congratulations are in order yet,' said Moldano, fixing him with a rather cold and glinty stare.

'Oh, come now, I'm sure you'll enjoy the position and fill it with distinction.'

'But you've neglected to ask whether I accept, or not.'

'Sorry. Do you accept?'

'No.'

J. T. sat up, feeling as though he'd just been slapped in the face with a wet halibut.

'Surely you ... I mean ... probably I should have presented the offer in more detail and asked more formally, but I didn't think we had to follow a strict protocol. On behalf of Burke College and the search committee, do you ... I sincerely hope you do ... accept our nomination as Principal?'

'No.'

'But ... hell's bells ... I'm not sure that ... you must have reasons.'

'Of course.'

'Couldn't we discuss those reasons? Probably we could work

something out. The president could, I'm sure.'

'I doubt my reasons would interest you greatly. My decision is firm. But my cause for declining may be more clear if you let me put to you, as chair of the committee, a few questions.'

'Oh, good, that might clear the air and lead us to a more satisfactory ...'

'First, was the recommendation of the committee unanimous?'

'Was it...? Not exactly, er, I don't remember that there was a formal motion to make it unanimous, no. One other candidate was considered. But the entire committee agreed that I should make the offer to you.'

'I see. Let me mention that yesterday I was given some information, gossip really, but credible, that there was a split vote between myself and – another candidate. Is it true, Professor McLaughlin, that you as chair found it necessary to break the tie with the casting vote?'

'More or less, yes. I voted for you.'

'More or less. And would it be true that you voted for me because I'm a woman?'

'The committee's discussions were supposed to be confidential, entirely, but it seems somebody is leaking like the Russian navy.'

'Still, it's true, is it, that you told the committee that you favoured my candidacy because of my gender?'

'There were a lot of other factors, positive factors, but I told the committee that all things being equal we should recognize the gender imbalance in the college and lean to the woman.'

'Lean to, I see. Thank you for being candid. And so I'm led to believe that I would not have been chosen if I were not a female.'

'I didn't say that.'

'But you do admit that your vote was determined by my gender?'

'Well, don't you agree that women should be given some preferment around here? That we need more women in visible executive positions?'

'I do agree. Women should be given every opportunity. But equally. On merit.'

'It was merit that made you such a strong candidate.'

'Possibly. But not enough merit to obtain the votes of more than half of the committee.'

'You gained a clear majority.'

'Only after you so kindly pointed out my gender, which may not have been apparent to some.'

'I'm not sure you understand, it was ...'

'I believe I understand perfectly. On a split vote, I did not win. What tipped the balance was not merit but sexism, or sexist condescension. Gender apart, I'd have come second. And so I must decline the position. I will not be patronized. I could never feel comfortable being a token woman.'

'The committee will be terribly disappointed.'

'Perhaps so will half of the college, all of whom have undoubtedly heard of the, may I say, somewhat casual process by now. Really, you should have taken steps to ensure confidentiality, otherwise your proceedings are badly compromised. At any rate, you have my answer. No. I think, if you'll excuse me, that our conversation is finished.'

J.T. got up and moved toward the door, shaking his head in consternation and mumbling his regrets.

'One last thing,' said Moldano.

'Yes?'

'Is it true that someone on your search group referred to me as, quote, "a tough broad"?'

'Oh. It's possible that ... but I'm sure it was meant in an admiring way, you know, the way Sinatra used to refer to his favourite women.'

'Sinatra. Indeed. Good day, Professor McLaughlin. And I'll mention that I may be taking legal advice on this matter to protect my professional reputation. Please close the door as you leave.'

* * *

Panic. No appointment. The college would be buzzing with gossip, maybe snickering. Legal advice! What to do? What fresh hell was this?

J.T.'s nail-biting dismay was such that when he got back to his office he forgot to pull the vodka bottle out from behind Schumpeter. He sat behind his desk with his chin in his hands for some time. Went outside to smoke two cigarettes. Came back to ponder these new circumstances.

Finally he decided that the only course of action was to canvas the committee by telephone, alert them to the situation, and request their agreement that an offer should be made, quickly, to Peter D. Cooke. Within an hour he'd reached the four faculty members and obtained their consent. Winston K. Ramsammy sent in his vote, yes, by hand some time later. He could not reach Kravnik, which may have been just as well for his blood pressure because he had little doubt as to the source of the gushing leaks and his main difficulty. Poisonous bitch. Did she have particular reason for wanting to make trouble, or was it just the nature of the beast?

A phone call to Cooke gained him some hope, an appointment in Cooke's office at five the next day. J. T. had suggested they meet for drinks at the faculty club, but agreed that might be too public. Right. Cooke's office. He'd be there.

Private or not, the interview did not go well. Peter D. Cooke heard him out, listened quietly to the proposition, and sat for a while in stony silence.

'I do hope you'll consider this proposal favourably. It's a good fit, don't you think? The committee is convinced you'd be able to handle the position with ease and skill and ...'

'No. I'm afraid not.'

'No? You do understand that the terms are negotiable? It's a great opportunity. We think –'

'No. It's not my cup of tea. Definitely not.'

'I'd have thought that –'

'That I might be flattered to be your second choice? After Claudia Moldano. Excellent woman, certainly, but if she is your first choice, by all means pursue her. Just don't offer me someone else's leavings.'

'It's not like that. She had reservations because she's a woman, I mean, she didn't leap at it, because she's female.'

'Come on, McLaughlin, I've heard the news on the faculty grapevine. Everybody has. She told you to piss up a rope because you, your committee, insulted her.'

'We did not.'

'And now you're here to insult me with a desperate offer to get you off the hook. Second best, let me assure you, is not what I'm about. Do you really believe I could take the leadership of the college with everyone down to the lowest teaching assistant knowing that I was second choice? An afterthought? No, sorry, it's not on. Under the circumstances, I'm not interested.'

'Look, let's go and have a drink and discuss all this. I'm sure that we can reach some –'

'I think not.'

* * *

That evening, in despair, J. T. sent out messages that the committee should, must, reconvene at eight o'clock Monday morning. He picked at some frozen chicken dinner, couldn't stand it. Reached for a bottle of Bell's scotch. Decided that he had no bloody idea what to decide. Drank himself off to sleep. Woke up at three a.m. in a flop-sweat. Told himself that it was necessary to imagine Sisyphus happy. He couldn't.

What would Pepper recommend? She was so sensible. Maybe she'd see a way out of this mess. He'd phone her in the morning. Eventually he said what the hell, decided not to get up for a drink and drifted back to sleep.

32

Zinger and McLaughlin were in the garage, J. T. with his head under the hood of the Model A, Zinger sitting on a crate with a bottle of beer in his hand. It was a brisk, cool evening at the beginning of November. J. T. had bought another, larger space heater which he hoped would keep the garage warm enough to work in through most of the winter. He'd also set up an additional light standard which he could move around to shine on the machine wherever he needed it.

'So how are things going,' J. T. asked, reaching for a wrench, 'with Cathy, whatshername, Boychuk?'

'Wonderfully. She's smart and round and lovely. Been helping me with improving my novel. Great girl, but hard to con. I mean, I told her I owned a big gopher ranch in Saskatchewan, but she's from the West herself, Lethbridge, so she just laughed at me.'

'Good for her. And what do you do on dates? Movies?'

'Yeh, we go to a few movies. She takes me to book launches and a few literary parties, just us world-renowned authors getting together, you know, mostly in attics or basement flats, drinking from jam jars. Most of the scribblers I've met are just so fucking poor, man, it makes you weep. To most of them I seem rich.'

'Floated a few more loans, have you, that the marks have no hope of getting back?'

'Aw, ye of little faith. No, the celebrated Springer entrepreneurship has bounded back into play. I sell a small brochure, through the mail, on How to Beat the Ponies: Never Lose Money at the Track...'

'By staying away and never betting, I suppose.'

'It's good advice, yes, worth every penny. And I am the proud distributor of a Financial Newsletter, *Market Zingers*, culled and elaborated from the Report on Business of the *Globe* – subscriptions only forty dollars a year, selling very well. For a time I had a pyramid scheme going out of my post office box, but so far the results have been disappointing.'

'Wait a minute. Not the P.O. box you had me rent for you before you arrived?'

'The same.'

'Shit, Zinger, that box has my name attached to it! I had to pay in advance and give them a name with my cheque, and you're running an illegal pyramid scheme out of it?'

'I always think that an academic title gives a certain cachet, don't you? But I'd never let you go to jail, J.T. Your faithful friend would always go your bail.'

'Mother of God. Thanks awfully.'

'You shouldn't take the Lord's name in vain, boy, because another of my projects, with some bright-eyed investors and the Toronto School of Theology – there's always good money to be had in religion – is to set up a huge display or museum which tells the story of our Lord Jesus in, wait for it, a series of life-size tableaux with wax figures, like Madame Tussaud, very life-like, admission only ten dollars. I'm calling it "The Christorama".'

'Good name, Zinger, except I have to tell you, it's already been done.'

'What? Surely you jest. Who would do such a thing?'

'There is a wax-figure Christorama on a highway in Quebec, just north of Montreal.'

'Why those greedy, unprincipled, scheming bastards! Trying to deprive a poor Saskatchewan boy of an honest living. I should have known that those credulous *maudit* Frenchmen would debase anything sacred. It's outrageous.'

'Isn't it? But that's free enterprise for you. Hand me those needle-nose pliers? Thanks. Bloody valve is stuck. What's all the extra money for, Zinger, alimony?'

'I'm a bit behind on some of that, yeh, and I might have one or two outstanding debts floating around ...'

'Like, a thousand to me.'

'I haven't forgotten. Trust me on this. And I need a little extra for weekends with Cathy, out of town. She has only a small flat, and a roommate, and she's not entirely comfortable being in my spartan digs in college. Say, you might like her roommate, another editor.'

'I'm a bit preoccupied at the moment. Tell me, where is it you go for your nefarious weekends? I think I can see a time – in the future –

when I might need to know some good out-of-town inn or resort. Not my usual thing, you understand.'

'You young rogue, J. T. With Pepper? Hey, I do hope with Pepper.'

'I didn't say that. Just said I might, some time, you know.'

Zinger sang a few bars of 'Be prepared, that's the Boy Scouts' marching song, be prepared ...', accompanying himself on air guitar and chuckling quite a bit.

'I'll be damned,' he said. 'Well, usually, Cathy and I just drive out into the countryside until we see a place we like, or she looks through the Out of Town listings in *Toronto Life*. But I'll make a little list for you.'

'Yeh, do that. Just in case. Now hand me the biggest screwdriver you can see on that bench, will you?'

'OK. This one? What the hell is it you're doing now? And what's this yardstick for? You trying to measure your chances of getting this heap to run? Might need only a six-inch ruler for that.'

'No, she'll run. See, I've drilled eight holes in the stick. That's one for each valve. When I take them out, I put each valve in a hole in sequence so I don't get them out of the right order.'

'Damned clever, these professors.'

'That's a true thing. Once the valves are out, I'll remove the timing case cover, then the camshaft and timing gear. The next step will be to boil out the engine block in a tank of acid chemicals. Neat, huh?'

'If you say so, buddy. I think you're emotionally involved with it. Brownie points, though, for really caring about this car.'

'Some, yeh. Keeps me busy.'

'So what's the point, why are you restoring it? Not for profit, I'd guess, and not to impress the rich and powerful. And if you were rational, as you like to pretend you are, you could buy one already restored and just drive away and Bob's-your-uncle.'

'That wouldn't be the same at all.'

'Maybe it's nostalgia. I remember you had a Model A coach, two-door, when we were undergraduates, after the '29 Chev packed up. Ugly as sin, I thought, painted bright yellow, and hard to start. Ragged and broken seats with coil springs sticking up. I used to tell you, harm can come to a young man on those springs. I hated that car of yours, actually, hated it like an unfilled bra, hated skinning my knuckles on the crank to get it started while you sat behind the wheel and issued orders. But there were, by God, some memorable amorous tussles in the back seat, eh? Was it Connie Chandler who got her dress torn on those springs? Closest you ever got to a bodice-ripper, and you got even that wrong, and she made you pay for the repair bill. But your Adelaide A here doesn't even have a back seat for the hurly-burly.'

'Rumble seat. Yeh, I sure do remember, but it's not that. I'm stubborn about this, but I don't guess it's the nostalgia thing. It's that this roadster is mine, I'm doing it, I'm restoring it, with my own hands.'

'Ah. Hmmm. Like your father's boat. Is that it? Whatever became of that boat? It got sold?'

'I thought you'd remember. I was sure I told you about that years ago.'

'Can't say you did.'

'Well, that's enough on the A for one night. Come on in to the house and I'll tell you that glorious tale of my father's nautical adventures.'

With bottles of rye and scotch, an ice bucket, glasses, a pitcher of water and two bags of potato chips on the glass coffee table, they settled into the leather chairs on either side of the fireplace. J. T. had laid a fire earlier and now put a match to it. To take the chill off the house, he said; there's nothing like a fire to brighten an evening and warm the heart. Into the CD player he'd previously put discs of Serge Challof, *Blue Serge*, and what he considered the best jazz record ever made, Bobby Hackett and Jack Teagarden, *Jazz Ultimate*.

They put their feet up and talked idly for a while about the U.S. election and Cathy's editing of the book and the search committee and how Zinger had sat in to audit a lecture on U.S. history by Pepper. She spoke with feeling about FDR and the New Deal. At the end, a student had asked her what the 'relevance' of all this history was to him. Pepper had replied, 'I wonder what your relevance is to it?'

'She's a good woman, that Pepper,' said Zinger, 'a really great broad. Classy. How you getting on with her, anyway?'

'Fine, I think. We've had a lot of lunches, and two dinners, and we're going out for dinner again Saturday night at Le Paradis.'

'Oh felicitous name, oh excellent woman. I applaud you, J. T. Really. It's her infectious laugh that I like, and her bottomless eyes.'

'Yes.'

'That's all you're going to say?'

'Yes.'

'Uh huh. Then tell me, before the night becomes too long or the cock crows, what was all that shitteroo about working with your hands? I'd say you were about as handy as a pumpkin. You've always been a book man.'

'Well, books are the most important thing, after people, of course, and books are what you live by. But every now and again, I get this itch to make something more, I don't know, more simple. And I'm between books anyway, and maybe between marriages, as you keep saying, and my kids are away at school and I live alone, so I have some kind of need to put something together, tangibly, and I guess the Model A is it.'

'Like your father's boat?'

'Like that, yeh. He tried so hard. When he died he left deep puddles of debt and drawers full of penny stock in defunct companies, all worthless, enough disappointments to paper a room, but he meant well and he built some things, and I sort of hoped to keep some of what he'd made himself. But it was not to be.'

J.T. sighed and refilled his glass, poked the fireplace. Zinger waited.

'When I was in grade eight he bought that cabin in the Qu'Appelle Valley, Lake Katepwa, and your family's cottage, of course, was fifteen miles west on another lake, so I didn't know you then. Our place was at the wrong end of the lake, not where all the kids gathered and hung out around the main store, and I was too young to drive, and I felt cut off from the gang, close but not quite there. So I took some of my money, savings from my paper route, and bought a kayak. I wanted a boat in the keenest way, but all I could afford was this little runty kayak that I bought from a high school kid for, I think, fifteen dollars. Canvas over a light wooden frame. Short and wide, hard to manoeuvre, with some patches on the fabric. I painted it green and called it *My Leaf*, and I paddled the blessed little thing down to the other end of the lake most every day to be with the other guys, well, mainly to see Marie Rowan, the girl I had the hots for. I'd have paddled to Fiji and back if I thought I could just sit and look at her. But my mother was always scared that the *Leaf* would sink, and my dad snorted that I should stay home or build my own boat. Called me lazy. Said he could bloody well build a boat, it wasn't too hard. He just needed some plans, a blueprint, that was all.'

Zinger munched some potato chips and stared into the fire.

'So I went to the public library in the autumn and went through three years' back issues of *Mechanics Illustrated* looking for plans. Finally found instructions on how to build something called a "Sea-Flea", a fourteen-footer designed for an outboard that could handle the waves on Puget Sound, wherever that was, and it seemed a likely sort of craft, the right size, and stable. So I brought him these plans and showed him, maybe goaded him into it. See, I was too bloody dumb to understand that he couldn't afford to buy a boat. I knew we were not well off, maybe poor, but a boat? How much could that cost?

'But yes, he'd build it. Got some wood together, oak from scrap wood where he worked for the keel and frame, plywood from a lumberyard, and he borrowed some tools and some space in a warehouse behind his office. 'Just trying to teach the boy to be handy,' he told his boss.

'Through the winter, a lot of evenings and most weekends we worked on it. We – I just held boards and fetched tools and passed him screws or bolts or glue or what he needed. Dad was never much of a talker, just worked away, got on with it.'

'Did he know what he was doing?'

'Maybe. Maybe not. Trial and error. But I thought his skill was amazing. I was, well, proud of him for doing it, you know? And as it started to take some form and we screwed in the plywood sheets, shaped to the frame, and built the top railings and the footboards and the seats and it began to look like, gee, a real boat, I was so happy you'd think he'd given me the *Queen Mary*.

'Well, we got her finished, finally, and stained and varnished, and although varnish on plywood doesn't exactly make it like elegant cedar I thought it was the most perfect piece of work I'd ever seen. God, Zinger, I loved that boat. I can still tell you, to this day, where every board and rib and every screw went in, I can still see them, and to me it was a triumph, a work of art and a thing of beauty. I could rebuild it today from the pictures in my mind. And it was going to be my ticket to ride, to cruise down to the store and the dancehall where the gang hung out, where Marie Rowan might let me kiss her behind the ice-cream stand, and I'd take her out on the lake and she'd be astounded by my maritime skills and the craftsmanship of my father's wonderful boat.

'And don't you remember it, now? Don't you remember that it floated like a dream, like a sleek schooner cresting ocean waves, and when you and I went out to my folks' cabin, just the two of us that spring weekend with no parents, and cans of beans and Spam in knapsacks and we took the bus from Regina to Lebret and we hitch-hiked in to the cabin ...'

'We walked. Three miles.'

'Right. Seemed like twenty, yeh, and we took the boat out on the lake in the moonlight and drifted around and discussed the eternal verities while the loons called. Jeezus, it was heaven.'

'What I remember best,' said Zinger, 'was putting those two deck chairs, canvas sling-back chairs they were, orange, into the boat and stretching out that day, the next day, in the warm June sun with our feet propped up, and I painted valley scenes on a board with my first set of oils, and you read – you had a Louis Untermeyer anthology of modern poetry with you from the school library – or more accurately you lectured me, even then, on Hemingway or Atlantis or astronomy or Kipling or whatever the hell your passing enthusiasm was at the time. And you bored my ass off.'

'I never did. I edified you no end. Broadened your horizons.'

'Like hell. But another thing I remember was that we took the boat one evening all the way to the other end of the lake to Lebret to buy a case of twenty-four beer. I got an older guy to go in and buy it for me at the hotel, tipped him a buck. Drewry's India Pale Ale. Ambrosia. And we drank and read and argued all night by the light of a Coleman gas lantern. Not bad days, those. Good times. And we thought we'd live forever and wondered if forever would be long enough.'

'Too true. We did.'

'All that and fried Spam too, and we thought we were kings. But what I don't remember, J. T., is why we rowed, with oars, all the bloody way to Lebret and back for the beer. Why was that?'

'Sure beat walking, and didn't slow the drinkin' of 'er none. But we rowed because we had no outboard. Dad had built a motor boat but had no motor.'

'None at all?'

'That was when I finally began to realize that he had no money. Zilch. Couldn't afford an egg-beater. Said he'd get one later. And many weeks after that he did come home with a poopy little thing, a puny

Eaton's "Viking" five-horse, second hand, that could barely move the skiff and made the most atrocious racket. It sat up too high on the back of the boat, the transom, for the exhaust to be fully in the water, so it banged away and made the most godawful noise without producing much movement.'

'I thought I remembered a bigger motor than that.'

'You do. What happened was, when Dad was in the city and I was at the cabin with Mom, I took the five-horse and traded it up with Mr Fay who ran the boat rentals at Katepwa Point. I gave him the five, and all the money I had left in my bank account from the paper route, and promised that I'd work for him without pay for, I don't know, thirty or forty hours, looking after his canoes and row-boats and bait sales on weekends, and what I got – again second-hand but I thought it was great – was a sixteen-horsepower Johnson "Seahorse", quiet and shiny, with enough power, just, to raise the bow and make her plane and skim along at a lovely speed, shooting through the waves and leaving a white wake and making a breeze. And didn't I think it was grand? I thought that Marie Rowan's virtue was in dire peril and that I was a dashing seaman, proud First Admiral of the whole lake and a threat to all woman-kind. The motor would throb like the heartbeat of Neptune and the boat would rise and zoom and oh, dear God, but I loved that boat. It was my pride and joy, my *Rosebud*.'

'Your dad was pleased?'

'Not a bit, no. That was the thing. He was angry, sulked, said the five-horse was better for fishing and he could have lowered the transom, and that the boy was putting on airs and trying to show him up. He resented it. A lot.'

'Then, what happened to the boat? Sounds as though you'd have kept it forever and offered it to some marine museum.'

'What happened was, years and years later, when I took my first-born daughter, Jocelyn, home to Saskatchewan to visit – Trish had been out there once and refused to go again – and my parents both made the most enormous fuss over Joss, who was just three, travelling in a little plaid kilt outfit with matching tam, cutest thing you ever saw, and Dad did that thing with the doughnut tree, do you remember? Festooned a little tree in the back yard with doughnuts. Joss was delighted. But when we got out to the cabin, the boat was gone. I was astonished, devastated. Where was my boat?'

'OK, and where was it?'

'Sunk. He sank it.'

'Shitty pies. How? Why?'

'My mom explained to me that Dad had always been embarrassed by the boat, ashamed, because it was not like other people's, it was the only home-made tub on the lake, didn't I understand that? You can put several coats of mahogany stain on plywood and it still looks like plywood. And the motor had not been bought by him, but by me. So when he eventually got a chance to replace it, and I was away in Toronto, he sold the motor and towed her out to the middle of the lake with the new boat and chopped a hole in her bottom. He sank it.'

'But he had a new one?'

'Did he ever. An abomination, I thought. Turned out that his boss at the office had taken in a boat and motor as a trade-in on some machinery or for a bad debt or something, and let Dad have it for a very low price. Didn't you ever see the sonofabitch?'

'Don't think so.'

'He didn't have it long. It was, Krist, it was a bigger craft, fibreglass hull, plastic fucking seats, a huge, loud ninety-horsepower Mercury motor on it, white, with '60s great vulgar fins sticking up at the back like a '67 Chrysler ponce-mobile and the white paint had – can you stand it? – gold flecks in it. And stripes, red ones. Couldn't have been more garish or ugly if the sucker had been painted purple. Jeezus. He was actually proud of it. I was just sick when I saw it. Sick.'

'Does sound garish.'

'So the gods of the lake reached up and seized it in a clutch of retribution, pulled it under.'

'I don't follow.'

'Well, I'd talked about the old boat to Joss, and she insisted that Grampa take her out for a ride on the lake right away, tho' the waves were a bit high. I wouldn't go. We bundled her up in a life jacket and off they went. Although the wind got stronger, Jossy insisted that she wanted to fish, and Dad would do anything to humour her. He throttled right down to idling, trolling speed, and put out a line. Trouble was, the line caught around the propeller and wouldn't break, he couldn't cut it loose, and somehow it tangled more and got fouled in the gear mechanism and pushed the motor into reverse. It backed into the waves with a mind of its own, and big waves came rolling over the back into the boat, filling it up real quick, and before he had the wit to turn the motor off it began to sink. I'm sure he was more worried about his grandchild than he was about anything else, more than he realized the heavy weight of the big Merc motor, and it began to tilt back and bloody sink. He got hold of Joss and told her in a casual way that it would be OK, everything would be all right, they'd just get wet, be going for a little swim, and Joss thought it was all a great joke, and moments later down it went and left them floating away in their life jackets with Joss whooping with laughter. I guess she thought Grampa performed tricks like this every day. Some people on shore saw them and picked them up in a bigger boat and brought them home. All Joss said was that next time she hoped they'd catch a fish. Gramma went hysterical, and Grampa didn't say a thing for the longest time, not a thing.'

'Was he able to raise the boat later?'

'Nope. Couldn't. Too deep. So he lost his new boat and I'd lost my old boat. All gone. I guess I never entirely forgave him for that. Damned fool.'

'And who gave you the right to forgive or not forgive?'

'That's what young men do, that's how they grow up, by judging their fathers.'

'Did any son ever understand his father?'

'Maybe not. Shortly after that, he got sick and sold the cabin. Gave up.'

'I'm sure he was sorry, just as sorry as you were. He was close, so close, for a while at least, to having the boat he wanted.'

'Close only counts in horseshoes and hand grenades. Don't tell me about close.'

Zinger shook his head and muttered ruefully, then began to laugh. 'Close is the story of my life,' he said. Even J. T. began to laugh.

'And you're telling me that's the reason, one of the reasons, you like old cars and hand-made things, and you don't like glitz and plastic? One reason you're restoring the Model A?'

'One reason, yeh.'

'I'll be damned. I never knew that. Well, well. Who'd of thunk it?'

- 33 -

While they were having coffee one morning, Pepper told J.T. that she'd been invited to give a guest lecture at Queen's on a coming Friday. Would he like to drive out with her? They could be there in time for him to have lunch with the two of his kids who were there, Jocelyn and Robbie (wee Davey was a freshman at Western). Sure, he'd love to go. It was arranged that she would pick him up in her car, it being newer than his station wagon. The fact of the matter was that Pepper wanted to drive, didn't want him to drive, particularly on the way back in the evening, because who could guess how much he'd have had to drink by then? J.T. would be sorry to miss the regular Friday lunch at P.O.E.T.S. Corner, but could not pass up an opportunity to go driving with her.

On the appointed morning J.T. had overslept and Pepper arrived early, at eight instead of eight-thirty. He was standing in his living room in a bathrobe, drinking coffee, when he saw a car pull in to the driveway. It had not occurred to him that she'd be coming into the house, which was in characteristic shambles. What to do? He put the coffee cup down. Newspapers all over the floor. He gathered up an armload of papers and hurled them into the cold fireplace. A pizza box he grabbed from the floor and decided to put it, where? Where? Stuffed it under a cushion on the sofa. Picked up a half full glass of scotch from last night and put it behind a chair, making a quick pass at the coffee table, using his arm to sweep some stale potato chips into the magazine rack. Better. Not good enough, but better. He ran to the door to open it for her.

When Pepper walked in she smiled uncertainly, crinkled her nose and sniffed. He knew that he did not smell because he'd had his regular shit-shave-shower-shampoo only fifteen minutes earlier. They walked into the kitchen so that he could pour her a coffee. She sniffed again. The kitchen, he realized, was far from pristine. Dishes were stacked in the sink, and a distinct odour of last night's corned beef and cabbage lingered in the air. Quickly he cleared away a place at the breakfast table then found some cream and sugar. Poured. Turned on the exhaust fan over the stove. Grinned sheepishly. It's the butler's day off, he said. He asked her to take her coffee into the living room and be comfortable. It would take him only a few moments to get dressed.

He noticed that she was wearing a middle-blue pantsuit with a long jacket, a white (what were those called?) bodice thing under it, a heavy silver necklace, and – really? – running shoes. I have heels in the car, she had said. And no make-up except a slash of lipstick; with her perfect complexion she had no need of it. Upstairs he pulled on a pair of grey flannel pants, a grey shirt with a small stripe, a dark blue corduroy jacket. He selected a red silk tie. Does one wear silk with corduroy? Maybe not. He substituted a plain knitted tie but didn't put it on, shoved it in his pocket. Tassel loafers. Noticed that he had on brown socks. Where were black ones? Whatthehell.

When he got back downstairs he picked up a trench coat from the banister. Ready, he said.

'We're OK, we're in good time. Do you mind if I ask about your cleaning woman? I want to give her a prize.'

'Um, my last cleaner quit, actually. The last two.'

'I can see why.'

'What sort of prize?'

'Least Effort and Worst Filth North of the Great Lakes. Really, J. T., you've got to call in a salvage crew or possibly a fumigator. This place is an ungodly mess and very whiffy.'

'I guess it is, yeh.'

'I found a canister of air-freshener in the kitchen, but it was your garbage that smelled worst, so I put it out the back door. You'd better dispose of it. And look what I sat on in the living room – a pizza box.'

'I wonder how that got there? Maybe the last time one of the kids was home. A party or something.'

'Or something. And what's in your refrigerator would give you a good start for biological warfare. Look, I'll give you the name of my cleaning woman, but you'd better call a professional service first, like Molly Maid, to shovel out the worst of it. Maybe bring a dumpster.'

'Hey, it's not that bad. Is it?'

'Could be worse, I suppose, although I'm not sure how. And how do you notice the changing seasons when you can't see out this dirty window? I'm sorry to be critical, but wow, this place would make the

Black Hole of Calcutta seem bright and fresh.'

J.T. led her out the back door on the pretext of getting rid of the garbage but really so he could show her the Model A in the garage. It didn't look like much yet, he admitted, but it would be a thing of beauty and joy forever when it was finished.

'A Model A!' she exclaimed. 'Wouldn't my dad love this! The Senator has a thing for antique cars. And a rumble seat! I haven't seen a rumble seat since I was a little girl. Hot damn.'

She continued to poke and prod, asking intelligent questions, and oohed and awwed and made gurgling sounds of appreciation deep in her throat. J.T. thought that if maple syrup could purr it would sound like Pepper Pemberton.

Presently they went back into the house, J.T. locked up, checked the cats' food and got a small over-night bag – 'just in case,' he said, 'and some books and gifts for the kids.' Pepper eyed it quizzically, but he noticed that she had a small bag in the back seat of the car too, beside her briefcase. Her car was a silver Mustang, not new but shiny, with black leather upholstery. 'Nice wheels,' he said.

Soon they were rolling up the Don Valley Parkway, north to the 401, then turned east toward Kingston. The November sun was bright and Pepper drove fast. They listened to CBC radio for a while, then Pepper popped in a tape of a sprightly Mozart piano concerto, number 21, her favourite, she said. A morning without Mozart, he remarked with a smile, was like a morning with Teddy Kravnik, but Pepper didn't want to talk about that. Not on such a lovely day. The last flaming leaves of autumn were still on the trees and the sky was a brilliant blue and they saw two hawks gliding and a long V of geese flying south. The miles slipped by.

She asked about his two children at Queen's and he told her all about them. He asked about her two kids in high school and she talked about them with obvious pride. Their grandparents were paying for private schools for them. And their father? His parents were rich, she said, and he still accepted or borrowed money from them, which told you something about his backbone, but he paid only minimal child support. A mean man with a terrible temper. She'd booted him out eleven years ago. She'd worked nights as a librarian and done some contract research work for a history professor to put herself through grad school. The Senator had offered to lend or give her money to do the Ph.D., but she was jealous of her independence and it had been all right. There'd been some lean times, but it all worked out.

'Doesn't sound too easy a time.'

'It wasn't, no.'

When she said nothing more, he respected that with silence for a few miles.

As they drove on from Picton to Belleville J. T. spoke about how the area had been settled after 1776 by United Empire Loyalists and what Harold Innis had written about the square-timber trade and the burning of stumps for potash and the establishment of farms. Pepper of course knew most if not all of that, but didn't let on and let him talk. Before the cutting of the hardwood forest, he said, a squirrel could travel from Trois-Rivières on the St. Lawrence all the way to Windsor in the southwest, from tree to tree, and never touch the ground. She'd heard that before too, but smiled appreciatively. A girl had to know when to listen; at least he wasn't talking about himself, or even about Trish, 'Erstwhile', as he often called her. She put a Mozart flute concerto on the tape deck and let her mind wander to her upcoming afternoon lecture.

In Kingston, she left J. T. downtown near Chez Piggy's where he had arranged to have lunch with Joss and Robbie, and drove on to the handsome Queen's campus by the lake. They'd agreed to meet for cocktails on the roof of the Holiday Inn overlooking the harbour.

McLaughlin arrived at six-thirty, fairly sober, weighted down with Wolfe Island cheddar cheese from Hugh Cook's fabulous old general store, after a long lunch with his kids. Pepper was glowing with the success of her lecture on Sir John A. Macdonald and the hospitality of Queen's excellent history department. At the roof bar, she ordered a Margarita with salt on the rim, and he had a double Beefeater martini on the rocks. It had been a very good day.

'Don't you think we should be moving along,' Pepper asked, 'if we want to get back to Toronto in good time? Or do you want to have dinner here first?'

'No rush,' J. T. replied, luxuriating in her obvious pleasure at the reception of her lecture and his own happiness at seeing Joss and Robbie. 'Let's have one more.'

Pepper ordered Perrier with lime. He didn't.

They kicked around several possibilities as to where they might have dinner. Pepper's favourite spot in Kingston was Chez Piggy's, but she knew he'd had lunch there. No other suggestions seemed immediately to click with both of them. A two-and-a-half- hour drive back to Toronto before dining didn't hold much appeal either.

'Maybe we could,' J.T. essayed tentatively, 'break the trip and eat down the road in someplace like, I don't know, Belleville.'

'Why there?'

'Well, the thing is, I know a place near there that's a charming inn. Called "Mary's Retreat".'

'You know it? Been there before with Erstwhile, have you?'

'No, nothing like that. I've never been there, in fact, but it was highly recommended to me.'

'Ah, the plot unfolds. Recommended by whom?'

'By Zinger, actually.'

'Why am I not surprised?'

'I mean, it's only a suggestion. Would that, um, interest you?'

'Might. It's a hotel, you say?'

'An inn – but we don't of course have to stay after dinner or, anything. Unless you'd like to.'

Pepper laughed.

'I'm a big girl, J.T. I get the message. It's a nice message. I'd be happy with that.'

'Thank God.' He emitted a huge sigh of relief.

'Thank God, or thank Zinger, as you may choose. Or thank my foresight.'

'Your ...'

'You might not be amazed to learn that I brought an overnight bag with me, and told my babysitter to stay the night, stay till morning, because I might be late. My kids will be surprised; they keep me on a curfew just as I do them, have done ever since the three of us have been on our own, but I'll phone them. It'll be OK. Come on, lad, let's blow this pop stand. Let's go.'

And they went, holding hands like teenagers and wreathed in smiles.

They only trouble was, although they found Belleville easily enough within an hour, they couldn't find the inn. They stopped to ask directions, but the first person they asked, 'wasn't from around these parts,' and the second scratched his head and allowed as how he'd never heard of Mary's Inn. J. T. pulled out the instructions as Zinger had written them down and went over them again. Had they taken the wrong exit off the 401 throughway? The Shell gas station mentioned on Prince Road didn't seem to be there at all. Wondering aloud whether Zinger had, by accident (or by design?) misled them, they drove up and down and in circles for another twenty minutes until finally Pepper cried,

'There it is! We've driven right past here a long while ago without seeing it. Maybe its neon sign is out.'

There was a main building, some smaller outbuildings, and a large indoor pool, under a glass canopy. But the main building was curiously unlit, with only some night lights on. A sign announcing 'Mary's' was barely visible.

'Odd,' said Pepper, 'almost spooky. Well, at least they don't exactly cater to a late-night crowd of young swingers. It won't be noisy.'

And it wasn't. A portly woman who responded after some minutes to the bell of the reception desk said 'Welcome' without much enthusiasm.

'You'll be Mr and Mrs McLaughlin? We were expecting you much earlier.'

'Delayed,' said J. T. 'Had some slight difficulty finding you.'

'Really? I'm sorry. Most of our clients are regulars and know their way.'

'Regulars?' inquired Pepper, feeling just a wee bit uneasy.

'At our spa, regular guests.'

'I see.'

'Did I need a reservation for dinner?' J. T. asked.

'No, just for the room, of course, not for dinner. Anyway, the dining room closed at eight and it's now, dear me, almost nine-thirty. Dinner's over. But I suppose I might be able to find you some, I'm not sure, cheese and crackers if you haven't dined, or even a sandwich.'

'I'm sure that won't be necessary, thank you,' said Pepper, in her grandest and most assured tone. 'J. T., take the car, here's the keys, and go into town and find us some simple take-out snack, anything will do. But be careful to note the directions and not get lost again. Good. Here are our bags. Now if you'll be kind enough to show me to our room? Thank you.'

Nothing fazed Pepper, although she had some doubts about the place. On the way up the stairs with their minimal luggage she quizzed the receptionist and began to get the picture. She bit her tongue to keep from giggling.

When J. T. got back, some twenty-five minutes later, he brought a pizza, tomato and pepperoni and anchovies, double cheese, from the only fast food joint he'd seen that was open on the edge of town. He hurried up the stairs to their room, eager in more ways than one, feeling that his hunting-and-gathering expedition had been quite a success. Well, a success within the very limited range of local, after-hours gourmet possibilities. But he looked around the room with surprise.

There sat Pepper, in a sleek black silk dressing gown beside a roaring stone fireplace, calm as could be, leafing through a magazine. 'Welcome,' she said. 'Welcome to St. Mary's Catholic Health Spa and Retreat.' She dissolved in giggles.

'What?' He put down the pizza box and looked around, astonished. 'What?'

Pepper started to laugh.

Apart from the fireplace and windows looking out to the south, to the town and to Lake Ontario, the room was large, with a high vaulted and beamed ceiling, not unattractive, with easy chairs and a sheepskin rug in front of the fireplace. A small bathroom off to the right. On the wall to the left were two wooden beds, single beds, each with a large and garish crucifix above the simple headboards. Jesus wept. J. T. almost did too.

'It's a good thing you made reservations,' said Pepper. 'Else-how might we have ended up sleeping in a ditch, or in the car, or even in some luxurious suite in a downtown hotel in Kingston. The place has a certain *je ne sais quoi*, an unexpected charm, don't you think? The cru-cifixes add a nice touch.'

'I don't believe this, I don't bloody believe ...' J. T. stammered. 'Did you ring for glasses and ice? Room service? What the hell is going on here?'

'No glasses. No ice. No room service after nine p.m.'

'But, but, I thought ...'

'I'm sure you did. And I'm sure Zinger knew even better what he was doing. The bastard. But it's great, in its own very peculiar way, I think it's grand.' She threw back her head and laughed uproariously. 'You've been had, J. T. You've been had, and it's a great joke. Zinger was having you on. I love the guy. This is marvellous.' She couldn't stop laughing. 'Do you think he was trying to tell us something? I wonder how in hell he discovered the place?'

'Cunning,' said J. T. 'Dirty low-down cunning and a totally warped mind. I'll get him for this.'

'No, no,' said Pepper. 'Tell him something else. Don't let on. Tell him we stayed in the most elegant suite in the best hotel in Kingston. With perfect room service. With caviar and flutes of champagne. That might have been good. But this is unforgettable.'

J. T. blinked and muttered. Went into the bathroom and came out with a soap dish, which he used as an ashtray, and a toothbrush glass. He took a bottle of vodka out of his suitcase, poured a hefty slug into it, offered Pepper a drink.

'Well, I see you've brought some 7-Up with you from downtown. I'll just have that. It's still cool, if not cold. Thanks. And just look at this pizza,' she said, opening it. 'By gosh, double cheese! Is this romantic, or what? How charming that my day should begin and end with a pizza box.' She tore off a big slice, bit into it avidly, and let some grease run down her chin. 'Excellent stuff, J. T. Have some. When in Rome, or even when in Belleville ... Yum. I was getting hungry. Pass the 7-Up, will you? Is there a napkin?'

J. T. cursed and swigged from the tooth glass and cast dire imprecations at Zinger and swigged again and finally sat down by the fire. Took a few bites of pizza. And finally began to laugh too. Pepper laughed even harder. She laughed that hearty, lilting laugh until he began to feel better about it all. Much better. She laughed until she thought she'd split. Laughed until her dressing gown fell open. She seemed in no hurry to close it.

J. T., in rather more hurry, lifted her up and carried her to one of the wooden single beds. They smiled at each other, laughed, squirmed, caressed, laughed some more, caressed some more. Ah, was this not compensation? Was this not happiness?

J. T. stopped and got up.

'Where in hell are you going?'

'I'm, ah, turning the crucifix to the wall. I don't like to be stared at.'

'Oh.'

He got back into the narrow bed.

Some time later, some ardent and sweaty and tumultuous time

later, just as she was beginning to moan and arch and sigh, just as he was beginning to rejoice in his new-found vigour and beginning to re-learn arts and moves and even words that he thought he'd forgotten, just as the theme of Wagner's *Liebestod* was beginning to rise and ripple through her mind...

CRACK.

The bed broke.

Unused to such strenuous activity, the wooden slats under the mattress moved, gave up, broke, with a loud crash. They both tumbled onto the floor.

'Fuck!' shouted J. T.

'Yes, please!' said Pepper.

And they sat on the floor, and laughed, boisterously laughed and hugged each other and laughed some more, and kissed, and sat there, stunned. From next door there was an insistent banging on the wall.

'I'll be damned,' was all J. T. could say.

'Maybe, just maybe,' Pepper said, wiping tears of mirth from her eyes, 'Zinger did us a favour, a big favour.'

'How do you mean?'

'Maybe he's given us a chivaree, a reception, an intimate reception, without even knowing it.'

'Maybe he did. Maybe. Come here.'

And they put the sheepskin rug to good use, very good use, until much later in the night.

It had been a very happy day. It was an even better night.

Finally, J. T. fell asleep on the rug. Pepper gathered herself up and covered him with a duvet and went off to sleep in the other unbroken bed.

In the morning, he was somewhat bleary eyed but they were relaxed and amused and delighted with themselves. They dressed and kissed and looked out to the south to the wonderful view. Pepper said there might be something to be said, after all, for a Catholic health spa. J. T. only grinned.

At breakfast, McLaughlin recognized two priests from the faculty of St. Michael's College. Were they on a retreat? Did they recognize him? Who cared? At the long refectory table, the faces of the other guests were quite stern, unsmiling. Pepper found it difficult to butter and eat her blueberry muffin with one hand, her unringed left hand kept carefully under the table.

A chambermaid came up and whispered something into the ear of a reverend father who seemed to be in charge of the spa, something about the broken bed in room 202. Pepper and J. T. smiled gamely at the assembled company and drank their coffee in haste, soon gathered up their bags from the lobby, stopped at the reception desk (where the portly clerk gave them a decidedly odd look), paid the bill and departed. Pepper let him drive.

'Do you think I can find the highway? Broad daylight helps.'

'I think you can,' she murmured drowsily. 'I'm sure you can. Did you notice that I took a splinter from the True Bed of Christ for a souvenir?'

'Aw, Pepper, look, I'm terribly sorry about that place, the mix-up, all that.'

'Don't be sorry. Not one bit.' She laughed, a languid throaty laugh. 'It was an experience. Was it ever! I simply must tell the Senator.'

'Really? You'd tell him?'

'Sure. I can hardly tell my kids, can I? And we are saying absolutely nothing to Zinger! But I've got to tell somebody.'

'Won't your dad, er, mind?'

'Not at all. He'll be amused as all hell. Exactly his kind of story. Just my luck, at long last I'm off for a naughty night, a Bunbury, with a nice man, and I end up on the floor. Marvellous. I simply can't tell you how seldom I've drunk warm 7-Up in a Catholic health spa and broken a bed. And been kept awake, actively awake till four a.m. and then breakfasted with priests and, in this lurid age of extreme sexual permissiveness, kept my naked left hand under a table. Not your normal everyday Harlequin novel, is it?' She laughed again. 'But it was all such fun.'

He looked at her with profound appreciation, almost as though he'd never really seen her before.

'I ... I think I love you, Pepper.'

She reached over and squeezed his hand.

'Why, Professor McLaughlin, I do believe you may have some tiny touch of the romantic somewhere in your soul after all.'

'Yes.'

'Drive,' she said, 'just drive. I might take a nap.'

- 34 -

Four more weeks went by before the search committee made any real progress toward a decision. After the disastrous experiences with Claudia Moldano and Peter D. Cooke, the next meeting was spent mainly in extended explanations by J. T., expostulations and expressions of regret by others, and recriminations exchanged between various members over the obvious leaks and rapid spread of gossip about the committee's deliberations that had done so much harm. Several members, particularly Osbourne and J. T., looked very pointedly at Theodora Kravnik when they stated and restated the fundamental imperative that the committee's internal affairs must be kept private and confidential, but Teddy only glowered and looked daggers back at them. She said nothing, but it was abundantly clear that she was no friend of the chair.

The next two weekly meetings were devoted to a somewhat frantic search through lists of names that had been considered in the first round. Some solid and worthy people were again discussed, and again none seemed as outstanding as Moldano or Cooke, none seemed to attract much warm support. The name of a very fine scholar-administrator from nearby York University came up, but after an initial flurry of interest, all seemed to agree with the sensible Myrt Gold that it would be unseemly, 'poor form' she said, to raid a sister institution for a job at this level. For a president, perhaps, but not for a college.

And so they went around and around like a dog chasing its tail, with the same negative result. Considerable time was spent on a helpful proposal by Norbert Norton that they examine a list of all present departmental chairmen – oops, chairpersons – but that suggestion too went nowhere. As the names came up they were quickly shot down: too old; too young and inexperienced; too unpopular, even with her own department; too confrontational and ornery; too lacking in personality and leadership skills; too shy ...

By the end of the fourth meeting they were all discouraged and quite fed up. The chair was increasingly uncertain as to how to proceed.

'Too bad about Morley,' Sam Osbourne was heard to mutter.

'What was that, Sam?' J.T. asked, ready to grasp at almost any straw.

'Our man from Drama, Morley Snelgrove. Too bad he's so flamboyantly gay.'

There was a long silence. You could almost see the balancing act in the minds of the committee, the five faculty members if not the two student reps calculating how much, how very much they wanted to reach a decision and a conclusion, but how reluctant they were to recommend someone whose sexual orientation made him a, what could they say? a bold – perhaps too bold – choice. As they mulled this dilemma, no one seemed to want to be the first to speak.

'I appreciate your suggestion of Morley,' J.T. said. 'It's, um, interesting. He does look a more reasonable possibility than he looked a month ago.'

Still silence.

'Gay. Big goddamn deal, being gay,' said Winston Kennedy Ramsammy. 'Now if he were a person of colour, a black, say, or a brown like me, I'm sure he might have trouble being taken seriously. But the guy is white, a respectable WASP, accomplished, and popular with the faculty. Does anyone really care about his private life? Does it matter?'

'It would bloody well matter to the board and to the president,' Sam Osbourne commented. 'Not necessarily to me, you understand, but to the fundraisers. It's a public image thing.'

Further silence. Pepper decided to take up the cudgels.

'I've got a lot of time for Morley Snelgrove,' she said. 'We've reviewed his credentials weeks ago, and we all found them impressive. I've thought about him since then. He's respected, popular, a man who's reached the top of his profession against some odds. A genuine scholar and a proven commodity. This committee was not appointed to do fundraising. That's not our job. We weren't charged with finding a person who'd win a popularity contest with the Board of Governors or with bankers on Bay Street. Not at all. What Morley does behind closed doors is of no interest or concern to me. Among the senior administrators on this campus, if we tallied up how many pricks were stuck into inappropriate places, how many secretaries and research assistants get diddled, how many junior professors owe their Ph.D.s or their jobs to their supervisors with bulging libidos, how many, I wonder, how many would come out smelling like daisies? So why would we rule out Morley simply because he is open and up front about what he does off campus and between the sheets? At the very least, he's honest about his sexuality, so in a world of liars and cheats and sexual predators often hiding behind office and pseudo-respectability, I'd give him full marks for being a straight-forward guy. Homosexual? Why, of course. But does that matter? Not to me, it doesn't, no.'

Pepper sat back, possibly a little surprised at the heat of her own outburst. Myrt Gold looked at her with frank admiration. Osbourne and Norton studied the papers in front of them as if looking for some revelation from the files. Kravnik and Ramsammy didn't actually applaud, but looked at Professor Pemberton with respect and approval. But nobody else seemed eager to speak.

'It might be a tough sell,' said J.T. 'I have some serious doubts about how the president might receive such a nomination. Today, though, the clock is our enemy. It's now after nine and there's a class lining up outside waiting for us to vacate this seminar room. Think about this, think hard, I'd urge you, and we'll reconvene in a week's time. Adjourned.'

* * *

'That was a superb dinner, Pepper,' said J.T.

She had invited him, after the previous search meeting, to her house for home cooking, something that J.T. had missed, a lot, in recent months. In fact he'd invited himself, saying he'd bring a prime rib of beef if she'd cook it. Her home in the west end, near the Bloor West Village, was a modest but elegantly decorated three-storey semi-detached. The walls were painted mostly in warm beige-pink tones and pale yellow, displaying prints by Riopelle, Norval Morrisseau and Vasarely, as well as two soft and delicate monoprints by Ann McCall. In the dining room were numerous large pieces of antique silver, tea and coffee pots and serving dishes, and a fine Persian rug, legacies from her late mother.

The two children, Lindsay and Stuart, were on their best

behaviour, not knowing what to expect from this tweedy and somewhat shaggy professor. They were careful and a bit guarded, knowing very well that their mother must like him or she wouldn't have gone to so much trouble. J. T. thought Stuart was a handsome fellow: he was interested in doing a university degree in international relations; Lindsay, the younger of the two, was studying at the grade ten level at Havergal, but writing poetry under the sway of Emily Dickinson. Later, while helping their mother clean up, Stuart said J. T. seemed like a good guy, cool. Lindsay told her mother that she thought Professor McLaughlin was, like herself, a bit shy, but smiley, and as appealing as a Labrador retriever. For his part, J. T. thought that Lindsay had the face of a seraph, and luckily, her mother's infectious laugh.

Dinner had been a shrimp and avocado soup, the roast beef medium rare, followed by a homemade wild blueberry pie, with a minor Burgundy that J. T. had brought, port following the coffee. Pepper had tried, successfully, to set a casual and relaxed tone, wearing DKNY jeans and a pleasantly bulging pale yellow shirt.

'Yes, a most excellent meal. I don't know many academics who can cook like that, Pepper.'

'Thank you, kind sir. We don't have a lot of guests or eat like this most nights, but I wanted to signal the children that you might be, um, worthwhile. From my former days of grinding away in grad school, you should see what I can do with wieners and beans.'

Over port they talked a while about their mutual worries over the search and about what a stir they might cause if they recommended Morley.

'On paper,' said Pepper, 'the gay thing apart, he's more than appropriate, maybe our strongest candidate. Excellent track record as an administrator. It just took us a while and a couple of setbacks to see that. I've turned it over and over in my mind, and I think it's high time the college acknowledged contemporary realities.'

'Agreed. You do, and slowly I've come around to your view. But will the president? There might be a major flipping fuss. Would you be ready for that?'

'Sure. Merit, that's all we should be considering. Just merit. Simple.'

They decided that Pepper would have a quiet word with Myrt

Gold. J.T. would try to take some soundings from Osbourne and Norton. There seemed little doubt that Ramsammy and Kravnik would go along.

'I'd better be going along myself,' said J.T.

'I sort of wish you didn't have to drive so far, maybe stay over, but I'm not sure the kids would be ready for that.'

'We must be careful not to shock the young. Anyway, I didn't bring my crucifix.'

* * *

The committee, much sobered by the earlier fiascoes with Cooke and Moldano, met the following Monday to review the file on Morley Snelgrove. Two good books, a stack of articles in major journals, a former chairman of the Drama Department, certainly a prominent and outspoken advocate of the Gay Alliance, but also a personable and popular figure with the faculty, director of several major productions at the Hertz House campus theatre, and occasional drama critic on CBC radio. Everybody knew Morley. Everybody liked Morley. But a gay principal?

'Are there other new names anyone wants to raise for our consideration?' J.T. asked.

None.

'Have you all thought about this and reviewed the file?'

Nods all around the table.

'Is there a motion?'

Pepper cleared her throat and sat up straighter, ready to speak, but was pre-empted by Myrt Gold before she could say anything.

'I've given this a lot of thought,' said Myrt, 'and been impressed by Professor Pemberton's strong statement at our last meeting. Thank you, Pepper, for being so direct. I think you might be my seconder when I move, with optimism but some trepidation, that this committee recommend Morley Snelgrove for the office of principal.'

'Second,' said Pepper.

'Do you think,' J.T. asked, 'that we've thrashed this out more than enough? Do you think we're ready for a vote?'

'It can't be avoided,' said Norton. 'But let's dispense with the paper ballot formalities and vote openly by show of hands.'

'Agreed,' said Pepper and Myrt and Ramsammy.

'Right,' said the chair. 'All those in favour of Myrt's motion? Let me see: Ramsammy, Kravnik, Gold, Pemberton, and myself. That's five. Opposed?' Norton raised his hand.

'I've decided to abstain,' said Sam Osbourne.

'Noted,' said J. T. 'And evidently the vote is five to one, with an abstention. I wonder, given our problems in the past, whether there might be a motion to make the decision, now obviously taken, unanimous?'

'I think,' said Norton, 'that I'll resign from the committee. That will give you your unanimity.'

'Aw, Bert,' said J. T.

'Evidently the world has changed and passed me by,' said Norbert. 'I'll withdraw. I wish you all well. No hard feelings. And good luck. You may need it.'

'Aw, Bert,' J. T. said again.

But the meeting was over. The decision had been taken.

'Not a word, now, no gossip or leaks until I check with the authorities.'

Nods all around.

J. T. and Pepper took Myrt Gold along with them for coffee, wondering whatthehell they'd done. They were partly happy, partly sad and full of doubts. Myrt told Pepper that she thought she was one gutsy lady.

'She's that,' said J. T.

* * *

McLaughlin phoned to make an appointment with the president. A secretary called back to say he could have ten minutes at eleven-thirty on Thursday morning. It was important, said J. T. Nothing before that? No.

His departmental chairman encountered J. T. in the hall on Tuesday, and pressed his usual inquiry about the search committee. What was taking them so long?

'I think,' said J. T., 'we're ready to make a recommendation.'

'About bloody time,' said the chairman. 'So who is it?'

'I've made an appointment with the president for two days hence. The committee had quite a struggle.'

'I heard,' said the chairman, 'about your earlier farting and fumbling. Bad show, I thought. But things have shaken down, now, have they?'

'I think so.'

'Splendid. No leaks and goofs this time, eh? You finally got control of the situation, I hope.'

'I think so, yes. We're going to recommend – I can't tell you the name yet, you understand – a gay!'

'Ho, ho,' laughed the chairman, 'a gay. Sure you are! You're a great kidder. McLaughlin, I had some doubts about you, but seriously, your committee has finally come up with a nomination?'

'We have. Unanimously this time. I have to tell you, we think we have a strong runner, an excellent choice.'

'Who is it?'

'You'll have to wait till I inform the president.'

'Quite right. Understood. But you can tell me quietly. Not another woman, I hope?'

'No.'

'Thank God for that, at least. It's getting so difficult to appoint anybody around here who's not a woman or a visible minority person that soon we'll have no proper chaps left in the tenure stream. Damned foolishness, don't you think?'

'I'm not sure,' said McLaughlin. 'Times change. But you'd better get ready for it. Our choice is a homosexual.'

'Sure it is,' said the chairman, slapping him on the shoulder. 'Sure it is. You have a great sense of humour, McLaughlin. Now, if you'd only show the same imagination in your publications …'

J. T. turned away and left him, wondering if the chairman's was likely to be typical of the general reaction. He shuddered.

* * *

'This better be important, McLaughlin. Normally I couldn't see you till next week,' barked the president.

Dr Thornton P. Naugle (Ph.D. Management Studies, '59) was a tall and imposing figure, about six four, lean and spare, immaculately tailored. His thick grey hair was cropped short, his face sharp-featured, his eyes hooded, and a pencil-thin black moustache marched across his upper lip. He had the big booming voice of one used to command, and was now in the fourth year of his third five-year term as president of Chiliast U. Thornton Naugle had the reputation of a trouble-shooter, a fast-gun tough guy who'd been brought in from a deanship in a California college to bring some fiscal order to Chiliast during a time of financial crunch. He was accustomed to power, accustomed to having his own way, and bullied his Deans with a ceaseless bombardment of curt memoranda. Naugle had all the humour and subtlety of a chain saw. He made his impatience at being interrupted abundantly clear.

'I had to get you in between the dean of the medical school and the building committee. It's about your search, is it? God knows you've taken long enough. So spill it.'

'We nominate, the committee nominates, Professor Morley Snelgrove.'

The president blinked and his jaw fell.

'Snelgrove! But he's a fag! A flaming queer! Always lipping off in public about the bloody Gay Alliance. You can't be serious. What's wrong with you people?'

'Nothing's wrong.'

'How many people know about this?'

'Just the committee and yourself. Sir.'

'I hope to God your piddling little committee hasn't leaked this all over the floor of every faculty lounge on the campus, like last time.'

'No.'

'Then it can still be stopped. Let me think. This is one sweet screw-up, McLaughlin. You can tell your committee that.'

'We know – at least, we anticipated some surprise, even some controversy. But the committee has spent weeks and weeks on this, and we're resolved, unanimously.'

'Think of the consequences, man. Think of how the fundraising drive will be crippled! No, I'll do everything I can to stop this nonsense. I suppose if you insist I'm obliged to report this nomination to the board, embarrassing as it may be, and I'm sure they'll squelch it. But there's no meeting of the board now till, let me check the dates, after Christmas.'

'Couldn't you just go ahead and authorize me to make the offer to Morley, and then make the announcement?'

'I could. But I will not. It's out of the question.'

'A delay might harm the process.'

'Delay? You've been farting around about this since October, and you talk about delay? I'm not delaying this, I fully intend to stop it.'

'Well, I expect the search group might resign. Probably I'll have to resign as chair. But you realize that might mean, ah, going public with the story? Some member of the committee would surely do that. As chair, I guess I'd feel I had to do that.'

The president leaned across his desk, his eyes flinty.

'Are you threatening me, McLaughlin? Are you threatening *me?*'

'No, no. I'm just saying, there are some rules and procedures here, some due process.'

'Procedures? You might resign? Why, you keep on like this and you might be lucky to have a job to resign *from.*'

'I think the Faculty Association would back me up.' (And, he thought, thank God for tenure.)

'That bumbling association would make some noises, but lawyers would be involved, at great expense, and the whole stupid mess might be under negotiation or even before the courts for months, maybe years. Is that what you want?' He paused, looked out the window, steepled his long fingers. 'I hope you realize, my *dear* Professor McLaughlin, that I could make your life around here difficult, possibly quite miserable, if I had a mind to.'

'My life is already, um, a little hectic.'

'All this about some silly poofter,' said the president. 'Now see here, you just trot back to your undoubtedly well-intentioned, I'm sure reasonable, committee and report my – disappointment, and tell them they must reconsider.'

* * *

Later that day, he did. And they would not.

The end of the autumn university term was particularly welcome to Professor J. T. McLaughlin. Although it meant a large pile of essays and end-of-term exams to mark, the most difficult and numbing chore for any teacher, it was a good time of year. There was at least the satisfaction of knowing that Chiliast U., like almost all Canadian undergraduate institutions, refused to succumb to the widespread U.S. practice of substituting 'quizzes' for essays and written exams. 'Resolved that a line must be drawn somewhere,' as they used to argue at the Oxford Debating Union.

Several of McLaughlin's former graduate students were now teaching in the U.S. and one of them, a favourite of J. T.'s named Price, an assistant professor in North Dakota, reported in a Christmas e-mail that he was lumbered with 280 undergrads in one of his three courses. He had a mob of 160 students in Grand Forks where he worked, plus another 120 on the Bismarck, N.D., campus where his lectures appeared in a classroom on a giant TV screen. It was not exactly a warm and intimate educational experience for anyone. What to do about grading? Impossible, clearly, to read 280 essays, so no essays were assigned. Equally impossible to read 280 hand-written essay-type exams unless the load could be shared with at least one or two graduate student Teaching Assistants, but departmental budgets did not stretch to pay for many T As, certainly not for junior faculty members, and most smaller colleges did not have many graduate students who might have been Teaching Assistants anyway. The entirely predictable result was that the undergrads were graded by true-false or multiple-choice tests more appropriate to grade six than to university. 'Welcome to McEducation,' Price had written, 'Will you have fries with that exam?' The tests were all marked by machine, another triumph of technology over humanity.

The best thing about the holiday was having the kids home. It was a great satisfaction to have their energy and laughter in the house again. J. T. was so delighted and invigorated that he cut back on his drinking; some nights he just plain forgot about pouring scotch and drank only beer. Although they ordered in Chinese or Colonel Sanders a couple of times, the general desire seemed to be for home cooking, so he would whip up some of his specialties, beef short-ribs stew, corned beef and cabbage (which they pretended to enjoy), baked BBQ spare ribs with onions, or seafood pie. Several times when the weather was mild he'd don a parka and abuse some ribeyes or T-bones on the barbecue under the porch light. Joss wondered once or twice whether their mother should be invited for dinner, but this was not greeted with much enthusiasm, so the three youngsters took turns going over to her apartment where Trish generally thawed chicken potpies. Most nights the kids went out on the town with their friends after dinner, and J. T. was content to light a fire and read and listen to Beethoven or Benny Goodman. Several evenings he spent in the garage working on the Model A with the space heater going full blast. But most evenings he went out to movies with Pepper, or just drove over to her house where they sat and had coffee and sometimes watched a video. Pepper's tastes ranged from musicals and romantic comedies to blood-and-gore thrillers, although she managed to stay awake for yet another screening of J. T's old favourite, *Zulu*.

Some tensions arose over the logistics for Christmas. In this second year of their separation, J. T. realized it was Trish's turn to have the kids for the traditional turkey dinner. He offered to vacate the house so that 'Erstwhile' could come over and cook and hold the dinner there. Joss thought that was sort of sad, but it might work. J. T. had a standing invitation to dinner with Cutty and Alice. But as it turned out Trish decided that cooking might be too much trouble; she'd take the kids to the dining room of the King Edward Hotel for dinner. 'Aw,' said Davey, 'we'll have to get dressed up. I'd rather be at home.' But the King Eddie was decided upon. Pepper, at the same time, invited both J. T. and Zinger for the festive meal, which delighted Zinger, and caused McLaughlin to beg off with Cutty and accept Pepper's invitation with pleasure.

Jocelyn, Robbie and Davey decided they'd like to open their presents around the tree on Christmas Eve, so J. T. prepared a huge pot of Mississippi barbecue pork, with wild rice and coleslaw, and bought a lemon meringue pie from their favourite bakery. The four of them seemed a bit self-conscious and strained before dinner, trying to muster some enthusiasm by singing carols as they gazed into the blazing fireplace, but the mood lightened when J. T. came ho-ho-ing down the stairs in a rented Santa Claus suit with a bottle of champagne in each hand. They all hooted and laughed and had a grand time opening presents. The large, round, odd-looking object wrapped in red paper turned out to be a present from Robbie to his dad, a new but authentic steering wheel for the Model A that he'd sent away for, from a supplier in Hershey, Pennsylvania. It was a great hit. They all had a fine time opening and comparing presents with loud approval and happiness.

In the morning they slept in until almost ten a.m., when J. T. called them down for a mess of big fluffy blueberry pancakes and sausages, a holiday ritual.

At Pepper's that night, Zinger was on his best behaviour, bearing flowers and chocolates. He mentioned that his girlfriend, Cathy, was out of town with her parents. Pepper's widower father was not there either; she said he was at their Florida beach house with a new girlfriend. 'The Senator is a raunchy old character,' she said, laughing heartily. Pepper looked very elegant in a cream silk dress with a scooped neckline and small diamond earrings.

Gifts were exchanged over cocktails. J. T. had bought a chunky silver necklace for Pepper; she presented him with a handsome leather briefcase. He'd brought books for her children, two books of poetry, Patrick Lane and Lorna Crozier, for Lindsay, thrillers by Donald E. Westlake and Elmore Leonard for Stuart.

Dinner was excellent. A perfectly cooked free-range turkey with cranberry sauce, celery-apple stuffing and gravy is hard to beat. They put on silly paper party hats and gorged themselves.

Before the mincemeat pie with hard sauce was served, J. T. lapsed into a momentary lull, a blank space. It was one of those fleeting gusts of disorientation and irrational panic that can sweep through the uncertain mind. This is not my house! he thought. These are not my children. This is not my table. What am I doing here? Is my world ever going to straighten out and settle down? I must belong somewhere, but where? Could it really be here?

He shook his head to clear it. The moment passed.

When he resurfaced, Lindsay was asking shyly if 'Mr Zinger' was a professor too?

'Not a chance. I'm a journalist, and this year I'm back at school, reading about a lot of things, but mostly McLuhan. Do you know about him?'

Lindsay replied no, but Stuart said he'd heard about him in social studies class.

"Social studies," sighed Pepper. 'Doesn't anyone actually study history any more?'

'I wrote a poem about McLuhan just last week. It's a limerick,' Z. said.

'Careful,' said J. T.

'Never fear, it's clean. So maybe that disqualifies it as a true limerick.' He pulled a small sheaf of paper from an inside pocket, selected one, and read:

> I once asked Professor McLuhan
> 'Marshall, what are you doin'?'
> He replied with a wink,
> 'Trying to make people think
> How electronic viewin' brings ruin.

> 'As print becomes more obsolete
> Rationality suffers defeat.
> Too much watching the tube
> Turns you into a rube;
> It's your mind they're about to delete.'

'Zinger is also,' said J. T., 'a college president.'

'You are?' Lindsay asked, her eyes round and wide.

'Absolutely. I'm the founder, president, dean, and sole owner of the Prince Albert College of Journalism, Chiropractic, and Upholstery. I've just been revising and updating our curriculum. Got it here somewhere.' (He produced another sheaf of papers from another pocket.) 'We do a flourishing business in short courses by correspondence for ridiculously fat fees. In the summer term, for example, you might study –

> How to Make $40 per Month in Real Estate
> Zen and the Art of Burger Flipping
> Overcoming Self-Doubt through Pretence and Ostentation
> Burglar-proofing your Home with Cement and Rocket
> Launchers

Here's one for J. T. –
    Reducing Alimony Payments through Bankruptcy and
        Assassination
Or,
    Creative Suffering to Overcome Peace of Mind
    Career Opportunities in Catholic Health Spas.'
He grinned. 'Maybe you guys could help me with some more?'
J. T. decided to take a pass, somewhat miffed at Zinger, but Stuart
contributed –
    'Sinus Drainage through Knitting Needles and Firecrackers
    Rap Music for the Deaf and Dumb and Stupid.'
Zinger added –
    'Self-Actualization through Guilt, Ridicule, and Flossing
    Quality Control in the Workplace through Electro-Shock
        and the Lash.'
    J. T. sat back and relaxed, smiling at how merry Zinger seemed to
make the kids and Pepper as they bounced more preposterous titles
back and forth. It was hard to stay cross with Zinger, even harder not
to feel comfortable and, well, at home at this table, in this company.
When Pepper beamed that big incandescent smile at him, he felt as
though he'd just returned from a long journey to warm himself at a
welcoming fireplace.
    'Did someone mention "quality"?' Zinger asked. 'Now there's a
subject. Our friend B. J. Gandy says that is, or should be, the primary
subject of education. I'm glad you two youngsters are getting on with
your schooling; your mother says you're both doing very well. So you
won't be needing the help of the Prince Albert College, where we also
emphasize quality. It's the main thing. Professor Gandy says the
present educational system goes overboard for quantity. For numbers
and empiricism. He says if you can measure it, it's probably not very
important. Now, tell me, what does "quality" mean to you?'
    'Um, what is good, and what is better,' Stuart offered.
    'What is best,' Lindsay said. 'Degrees of excellence.'
    'Well said, good stuff. But how do you know, how can you tell,
what's better or best? Quality, like beauty, can't be measured, can it?
Now here's what I think you should do: each of you two write a short
essay on quality, coming as close as you can to defining it, and I'll put
up a prize of twenty dollars, no, hell, fifty dollars for the best essay.

Have we got a deal?'

Solemn nods all around.

'Difficult,' said J.T., 'but worth while. I wonder whether our esteemed College President from Saskatchewan would favour us with his own definition?'

'Trying to hoist me on my own petard, eh? Fair enough. Never let it be said that the Great Sage of the West lacked a response. I'd say, just for openers, that quality, like a lovely woman's beauty' – he raised a wine glass in an appreciative salute to his hostess – 'may be impossible to define, but is instantly recognizable when encountered.'

* * *

Later, when J.T. was driving Zinger home, Z. asked that he tell Pepper he'd send fifty dollars to both Lindsay and Stuart as soon as he had their essays. It would be a good intellectual workout for them, he said. 'There are more ways of teaching than merely lecturing, don't you think? That's how I run my college anyway, for fun and profit.'

'Fifty bucks is generous, though. Nice of you.'

'Aw, J.T., it's only money.'

'I don't think I've heard you say that before.'

'Sure, there are more important things. Happiness can't buy money, but it's still worthwhile. And I thought everyone was very happy tonight. Even, for a change, you.'

'Me? I guess so, yeh.'

'That's a fine and superior woman, my friend. You're very lucky.'

'You're right again.'

'Sometimes I think, J.T., that you are not just too up tight, but maybe afraid to be happy. That's the most relaxed and cheerful I've seen you since I arrived. Oh, you're a loyalist, I know, but don't be too loyal to your unhappiness. Living in an unhappy past is not where you belong. That would be a big mistake.'

'I've heard you say that before, Z.'

'So think about it. I might even give you a fifty-dollar prize too. Just as interest on what I owe you.'

'Should I hold my breath? Probably not.'

'Great things sometimes come to those who wait. Hark unto me, for I have spoken! And Merry Christmas. Good night.'

- 36 -

On the second day of the new term, McLaughlin's office phone rang and he found himself listening to the loud and insistent voice of President Naugle.

'I've checked with the university's lawyers and it seems I'm obliged to present your absurd nomination of Snelgrove to the board. That will be Thursday night, although I'm confident they'll reject it. Now here's the thing. The provincial Minister of Education was just on the blower to me telling – suggesting that I might find a suitable position here at Chiliast for a man we both know well, a business executive, a very big man on Bay Street with excellent credentials, but he's just been, ah, down-sized in one of those mega-corporation merger deals, the kind of merger that, shall we say, frees up a lot of high-priced talent like Jimmy Palmer – you know Palmer? No? A great guy who could be useful to us. He'd be a perfect fit. Jimmy has a lot of smarts. What do you say?'

'A perfect fit for what?'

'For principal of Burke College, of course! You're not very swift on the up-take. Ideal man for principal. Solve all our problems.'

'Um, what problems?'

'Why, making it easy to shuck off this Snelgrove faggot, and help us a lot with fundraising with the big players, not to mention earning important brownie points with the minister and probably the whole government. It's heaven-sent,' Naugle chortled. 'I'm just so relieved and delighted. I'll fax his CV over to you in five minutes. So I want you to reconvene your committee as fast as possible, certainly by Thursday, and we can wrap this thing up. You follow? You've got that?'

'I see it.' McLaughlin paused. 'What sort of academic interests or university experience does Mr Palmer have?'

'What's that got to do with it? He's a successful and prominent businessman, very hard-nosed. I want him. Isn't that clear enough?'

'Publications?'

'What possible …?' Naugle sputtered.

'He has academic degrees?'

'What? Palmer has an MBA. He has a Harvard MBA.'

'Ah. Another techie. Another bottom-line guy and a technician. Isn't that what's wrong with much of today's world? That instead of trusting the professionals who really know what's happening and understand the difficulties, we hire techie MBAs to head newspapers, broadcasting companies, hospitals, colleges, prisons, publishing houses, and even for godsake libraries? I think it's lamentable. I think it's vulgar. I wonder what Harold Innis would say about a man like that, turned loose in the Groves of Academe to shape us all up to business school standards?'

'To hell with Innis! He's been dead for years, and nobody could understand him anyway …'

'I could. Innis always said, when he was the chairman of this department and dean of the graduate school, he always said that the universities must always resist the attempts by business, and government, to undermine university freedom and independence. Universities must always defend intellectual liberty and freedom of the mind against control by Philistines. Innis also said that we had to resist the rising tide of mere measurement by the number-crunchers, mere quantification by the technicians, and that what this country needed was a good five-cent bullshit filter, otherwise social scientists might die laughing.'

'What in hell is wrong with you, McLaughlin? Are you presuming to lecture me on how to run this institution? You've got brass, I must say, even if you don't seem to understand reality. Now, just belt up, there's a good chap, and forget all this Innis nonsense. Reconvene your committee at once, show them Palmer's CV and get on with it. That's an order.'

'Reality? The reality is, Mr President, that the committee reached its decision weeks ago, unanimously, and I informed every member of your – reservations about our choice after our last little chat. None wanted to change our recommendation, and Professor Snelgrove seemed very pleased when I informed him. So, no, I will not reconvene the committee, not unless they ask me to. You can, of course, circulate this CV to them and make your wishes known; that's your privilege, but I very much doubt you'll get far by trying to bully them.'

'You mean, you won't do it?'

'That's what I mean. Sir.'

'There'll be repercussions, McLaughlin, *serious* repercussions.' Naugle was so angry that he utterly lost it, boiled over. 'I won't forget this! I'll have your balls for earrings ...'

'Earrings, Mr President? Did I hear you say you were interested in earrings? What a pretty thought.'

'Arrgh! Not earrings, no. But I'll nail your ass, McLaughlin, see if I don't!'

'Such imaginative imagery, Mr President. Nail my ass. How appropriate. I must share your thoughts with my colleagues, perhaps with Professor Snelgrove.'

'McLaughlin! I'm bloody well *telling* you –'

'No, you're not.' Click. McLaughlin hung up. He was more than a little surprised at the turn of events, but angry.

'Well,' he thought, 'I sure didn't do myself much good with *that*. Fun to do it, though; keeps the conscience clear. And as Zinger says, whatthehell, all life is six to five against anyhow.'

* * *

J. T. lost some sleep during the next two nights, wondering what schemes or retribution the angry President Naugle might dream up. It was worrisome. The Model A and his lectures distracted him somewhat, but Naugle preyed on his mind. And would the Board of Governors reject the nomination of Snelgrove? And leave the search committee twisting in the wind? Had he overstepped the bounds? How vulnerable was he to executive vilification?

And so he was very surprised to pick up the phone in the kitchen at eight-thirty on Friday morning and hear a woman identify herself as Angela Korchinsky.

'Yes?'

'My family donated Korchinsky Hall? Do you recall?'

'I do, yes, of course,' he replied tentatively.

'I've been on the university Board of Governors for years, and presently I am the board's chair, as you may know. We had rather a tussle at last night's meeting with President Naugle over a question in which I believe you're interested. The Snelgrove nomination?'

'Yes. My committee ...'

'I know about your search committee, Professor McLaughlin.

The president told us a great deal about it, although not in very positive terms.'

'Probably not, but ...'

'Please hear me out. Dr Naugle presented the nomination of Professor Snelgrove in a way that I found – surprising. He made light of it, rather, and seemed dismissive, unkind, and then went on to speak at length about Jimmy Palmer, a man I know slightly but don't greatly admire. I began to detect a whiff of rodent, you know? I'm acquainted with Senator Pemberton – I believe his daughter Jessica, Pepper – is a member of your search committee? Well, the Senator had joked with me at a cocktail party before Christmas that the university was becoming more and more difficult to administer, and how the selection of a new principal could become quite, er, contentious. He said no more than that, he's the soul of discretion of course, but I was grateful to be alerted that there might be a problem, a controversy before the board, and I was prepared to look closely at the nomination.'

'That's good, but I don't ...'

'Please. Let me continue. President Naugle made some rather slighting remarks about you personally, which did not seem necessary, and about the search process. I must tell you I thought there seemed to be some irregularities about your first selections, serious breaches of procedure which marred the process.'

'We tried to maintain confidentiality, but ...'

'I'm saying, IF you please, that this entire matter did not seem cut and dried, and so when Snelgrove's nomination was put on the table, accompanied by some snickering and some not very subtle innuendoes by Dr Naugle, I asked to see the man's CV. On paper he's impressive, more than acceptable. Clearly it was a question of his unorthodox lifestyle: his, er, sexual orientation.'

'Yes, but our committee ...'

'I'd be grateful if you'd do me the courtesy of not interrupting. I feel very strongly about this, and I didn't much appreciate Naugle's high-handedness. I reviewed the documents, circulated the CV around the table, gave everyone time to read and consider. I then asked for a motion that the nomination be accepted.

'And it was duly moved and seconded.'

'It was then that some heated discussion broke out, and the president, a man who is used to having his own way, more than is perhaps desirable, began to fulminate and expostulate. I think he may have damaged his own cause by the intemperance of his remarks, but it was clear the board was undecided, wavering. Image and fund-raising seemed to be at issue. But I knew that at least two members of the board had relatives and, er, close friends who were not straight. Gay. So I knew I was not alone, and I spoke my mind. I urged the acceptance of Professor Snelgrove's nomination as principal.'

'You did? Good stuff!'

'Absolutely. In the heat of discussion I might also have mentioned that I might want to rethink a previously announced donation from the Korchinsky Foundation of some seven million dollars to Chiliast University if Snelgrove were to be rejected merely on the grounds of his orientation.'

'You did? You said that?'

'Certainly. It seemed to me necessary and straightforward. If universities discriminate unfairly, whom we can trust? Your committee came to a difficult but sensible conclusion, and I insisted that the board must respect the recommendation of Snelgrove's peers. I then called the vote, and the motion was carried, narrowly, but carried. I must say I took some satisfaction in Naugle turning purple, but that's beside the point. I'm merely phoning you to say that your candidate's nomination was, along about midnight, confirmed as Principal of Burke College.'

'It is? He *is*? I'll be damned. I mean, thank you, Mrs Korchinsky. Thank you for telling me this. It's awfully kind of you to phone and let me know. I'm relieved, surprised. I'm very pleased to hear what you've said.'

'I got your home number from the university directory and thought you might not mind receiving this news so early in the morning. I hope I'm right.'

'You're right. Of course you're right. I'm very grateful, very. It's just such remarkable news.'

'And if anyone should happen to ask you, you needn't mention that one of my two sons is gay. Is that agreed?'

'Why, certainly. I didn't know. I mean, it's nobody's, that is, it's not ...'

'Exactly. And may I suggest that, on the evidence of last night's performance, if President Naugle makes any personal or uncalled-for, er, gestures toward you, as seems just possible if I read him correctly, you might let me know?'

'Mrs Korchinsky, I'm immensely grateful to you. Certainly I will. But I'm sure that this is all happily settled and over and done with now.'

'I would not be too certain of that. Keep your elbows up in the corners, as the hockey players say, and keep in touch. Nice talking to you, Professor McLaughlin. I think we both have reason to be pleased with this outcome, but it's a difficult world, isn't it? Good morning to you.'

J. T. was in his office at four-thirty one Monday afternoon two weeks later with Cutty, putting away some books and lecture notes before leaving for the day. Cutty had asked for a ride to his garage because his car was in to have a leaking radiator replaced, and was grumbling about the cost of auto repairs when the phone rang.

'Let it ring, ignore it. Let's get going,' said Cuttshaw.

'Might be a student, though. Only take a moment.'

'Hello? Professor McLaughlin? My name is Constanza de Fuentes. I'm chair of the Ethics and Standards Committee. May I have a minute of your time?'

'Ah, the political correctness guardians, the gestalt Gestapo. What can I do for you? I'm a bit busy at the moment. Could I call you back tomorrow?'

'I think I should inform you about a case that has come before us, and there's no time like the present.'

'I don't think I'd be much interested. I have no complaints for your committee, never have had. I'm sure you do good work, but sometimes it seems to me that you people tend to be rather, um, excessive in your zeal to safeguard us all from the evils of reality. Are you sure this won't keep? I mean, have you heard any good anti-Presbyterian jokes lately? Heh heh.'

'I'm afraid the name that's come up in a formal complaint is your name, and it's my duty to inform you that ...'

'MY name? You're joking. You're funnin' the ol' perfessor, right?'

'I'm afraid we don't usually joke about these matters. It seems there may be altogether too much unfortunate "joking" involved here. Statements made which may not be appreciated by some aggrieved minority persons.'

'Aggrieved? What on earth are you talking about? I'm an aggrieved person – just ask my divorce lawyer or my tax accountant.'

'I must ask you to be serious, Professor McLaughlin. My office has a file here, a fairly large file, listing a number of charges pertaining to statements made by you. I'll have the complete list delivered to your office by hand tomorrow morning. The charges, I should say, relate to sexism, religious and ethnic biases, and homophobic expressions of an extremely serious nature, all of which appear to violate explicit provisions of the university's Code of Conduct. You're familiar with the code, of course.'

McLaughlin rolled his eyes and slapped his forehead, whispering to Cutty that this woman on the phone was calling him a flaming great bigot.

'You? There's a laugh,' said Cutty. 'You of all people. Come on, cut her off and let's get going.'

'Ms de Fuentes, I'm not sure what you're driving at, but I really must go. I've a friend here I've promised to ...'

'Perhaps you don't appreciate the gravity of these charges, or their potential consequences. I assure you that I'm entirely in earnest, and I'm merely attempting to give you full and fair warning of what is at issue here. Our time schedule might be a little tight to arrange a hearing.'

'A hearing? My God. On what?'

'I'm trying to tell you on what. Shall I read you a few items from this dossier?'

'I suppose, if you feel you have to. (I'm sorry, Cutty, this may not be a joke.)'

'There's no humour at all involved here, please be clear on that.' Ms de Fuentes' voice crackled. 'It's alleged in this statement of charges that you invited some members of the Gay Alliance to join you in a chorus of "Sodality Forever".'

'What? Whatthehell? If I said anything like that it was just joshing with some students about how to nominate one of their members for an important job. I was helping them, for godsake, in my office. In private.'

'That could be, but ...'

'You're not telling me that some fiddling complaint has been brought by one of those boys? Or by the Gay Alliance? Why, my views, my record, on that score are ...'

'I'm not at liberty to say who brought the complaint. Our committee is obliged, of course, to protect our sources and safeguard the rights of those who bring information before us.'

'What about *my* rights? So it's our old pal Anonymous? I'll be damned.'

'It's alleged that you made disparaging remarks about two Muslim women to the effect that their veils and *hijabs* were Hallowe'en costumes.'

'I said, I might have said, that I *thought* of saying something like that, but I certainly did not say it to *them*.'

'Then how could someone report hearing those words from your lips? Allow me to continue. It's alleged that in a committee meeting, a search committee I think, you recited a lewd poem, a limerick, about – er – testicles.'

'Teddy,' he groaned. 'That Kravnik woman.'

'I beg your pardon.'

'Anything which might have been said in committee was in private, confidential, certainly not public.'

'It seems there were both student and faculty colleagues present who might well have taken offence, so it could scarcely be called "private". And it's alleged that a strong suggestion of alcohol was on your breath at the time – early in the morning, at that – so you might not recall with full accuracy what you said.'

'Nonsense. Bloody nonsense.'

'Kindly do not use profanity with me, Professor McLaughlin.'

'What profanity? Do want to hear some real down and dirty profanity about that Kravnik bitch? Er, witch? Shit, now you've got me doing it, all the correctness cant and evasive weasel words, is that what you want?'

'Some "evasive" circumlocutions, as you say, might in fact have avoided this difficulty, don't you think? Anyway, you'll soon see the full list of allegations.'

'Full? You mean there are more?'

'A few more, yes, not the least of which concerns a distinguished colleague, the Chair of Italian and Renaissance Studies, whom you are alleged to have referred to as "one tough broad". Does that ring a bell?'

'In private, and meant as a compliment.'

'In committee, it says here. May I point out that I'm relating these allegations to you at the earliest moment possible, as a courtesy …'

'A *courtesy*, you call it?'

'Yes, a courtesy so that you will have time to consider and to respond to these charges by a week from Friday at nine a.m. The committee requests that you meet with us at that time.'

'Friday? You mean *next* Friday? Bloody hell. What's with this rush to injustice?'

'Profanity again, Professor. That's not at all the type of response likely to endear you to the committee, believe me. We prefer to proceed briskly in matters such as this, and then too I might mention that President Naugle himself has taken an interest in this case. He has sent me a memo concerning your dossier, I suppose due to the numerous charges and their gravity, and suggested that we move along with dispatch. I hope that will be agreeable to you? There's ample time for you to seek advice if you wish.'

'Legal counsel, you mean?'

'If that's your desire, of course, but this is not a court of law and not a public hearing, merely a preliminary meeting to seek all possible clarification. Our group has the authority to investigate charges, assess their validity, and make recommendations.'

'What sort of recommendations?'

'Oh, regarding possible actions, and er, recommending sanctions to the president and through him to the Board of Governors.'

'Holy shit,' J.T. exclaimed. 'Holy ruinous shit.'

'Professor McLaughlin, I've warned you about profanity, and I must say your language is most deplorable. I do not intend to listen to any more of your verbal abuse. Good day.'

McLaughlin sat in stunned silence for several moments, looking at the telephone as though it had leaped up and bitten him.

'Now what the hell,' said Cutty, 'was all that about? It sounded damn odd. What's this burble about next Friday?'

'I'll … I'll try to explain in the car. I must think. Come on. I've gotta think.'

* * *

Once Cutty got the story straight, or as clear as the distraught McLaughlin could make it, he knew that his friend was in deep trouble. The two of them drove to Cuttshaw's house and got on the phone to call a council of war, or at least of defence. B.J. Gandy listened to what Cutty told him and proposed that they meet in two days, at noon. Off campus might be best; they'd meet at Dooley's. Meanwhile they'd all make inquiries and think hard about some strategy. B.J. urged them to include Francis Z. When Cutty wondered what Zinger would know about academic procedures, Gandy said that Zinger had keen and street-savvy fighting instincts, would take a lively interest, and might be useful in matters of public relations later on. J.T. shuddered at the mention of 'public relations'. Surely hearings like this were private? Gandy told him not to count on it. Things might get ugly, and J.T. already knew about leaks.

Cutty also offered to phone Pepper, saying how bright and sensible she was, but McLaughlin remembered that she had a Ph.D. oral exam with one of her students booked for that day at one o'clock. Besides, he said, he didn't want to upset her, or embarrass himself further at this point. Did J.T. want to stay for dinner? Alice asked. But he said no thanks, he was too strung out to eat.

That night, at home, McLaughlin fussed and fretted and paced the floor. He saw lots of irony in the situation but couldn't bring himself to laugh. Instead he backslid from his relatively moderate ways of recent weeks and poured such an excessive quantity of scotch down the inside of his neck that he slept very little and very badly. In his dreams he could hear the gurgling of his career going down the drain.

- 38 -

Cathy invited Zinger to her company's upcoming book launch party. MacDonald-Fraser was ushering in two books, one about gardening, one an expensive coffee table and soft-porn volume about Canadian supermodels, who would all turn out in expensive borrowed clothes and make-up as thick as banana cream pie. It was to be a lavish bash, a flashy event, Cathy said. Limitless wine and finger food. Big publicity cost big money, and the publisher was pulling out all the stops, hoping that the glossy magazines and weekend newspapers would feature the event. The *Globe and Mail* might 'monster' it, give it a big spread. Lovely new verb, that: 'to monster', the ultimate in PR and media play.

When Zinger arrived at the Sutton Place Hotel reception, he found a huge and noisy crowd, the usual suspects, waving, hugging, squealing, air-kissing and pressing flesh as they looked furtively over each other's shoulders for 'celebrities' they might buddy up to, harass, or be photographed with, even if they weren't entirely sure why the objects of their fleeting affections were celebrated. Almost everyone wore a nametag, like a suburban Rotarian, and if you needed a nametag you were by definition not a celebrity.

Just inside the door on the far left Zinger was confronted by a vast block of television sets, about forty of them, stacked four deep in rows of ten. Each was without sound and each tuned to a different channel. A battalion of telephones enabled a viewer to follow instructions and push a button for a numbered channel that would bestow audio unto the eager ear. The selection was huge, with something for even the most jaded electronic taste, including:

> WWF Professional Wrestling
> Lifestyles of the Greedy and Depraved
> Travel: Little-known Inns in Ulan Bator
> Your Health: Bladder Control for Geriatrics
> Hobbies: Train Your Pet Turtle to Fetch.

Just standard TV fare, thought Zinger, the banal byways of the Global Suburb.

On the far right a bevy of languid supermodels was draped along the bar. They all looked bored out of their tiny minds. Zinger got a drink and was relieved to see Cathy bouncing across the room to greet him.

'Come along and meet some of the models,' she trilled. 'Aren't they gorgeous?'

'Well, you won't have to worry about feeding them. They look like they don't eat at all, like they haven't eaten in months. Desiccated. Cadaverous. Are they all on tranqs?'

'Now don't be difficult. They're stunning, don't you think? Usually our PR people have to rent a dozen of them to dress up the room for a party, but since they're all in the book, they're here in droves. If you don't think they're gorgeous, why are you staring?'

'That's what they're *for*, Cathy, to be stared at. That's their profession. It would be rude *not* to stare. But I've seen more meat at a vegetarian picnic. Can they actually walk and talk in dresses that tight?'

'Of course they can. That's the fashion.'

'I guess so. Loose women in tight dresses or tight women in loose dresses, whatever's in style this season.'

'Now stop it. Come along and I'll introduce you as a famous author.'

'Don't bother, really.'

'You're being silly. You must agree they're sensational. God, I'd give a year's pay to look like that.'

'If you say so, but in my opinion if there was some flesh, possibly a smile or two, a roundness or a curve somewhere, some character in a face, and here and there a serious boob, the prospect might be greatly enhanced. Anyway, tell about those rows and rows of TV sets. What are they in aid of?'

'Oh, the whole party is being videotaped. When things get going, everything in the room will come up on a screen and maybe on the fashion program on CITY-TV on the weekend. The guests like to see themselves, the models love to see themselves, and Big Mac thinks the event isn't actually real if it's not on TV. He says anyone can come to a party, but if it's on TV it's *really* real.'

'Jeez. And him in the print business. What a beguiling thought. I suppose if the power goes off, an outage, he thinks the world stops spinning?'

'Shhh. Here he comes now.'

'Ah, the Alberta man. How are you?'

'Fine, thanks. From Saskatchewan.'

'You shouldn't admit that. No one's from Saskatchewan. So, isn't this a swell bash? The cameras will roll in any minute. Get me another drink, Cathy, will you?' MacDonald leaned closer to Zinger. 'What did I tell you about literary pussy? Is this hot stuff or what? These broads would give a hard-on to a mashed potato.'

'I wish you joy of it, Mac, but mind you don't cut yourself on one of those hip bones. Harm can come to a man that way.'

'Ho, ho, you're a great kidder, Singer. It's all for business, of course, great for business.'

'Will I have a book launch like this in March?'

'Maybe not quite like *this*, of course, but something, sure. Accounting would have to take the cost out of your royalties – let's hope there *are* some – so you might give some thought to what kind of a launch you'd like. Do you have an agent? No? Well, promotion costs other than transportation to interviews are outlined in some section of your contract. Cathy can explain all that. Here she is. Bye for now. I must mingle.'

'I suppose Mac told you how all this is good for business,' Cathy said. 'It's his favourite theme.'

'Yeh, I've been reflecting on the nature of commerce since he brought it up. Near as I can figure it, business – well, apart from inherited companies and "Thanksdads" – is mostly a big guy buying a good idea from some little schmuck, cheap, a large shark eating up small fish, and producing some load of crap, and shipping it out in trains or trucks, making sure that the cost of the thing is only pennies, while the high costs of packaging and distribution and advertising run up a score for related subsidiary companies where their idiot sons work. Then they have some brilliant incestuous mergers and sell their patents to each other while some accountant named Herbie works in a tiny office downtown to explain to the tax man that there's no real profit, not yet, after deductions, and keeps them out of jail while they all go to a courtroom or a country club to sort out their winnings, swilling martinis while complaining about the evils of government regulation and high taxes. Then they fire some staff and work the rest of you overtime without pay. I believe that's the essence of it. The main problem with business, I think, is that it's not very interesting, so the owners like Mac get bored and yammer about "stress", or get ulcers and die young. For what? A mug's game. Who needs it?'

'Maybe you do,' Cathy said, smiling. 'Maybe you need a job and a publisher.'

'Whatever. As long as you don't take it seriously. What I do need is to get out of here. Let's split.'

'Now you know I can't leave yet. I'm working; I'm a hostess. Mac would be furious.'

'But you worked in your office all day.'

'And much of last night, yes.'

'There you go. That's what I'm saying. The system ignores you and extends your hours and eats you up.'

'If you'd stop lecturing at me, I'd make one more tour of duty around the room and then we can slip away, OK?'

Z. had another drink and a couple of unrewarding glances down some necklines before he got the coats and stood by the door, waiting a bit longer for Cathy. Finally he went over and seized her arms and steered her away.

'Out. Out. We've gotta get out of here.'

He hailed a cab which took them to Baroote's excellent restaurant on King Street West. They ordered the excellent veal chops.

'I've been thinking of what you said about business and long hours,' she sighed. 'It's becoming so "normal" that we take the work load for a granted if we want to keep our jobs. Not much time to have a life. You're not all wrong. Damn, I can walk into any bar in town and listen to young lawyers talking about twelve- or fourteen-hour days, usually six days a week. Computer systems employees working at a furious pace with bleary eyes for twelve-hour days or longer. Young MD interns working in emergency wards for sixteen-, even twenty-four-hour shifts till they can scarcely see straight. It's all so ironic because technology, the computer, was supposed to make everything easier, save us time, create leisure. Fat bloody chance. For decades people like my dad in labour unions fought for the eight-hour day, and thought they'd won, but now most young workers in the city would find an eight-hour day a part-time job, a breeze. I'm just so tired, Zinger. It's a rat race here, and the rats have won. Maybe I'll quit and go back West.'

'Maybe you should. Maybe we should. But just let me get my book launched first and then we'll sort it out.'

'Sure, OK. I'll be glad to help with that.'

'Will I have to wade through all this publicity shitteroo, what we saw tonight?'

'Some, yes. You'll need the hype if you want the sales. That's just how it is.'

'I guess if you want to run with the wolves you've got to howl like a wolf. Well, I'll give it some thought. There must be ways. Maybe we can teach the wolves some new tricks.'

39

At Dooley's they got a quiet table at the back and the four of them got right down to it. How to get J.T. off the hook? Cutty outlined the facts of the situation succinctly and McLaughlin muttered some supplementary points and comments throughout. Cutty told J.T. to shut up and let him keep the matter in focus. What could the authorities do? he asked Gandy. What did the Ethics committee have power to recommend?

'Har,' B.J. snorted. 'Almost anything. I've never heard so many charges being levelled at the same time. This document from Ms de Fuentes is very extensive, distressingly detailed. It's difficult to predict what the committee will make of all this. The range and number of the allegations render a strong defence all the more problematic, I'm afraid.'

'But can you remember the sorts of recommendations they've made in the past? Just so we know,' said Cutty, 'what we're up against.'

'In the past? As I understand things, their findings have led them to urge anything from warnings and mild rebukes to enforced leave of absence without pay for a year. I think in one rather extreme case of sexual harassment they recommended withdrawal of tenure, dismissal.'

'Jee-zus,' said Cutty.

'Yes, things can get very nasty indeed,' B.J. nodded.

'Can we make any yards with a defence that all of these statements, OK, alleged statements, J.T., were made ...'

'I guess I'd have to admit that I did say everything they say I said. Guilty.'

'Don't say that,' said Cutty. 'I'm asking how far could we get, do you think, B.J., with a defence of privacy, that anything said was in his office, not in public, not in a lecture? Or in a committee whose proceedings were – were supposed to be – private and confidential? It's obvious that J.T. was only trying to lighten up some situations by being jocular.'

'I really don't think that the Code of Conduct or those ethics and standards people place much weight on humour,' said B.J. 'The privacy defence probably won't wash because in each case there were several people present, witnesses, both in his office and in committee. No, that won't be adequate, I think. I wonder why this woman has it in for you so much, J.T.? Kravnik? Is that her name? Do you have any doubt it was she who brought the accusations?'

'None at all. It's got to be her. Evil bitch. As to why she hates me, hell, I don't know. Maybe it's because I'm a man, or flippant, or she sees me as a representative of establishment power – now that's a laugh – or maybe because I rejected some of her nominations or because I part my hair on the wrong side, who knows? I think that she's just a twisted woman with a mean streak as wide as her ass.'

'Tell me again,' said B.J., 'why the president might be involved with this.'

J.T. reviewed that for him, emphasizing Naugle's opposition to Snelgrove. Gandy merely nodded.

'A line of defence,' Cutty kept saying over and over. 'Even if J.T. did not admit his comments, we could scarcely use denial as a tactic because, again, there are too many witnesses.'

'Maybe he could plead insanity,' Zinger grinned.

'You could say you were upset, J.T.,' said Cutty, 'that you were on heavy medication, didn't know what you were saying, were under the care of a doctor who'd dosed you, a psychiatrist. Plea for mercy on grounds of mental infirmity and distress.'

'The only dosage he was under was from the liquor store,' said Zinger.

'Oh, knock it off, Zinger. Could we make any headway with some kind of mental instability plea, B.J.?'

'Probably not. He was meeting his classes and chairing the committee and evidently functioning. So, no, even with medical testimony, which we don't have, I think not.'

'Damn. But can you propose any defence?'

B.J. shook his head. 'Pleading truth and good sense may be a defence in a libel action,' he said, 'but this would appear to be an issue of attitude, unacceptable expressions of opinion. That's why any defence is so damnably difficult. We're boxed in.'

Silence all around, until Zinger said:

'Attack.'

'What?' said Cutty.

'If in doubt, if cornered, the thing to do is attack.'

'But Zinger, how could we attack this Kravnik person? She probably wouldn't give a damn anyway. What's she got to lose? Nothing.' Cutty looked baleful. 'But J.T. has, well, a whole lot to lose. Guilty or innocent, one way or the other, he gets dragged through the shit. Even if he wins, he loses. He's smirched. So maybe Zinger is on to something. Accuse her. Charge her with, um, malicious slander, with character assassination. How's that?'

'Motive?' B.J. inquired. 'Any plausible motive?'

Another long silence.

'Wait a minute,' said Zinger. 'I'm still pondering "malice". A thought is forming. Maybe a most luminous thought. Now, you're sure that this Naugle bozo is supporting the action, maybe encouraging Kravnik? That doesn't sound sweet and neutral and presidential to me. And the de Fuentes broad actually said that the president was taking an interest? Pushing it?'

'Yes,' J.T. nodded, 'but what's that got to do…?'

'Quiet. *Wait* a bit. I'm still in attack mode, and the wily brain of your bold prairie tactician just sniffed a weakness in the enemy's phalanx.' He paused. 'I remember you telling me, J.T., that Naugle used some highly disparaging and intemperate language about your man Snelgrove, true?'

'Yes. Very. I was surprised.'

'Tell us exactly what he said.'

'Well, he was dismissive at first and then got angry. Said Snelgrove would be a liability, maybe an embarrassment. Said he was a queer, a faggot – I think the word "poofter" came up.'

'Good. Very good. Anything else?'

'Not that I recall …'

'But he used other insulting words? Think, man. Tell us more.'

'I think he said something about Morley being the type who would pee sitting down.'

'I love it,' said Zinger. 'Great stuff.'

'What's so great,' said Cutty. 'I don't see …'

'And you told me,' Zinger pressed on, waving Cutty aside, 'you told me that when Naugle phoned you about some other candidate, some suit from Bay Street, he bad-mouthed you as well? Did he threaten you? Keep thinkin', buddy.'

'He said he could cause me trouble, yeh. Told me he'd "nail my ass".'
'Excellent. This is wonderful. Go on.'
'He shouted something about "having my balls for earrings". I'm pretty sure that was the line.'
'Perfect. We've got him. Do you see it, B.J.?'
'I think I do, Francis, I see where you're going. But it's very dangerous stuff.'
'This is no time to be timid. It's a gotcha. We'll hang him out to dry. The ass to be nailed won't be J.T.'s, it'll be Naugle's. Oh, I just *love* it.'

'Do you mean,' Cutty wondered, 'do you really mean that we don't attack Kravnik, we actually attack *the president*?'
'You've got it. And we've got him. What's to lose? He's already antagonistic to J.T., to say the least. The beauty of it is, don't you see, J.T. already has a friend, a powerful ally, in the woman – is it Korchinsky? – who's chair of the Board of Governors, the board Naugle has to report to. It's delicious. Look, Snelgrove's appointment has already been announced, it's public, endorsed by the board. Naugle has slandered Snelgrove, the choice of McLaughlin's committee, and then uttered threats against J.T. If any of this becomes public, vivid quotations from chairman Thornton P. Naugle in the press, he's toast. He'll have to trade off dropping all charges against J.T. The faculty association, and probably the board, would demand his resignation. Burned toast. Hey, I'll bet even the bloody committee on ethics and standards would come after him, baying for his hide. Wouldn't *that* be a joy? You *gotta* love it.'

'Jeez,' said Cutty, 'going after the president himself is really pushing it.'

'We go for broke,' grinned Zinger, 'we go for gongs and glory and presidential gore. We nail the sonofabitch good and proper, and J.T. will be home and dry. The man from Prince Albert has led the charge of the cavalry over the hill once again. Not true, J.T.? Waiter! Bring us another round. Bring us each a touch, hell, bring us a whole bottle of Bushmill's best, the Black Bush, and four lovely large glasses.'

By this time even J.T. had fetched up a smile, still blinking and uncertain, as Zinger slapped him on the back, nearly knocking him out of his chair, and again Z. flashed a most sardonic grin of self-congratulatory triumph.

'Amazing,' said Cutty.

'Nothing if not audacious,' said B. J., 'but I believe Francis is right about "nothing to lose". I'm still trying to consider it every which way, and undoubtedly there are risks. But I believe it might work. Yes, I think it could work. We inform the ineffable Naugle that if he doesn't have the charges against McLaughlin withdrawn, quashed, we'll charge him with defamation and slander against Principal-elect Snelgrove, and with uttering quite extreme threats against J. T., tantamount to character assassination against one of his own faculty members. And, if worse came to worst we'd have the backup that Mrs Korchinsky and the board would be quite properly horrified. Yes, I do believe it will work. Congratulations, Francis. I'd never have thought of it – will you fill my glass again, Cutty? – but I do indeed think it could play out most agreeably.'

J. T. sat wreathed in smiles, still unable to speak, almost weeping with optimism and relief. He could only think, wait till I tell Pepper about this. Cutty, for his part, kept repeating, 'I'll be damned. Well, I'll be damned.'

* * *

Professor Morley Snelgrove, Principal-elect of Burke College, dropped by McLaughlin's office to say, again, as he had weeks before, thanks for the help in getting him considered for the appointment. Morley was dapper, a tall, spare man of fifty-three with iron-grey hair and a smooth handsome face. His suit was well cut, perhaps Savile Row, his smile engaging. He looked every inch, J. T. thought, the confident executive type.

'I've been thinking about it a lot,' said Snelgrove, 'and I'd value your opinions, on how to make the college a better place for students. Could we talk about that sometime soon?'

'Sure, but that will be a *long* talk.'

'Of course, J. T., of course. Maybe over the next year or so. I mean, to me the largest question is how to resist the commercial pressures and shift our education goals. As I see it, we should try to avoid just producing fodder for the mercantile society, to produce thoughtful citizens and not merely obedient corporate workers and passive consumers, do you see what I'm saying?'

'Morley, certainly, I do see it, and even although I don't have any

226

adequate answers, I sure like the questions you're asking, and that may be half the battle. But it *will* be a battle. Have we got a decade or two for this dialogue? You know, you sound a lot like my hero, Harold Innis, when he was Dean of the Graduate School.'

'I take that as a compliment, thank you. Anyway, when I saw your door open I thought you might have time to chat. I wonder if you'd fancy a drink? Perhaps a martini at the club?'

'Very nice of you, I appreciate the thought. But would you mind if we skipped the bar and just got a coffee? The thing is, I'm sort of off the sauce. Not on the wagon, not totally, but I'm trying to taper off, give the old liver a rest.'

'Ah, I understand. Good for you. I had to dry out once myself, years ago. But you don't seem to have the shakes or any visible symptoms, so I guess you're OK?'

'I think so, yes, thanks.'

'Many of your colleagues knew you were having a bit of a tussle with the bottle, and will wish you well.'

'Nice of you to say that, Morley.'

'There are some, doubtless, who are intolerant and censorious, but most decent people in the college realize it would be a pretty boring person who never had any problems at all. Most of us do, I'd say we all do. To be human is to be fragile, don't you think?'

'I suppose so. But are you trying to tell me something, Morley?'

'Well, just that I have a great deal of sympathy with victims of intolerance, as you might imagine, and I'm rather alarmed to hear rumours in the common room that you might be having problems with the Ethics and Standards Committee. Is that true?'

'It's true, yes. There are just no secrets around here, eh? I may have made some unguarded and facetious comments during the search process. Only wisecracks, you know, and alcohol doesn't improve your judgment. Somebody reported a version of my remarks to the Code of Conduct people, trying to embarrass me, and with real success. Bloody awful nuisance, but it might come right yet.'

'I see. Most regrettable. I think this Ethics outfit started out positively a few years back, trying to confront serious bigotry and protect minorities, but then became bureaucrats and barrack-room lawyers willing to listen to gossip and snitches and anonymous people with petty or paranoid grievances.'

'I can't disagree with that.'

'Hell's bells, if you were a bigot I could hardly have been taken seriously for principal, now could I? They'll have a hard time convincing any large group in the college that you're not a good chap. So if there's anything I can do, or say, or write on your behalf ...'

'I really appreciate that, Morley. You're most kind.'

'Not at all. Let's hope it all blows over. Now, shall we go and find that coffee?'

* * *

It had been arranged that Zinger would draft and type up the statement to Thornton P. Naugle and deliver it to the president the following morning. Accordingly, at 7:45 a.m., in his best dark blue suit, Z. waylaid Naugle at his office door and announced that he was a lawyer from New York, a specialist in libel, a friend and counsellor of a distinguished member of the Chiliast U. faculty. He had, said Z., important legal documents including a sworn deposition which he was instructed to deliver to the president personally.

'What? What are you talking about? Don't you know enough to leave it with my secretary?'

'Very sensitive documents, these. For your eyes only – so far, at least. I believe you'll find this quite absorbing reading.'

Muttering about 'damned foolishness', Naugle impatiently ripped open the envelope. He read the first page with mounting astonishment, turned white, sat down, read through the entire contents slowly, and turned a most remarkable shade of purple. There was a very long pause. He mopped his brow and stared at Z., who smiled back at him in an encouraging way. Finally Naugle cleared his throat and in a strangulated voice said:

'Under these circumstances I believe it would be appropriate for me to inform the Ethics and Standards Committee that there has been a grave misunderstanding and that there is no reason, none at all, to proceed with any charges against your client, unmitigated prick that he may be. As a gesture of good will I will further arrange that Professor McLaughlin will go on a research leave for the next academic year, at half salary.'

'Full salary, or ...' Z. smiled again.

'Quite so. Full salary, I agree. All charges and all unfortunate allegations are to be dropped, stricken from the record.'

'I congratulate you on your wise decision. It's been a pleasure doing business with you, Mr President. And do bear in mind that my law firm has a copy of these documents on file, merely as a precaution against any, ah, slippage. Good day to you.'

When Zinger hopped along to McLaughlin's office he found J. T. waiting at the door.

'Done. Done like dinner. Nothing to it. The old fart's all bluster. Like most bullies, he backed right down when poked. I was surprised, frankly, at how quick and easy it was.'

'Wow,' said J. T. 'Wow. I'm amazed, delighted, enormously grateful. I'd never have believed ... But I owe you, Zinger, I owe you large.'

'That you do, in fact. You owe me your life and your leave and your salary and your first-born daughter, but I may also think of something else. For now, I'll take a rain check, and maybe dinner at Biagio's with Cathy and Pepper.'

Then they both sat down and laughed with glee.

40

Over a dinner of sweetbreads at Le Select, Pepper said that her father was coming home from Florida to attend to some business.

'He says that I – we? – could use his house in Florida, and Reading Week is just coming up. What do you think?'

'That's the third week in February, right? Sure, it sounds wonderful to me. If my kids come home for that time, they'll be fine on their own, and I guess their mother can look after them, from a distance at least.'

'She wouldn't move back into your house?'

'I wouldn't want that, no.'

'I see. So it's settled then, just like that?'

'Just like that. And thank you. Thanks to your dad, too. It sounds grand to me.'

'I'm less keen on Florida than the Senator, but it's a very nice house, well equipped, on Longboat Key on the Gulf side. Far from the madding crowds. All I need in winter, all I need anytime really, is a warm sandy beach, and bare feet, and I'm a happy camper. Dad says he'll be happy to stay with my kids.'

'Florida, gee. Will the beds break, do you think?'

'We can try.'

* * *

On the evening before their departure J. T. had a light supper. He ordered an airline limo to collect him at six-thirty a.m. so that they could pick up Pepper at seven for an eight-thirty flight. He was upstairs packing a suitcase when he thought he heard the front door open.

'Hello? Somebody there?'

'It's just me.'

The voice was Trish's. Good God. Trish here, now?

'Aren't you glad to see me?'

'Well, sure, yeh. But the thing is, I'm just packing. Going to bed early.'

'Joss told me you're making a little trip.'

'In the morning, yes. It's Reading Week, you know? Be back a week from Sunday.'

'I see. So buy me a drink, sailor?'

'Um, OK, yes, but I'm serious about going to bed early. Just one drink.'

He went off to the kitchen for glasses. Trish asked for a martini. He poured himself a short scotch.

'You want to be fresh in the morning for her, do you? This woman you're dragging along.'

'Actually, she's taking me, I mean, it's her house. In Florida.'

'So I guess she's after you in a serious way, laying it all on. Making a play.'

'I wouldn't put it like that. She's a friend.'

'A very good friend, I take it. Name of Pepper. What a curious name.'

'Her name is Jessica. She's very nice. But look, I don't want to talk about her right now, OK?'

'I don't either.' She drained her glass and thrust it forward at him. 'What I do want to talk about,' she said, moving toward the kitchen bar for refills, 'is some other stuff. Like the children.'

'What about them?'

'Jocelyn thinks you're neglecting her, maybe getting ready to dump all three of them.'

'Neglecting? Dump them? That's preposterous. I talk to each of them by phone every weekend. They were here all through Christmas, remember? I write them notes, send them books. Send them cheques for petesakes. Is that neglectful?'

'And when they come home this week, you won't be here. You'll be off with some woman. Joss says she wonders if you'll be moving in with her. Or maybe moving her and her brood in here, to this house, taking up all the space. No wonder the kids worry.'

'Moving in here? That's never been mentioned, not once. That wouldn't feel right, be right, for anyone. That's just nuts.'

'So do you want to sell the house? Is that it?'

'I do not. Haven't thought about it.'

'I'd get half of the money, you know.'

'Is that what you want to talk about, money? Not now, Trish.'

This is not the time for it. I'm just taking a short trip, that's all.'

'Money counts, J.T. My producer has hinted that I try out for radio, that this TV gig may not last forever. I think he considers me as getting a bit long in the tooth for the camera. Oh well, a few more nips and tucks with the plastic surgeon. But what if I fetch up unemployed, if they don't renew me for next season? Then what? I'll be needing some money, you'll agree. Think about it.'

'I asked you to think about it, a year ago, two years ago. And you just blew me off. I remember you saying that you didn't intend to force me to sell the house, to keep it for the sake of the kids at least. And that you didn't want, wouldn't take any money, because you were a big deal on TV. When I pressed you repeatedly on the financial score, you kept saying that if I thought you were interested in gouging me for money I "just didn't understand" you, I "didn't really know" you. Isn't that right? Didn't you say that?'

'Then was then, now is now. Circumstances change. And as a freelancer, I don't even have a pension. As things stand, it wouldn't be too easy to sell the house anyway, the way you live like a troll and have let the place get run down.'

'I have not,' said J.T., reaching for the bottle of scotch.

'You have. It's a mess.'

And so the gloves came off, and J.T. came unravelled, and they fought. And drank. And fought some more. About what she'd said or hadn't said, about the kids, about the house, about money, about his tenured job, her rather shaky position, and his pension. Their voices were raised. Angry words were exchanged. Mutual hurts and recriminations were bandied about. Hours went by.

At some point, Trish got up and went upstairs to the washroom. She took her time. When she returned they had both calmed down a bit if only from fatigue. When they began to speak again it was in guarded tones, pain and guilt and regret hovering between them like a mist. They spoke in stilted and polite sentences with heavy silences in between. There was a touch of wistfulness in their voices, a grief for old wounds and happier past times, a need to stop and accept new truths but also a reluctance to turn away and make an end. The strain was palpable.

'Look, Trish, this is getting us nowhere. I've got to get some sleep.'

'Ah, your lady friend awaits. You aren't thinking of getting married again, surely.'

'Who said I was?'

'I think it's really neat, the freedom of being single, don't you?'

'Can't say that I do. Freedom, as you call it, gets lonely. As Kristofferson says, 'freedom's just another word for nothing left to lose."

'Oh pish tush, don't be so dramatic. I mean, we're separated and all, but we're not divorced yet. I've always said you were my best friend. What if I decided to come back, say, next summer? Or in a year?'

'Swell. A year. I'll just put myself in deep freeze. Hibernate until you deign to take things seriously. Cryogenics, is that what you want? No thanks. I've had enough of that.'

'So it's this bimbo you're taking off with, is that it? She's what matters, not me.'

'Pepper's certainly no bimbo. She's an absolutely first-class woman and a professor.'

'I know. Another bluestocking. I've seen her, had her pointed out on Bloor Street. Not bad looking I suppose, if you like the type. Hardly glamorous, though. I thought you always went for glamour.'

'What did glamour ever do for … anyone? Glamour's just an expensive illusion, not reality.'

'I expect you've had her on the side for years. Hot times on the desk around the romantic department of economics.'

'For godsake, Trish, I didn't know her at all until September, more than eighteen months after you walked out.'

'Maybe she just wants somebody to look after her in her declining years.'

'Pepper is ten years younger than I, or you for that matter.'

'Ouch. Well, it's all a mystery to me.'

'And none of your business. Absolutely none. I don't have to explain to you about anything. Now if you'll please just stop. Stop baiting me and just leave. I'm going to get some sleep.'

'Sure. Nice talking to you, sweetie. And about the money thing, I'm sure you know I have no intention of ripping you off. None. It's just that I want what I have legal rights to, that's all.'

'Legal rights. How about moral rights? I didn't leave you, Trish, you left me.'

'So what? My lawyer says ...'

'I'll bet he does. So it's to be lawyers and a battle, is it? Lawyers and nets and tridents until I'm busted. That'll be fun.'

This led to yet another round of shouting and denials and drinking and recriminations that went around and around, on and on, getting absolutely nowhere. Finally J. T. looked at his watch. After two a.m.

'Dear God, I've got to get some rest. Stop it right there, stop it and leave, now. I can't stand any more of this.'

Slowly, she left, and even more slowly he climbed the stairs. He realized that he was quite drunk. Dammit all. Packing to do. Where's my goddamn bathing suit? He'd do what he could in the morning. The alarm had already been set for six. Half undressed, he stretched out on the bed. He'd been bushwhacked, he realized. Probably quite deliberately. Great timing. Maybe her idea of fun.

And through his alcoholic haze he also realized that the fabric of their two lives, long ago tattered, was now totally torn. Whatever it was they'd once had, it was gone, irrevocably.

The finality of it all made him toss and turn. He felt as though he'd been sucked into a jet engine, and chewed up. Far too late to take a Valium or a sleeping pill. His mind churned.

What if she was right? What if he really did not understand her, know her? The deepest grief was not in the hassling and acrimony. The deepest grief was the shock of such a raw exchange of jagged words, the incomprehensible but undeniable fact that their emotions, once so warm and open, were now so cold, so closed. It was possible, as she said, that he had never truly known her, what she wanted, needed, had tried to make him understand. His sorrow was not so much a lament for what was past forgetting and could no longer be, but the apprehension that perhaps it had never been at all, that it was all a dream and a delusion shared by unknown selves. If she was what he had known, what he thought he had known and loved, if she had ever been what he believed she was, how was it possible for her to be what she was tonight? Which woman, which wife, was the real one? Had their trust, their warm interdependence, never been real? Had he, had they, been living a hallucination for all these years? Maybe we are all strangers to each other, to ourselves, creatures who assume roles without really knowing why, laughing and loving and still failing to connect or comprehend. Isolated in sweet naïve hopes and temporary illusions. Maybe he'd been living for years in a mausoleum of misunderstandings.

He shuddered. Sleep would not come. He thought, this must be what failure feels like. Hollow. An emptiness. A cold affront to his warmest beliefs. But his feelings were, what? – contradictory. Anger, confusion, remorse, sorrow. He felt profoundly sorry. For himself. For Trish. Sorry that in life there is nothing permanent. He curled into a despairing fetal position and gave it up.

Sleep finally overtook him, rounding off his doubts and fears with dark relief.

* * *

The jangle of his six o'clock alarm bell roused him from a stuporous sleep. He lurched into a cold shower, but even that did not bring him into anything more than semi-consciousness. His head hurt, his tongue was thick, his eyes were grainy and red. Was his suitcase packed? Another three golf shirts and a pair of sandals got stuffed in. Got down the stairs. Instant coffee and two Alka-Seltzers. No time for toast or cereal. The limo driver was at the door. He filled the cats' dishes. Turned out the lights left on from last night. Rubbed his eyes. Looked around vaguely as if he'd never seen his own house before. 'Show time,' he said, in desperate imitation of Bob Fosse, 'Let's dance. It's show time.'

In the limo he fumbled through his suitcase on the seat beside him until he found his electric razor. Flicked the switch to battery operation. Tried to shave as the car jounced along, but didn't get it right. Swore. Arrived at Pepper's house. Told the driver to honk. Too early, the Sikh driver said. Got out. Went up to her door. Knocked.

And there stood the Senator.

Not a tall man, about five foot ten, but with a bearing, a manner that commanded attention. Black hair, bright eyes. Immaculately turned out in white shirt, a Yacht Club tie, blazer, sharply creased flannel trousers. What was he doing up so early?

J. T. blinked and stuck out his hand.

'I'm McLaughlin.'

'Pemberton.'

'I've come to pick up Pepper.'

235

'And pickled,' said the Senator.

'Well, the thing is, I haven't had any sleep. I'm sorry if I ...'

The Senator turned away and called Pepper. J.T. looked at the back of his well-tonsured neck and wondered what to say. What could he say? What would Ann Landers recommend? I've come to take your daughter away on a nefarious outing? Swell.

The Senator looked at him quizzically, but said nothing. In the disconcerting silence, McLaughlin tried to think. A comment on the weather didn't seem much of a gambit. Then he heard himself say: 'Sir. We have something in common. I mean, I'm a father, too. I have a daughter. I know what you ... that is ... I promise that I'll take good care of your daughter, look after her.'

'Pepper!' The Senator shouted. 'Young Lochinvar is here. Will you *please?*'

J.T. groped for her two suitcases, stumbled back to the limo. The Senator drew Pepper back into the house.

'I'm not sure I believe this, Jessica. He's obviously drunk. At seven a.m. His face had that purple tinge from booze. His eyes are red, he's unshaven, and he reeks of alcohol. He babbled something about being a father. He's not coherent. Are you sure you want to go through with this? I've seen more prepossessing specimens on a bar-room floor.'

'He'll be all right, Dad. I don't know what the trouble is, I've never seen him this bad, but I can take care of it.'

'Jessica, I'm asking you, you wouldn't marry a fellow like that? Would you? Would you?'

'No, Dad, not unless he sobered up, got off the bottle.'

'Promise me?'

'Of course. I *am* sorry that you had such a poor first impression, but he's a good guy, really. And as your generation would have it, his intentions are entirely dishonourable.'

'*That's* a relief. Bye, dear. Have fun.'

In the car, Pepper patted his hand, looked at him searchingly.

'Were you out with Zinger all night? You look a wreck. Are you all right?'

'Not really, no. But I'll come around. Not Zinger. I meant to get to bed early, but ... I had a visitor.'

'Let me guess. Erstwhile?'

'Yes. She raked me over pretty bad. I'll tell you about it on the plane. I'm awfully sorry. But as the man said: Free at last. I'm free at last.'

'Is she doing her Eustacia Vye thing? Hardy's *Return of the Native?* Is that it?'

'Hunh? I don't remember that book.'

'You should.'

'If you say so. But now, just relax. Let's fly south.'

He fell asleep on her shoulder.

41

While J. T. and Pepper were away, an item appeared in a tabloid gossip sheet, *Frank* magazine, insinuating that one J. T. McLaughlin, professor of economics at Chiliast University, was the subject of an investigation by an ethics committee. He was likely to be brought up on charges of racism and sexism. He was a well-known disturber of academic feces, the report said, and often 'over-refreshed'. But what could you expect from universities these days, the report asked, when they appointed 'light-in-the-loafers' types as college principals and granted tenure to faculty bozos who flouted the Code of Conduct? Institutions such as these should be 'privatized', *Frank* concluded.

The major newspapers did not bother to pick up this minor and questionable story, which was just as well, but for a few days the gossip mills on campus churned it over. Speculation as to who submitted the piece caused a lot of chuckling and finger pointing. Was it Teddy Kravnik? Some extreme homophobe on the Board of Governors? Maybe a secretary in the office of the president? Zinger laughed at the ridiculousness of it all, but also on reflection saw it as an opportunity, and decided to exploit it. Anything, he thought, was fair in love and advertising.

* * *

Zinger then called a press conference for the end of that week, just in time to catch the weekend papers. His bait was the promise of juicy revelations about university misconduct and a shocking attack on the freedom of the press. Although he could not hope for a huge turnout, since flashy little press conferences were a dime a dozen and created yawns in most newsrooms, Zinger loaded up the room, the handsome Croft Chapter House in Burke College, with some reporters from the student newspaper and primed them with snappy questions to ask, telling them to wave and shout in front of any TV cameras that might show up. In fact, at the appointed hour a fairly large group of journalists and even two news cameras showed up, grumbling that it was a slow day for news and fully expecting to be bored. Zinger smiled with satisfaction, straightened his very bright tie, smoothed his hair back, and strode up to the lectern at the front of the circle of chairs.

'Good morning, ladies and women and gentlemen and men. As you see in my press release, I'm Francis Z. Springer, award-winning Western journalist, presently Journalism Fellow at this university. I have a book coming out in two weeks' (groans from several in the audience) 'from the distinguished publishing house Macdonald-Fraser. I wish to emphasize, just to allay your natural skepticism, that the publicity and marketing division of M-F have nothing to do with this press conference, absolutely nothing.' (Muttering from the journalists of 'Oh, sure.' 'I'll bet.') 'I assure you that our meeting this morning is entirely professional and academic. Please note that there are none of those familiar and lamentable PR persons in this room.' ('Well, that might be true, but ...')

'My book is about a hard-working journalist, one of those unsung, under-rewarded, salt-of-the-earth reporters we all know so well.' ('He's got that right!') 'A wonderful fellow, a credit to the profession of journalism. The book is a novel, its title is *J. T. and Me*, available March twelfth at better bookstores everywhere – that's just a footnote, as we say here in the Groves of Academe. That's of no consequence to our purpose here today. None at all.

'No, our subject here today is not art or literature, but, it grieves me deeply to say this, academic arrogance' (some journalists nodded at that) 'and gross social injustice. It's a blatant attack on press freedom, a cynical attempt to suppress publication. I am, my friends, the victim of a lawsuit. I am being sued. I, a dutiful working journalist and creator of an astonishing novel, a novel set in the professional world of the press that you and I share, have been singled out by a rogue academic, a man I'd formerly considered my friend' (here he pulled a long face and hung his head affectingly in sadness), 'as the target of serious legal charges. It's heartbreaking. His name is Professor J. T. McLaughlin, the man I'd actually mentioned in my novel – titled *J. T. and Me*. This McLaughlin person has all the resources of personal wealth and academic prestige behind him, while I have nothing, nothing left at all besides pride and dignity. And I am to be dragged, most unjustly, through the courts merely because I did him a favour, tried to give him the honour of bestowing upon him a place in the annals of our national literature.

'Now, this turkey, I mean, this elitist' (that always gets them), 'this ivory tower person, alleges that I have appropriated some inconsequential old letters of his, letters dating back years ago when we used to be friends, and made some marginal and fictional use of them in my novel. This suggestion would be unlikely enough, since we all know that academics can't write, but it's all the more preposterous because of its source, because this man McLaughlin is a notorious person. Why, it was only recently that he was written up in *Frank* magazine as a woeful specimen. The February twentieth issue of *Frank*. Which is why I say he's a well-known malefactor. No morals at all. It's a preventive legal manoeuvre, libel chill of the worst kind, trying to stop publication.'

'What's he suing you for?' came a voice.

'A million bucks. Plus costs. Claiming damages for pain and loss of reputation. Which is ludicrous. Now, as fellow working journalists, you're well aware that an ordinary scribbler like me, a poor boy from Saskatchewan, hasn't got a million bucks. I think he's doing it just to achieve some cheap notoriety. It's shameful.'

'No, I meant on what specific legal complaint is he suing you, what charge?'

'Oh, I think —' (oops, he hadn't thought of that). 'I think he's alleging malice, and, er, breach of promise.'

'Breach of…?'

'He claims that I promised not to refer in print to his sordid background or allude to any of his experiences as a junior lecturer, willing to stoop to anything to obtain tenure. And we all know about academics and tenure, don't we, eh?' (Knowing nods and chuckles.) 'But he cannot stifle our precious freedom of the press!'

One of the student journalists chirped up.

'Is there a trial date set?'

'No, but my date of publication is March twelfth.'

'Tell us,' put in another student journalist, 'the title again.'

'*J. T. and Me*, MacDonald-Fraser, priced at thirty-three dollars. Any other questions?'

'Are you going to countersue this guy?'

'That will be decided by my lawyers. But I doubt I'm prepared to demean myself to that extent. I'd rather be forced into bankruptcy.'

'Can we interview the guy?'

'No, he's out of the country.'

There being no other questions, Zinger made some further heated pleas for freedom of the press and denounced the evils of frivolous libel suits designed only to prevent publication, and the conference came to an end. Zinger urged them to leave him their cards and he'd see that they were all invited to his book launch party.

'There'll be free booze and naked women.'

'Really?'

'Really. Have I ever lied to you before?'

- 42 -

Zinger loped along the street singing to himself, dreaming of fat royalties and amusing himself with new words to an old refrain:

> 'Mine eyes have seen the glory of the coming of the loot.
> I am trampling out the vintage where the grapes of truth are moot ...'

Zinger had invited J. T. and Gandy for a slap-up lunch at Mel's Montreal Deli on Bloor Street West for proper blintzes and smoked meat sandwiches. Mel's was aces, he thought. He wanted B. J. along as a buffer because McLaughlin was still steamed, furious, about the lawsuit story. J. T. had left some extremely angry voice-mail that burned Zinger's ear. Two of the Toronto dailies had given Zinger's press conference a bit of space, if only on pages 16 or 19, but enough to cause some small ripple of interest or amusement, and there were sixty-second items on two television news programs, as well as a follow-up squib in *Frank*. Zinger was much pleased, as if his fifteen minutes of fame had come early, or just in time. Already there were inquiries to his publisher about radio and television interviews concerning the 'highly controversial' book. He'd created some 'buzz', and that might be enough to make a difference.

He recounted to Gandy and J. T. how he'd granted just two selected pre-publication interviews, as 'favours' to friends in the media, he said. In one, he talked about how his agent (I must try to get an agent, he thought) was negotiating with United States and British publishers for advances in the mid-to-high-five-figure range, and how he was considering some offers for translation rights into German, Italian and Urdu. An auction for the film rights would be held after publication in New York, with colossal sums being casually tossed about.

'Is some of this publicity stuff true?' Gandy wanted to know.

'Ah, it was you who reminded me of McLuhan's view that advertising isn't a matter of being true or false, B. J., just a matter of image and impact. In my modest way, I've been polishing up my image.'

'At my expense!' J. T. snapped.

'There's no expense. It's all free if you know how to do it.'

'So you lied and dragged me into your grubby little scheme with this bizarre lawsuit crap without telling me.'

'I couldn't tell you because you were away, lollygagging in Florida. I didn't think you'd mind.'

'Mind? I bloody well *do* mind. People have been asking me about it ever since I got back. Snickering. It was a low trick, Zinger.'

'Aw, it's just for the hype. No one will take it seriously. Once you'd appeared in that tabloid, the damage was done. But no one will remember it next week. Just a gag for publicity.'

'Bloody bad publicity for me. And what was that crap about my being under some investigation?'

'Just more journalistic filler, probably nothing at all. But there is no such thing as bad publicity, J. T., that's how you get ahead. I've gotta penetrate the market with something bizarre so that I can break out beyond Canada, hit New York, and cash in on some big international sales. No one in New York has ever heard of you, so you're not hurt one bit.'

'It hurts that you'd take advantage of our friendship like this. And lie about it, that's what gets me. God knows what you've said in your goddamn book.'

'I'll give you a copy next week. A free pre-publication copy. And you can come to the launch party. What more could you want?'

'A little consideration, a little decency.'

'Decency isn't a word they use much in the public relations industry. Shit, how do you think the big corporations conduct their advertising campaigns, boost their sales?'

'McLuhan,' said Gandy, munching a cheese and blueberry blintz, 'always said that advertising was war. They talk of an ad "campaign", about "blitzing" the market, attacking the competition, an aggressive ad strategy, "capturing" market share. All very military, he said.'

'An assault on the mind of the consumer.'

'Surely there are things that you don't 'market', J. T. said.

'True, there should be,' B. J. replied. 'But we market human beings, buy them and sell them at a price, and call them "labour". We market nature, if you please, and call it "land", a factor of production, a "resource" to be bought and sold. Never underestimate the power of market, raw and crude as it may be.'

'Oh come on, B.J., you're not saying that we should "market" friendship?' said McLaughlin. 'You're not saying that we should buy and sell education, university degrees, or health care, an essential community need, regardless of ability to pay? When they "market" religion on television, we say that's vulgar.'

'You're right, of course. The best things should not be bought and sold for a price,' B.J. nodded. 'Some things should be beyond price.'

'Like love? Friendship?' said J. T., glaring at Zinger.

'Agreed,' said B.J. 'Which is a major reason why I hold the contemporary corporate world in such contempt. Everything tends to be demeaned by "pricing". That's why, you see, when we give a gift, something personal and emotional in the realm of human feelings and reciprocity, the first thing we do before we wrap a gift is to take off the price tag. Anything else would be crass.'

'I didn't "sell" J. T.,' Zinger objected. 'I know he's not for sale. No harm intended. I merely used him as a means, an innocent and jocular means, of pushing into the orthodox system, getting some attention and distribution for my book. I don't need to listen to a load of pseudo-philosophical crap about "marketing". It's obvious that the corporate media system is stacked against the little guy, against, well, art.'

'Francis has a point,' said B.J., picking up his smoked meat on rye. 'There's no doubt that the system is now "stacked", as he says. These days the sprawling mega-corporations, the giant global media companies, are owned by fewer and fewer bosses, merged into vast conglomerates, that we tend not to notice the higher degree of vertical integration.'

'Vertical integration?' J. T. asked.

'I mean,' said B.J., 'instead of there being just book publishers, there are now integrated mega-corporations which span the globe, combining ownership of newspapers, magazines, books, radio, movies, music and records, television broadcasting, and cable, packaging and flogging the same content, so that the "product" is becoming homogeneous, the filtered views and narrow values of fewer and fewer giant corporations offering more and more television channels and diverting "content", but fewer and fewer points of view, less and less real choice, more banality. And so, I gather, Francis will go to any extreme not to be marginalized, to break into the market.

I can't say that I approve, but there it is.'

'Exactly,' said Zinger. 'Say a magazine spots and uses a good piece, a good "concept". If the magazine has a book publishing wing it passes the idea along and a book is "developed" and then touted and "monstered" into a bestseller. Then the same company's film unit makes it into a movie, bangs its publicity drums again, and morphs it onto its television network and its cable system for international distribution and recycling. Everything bundled by one parent corporation, no competition, and everything slides along as slick as snot. Very smooth, so smooth that most people don't notice it. Power, real, but invisible, eh?'

'And of course, these giant networks never question the dominant market system,' said Gandy, 'or criticize the corporations that pay for advertising, or the governments that "deregulated" them. And we know how rarely U.S. news broadcasts report resolutions in the United Nations General Assembly condemning American aggressions against say, Grenada or Chile or Nicaragua or Cuba. Which is a principal reason why ordinary "consumers" are awash in so very much "information" about the world, but get so little understanding of it, so much bland "As If" and so little reality. This is surely one of the biggest questions of our era, and not just a matter of media and communications technology. The end result is an increase in global wealth, very inequitably distributed, and cultural deprivation for all. Here's my basic question: if, in the most optimistic scenario of the future, market globalization is triumphant and people are all coloured café au lait, all shopping cheerfully in the same malls, all prosperous, satisfied, accepting similar "free enterprise" assumptions and mythology, swilling Bud Lite as if it were real beer and eating identically packaged fast foods, monolingual, unicultural, probably all of one religion – consumerist or atheist, I'd expect – what would be the price we'd pay for all of that? What cost?

'The benefits could turn out to be huge,' he continued: 'prosperity, possibly even an end to war and nationalist or ethnic conflict and slaughter. Not inconsiderable benefits, I'd agree. Most significant. But would the result not be merely crashing uniformity? Boredom? Har! I don't know. I've cogitated upon this issue, maybe the most pressing issue of our day, but always I come down on the side of particularism, for the preservation of unique pluralistic cultures, I might call them "civilizations", and against McWorld. Have we humans come so far, only to leave mere businessmen in control of everything?'

'I'm with you, B.J.,' said Zinger. 'Did I show you my new poem on this subject?'

'I don't recall that you did.'

'Goes this way:

IBM, Bill Gates, Disney and Shell
Built a global commercial pussy cartel,
And by planned obsolescence
So controlled detumescence
That a poor man could not get a smell.'

'I like that. Har! I like that extravagantly,' B.J. laughed. 'Vulgar, but pointed.'

Even J.T. managed a small chuckle.

'But you haven't told us about your Florida trip. How was it?' Zinger asked.

'Wonderful. We had a great time. We walked miles on the white sand, ate hush puppies, shrimp and soft-shell crab. Read a lot, talked a lot, also did some brisk swimming. I eased up on the scotch and drank mostly wine, California wine, which is quite good. Pepper was a great joy, made me relax.'

'I'll bet,' Zinger said with a leer.

'Don't be difficult, Francis,' Gandy wagged a finger. 'Pepper is my esteemed friend.'

'Yeah,' said J.T., 'don't be difficult. You've caused enough bloody trouble already. I come back from a tremendously enjoyable holiday, happy as a lark, and find out my name is in the papers as suing my oldest so-called friend for a cheap publicity stunt. I'm still bloody furious.'

'Aw, J.T., back off. It's all over and forgotten, a trifle. I promise not to bring a countersuit, how's that? And, hey, didn't I save your sorry ass with the Naugle problem? Didn't I?'

'True, but….'

'J.T. has every reason to be cross with you, Francis,' said B.J.

'I suppose so, yeah, but I may be able to make it up to you soon in another way. You'll see. It's just that sometimes I get carried away. Let's have another beer. I'm buying.'

43

At eight-thirty in the morning B.J. Gandy telephoned Zinger. 'Francis,' he croaked, 'I'm glad I reached you. I need to ask a favour.' 'You'll have to speak up, B.J., I can hardly hear you.' 'That's the thing, Francis. I have laryngitis and perhaps a touch of the flu, but I'm scheduled to appear on a TV talk show this very afternoon and I simply can't do it. I'd be extremely grateful if you could fill in for me.'

'I suppose I could try, B.J., if it matters to you. What's the topic?' 'It's McLuhan, the anniversary of the publication of his *Understanding Media*. It's just an afternoon talk show, not at all important, but the program runs live, you see, and I hate to let the side down. Because you've read that work recently, and a lot of Marshall's other books, I hoped that you could … gulp, wheeze.'

'You sure don't sound in great shape, B.J., so yes, I'm willing to try, just as long as nobody thinks I'm some kind of an expert. Whatthehell, I guess I might get away with faking it for a few minutes if it would help you out.'

'Splendid. I'd be profoundly grateful. Possibly I should mention that the host – interviewer person is someone you know. Patricia McLaughlin. Doubtless she'll put you at your ease.'

'Trish? McLaughlin? Well, I'll be damned. That might prove interesting.'

'I don't mean it invidiously, but I have little doubt that you'll know more about McLuhan than she will. So you might be helping everyone out all 'round.'

Zinger chuckled and agreed. Gandy gave him the details of time and place, and rang off with further expressions of gratitude.

Z. sat and thought about this unlikely turn of events and then had an idea, a somewhat wry, even twisted idea that made him laugh out loud. He hummed to himself as he looked up Pepper's office phone number.

Z. explained that he'd just had a call from B.J. asking him to try to locate Pepper and to beg a favour from her. Because Gandy was slightly ill, could she replace him at a minor speaking engagement later in the afternoon? All quite casual, he said, and would be a real favour to her old friend. Some brief chat on TV about McLuhan, on whom she was becoming an expert.

'Anything for B.J., of course. But it's odd that he didn't phone me himself. I've been here in the office since eight-fifteen.'

'Oh, I'm sure he tried earlier, but just missed you. When he called me at eight he didn't have much voice left, and I promised him I'd do my best to locate you. You'd be helping him out in a big way.'

So Pepper agreed to skip a curriculum committee meeting and show up at the time and place specified, regretting only that she wouldn't have time to go home and change. Z. thanked her on B.J.'s behalf and somehow forgot to mention that the interviewer would be the erstwhile Mrs McLaughlin. It would be a shame to bother her with trifles, Z. smiled to himself. His sardonic grin spread wider as he thought how amusing it might be to manoeuvre J.T. to the front of a TV set, perhaps in the Faculty Club, to witness the encounter.

* * *

The producer of the TV show was a bright and beautiful young woman named Liz. She usually tried to elevate the tone and content of the program, often choosing challenging non-fluff topics, but was hampered by a small budget and an inadequate research staff for a quick daily show. She explained to Trish that the prepared questions on the 'greens', the suggested outline and content for the half-hour, were probably a bit thin. But then, to most people McLuhan was not easy reading, and what could you expect? Trish replied airily that there would be no problem; she would just toss around a few catchphrases like 'Global Village' and Professor Gandy would carry the ball. She knew him, and regarded him as garrulous if maybe a bit soft in the head.

'Well, that's the other thing,' said Liz. 'Gandy cancelled on us and is sending a substitute.'

'Oh? Who?'

'Another professor who is said to be writing about McLuhan, a woman named Pemberton.'

'What? Jessica Pemberton? No way. Scrub her. Scrub the topic if we have to. I will not have that woman on my show!'

'Why on earth not?'

'I have my reasons. I know about her, and she's just another pretentious bluestocking bitch, probably desperate to get her face on TV.'

'When she called me this morning to confirm she sounded very with it and rather nice.'

'Nice my ass. She's poison. Get rid of her.'

'Trish, be reasonable. It's far too late to make another change. She'll be on her way here by now, and we go to air for pete's sake, live, in an hour, less than an hour. It's a go, gotta be.'

Trish continued to fuss and flap and object. Finally Liz sighed and put to her the bottom line.

'At this point it would be easier to get a substitute host, maybe a staff announcer, than to get another guest. Is that what you want?'

Trish gulped and glowered, and caved in.

As they say, the show must go on.

* * *

When Pepper arrived in the studio and was introduced by Liz to the crew and to Trish, the guest was no less startled than the host had been to discover the unlikely identity of the person facing her. The two women settled into plush chairs on opposite sides of a coffee table on the set and, while technicians miked them and Liz murmured words of encouragement and instruction, the two eyed each other warily like dogs at an unexpected encounter on a path in the woods sniffing each other with extreme caution.

Trish was coated in theatrical make-up and thick glistening green eye shadow. Pepper was content with lipstick and a light dusting of powder that was all the make-up girl could persuade her to accept. Pepper's dark blue suit with knee-length skirt and flat shoes, no jewellery, seemed austere beside Trish's bold fuchsia blouse, abbreviated miniskirt, killer heels, and heavy gold bracelets. Pepper regarded Trish as overdone; Trish saw Pepper as a drab mouse.

'Is that suit a Giorgio Armani?' Trish inquired.

'No, it's an Armani knock-off, a bargain, but appropriate for the classroom.'

'I'm sure it's very – serviceable, dear,' Trish purred. 'And I suppose you're very nervous about appearing on television?'

Pepper returned service with a volley and a cool smile. 'Nervous? Not at all,' she lied coolly. 'I've had to do a lot of TV interviews to discuss books I've written. My only problem has been with interviewers who haven't read the books, but I was always able to carry them through it. I've never taken television too seriously.'

Liz started the countdown to airtime, thinking to herself that there was no doubt that this guest could handle most anything thrown at her.

It was Trish who seemed a little tense as she read the introduction from the teleprompter scroll. Although the intro styled Pepper as 'Professor' and 'Doctor Pemberton', Trish began by addressing her guest as 'Miss' Pemberton. Pepper replied by calling Trish 'Mrs McLaughlin.'

'Do call me Patricia.'

'Whatever makes you comfortable.'

'So here we are on the fortieth anniversary of the publication of *Understanding Media*, the book that established McLuhan as the oracle of the electronic age, the champion of TV ...'

'No, no, the enemy of television. He hated it, warned us against its effects, warned us that TV was changing and undermining rational Western civilization as we have known it.'

'Surely he wouldn't have written so much about something he was opposed to?'

'Authors of mystery novels write about murder, but generally they're not in favour of it.'

'But he popularized writing about TV, and gave us new insights into it. Some say he was the most important thinker since Darwin and Freud, although I guess there were others who dismissed him as a clown and an incomprehensible intellectual *poseur*.'

'There are two McLuhans, don't you think? One was the entertaining joker who tossed off one-liners and aphorisms. The other was the serious scholar who provided us with new understandings of media and their dangers. He built on the work of Harold Innis, extended it, and I'd say anybody who used Innis so brilliantly must be a serious thinker.'

'Innis? What's Innis got to do with it? I mean, I know an economist who wrote a book on Innis ...'

250

'I believe I know that author too.'

'I'm sure you do, dear. But he said that Innis wrote about cod fisheries and the fur trade and all that dreary stuff.'

'But the later Innis used the same approach that he'd applied to economic history, studying, not content, but patterns and results and *effects* of trade, and turned that approach to the study of communications, methods of conveying information, the nature of information itself.'

'How very odd. How could anyone study "information"? That's not a real subject, is it?'

'Oh yes, absolutely. Innis examined the impacts on society of different methods or technologies of transmitting information in ancient Babylon, Assyria, Egypt, Greece, looking for patterns. He couldn't speak or read those languages, of course, but he –'

'Wait. Just a minute. I know when I'm having my leg pulled, and I know you can't study "information" in languages you don't read.'

'But that's the point, you see. He examined the *effects* of their media, not the content. For thousands of years scholars had studied content, and only content, then along comes a great innovative thinker who asks the big new question: how does the method or medium of transmitting content affect society and men's minds?'

'You're not saying that content doesn't matter!'

'Of course it matters. But maybe it matters less than the effects of the various media that convey the content and have different impacts on human civilization. The question is, not the information itself, but how the information is delivered. It's the medium that's the message.'

'I might be getting lost here. We'll have to take a break for our commercial messages, or ha, ha, content, and when we return I'll ask you again how in the world anyone can pretend to study a subject so nebulous as "information". We'll be right back.'

* * *

After a three-minute pause to sell shampoo and fast food and deodorants, during which Trish stared at her guest in frosty silence and Pepper idly toyed with a water glass, they picked up the theme again. 'It might be helpful,' Pepper argued, warming to her subject, 'to regard most of our major institutions as, not so much bricks and mortar, but information systems, or systems for the delivery of information. Churches, schools and universities, political parties and governments, organized professions, and even science itself, and certainly the supply and demand signals of our dominant institution, the market, can be regarded as networks for the transmission of information, similar to what we laughingly call "the media". Then too, what we describe as "human consciousness" may be simply or mainly the ability to process information. For instance,' Pepper asked, 'how do you regard your own physical body, Mrs McLaughlin?'

'My own...? My body? How do you mean?'

'Your body, like everyone else's, is the creation of your genes, built from the double helix of your DNA code, which is a biological information system, the root of life.'

'I've never ... I mean, I've never thought of it like that. But wait, we've come a very long way from McLuhan if we're going to chat about DNA and my body ...'

'It would never do to be deflected by your body, Mrs McLaughlin.'

'Uh, right, so let's get to the Global Village.'

Pepper took some time to run through how, compared to writing on papyrus or words in print, electronic media such as TV and the Internet overcome, obviate, Innis's prime categories of time and space and create an instantaneous organic community or environment of information. So is print different from TV mainly in that it's too slow? Trish inquired. No, Pepper replied, it's mainly that print is linear, mechanical, logical, rational, and tends to produce things like mathematics, science, individualism, bureaucracy. Television on the other hand undermines, attacks the rational mentality by producing images, impressions, glamour, edited glimpses of reality. TV speaks to us in only one ephemeral voice, the voice of entertainment, and tends to reduce everything – religion, athletics, politics, art, intellectual argument, even war – to entertainment. That's what McLuhan means by TV attacking reason, creating short attention spans, mainly emotional responses, juvenile and jangled brains. McLuhan's point is that TV is non-rational. Advertising, which TV does supremely well, doesn't attempt to persuade us through reason, but to beguile us with favourable emotionally charged impressions, feelings.

'So now you're saying that television is irrational?'

'No, what I said was *non*-rational, fleeting, and principally emotional. As McLuhan's disciple Neil Postman says, we're in danger of amusing ourselves to death.'

'And so, Miss Pemberton, are you one of those ivory tower intellectuals who prides herself on not watching TV?'

'No.' Pepper bristled at Trish's mocking tone, and a dangerous glint appeared in her eyes. 'I watch the news, *60 Minutes*, a lot of PBS, sometimes even Dr Phil. Just the other day, come to think of it, he had a woman on talking about rebellious teenage girls, quoting André Maurois that "to acquire culture is to prepare yourself for love." She added that to acquire makeup and glamour is to prepare yourself for showbiz and disappointment. So true, don't you think?'

Trish glared and sulked, apparently at a loss for words, so Pepper pressed on briskly.

'But that's merely content, you see, just entertainment. It's the *medium* that's the message, as McLuhan says. It's the impact of TV that affects our entire nervous system, creates a new electronic environment, and alters our consciousness.'

'It's time for another non-rational break for a commercial,' said Trish sharply, and turning to the camera snubbed her guest with the comment, 'More from the professor lady in a moment.'

* * *

Following the interval, Trish counter-attacked, defending the strengths and importance of TV news, pointing out how immediate and dramatic and compelling it usually is.

'Sure,' Pepper countered, 'if it bleeds, it leads. But what can't be conveyed in thirty-second video clips and sound bites and lively images is *why* something happened in Iraq or China or Washington. There's little or no attempt at what print can do, such as interpretation and perspective and analysis, so that with print we get toward causes, understanding, even truth. TV gives us instead snap impressions and what many call "infotainment", not information.'

Trish shook her head. 'TV news shows us the truth. The camera doesn't lie.'

'Doesn't lie but often misleads, usually omitting the underlying reasons *why* events happen. It's a show, eye candy. Distortion. Television can be a huge and pervasive weapon of mass destruction. It sacrifices perspective, linearity and rationality in favour of mere images and fleeting impressions. It lets political leaders stand in front of a camera and deliver carefully scripted speeches that sound plausible, without asking whether the speaker ought really to be regarded as a mass murderer or a war criminal, like Kissinger or George Bush.'

'Wait! Stop. You can't say that on TV!'

'I just did. Look at the long record of the Cold War.'

'But, when you compare the freedom-loving U.S. to the Russians or –'

'Oh come off it. Does TV really inform us about power and reality? Look at the scorecard of aggression. Both sides have acted badly, not just one. Since the Iron Curtain fell in 1945, how many states or governments on this side of the curtain have the Russians invaded or overthrown? Afghanistan? They tried it in Greece in 1946. Cuba, with missiles? I'll give you Cuba. But that's three.'

'Well, Poland? Hungary?'

'They were already in Soviet control since 1945. On the other side of the scorecard, however, when you total up the fascist states the U.S. has supported with "advisors" on torture and death squads against peasants, or democratic governments the U.S. has overthrown, or countries they've actually invaded, we have Vietnam, Chile, Panama, Grenada, Guatemala, El Salvador, Lebanon, Nicaragua, Dominican Republic, Cuba and the Bay of Pigs, Afghanistan, Iraq twice … do you want me to go on?'

'No, no, but …'

'My simple point being that this sort of perspective, this sort of scorecard, is never, but *never* available to the Americans, the very decent American people, on TV news. They don't know. TV hides it. None of this makes the Communists sweetie pies or good guys, of course, but it does help you to understand why the Americans are regarded as rude imperialists and frequently as terrorists by much of the rest of the world.'

'Well, Miss Pemberton, I'm afraid we're running out of time, and we've strayed a long way from McLuhan.'

'Not really. But OK. How much time's left? Two minutes? Right. Let me offer this short quote from Jason Meyrowitz that I often throw at students and even friends at dinner parties to see whether they get it, or disagree. It goes, "To understand TV news we must recognize it as a distinct genre, not reducible to word-based forms of analysis."

How would you react to that?'

'I'd say you're being facetious again. I'd say *anything* can be reduced to word-based analysis, except maybe magic and deception.'

'Exactly, deception and emotional misleading of the viewer. Smoke and mirrors. People who've read McLuhan usually accept the Meyrowitz view as serious if not obvious. Those who don't understand McLuhan say it's nonsense. But it's the emotional and sensory impact of TV that's beyond words. It's mysterious and powerful, like sex. Ineffable, like love. Beyond words.'

'Gee, I'm sorry, our time's up. But I want to thank my guest for appearing today. We have only scratched the surface of this fascinating topic.'

'It's been great fun to scratch surfaces with you, Mrs McLaughlin.'

Quick cut to a commercial for indigestion pills.

* * *

Zinger snapped off the TV set in the Faculty Club and let out a whoop. 'J. T.,' he bellowed, 'we've just seen one of the most delicate carving jobs I've ever witnessed. That Pepper, she wields a mean stiletto. She's one classy lady, and smart as a whip. Imagine that, with zero preparation for a high-speed game, and she came out a winner, just aces.'

'You're right, Z., it was impressive.'

'I almost felt sorry for Trish. She was out of her depth, over-matched.'

'Yeh. I suppose so. It wasn't her kind of a subject, of course, but … Yeh.'

44

J. T. continued to be plagued by insomnia. Long interviews with his divorce lawyer and his accountant recently had done nothing to raise his spirits. He had trouble concentrating on his work; even his lecturing seemed below par. He was ragged in the college common room about being a bigot, and lawsuits, and appearances in *Frank*. He began to fret and sulk and worry even more.

He tried, with a warm break in the March weather, to work in the garage on the Model A. He tried to write, to finish an article on Schumpeter, but nothing seemed to flow. Lengthy phone conversations with his kids gave him pleasure, but he was extremely nervous and tense, had trouble sleeping. He found an old vial of tranquilizers, Valium, and put it beside the bathroom sink. He swallowed one.

Later, before falling into bed, he took two serious belts of scotch and those relaxed him, put him to sleep. But around two-thirty a.m. he woke with a start, his mind whirling, dreads and apprehensions firing bright flashes in his head. Got up. Tried to read. Paced the floor. His watch said 3:20 a.m. Must get back to sleep. Took another finger of scotch and another Valium. Hadn't he had one, or two of those pills about eleven? Didn't remember. Went into the bathroom to pee. Slipped in some water on the floor. Fell. Banged his head on the edge of the bathtub. Blacked out.

* * *

At about two-thirty the next afternoon, Pepper phoned Cutty's office. She said she had an appointment for lunch at noon with J. T. but he had not shown up, and had not phoned to cancel, which was not at all like him. His phone rang, but there was no answer.

Cutty said that was strange, and that J. T. had not been in his office all day either. Seemed to have missed his two o'clock lecture, and hadn't called the department to cancel it, which was even more odd.

Pepper thought something must be wrong. Was she being silly to

worry? No. Did Cutty have a key to McLaughlin's house? No again –
but he knew where the extra set of house keys was kept in the garage
since the time J. T. had locked himself out. He'd go over and check right
away. She'd meet him at the house, Pepper said.

Within half an hour the two of them let themselves into the
house. They called up the stairs. No answer. Cutty went up to the
bathroom and found J. T. on the floor, in pyjamas, out cold with an
obvious lump on the side of his head. Doubtless a concussion.

They decided to call an ambulance and have him checked over in
Emergency, just to be sure, even though there was not much the
medicos could do for a concussion. While they waited they brought
him around to at least semi-consciousness with a cold compress.

Two hours later, they drove him home again. The doctors told
them to keep J. T. awake for at least twelve hours, sixteen if they could,
and keep alcohol away from him. He agreed easily to no booze; liquor
was the last thing he wanted, he said. Yeah, it was true, during the
night he'd combined scotch with maybe two Valium, he couldn't
remember. Pepper found the bottle of pills on his bedside table, open
and spilled. Dammit all, she cursed, and flushed the bottle's contents
down the toilet.

It was agreed that Cutty would stay with J. T. until nine p.m.
Pepper would go home and feed her children and return at nine for the
next shift.

From nine until very late at night, Pepper plied him with coffee
and kept prodding him to stay awake. The two of them talked and
talked until the small hours. He said his head hurt too much to watch
a video. She put a couple of Django Reinhardt discs and an old Eddie
Condon anthology on the CD player in an attempt to keep things
upbeat, and kept him talking. She had him recount the stories, again,
of how he and Z. were a debating team in high school, anything to jog
his memory and keep him awake.

It was after two a.m. when J. T. finally got around to blurting out
the question that had been on his mind for weeks.

'When we got all this straightened out, my head and everything,
would you consider – you know I love you, Pepper – consider
marrying me?'

'Don't be daft. You're not divorced yet.'

'I know, but when that's done with? Finalized? Would you?'

'I care about you, J. T., very much. You're a lovely guy. You're smart and you're kind and you're funny. But, no. I'm sorry, no. Not unless you were to kick the bottle and got off the booze. Then I'd think about it.'

'I really do believe that's behind me. I don't *want* a drink now. I'll certainly promise you not to get drunk any more. No vodka in the office. I mean, the cocktail hour, sure, but not the heavy drinking.'

'Easy to say. You've been half-ripped for, what? two years now?'

'But I'm not a real drunk, not a regular lush, believe me. I wouldn't want you to be married to a lush either. I'll cut it out, cut way back, honest. I don't think I'm a genuine alcoholic, it's just that I tend to be compulsive, and after my wife left I was really down.'

'I know, depressed and self-destructive. I've tried to get you to admit that you were focusing your anger on the wrong person. It's not yourself you should be angry with.'

'Yeah, I know. I see it. Just didn't want to admit it. Blaming her seemed so, I don't know, disloyal. Disloyal to our previous life.'

'You're a loyalist, God knows, J. T. But there comes a time....'

'Yes. And now I feel as though that's behind me. I guess I wasn't following what the economics textbooks call enlightened self-interest.'

'B. J. and I have often wondered why you economists believe that self-interest is usually enlightened. Historians would say there's precious little evidence of *that*. And just last night you were enlightened all over the bathroom floor.'

'It's true. You're right. But the thing is, Pepper, crack on the head or not, I really feel – I'm really determined – that drinking as a defence mechanism is over with. It sure didn't work. I guess I'm completely tired of it, tired of being numb. So I'd promise you, maybe not a rose garden, but at least no more hiding in the sauce.'

She looked at him searchingly.

'Why, my dear Professor McLaughlin, I almost believe you. I want to believe you. And if you're still sober in, say, six months, I do hope you'll ask me that question again.'

- 45 -

'Now this is some party,' said a reporter from the *Sun*.

'Too right, it is,' said his friend from the *Star*. 'I was just on my way home, you know, when I remembered this guy's weird press conference about libel chill and that he'd said there'd be free booze. Well, I thought just another bloody book launch party, maybe bloody wine and cheese, eh? But this, it's something else.'

They both gulped at their whisky as a semi-naked woman sauntered by and another cavorted on the stage.

'I'll tell you, now, I'm sure glad I happened to remember this invitation. A strip joint, yet. The predictable little book soirée, it is not. I called back to the paper to get a photographer buddy of mine to hustle on up here, and he's on his way. Said he'd call another pal of ours from Channel 9 to come along with a video camera. Lotta people here already, eh? Jeez, it's a different sort of happening.'

Francis Z. Springer, author and self-appointed PR hypester, stood in a corner with Cathy Boychuk, a large glass of rye, and the beaming countenance of a very cheerful con man.

The room was a long narrow one with a mirrored bar running down one side, and on the other a stage illuminated by bright waves of strobe lights. Cheater's is a club devoted to the art of the strip tease and the pushing of drinks. The stage was constantly occupied, and between featured appearances, young delectables wandered among the tables looking for laps to dance on. The atmosphere was startlingly non-literary.

'But the invitations you had me print up,' said Cathy, 'just said Cheater's, 2087 Yonge St., and I thought Cheater's was an odd name for a restaurant, and here we are in a goddamn strip joint. With table dancers. I mean really, Zinger. This isn't at all what anyone expected, or what the company expected, or what I went into publishing for, with a fine old family firm. Mac will be horrified.'

'I doubt it. He's already here, somewhere, and I told you Mac and I were on the same wavelength. It was you, after all, who told me that your flack guys often "dressed up" a party by hiring models, so I thought it might be a nice change to undress the occasion with naked ladies, sort of *reductio ad absurdum* as the scholars say. And it seems to be working, don't you think? I recognize several journalists from my press conference, and here comes a television guy with a camera. Well, well. See, I tried to hire a few of the girls from here, but when I got talking to the manager about a group rate, it occurred to me that I should just rent the whole place, dancers and all for three hours, six to nine. The manager is happy because he's got a pretty big crowd and is moving a lot of booze. The girls are happy because they've got a more up-scale and appreciative audience than usual. I'm happy because I might squeeze some bit of publicity out of it. Everybody wins.'

'Must be costing an arm and a leg though.'

'Nah, not all that much. What the hell, it's only money. What's a few bucks here or there to an artist like me? Besides, I'll bet you a dinner at Le Select that Mac will be so knocked out by this and have such a great time that he'll be happy to pick up the tab and hardly notice it. He knows damned well he can't buy publicity like this for any price in some drab reception at the Royal York or the Yacht Club, and it's a tax deductible expense anyway. So relax. Enjoy. Maybe nip over and see whether you can interest some of those press guys in an interview.'

Cutty arrived with Alice and was quite amazed, said Zinger had out-done himself. J. T. and Pepper rolled in, he with his eyes round as saucers, she laughing her head off.

'I must phone the Senator to come over,' she said. 'He'd appreciate this.'

And when B.J. walked in he stopped short and kept saying, 'Oh my. Oh my.'

Shouldering his way through the growing crowd came Big Mac, beaming with the joy of promotional dollar signs in his shining eyes. He had a delectable on each arm.

'Springer! By God man, this is fabulous, it's tremendous. Why didn't I think of this? It's a good thing Mrs MacDonald didn't want to come along tonight. What we have here, by God, is the best decorations and the best dope in town.'

'Careful what you say, Mac,' said Zinger. 'Most of these ladies are ecdysiasts, artists, very refined, mostly students working their way through college – you know how steep tuition fees are. Superba van Snoob here is an art and archaeology major, didn't you say, Superba? And Miss Rosie Dawn is an M.A. student in English literature.'

'Splendid,' said Mac. 'You must come to work at my publishing house.'

'Did you say, dope?' Cathy asked.

'Sure thing,' said Mac. 'There are two dealers doing quiet business at the bar and a couple more in the men's room pushing a few ounces. It's a circus in here, I tell you. Bloody marvellous.'

'Dope?' said B.J., moving up at Zinger's elbow. He repeated 'Oh my' a few more times.

'Just some marijuana, I guess,' said Zinger.

'I think you've gone too far this time, Francis. The view is most edifying, I admit, and I'm deeply sensible of your desire for ballyhoo and puffery, but this seems beyond the acceptable. It's garish, it's trickery.'

'But B.J., it's a cunning array of stunts, as Dr Spooner might have it, wouldn't you say?'

'I don't approve,' Gandy sniffed.

'It's not your approval I need tonight, it's the attention of these press boys I'm after. Excuse me, Cathy is waving at me.'

Meanwhile, Cutty and J.T. had bellied up to the bar.

'Double scotch,' said Cutty, 'water, no ice.'

'Just a beer for me, please,' J.T. said.

'You're really cutting back, are you?'

'Yup. And I don't much miss it.'

'Good on you. Real good. Say, look at Alice and Pepper over there by the stage.'

Pepper was saying something amusing while she swayed and bopped to the music. They both were riveted by a stripper with impossibly long legs, wearing two red scarves and little else.

'Do you think we should get up on the stage and show her how it's done, Alice?'

'Pepper, you *wouldn't*. You're so competitive.'

'Damn right. But relax, I'm not serious and anyway, there are photographers popping away everywhere you look.'

Zinger was on the other side of the room drinking and backslapping with two journalists.

'Drink up, lads, it's all on the house. Hey, do you think there's anyone here from the Governor General's Awards selection committee?'

'Are you expecting a G.G. nomination, Mr Springer?'

'Oh, I suppose so, yeah, but it's the Pulitzer my agent says I should have my eye on, although the Booker Award might be nice. The auction for my British rights won't be till next month.'

'Auction?'

'Sure, I don't yet know which London publisher will be successful, and I can never remember what the Limey pound is worth, but they're talking high five figures, you know? Might make it worth a short trip across the pond.'

'Gee, you're a very lucky man, Mr Springer.'

'Call me Zinger, everybody does. But we all make our own luck, eh? I was saying to Maggie Trudeau just a moment ago – she's over there at the table at the back with some stoned musician or other – I was saying you have to find your own comfort level. Maggie's a great friend.'

'You mean that's the ex-prime minister's wife over there?'

'Absolutely,' said Zinger. (Although it was a pretty look-alike he'd hired from an agency).

'I'll have to nip over and interview her,' said one of the journalists, straightening his tie.

'You do that, pal,' said Zinger. 'I'm just sorry that my art dealer from Prince Albert couldn't be here.'

'You buy art?'

'Some. But I paint a little. There's a show on now of my work, mostly landscapes, back home in P.A. at the David Mason Gallery. Selling quite well, I'm told.'

J. T. drew Zinger aside.

'I don't remember a Mason Gallery in P.A. There's a great antiquarian bookstore of that name here in Toronto, but I don't remember a gallery ...'

'There isn't. I just made that up on the spot to show the range and scope of my amazing talents. But by the time anybody bothers to check that out – and most probably they won't – the news of how I rival Matisse will already be in print. See, I almost had even you on the hook with that one, didn't I? Don't you go getting gullible on me, buddy. I'm juggling enough magic balls in the air as it is. Hey, wait, I see B.J. heading for the door.'

Zinger rushed over to Gandy.

'Not leaving so soon, B.J.?'

'Yes, I fear I'm getting too old for mob scenes like this. But isn't it dangerous, all this – what do you say? – "pot" in the air?'

'Nah, not much risk, I think. It's a private party, closed.'

'Well, I've told you that I don't find this entirely agreeable, Francis.'

'You of all people, B.J. It was you who put me up to this lark.'

'I? Put you up to ... What in the world are you saying?'

'Sure. You. Let's step outside, shall we? Listen to me, old friend. I've learned a lot from you, and I'm grateful. It was you who told me about "infotainment", the substitution of hype and spoof for news or fact. If they want infotainment, then I'm just the guy to lay it on them. It's easy. And I'm having fun, B.J., a lot of laughs. It was you who told me to read McLuhan on advertising, advertising as war, right? So, I'm on the attack. That's all it is. I may be a bastard, but you have to be a bastard to break in, and bastards have more jollies. I know you think I've pushed all this too far, and I'm sorry you think so, with the table dancers and all, but artists have always regarded aesthetics as more important than ethics.'

'Have you now promoted yourself to "artist", dear boy?'

'Nah. Not at all. I'm a writer, and maybe a middling-good writer at that. Just a scribbler with something to sell, but I'm a dynamite promoter. So, I'm using a few tricks to flog the product. Don't blame me for it.'

'I don't really mean to be censorious, but ...'

'B.J., think about it. Who should be blamed? It's one of your real questions. You can lay a guilt trip on me if you like, or blame the media for wanting novelty, the bizarre, anything different. You could blame the gossip columnists and the reporters for being patsies, taken in by obvious bullshit. You could blame the editors and the owners of newspapers and television networks who are so eager to transmit anything grabby or unusual for sales and ratings. Hell, you can blame the public for wanting such nonsense, for being eager to buy it, lapping it up. So do you blame me, just for playing the game, or do you condemn the entire freaking media system? Am I pandering to them, or are they pandering to me? And to everyone else?'

Gandy sighed like a man who had lived hundreds of years and was no longer surprised by anything.

'What a silly world it is, Francis. What a cynical world. You do make a case, I'll grant you, much as I find the whole thing deplorable. So, I'll just wish you good luck, and good night.'

'Thanks, B.J. And don't take it all too seriously. I don't.'

* * *

The next morning, Saturday, Cathy and Zinger bought all the papers, local and national, and took them to McSorley's Wonderful Saloon on Bayview Avenue to peruse over brunch.

'Your party got quite a bit of ink in two of the local papers, Z. Apparently, the place got raided after we left.'

'Un huh. Serves them right.'

'And there are some reviews here, thanks to our early distribution of pre-publication copies from the sales department.'

'Read me one or two, will you? There's one here that calls me "an authentic Prairie Thistle". I like that.'

'And here's one that says: "The book has energy and eccentricity and wit."'

'Can't make much use of that. It's okay, but not what I'm looking for.'

'There are some other favourable notices, "a comic romp," says the *Sun*. But there are some negative ones, too.'

'To be expected. Probably a genuinely perceptive critic, or some bitter schmuck who's written a failed book himself.'

'This one says: "Don't buy this book. It's incredible what a travesty it is. You'll laugh out loud at the pretension and ineptitude of the author." *The Calgary Herald*.'

'Excellent. We can use that, quote it in publicity releases or on a poster. Great stuff.'

'But it's dreadful; it's unfair.'

'Cathy, come on. Don't you see it? We only need a little cut here, an ellipsis there, and it'll read: "… buy this book. It's incredible … You'll laugh out loud … *Calgary Herald*." See what I mean?'

'That's wicked.'

'Yup. But too good to pass up. Let's eat. We can read the rest of this crappola later.'

Cathy had elected to be the PR rep who shepherded Zinger on Monday from one radio or television interview to the next. After his second appearance of the morning, on CHUM-FM, she upbraided him.

'You cannot come on like that with gruff and monosyllabic replies! Who do you think you are, Mordecai Richler?'

'He made me mad. Did you hear how it began?'

'No. I was talking to the program manager, behind the glass, saying thank you.'

'The son of a bitch asked me if I, as a journalist, found writing easy, so I gave him the old Stephen Leacock retort: "Writing is no problem, really; you merely jot down things as they occur to you. Now, the jotting down is simplicity itself, but the occurring, ah, that's more difficult."'

'Okay, so what went wrong?'

'The twit just looked at me blankly and asked: "Who's Leacock?" I coulda decked him.'

'Oh, dear. Well, I'm sure you'll do better with the next one.'

'I hope so. Bloody young electronic kid with no sense of anything but today, immediacy, and an utter disdain for the past. Is there no history any more? FAWK, I say.'

* * *

The next appearance was on a morning television show. Zinger wondered whether any sentient beings watched television in the morning.

'Seems like it might have been fun to write,' said the big-haired hostess with award-winning stiff eyelashes. 'Do you enjoy writing?'

'Some, yeah, but it involves a bit of time and sweat. As the great Northrop Frye said, "No, I don't always enjoy writing, but sometimes I enjoy having written."'

'Is it true, as you've been quoted in the press as saying, that you expect a nomination for a Governor General's literary award?'

'I do, yes, certainly.'

'But there's no separate category for humour, and your book, from what parts I've had time to read, seems to be comic.'

'Yes. So?'

'I mean, comedy never wins awards. It's not, well, serious.'

'Ah, I see. Okay, just think of the best comic writers for a moment. Who would you include? Falstaff and Polonius weren't created by Jerry Lewis you know. Cervantes, Rabelais, Swift? I'd throw in Dickens, Aleichem, Mark Twain, Molière, Waugh, Flann O'Brien, Paul Quarrington. Maybe Saul Bellow for *Augie March*. Not a bad list of "serious" writers, eh?'

'Um, well. You mentioned Mark Twain. Would you say he's an influence on you?' (Ms Eyelashes was clearly groping.)

'Certainly. I line up with those who say that *Huckleberry Finn* is one of the greatest books of all time.'

'And Huckleberry was a comic novel, I guess.'

'But also, you see, great literature.'

'A boy on a raft is "serious"?'

'That wasn't Twain's subject. His subject was slavery. How's that for serious?'

'So you'd compare yourself with Twain?'

'Some. And also Sarah Binks.'

'I … think we'd better break for a commercial message here.'

And there followed a swell ad for underarm deodorant.

As they left for their next appointment, Cathy said that long eyelashes might not be the best qualification for a television interviewer.

'Aw, she was all right. Easy to deal with. She was probably a philosophy major in university.'

'Why do you say that?'

'She's just got everything in slots and categories, probably a Platonist, you know. Comic, serious, thriller, crap. Plato reasoned well, but he was a solemn and rigid bastard, opposed to the poets and not much fun.'

* * *

'For the next show, Zinger, we've got to be there early. It runs live, and this guy, Martin Capon, is a big deal in showbiz reporting, and he knows it. Considers himself a real hot-shot.'

'He does, eh? Well, well. I've seen promos for his show once or twice. A bit smarmy.'

After make-up and sound checks and other preparations, they got settled in swivel chairs in front of the cameras.

'You've had a lot of media play since your book appeared. I guess you can now call yourself a celebrity. How do you account for that?'

'Luck. Talent. A great publisher. Maybe the power of prayer.'

'And maybe a lot of self-promotion.'

'Some, possibly.'

'I mean, for example, that you've told the press that you have a big movie deal in the works.'

'I might have mentioned that.'

'But you and I both know that no one can make a movie of a book of *letters*.'

'Why not?'

'Well, there isn't even any dialogue.'

'Letters are all dialogue, just people talking on paper.'

'And you insist this could be the makings of a movie? Tell me, how would you do that?'

'I'd hire a really good-looking mailman.'

'I see. So why do you write?'

'Why? Because I can't dance. And those other things, need and greed. I need to write, and I don't mind getting paid for it.'

'And why comedy?'

'Because I have no sense of humour, and want to cheer myself up. Besides, I think a writer has an obligation to be entertaining.'

'Your style has been compared to W.O. Mitchell's. Would that be a good comparison?'

'No, and certainly no favour to W.O.'

'But you both wrote about Saskatchewan.'

'That's brilliant. You're *so* clever. Shakespeare and P.G. Wode-house both wrote about England, but their styles were slightly different. But say, Martin, did you like the section set in Vancouver?'

'That was one of the best parts, yes.'

'There's no section set in Vancouver.'

'Oh, well, I thought ... actually, there were a few parts I didn't have time to read. In the middle.'

'Then why talk about it?'

'He's just kidding, folks,' he said to the camera with a toothy smile.

'No, I'm not kidding, folks.'

'Ha, ha. Seriously, how long did it take to write the book?'

'How long? What's that got to do with anything? All my life, I guess.'

'So the book is autobiographical?'

'No, it says on the cover – see – a novel. Fiction. And of all the forms of fiction, autobiography is the most egregious. My main thing is bouncing high off reality to fun. Hyperbole.'

'I notice that some of the reviews said you use some old limericks, maybe borrow and recycle some old jokes?'

'Yup. And I notice that you, not having read the book, borrow and recycle other people's reviews instead of doing the work yourself.'

'Wait, there's a *big* difference here.'

'Is there? I steal a joke and call it "research". You steal from reviewers and call it "showbiz". What difference? It's all theft, and takes a lot of chutzpah, Marty.'

'Are you calling me, Martin Capon, a thief?'

'If the cap fits ... but no, I'm calling you a B E N B P.'

'What's that?'

'A Big Ego No Brain Phony.'

'Why, I've never been so insulted in all my life. And on my own show! This is *my* show!'

'And it runs live, I think?'

'You bet it does.'

'Then, dear folks out there in vacuum land, your brilliant and lovable host, live, will now entertain you for the next nine long minutes, solo, with his own wit and wisdom. Or else with nine minutes of dead air and knuckle cracking. I'm outta here. 'Bye.'

The next day the gossip columnists had sport with the great Martin Capon's sputtering incoherence, and Francis Z. Springer, daring buccaneer of the airwaves, got even more ink, which was, of course, what he'd intended.

* * *

Two days later McLaughlin was to meet Zinger at City-TV after what he said would be his last scheduled Toronto talk-show gig. They'd have a beer after it was finished. Zinger allowed that the hectic week of interviews had begun to grind on him and bore him. Being a self-made and self-proclaimed celebrity was not much fun any more, more like work. J.T. thought he'd arrive early and watch Zinger do his thing in the studio.

But when J.T. got there, Zinger was nowhere to be found. The receptionist said Mr Springer was late and hadn't checked in yet. Odd, thought, J.T. He waited another ten minutes, then went back out to the street to smoke, wondering whether or not he should stick around.

At the end of the block there was a small crowd gathering, a slight commotion. J.T. strolled toward it. What was that the people were grouped around? A big cardboard box?

Zinger had found (outside of a frat house on St. George Street, he said later) a huge carton in which a refrigerator had been delivered. He'd rescued the box. He'd carved two eyeholes in the front at the top. With some bright red paint he'd printed under the eye-holes: 'No interviews, please. Private Citizen.' On the back, in larger letters, he'd printed the title of his book. Balancing the box from the inside on the top of his head, he had a few inches from the ground to move his feet and make the box walk, and the improbable spectacle made the gathering crowd hoot and laugh.

'What are you selling, man?' shouted a passerby.

'Nothing at all,' came the muffled reply. 'I'm merely trying to preserve a dignified anonymity in the face of a shattering media onslaught on my privacy. Please step out of the way.' And marched on toward where J.T. was standing.

'That's you inside, is it, Zinger? You're looking good. Your costume is maybe a little square, but it hides your ugly kisser.'

'Hard to smoke in here, though.'

'Do you want me to cut an air-hole in the top?'

'Yeah. I should have thought of that before. Ah, the price we celebs must pay to avoid the harsh glare of the media spotlight.'

'Where are you headed?'

'I was proceeding east, if you please. Do come along.'

'East toward City-TV?'

'That general direction, yes. But, as always, I'm resolutely desirous of avoiding exposure to the vulgar intrusion of the cameras. I have rocketed from nonentity to only semi-obscurity in just two weeks, so I thought I'd send it up a little. One becomes so weary of being exploited by the media Charlies. But the crowd seems to be getting bigger. See if you can't clear a path for me, will you?'

'Sure. How far do you want to walk?'

'Just until we see whether the television mountain will come to Mohammed. I'm betting it will. If my keen journalistic instincts are correct, the front reception desk will call up to the studio and they'll send out a remote video crew to intercept and abuse me. It's getting to the point where a quiet ordinary citizen can't even take a walk on a public thoroughfare without being accosted by some dolt with a microphone. Ah, look, here they come now, just as I told you. Lights and cameras. Shall we linger and see what they want?'

'Doubtless. Jeez, Zinger, I never thought I'd be standing here on Queen Street talking to a fucking box.'

'But it makes a great visual for television. That's the only trouble with books, they don't lend themselves to photo ops.'

'I suppose I'm meant to see some deep literary symbolism in this packing case.'

'Nope. I'm just fed up with being only another pretty face. But now that you mention it, maybe I should concoct a symbol for the television boys. Possibly: I write from imagination and memory, and memory is a box like this in the attic. Or how about: I am the True Ark of the Media Covenant. No, for that the box would have to be empty. I'll study on it. The only thing I know for sure about containers is that I'll be in a remainder bin soon enough.'

'So, you believed all the time the cameras'd come out to you?'

'Sure. *Incognito ergo gloria sum.* It's the perversity thing. As the Wife of Bath said, "Deny us thynge, and that desiren we." They're suckers for the unexpected. Tell you what. Wait around for just a bit while I dazzle them with my J.D. Salinger act, evasive, getting my box on the box you might say, and then we'll go for a beer. It's thirsty work, being anonymous. See you later.'

46

'I got it going! Cutty, hey, Cutty,' J. T. shouted as he rushed down the hall and burst into Cuttshaw's office, 'Adelaide, I got her running!'

'That's nice, J. T.'

'I mean, I've got 'er here. Come on out to the parking lot and see. Running like a charm. Come on!'

'The thing is, I've got all these essays to mark, you know? I'm rather busy.'

But J. T. dragged him out to behold the splendour of his automotive accomplishment.

'There she is! The perfect Model A Roadster. Isn't she spiffy? Wait'll I start it, I'll let you hear how she runs.'

'J. T., it hasn't even got any paint on it. Just some grey undercoat.'

'But she will have. I'll take 'er to the body shop for a paint job next week. That's only cosmetic. Who cares about that?'

But Cutty's attempts at enthusiasm remained restrained. Still, he could not help but smile at his friend's excitement. Different strokes, he thought.

What happened was, while Zinger was away on a further book flog in Halifax, Montreal and Vancouver, and while Cutty had his head down working on his book on international trade, J. T. had taken advantage of a warm spell in the weather at the end of March and had put on a big push to finish the mechanical work on his own, and succeeded. Without a lot of scotch as a slowing factor, he worked efficiently. When the seats came back from the upholsterer on Saturday, he installed them quickly, and on Sunday he was ready for some finishing touches. Pepper came over Sunday afternoon to take down his curtains to be sent out for cleaning and brought Lindsay along to help. While they were there Stuart came by from a friend's house to see what they were doing and joined J. T. in the garage.

'How's it going?' he asked.

'Wonderfully,' said J. T. 'I'm almost ready for the big test. Hand me that wrench, will you? Great. This, Stu, this is the *pièce de résistance*, the real thing. I will now demonstrate how a master mechanic does it. First, I'll just check the brakes – see how well the pedal operates? Perfect. Distributor cap seems tight. With these cars, you see, there's none of that fancy crap about not being able to repair anything without some engineer putting in an entire new computer chip to regulate the carburetor. Here, watch, you just turn this needle valve with a screwdriver, right? Then it's simple gravity flow from the gas tank here, see? Then I'll adjust the steering to be sure it's tight, like that. And I'll check the radiator hoses to be sure there are no leaks. There we are, lad, there we are and Bob's your uncle and we're all set to fire she up. What do you think?'

'I think it's swell. You sure know what you're doing. What oil do you use, summer or winter grade? 10-W-30?'

'Oil,' said J.T. 'Oh mygawd, OIL. I'm glad you said that, Stu.'

'Said what?'

'Don't tell your mother, but I almost forgot to put oil in the motor. Jee-*zus*, what a goof that could have been. The engine would have seized up. I think you just saved me from a terrible mistake and rescued the whole motor from the junk heap.'

'I did? Gee, glad to help.'

Once the oil was poured in, J.T. breathed a great sigh of relief.

'Here,' he said. 'I'll let you do the honours. Climb into the driver's seat and I'll show you how to start it.'

'Lubrication really matters, huh?'

'Sure does. I'm hugely grateful.'

'Mom says you were over-lubricated yourself for a while there. Is that right?'

'It is. Your mother is usually right. But we were sure as hell under-lubricated today. Now, this is what you do.'

So Stuart followed instructions, glad not to have another lecture on the theory of the internal combustion engine like he'd had from J.T. once before, and he pulled out the choke and hit the starter and, zap, it started. Began to tick like a sewing machine.

J.T. laughed and punched the air and capered around the garage in high glee.

'Keep it in neutral, Stu, with the hand brake on, and run and get your mother and Lindsay. We'll take them out for a spin.'

Soon they were off around the block, then west on St. Clair as far as Yonge Street, J. T. in ancient goggles driving with a demented grin, Pepper waving grandly at bemused strangers, Lindsay and Stu in the rumble seat, slightly embarrassed but getting a kick out of it.

When they got back to the house, chilled but happy, Pepper made hot cocoa.

'Do you have any champagne around, J. T.?'

'I think there's some cheap Spanish bubbly in the cellar. Shall I get it?'

'Do. Lindsay has made you some cookies, and I brought along a chocolate cake I made. We'll celebrate, and we'll pour a festive glass over Adelaide's front to christen her.'

So they did that, and had a great time, gorging on cake and cookies, drinking sparkling wine, and laughing at J. T.'s attempt to explain how he was sure that an adjustment to the carburetor would coax the Model A's speed up to more than forty-five miles per hour.

'I'll get my camera,' said J. T., 'so I can get some pictures of this for my kids. I wish they could have been here, but it's almost exam time. I guess I can't have everything. Today was damn close, though.'

Pepper said she had to hurry home to cook dinner. The Senator would be there, and they were having a leg of lamb. Did J. T. want to come over to her house about seven? Enthusiastically, he did.

'You're a bit of a nut and an odd-ball, but a nice nut, and I think you know I love you.' She kissed him. 'So if you want to, and if you're still sober after your divorce comes through, ask me again and I think I might just marry you. Yes.'

'Wow, Pepper, wow. Tremendous. I'll certainly be sober, have been for weeks.'

'I know. But if you're not, you won't see me for dust, remember that.'

'Not a problem, young lady, none at all. Hot damn, wait till I tell Zinger about this. He'll be amazed. I'm a little amazed myself. And your dad will be there? Shall I, you know, get all formal with the Senator and ask for your hand in marriage and all that old-fashioned stuff?'

'Don't be silly. He already thinks you're a bit batty. See you at seven.'

47

When Zinger returned from his book tour he took Cathy off for a long weekend in New York where they ate in the Oyster Bar at the Plaza and the Carnegie Deli and once at Sardi's. They did all the standard tourist things and visited the Met and MOMA and the Guggenheim. They didn't make any book deals, hard as they tried, but Cathy told him when they got back to Toronto that Big Mac had managed a sale in Britain, partly on the basis of reviews and quite satisfactory sales in Canada, partly on the basis of a videotape of the big box interview. It was an advance of only one thousand pounds, she said, but not bad at all. Zinger allowed it as how it was much better than a kick in the ear with a frozen boot and might see him through till July.

So Zinger rested himself up for a few days after the rigours of the book tour and New York, and then re-surfaced to invite Gandy and J. T. to dinner, for beer and oysters at Rodney's.

'Tell us about your travels, Francis.'

'Oh, standard stuff, I suppose. Tiring. The old *veni, vidi, Visa* thing. I always spend a little too much, God knows. But I'm expecting some cheques soon, one from the U.K. and one from – downtown.'

'Sure you are, and maybe you'll pay back what you owe me,' said J. T. 'Should I hold my breath?'

'Patience, ol' buddy. All will come out well. I'm serious about anticipating a satisfying flow of fiduciary instruments very soon. Ask me next week.'

'Uh huh. I will.'

'J. T.'s news is also most salutary,' said Gandy. 'Pepper says she's willing, contrary to all good sense and justice, to marry him next autumn. Isn't that splendid?'

'Marry!' said Zinger. 'You do get carried away, lad. I urged you to date her, but marriage? Holy shit. I guess you might try living together, but you don't need a licence for that. The girl must have lost her mind. No sane woman would take you on, J. T., not on a bet. I can't believe it. What do you think of this, B. J.? You're the most experienced man here.'

'Experience,' said B.J., 'is just another word for having made almost every mistake in the book. I was divorced once, and later I became a widower. Did you know that?'

'I didn't,' said Zinger. 'But do you think the boy is being sensible? I mean, Pepper has two kids, and he already has three. He's not even divorced yet, but ready to tie another knot. Doesn't seem rational to me.'

'Which is exactly why outsiders cannot judge, Francis. It was the great David Hume who taught us the basic truth, that rationality is not how we choose. Reason is a useful tool to help us accomplish ends and goals, but those ends, those choices, will always be set by non-rational desires. Rationality is just a means towards ends, often mad ends. So if J.T. is happy, and if he and Pepper want this and are happy, then I'm abundantly happy too.'

'I just don't know about you, J.T. It seems awfully impulsive and dicey to me. Talk about emotional snakes and ladders. You're up and down like a toilet seat.'

'No accounting for the anfractuosities of the human mind, Francis. And J.T. is a good man. Pepper will see him right. The warm Indian summer of the heart can be wonderful as the years advance on us.'

'Zinger, when did you become such a great expert on marriage? Here I thought you'd be happy for me, instead you're giving me a hard time. You, with the terrific record of three divorces, you're going to dish out advice? I'm laughing.'

'Just trying to make you think, for godsake. Maybe save you from yourself, maybe be helpful to Pepper. Hell's bells, man, when I first got here in September you were moaning about Trish. Does that still count?'

'No.'

'He says no, B.J. What do you think? Can you tell me you're in love with Pepper? In so short a time?'

'Yes.'

'He says yes. I'll be damned. He says he's in love, B.J., whatever that's supposed to mean. These days it usually means a swift roller coaster from honeymoon to acrimony to alimony I'd say. It's *such* a heavy trip. It's dangerous, let me tell you. I can't believe you'd roll the dice again so soon and take such a bloody great risk.'

'Look, Zinger, I don't know what you're playing at, or what this cross-examination is in aid of, and I guess I don't perfectly know what love is either, but I can tell you that Pepper is – very dear to me. Precious. I'm hugely grateful to her. I wouldn't hurt her for the world. I love her. And I've given her my word about the booze. I'd never go back on my word, can you understand that? I want to try to make her happy, that's all. I think that's what love is all about.'

Zinger regarded him solemnly for a few moments, examined his face minutely, and then broke into a big grin.

'One of his best Boy Scout answers, wouldn't you say, B.J.? Not bad at all. I think we might award him a passing grade. I'm more than somewhat reassured. Uncle Zinger might bestow his blessing on you yet. Come to think of it, I long ago arrived at the belief that any two people who are at all attracted to each other can live quite happily together if they're mature and reasonable.'

'I suppose that explains your track record of divorces,' said J. T.

'Certainly. I'm not reasonable.'

'I'll drink to *that*,' said J. T.

'And I too,' said B. J. 'But Francis is not wrong to remind you how difficult these things can be. Children, new relatives, divided friends and loyalties, financial considerations. I expect you'll have to sell your house, move Pepper into some new dwelling for a fresh start. All very difficult, J. T., most taxing. I'm reminded of something Keats wrote, I was reading a collection of his letters just the other night. "There is nothing stable in the world; uproar's our only music." Do you like that, J. T.? Oh, I like that immoderately.'

'That's about it,' said Zinger, 'yeah. Uproar and tumult lie in wait for you, my friend, and refugee status. You'll find out.'

'How do you mean, refugee?'

'I mean that in a second marriage, trust me on this, you're something like a refugee from your past. You have to learn a whole new language, drop the previous patterns of pet names and endearments, your old ways of doing things, forget the former family in-jokes, and live with the fact that whatever the tug of previous habits and emotions, you can't go back again. You're cut off, totally, obliged to learn new ways in an unfamiliar world. It's not easy. You're adrift. In some sense, you've got to dream yourself a beach.'

'What do you mean, beach? Shipwreck? It can't be all that bad.'

'In many ways, good. All things old can be new again. But I thought you knew that William McIlvanney poem about a beach, surely I've quoted it to you before. No? Glasgow writer, one of the best contemporary novelists and a great favourite of mine, a helluva poet. This one walked right in and hung up its hat in my mind. I have it by memory, I think:

> And so adrift in unknown selves we lie
> Abandoned to dark plucks of circumstance
> Not knowing what will come or what we'll do
> Or where the tides of sleep will wash us and
> Shy from the sculling shapes that feed on mind,
> Feel every certainty drift out of reach
> And sigh and hold each other, tryst with touch
> To share what is not shareable, and know
> The jerking terror of time's undertow
> And madly try to dream ourselves a beach.

'Now that, by gawd, is a man who *knows*.' J. T. stared at him, blinked, and stared some more.

'Oh. Oh my,' said Gandy. 'For a time I was concerned that you were turning into a Philistine, Francis, but I am relieved and gratified to learn that I was wrong. Har!'

'Say it over again, Zinger, slowly.'

'I'll do better than that, I'll write it out and leave it in your box at the college. Consider it an early wedding present, and obviously one of inestimable value – although I have one other little thing in mind to offer you later. Waiter! Yeah, bring us another three pints of this excellent Bass ale. We have something to celebrate. My young friend here is engaged to be married.

'So here's to you, J. T., ol' buddy. May the gods smile on you.'

48

The next Friday they were gathered for their regular lunch at the P.O.E.T.S. Corner.

'Well boys, this is my farewell party,' said Zinger, returning from the men's to the big round table at Dooley's. 'I've told the bartender to bring us a round of Black Bush.'

Most of the regular lunch bunch had already left, but J.T. said Pepper was going to meet him there to go shopping, and Cutty and Gandy had been asked by Zinger to linger too.

'Farewell?' Cutty asked. 'Where're you going?'

'Home. Leaving next week.'

'But term isn't over,' said J.T. 'Not over till the exam period is finished in two weeks.'

'Well, I'm ready to get on the road. I'm delighted to report that Cathy says, no, she doesn't want to marry me – thinks I'm not a good bet – but she's coming along, and we'll try living together back in Saskatchewan. So we're off.'

'Damn,' said J.T. 'I thought you might stay on longer, maybe a few years, maybe ...'

'I couldn't do that, J.T. Sure, I've been offered several jobs here in PR, but that's no life. If diplomacy is saying "good doggie, nice doggie", while you reach for a brick, PR is just lying and pimping for a client.'

'But you did that for yourself,' Gandy noted.

'That's different. Just doing it as a job is no fun. As for journalism, a lot of the press boys I've met here in the east are mostly garbage collectors, picking up PR handouts. Trouble is, they then inflict their garbage from the Imperial Centre on the rest of the country and expect us to like it. All too smelly. No, I'm off.'

'Sorry to hear that,' said Cutty.

'Now about that thou I owe you, J.T.'

'Oh, swell. You're going to buy me a jar of whisky as interest on the loan and send me the rest of it from Prince Albert, some day, right?'

'Better than that. I've got a cheque here for the full amount, plus interest. Quite a lot of interest.'

'Sure you do. And it will bounce like a kangaroo in heat. Why would I think any cheque of yours would be good?'

'If you'll look at it, you'll see that it's a company cheque, drawn on a company called Horn-Abbot, not on me.'

'Whaddya mean? Let me see it. Oh great, it's made out for fourteen hundred dollars. What's the con?'

'Look again. It's fourteen thousand.'

'So the joke gets bigger, eh? And the joke's on me. Zinger, you're such a pain in the ass; I was going out later to buy Pepper a ring, and I wish I could afford a bigger stone but I can't. And here you are making bad jokes about this debt.'

'You can afford it, J. T.'

'I wish.'

'No, really. Trust me on this. Do you remember that I told you I invested your thou?'

'Bought me some shares in a moose ranch, did you? Thanks a lot.'

'Will you bloody well listen? One afternoon here at Dooley's, back in October, you guys had all gone but I was staying on to hustle a waitress I fancied, and two guys came in asking for your P.O.E.T.S. table, so I invited them to sit and bought them a beer. Interesting fellows. I pegged them right away for rogues and con men, so naturally I liked them – clever and likeable con men.'

'Takes one to know one,' muttered J. T.

'Of course. But they had a box with them. Said it was a game they'd developed with Tom Naylor, a bright McGill economist. Very handsome box, great design. Looking for investors. Said it was called "Dirty Money" or "Hot Money" or some such shitteroo. So I played it, and I bought them an extra couple of flagons of ale and we played some more. All very jolly. Nice guys.'

'What did you say the name was?' Cutty asked. 'Not "Hot Money"?'

'Yeh, that's it. Biggest thing in board games since Trivial Pursuit. Might even rival the great smash hit of Trivial Pursuit. "Hot Money" is *THE* new fad, based on how to make, launder, hide dirty money made from guns, drugs, or tax evasion, the real game of high finance.'

'My kids play that all the time. Alice and I play too. It's a big hit.'

'Pepper's kids got one at Easter,' said J. T. 'They love it.'

'Oh my,' said Gandy. 'I've heard of that. A grand success story.'

'Sure,' said Zinger. 'Sales are rocketing. It's taken off like a big-assed bird. Anyway, I had some room left on one of my overdrafts, so I gave them, invested, two thou. One for me, and one for you, J.T. Seemed like an amusing idea at the time – I was drinking martinis – and I thought it could be a good tax loss anyway, backing Canadian enterprise and all that.'

'You mean, you put my thou into that game? You bought me a share of Hot Money? Are you saying this cheque is actually good?'

'Absolutely. That's what I'm trying to tell you. It's for real. Enjoy it in good health.'

'I don't believe this. The bank will just laugh at me, won't it?'

'Nope. Not if they want your business, our business. We're fat-assed capitalists. Dividends are swell, I think.'

'Jeez. Fourteen thou! I'm stunned. I'm amazed. But won't your two inventors just disappear now that they've made their hit?'

'I doubt it. Last week I was at the company's annual meeting, a grand booze-up it was, and the boys assure me there's lots more where that came from. They're just getting started. Going on a licensing arrangement with Parker Brothers for U.S. distribution, and setting up an off-shore company for translations and foreign sales. The boys tell me we'll be collecting dividends for years.'

'I don't suppose they said how much?' Cutty asked.

'No one knows for sure, of course, but some numbers were mentioned. Like, give or take a few, a quarter of a million, maybe a half.'

'A half …,' J.T. gulped, 'a half million?'

'More or less, yup.'

'Kick me, Cutty, I think I'm dreaming.'

'Not,' said Zinger. 'I think it's for real. In the game business and in the bars along Bay St., they're saying it's the damnedest investment for multiple returns of the decade.'

'Halle – flipping – lujah!' whooped J.T. 'This is astounding, tremendous. I'm going to get down on the floor and turn a somersault. What a great guy you are, Zinger!'

'My ol' daddy always said, if you can't be good, be lucky.'

'Now steady on, lads,' said B.J. 'This is mostly future money, "maybe" money. Don't get carried away. And whatever amount you might be talking about, it will be spread over several years, and it's all before taxes, before alimonies and gifts and impetuous spending, perhaps before lawsuits and disappointing investments. Best to keep a lid on it till you see how it plays out. Wait till it's in the bank, at least.'

'But B.J., we're rich,' shouted J.T. 'No matter how thin you slice it, we're rich!'

'Might could be,' said Zinger.

'It's my considered opinion,' said Gandy, 'that money isn't very important. Necessary, but not important. Always remember, lads, it's only money. Not health, not family, not creativity. It's not love or friendship, it's only money. And often a burden.'

'Try me,' J.T. grinned. 'It's a burden I'm willing to bear. What will you do with yours, Zinger?'

'Haven't really thought much about it yet. Are you making plans already?'

'Damn right I am. Holy shit but it's exciting. With my year off, and if Pepper can arrange a leave from her department, we'll go ... we'll probably go to Paris and rent an apartment on the Left Bank. Maybe a villa in the south of France for a couple of months.'

'The Riviera might not be an ideal place for academic research,' Gandy said.

'OK, maybe one month. Where will you go, Zinger? I mean, think of it, wow, London, Rio, Barbados, Rome, Tahiti? Where will you be headed?'

'I told you,' Zinger said, 'I'm going home.'

'No, but where will you go first, before that?'

'No place at all. Home to Prince Albert. I miss the old place. I miss the old newsroom. I miss the hustle and bustle of newspapering. After all the hype and nonsense about the book, it will be great to get back to real writing about real things. I'll take the back roads west, the greener small highways, and roll on out.'

'But, but the world's your goddamn oyster, Zinger.'

'Might be. I guess I'm not really a great hand at travelling. Hey, it was B.J. here who taught us years ago that much of the point of education is to realize the largest expanse of space is not across continents but in the limitless territories within the mind. At most I might put a down payment on a small cabin on a secluded lake, and buy a canoe. Maybe you should come back to Saskatchewan with me for a while before you go charging madly off in all directions.'

'Not bloody likely. I'll visit you, if you like, but it's *la belle France* for me. Anyway, Zinger, I wish you'd stay on with us a while in Toronto. Pepper would like that, too.'

'Can't do it. This place is too confining. Oh, I had a good run here, enjoyed it. I got what I came for, and more. I got some time to read, a book published, I got Cathy and a nice change and a few laughs and a ride in a Model A, and I suppose a satchel full of lovely windfall money to boot. Can't complain. Besides, the money will buy me another chance at fatherhood. I mean, I can lay a bundle of cash on my son John as a trust fund and get his attention, buy him a car for graduation and get another chance to be a real dad. That will be a great satisfaction. Hell, I might even catch up with some back debts for alimony.'

'Now you're talking,' said J. T.

'Sure. And what did I tell you last fall about luck, about LRUC, the Law of Random Unexpected Consequences?. Now maybe you'll believe me. If you hadn't let me borrow that thou, and if I hadn't come to Dooley's with you, fortune wouldn't have smiled on us so pleasantly, would it?'

'I guess you're right, Z. I'll always be grateful to LRUC.'

Glasses were raised. Grins and backslapping all around.

'But how can you call Toronto "confining", Francis?' B.J. inquired. 'By comparison, Prince Albert is tiny.'

'I dunno, maybe "impersonal" is the word. Apart from you guys and the university, I find it hard to fit in or make a niche for myself. The city seems to leave me feeling anonymous. People here are so obsessed with their work as cogs in the machine, as blips on the electronic circuitry, terrified of being downsized, that they don't seem to relax or have real lives. It's all hurry-scurry and the frantic headlong pace. Not for me.'

'Why do you say "real lives"?' J. T. put in. 'Particularly now that you have extra money and a wider choice, to me Prince Albert doesn't seem very "real", just a marginal town, "out there".'

'Do you call Toronto "real"? Damn, it seems to me a place that pretends it works, but doesn't. The ravines are being filled in by developers and highways. The main street, Yonge, is a narrow strip with a bad case of the uglies. The true main street is University Avenue, but it's arid and desolate, has no serious bistros or sidewalk cafes, no life, and is cut off from the lake at the bottom by Stalinesque buildings, truncated. To me, Toronto is its thruways, usually clogged, shunting glassy-eyed commuters brimming with angst and road rage from one brutal high rise of glass and concrete slabs to another exactly like it. It's an "As If" city, pretending to be important and lively, but it's not. It's a place where you step over the homeless on the sidewalk to go to the opera. No, if this is reality, it's too nasty for me.'

'It gets better, the longer you live here,' said Cutty. 'You get used to it.'

'That's what I'm afraid of,' said Zinger.

'Pepper and I hoped,' J.T. insisted, 'that you'd stay on at least another year. Get a job, write some more, stay for our wedding. I mean, if you go back to P.A. you'll stagnate.'

'You think so? Nah, not me. I'll be one of the lucky ones. Out of the rude crowds, away from the grubby promoters and the cold asphalt canyons, out of the traffic jams and the smog. I'll be where I can feel more real and more alive. I'll be closer to the lakes and woods, maybe closer to myself. I can walk to my office in ten minutes without listening to bloody helicopter traffic reports. I can walk home from a poker game at dawn and see the sunrise without being cut off by monstrous high rises. No, I'm not a city man. If I stayed here I'd probably slide into the vast pool of inflated self-congratulatory media mediocrities, eating tofu and swilling decaf lattes, endlessly exchanging identical flatulent opinions with the other dummies. The city has little use for anyone except conformists and robots and phonies, and all too uptight. It's no place for a Cavalier. The Roundheads have won. I'm outta here.'

J.T. and Gandy looked at each other, realizing that Zinger had it right, or at least right for him, and that argument would change nothing. Zinger's timing was always eccentric, often abrupt. McLaughlin sighed, finally having come to believe that much of life was knowing when to grab on and when to let go.

'So, I'm off,' said Zinger, draining his glass. 'Give my love to Pepper. She's too good for you, J.T., but bless her feisty heart. I'll drop you a postcard. The moving finger writes, and having writ, pissed off, eh? And as the feller said, "Remember me in your smiles and wine."'

'I wish you the very best of good fortune,' said B.J., swirling the whisky in his glass. 'L'chaim! To life!'

Acknowledgements

Permission has been granted by the publisher for the reprinting of the poem, 'Concerning Stars, Flowers, Love, Etc', by John Newlove from his book *The Night the Dog Smiled* (ECW Press, Toronto, 1986).

The untitled poem by William McIlvanney is the frontispiece to his book of short stories, *Walking Wounded* (Hodder and Stoughton, London, 1989). Reprint permissions, unavailable at the time of this printing, will be formally acknowledged in subsequent editions if so requested.

For critical suggestions and encouragement during several drafts over four years, the author wishes to thank David Cobb, Dean Cooke, Elsa Franklin, Nada Harcourt, Linda McKnight, Julian Porter, and Eric Wright. Sam Solecki generously buoyed a flagging spirit. Christina Greenough struggled bravely through several re-writes as typist and copy editor. Doris Cowan meticulously prepared the final manuscript for the printer. And many thanks to Tim and Elke Inkster, publishers at the Porcupine's Quill.

About the Author

Jack MacLeod (aka McLeod) was born in Regina, Saskatchewan in 1932. He earned a BA and MA in economics at the University of Saskatchewan before taking a Ph.D. in political science at the University of Toronto where he taught from 1959–1996. An experience in Budapest during the Hungarian Revolution in 1956 led him to begin writing political journalism, some of which appeared in the *Globe and Mail*, the *Toronto Star*, *Saturday Night*, *Books in Canada*, *Canadian Forum* and the *Journal of Canadian Studies* as well as on the CBC. MacLeod published several academic works with University of Toronto Press, Oxford University Press and McClelland and Stewart and two political science textbooks. His two previous novels, *Zinger and Me* and *Going Grand* were on the bestseller lists.

He is married to Cynthia Smith and together they divide their time between homes in Toronto and Muskoka. They rejoice in three children and three grandchildren.